MURDER ON DECK!

Murder on Deck!

SHIPBOARD & SHORELINE MYSTERY STORIES

EDITED BY

Rosemary Herbert

New York   Oxford

OXFORD UNIVERSITY PRESS

1998

Oxford University Press

Oxford   New York
Athens   Auckland   Bangkok   Bogotá   Bombay
Buenos Aires   Calcutta   Cape Town   Dar es Salaam
Delhi   Florence   Hong Kong   Istanbul   Karachi
Kuala Lumpur   Madras   Madrid   Melbourne
Mexico City   Nairobi   Paris   Singapore
Taipei   Tokyo   Toronto   Warsaw

and associated companies in
Berlin   Ibadan

Copyright © 1998 by Rosemary Herbert

Published by Oxford University Press, Inc.,
198 Madison Avenue, New York, New York 10016

Oxford is a registered trademark of Oxford University Press

Library of Congress Cataloging-in-Publication Data
Murder on deck! : shipboard & shoreline mystery stories/
edited by Rosemary Herbert.
p.   cm.
Includes index.
ISBN 0-19-508603-1
1. Detective and mystery stories. I. Herbert, Rosemary.
PN6120.95.D45M84   1998
823'.0872'08—dc21   97-908

135798642

Printed in the United States of America
on acid-free paper

To the memory of my Dad
With love

So much depends upon the red canoe
Beside the white birches.

CONTENTS

PREFACE

Here is a volume designed to be placed in the lap of luxury, to be read when one is literally on holiday—or when one wishes to be. Mystery stories set on shipboard or shoreline can be read in those places, in deck chairs or on blankets on summer sands, or they can be savored in any season in the classic library of the armchair detective. Unabashed escape reading, such stories may be expected to take the reader into different worlds, whether they be the nightclubs on board luxury liners, the shining sands of holiday resorts, or the treacherous decks of military transport ships. The sense of being abroad—or on board—and cut loose from one's ordinary life provides the thrill of escape. But, as this anthology proves, the shipboard and shoreline milieus can also be used to launch the reader into thinking about inescapable issues and aspects of human nature.

Many of the stories in this volume illustrate beautifully W. H. Auden's view of detective fiction. His poetic take on the genre supposed that the peaceful idyll of the Great Good Place was shattered by the intrusion of crime—in particular, murder—forcing the detective to step in and restore peace and order to society by identifying and expelling the criminal. Like the English country house that formed the setting for so many of the murder mysteries that Auden enjoyed, the cruise ship and holiday shoreline are places of comfort, populated mostly by privileged people, with orderly routines underlying lives of civilized ease. In such places violent death makes a striking contrast before the solution of the crime reassuringly restores order.

Certainly stories like M. McDonnell Bodkin's "The Ship's Run," Agatha Christie's "Problem at Sea," Viola Brothers Shore's "The Mackenzie Case," Edward D. Hoch's "The Theft of the Bingo Card," and John Mortimer's "Rumpole at Sea" fit this bill. Set on luxury liners where the circle of well-off suspects is conveniently circumscribed by the surrounding seas, these stories show that murder is just as likely to occur during one's idle hours on holiday as in everyday life.

While the passengers scramble for alibis as desperately as they might seek lifeboats on a foundering ship, the sleuth, generally on vacation him- or herself, quickly finds that the occasion has become a busman's holiday. On board a *Titanic* that does not sink, Bodkin's hero investigates a high-stakes wager on the speed with which "the world's largest and fastest passenger boat afloat" returns across the Atlantic from New York; Christie's vacationing Hercule Poirot is prevented from nursing his *mal de mer*; Shore's Gwynn Leith cannot resist following up hunches that rise as certainly as the tides; and Hoch's professional thief, who had sought to leave his work on shore, is assured more work at sea when he is hired to locate a bingo card that is at the heart of a high-stakes game of international dealing. Even John Mortimer's barrister, Horace Rumpole, collared by his wife into a second honeymoon cruise, finds that he can escape neither the company of a dreaded judge who shares his ship nor the questions of justice that beleaguer him on land and at sea.

Another story where luxury and privilege are presumed is David Winser's "A Boat Race Murder," in which murder strikes amidst the elite Oxford rowing tream. Winser shows that competition can stir up dark undercurrents among his white-clad boaters, despite the assets that the crew members possess. The urge to compete is carried to an even greater extreme in David Ely's "The Sailing Club," a chilling tale of corporate thrill-seeking on the high seas.

Murder, however, is not confined to the orbit of the rich. The denizens of a rural Mississippi backwater discover a riverside crime in William Faulkner's "Hand upon the Waters," a tale in which the Nobel Prize–winning author illuminates the dark human impulses that lead toward violence.

An atmospheric canal and lock form the stage for Georges Simenon's dramatic tale of jealousy, "Two Bodies on a Barge."

Readers can get away from it all—geographically if not philosophically—in other international scenes shown in this volume. Gabriel García Márquez sends ghostly ocean liners through a Caribbean bay in "The Last Voyage of the Ghost Ship," and, in "Ferry Noir," Chris Rippen launches his ferry across international waters from the Continent to Britain, carrying illicit cargo and a passenger oppressed by paranoia. This is Rippen's first story to be published in English; the Dutch author wrote it especially for *Murder on Deck!*

The Far East is the scene of the crime in both Saho Sasazawa's "Invitation from the Sea" and Janwillem van de Wetering's "Messing About in Boats." In Sasazawa's story, five strangers are summoned to meet at a Japanese resort hotel, each having received an invitation signed only, "The Sea." A journalist among the invited guests discovers the sad history that links the company. Van de Wetering's little tale of misogyny describes a boating outing undertaken by a Dutch professor and his all-too-attentive Japanese secretary. The author rewrote his 1985 story of the same title for publication here, providing a more definitive conclusion while retaining the enigmatic quality that makes this tale memorable.

British author Peter Lovesey sets "Where Is Thy Sting?" on an Australian shore. Here a con man drifts into and interrupts the sad but loving routines of a couple coping with the aftereffects of the husband's stroke. This poignant portrait of a marriage also succeeds as a clever tale of entrapment.

Disposal of murderous remains is attempted in Catherine Aird's witty

"The Man Who Rowed for the Shore." There is never a question of whodunit here. Rather, the reader wonders, "Will he get away with it?"

No anthology of crimes on the water would be complete without a classic case of a corpse surrounded by a pristine stretch of sand proving no one had approached the victim. The master of impossible crimes, John Dickson Carr, presents such a puzzle in "Invisible Hands."

The will to apply legal expertise to a puzzling case is the focus of Martin Edwards's "With a Little Help from My Friends," an original story written for this volume. Edwards, who is a solicitor practicing in Liverpool, England, has his story of promises made in the past turn on a point of law.

The stories in *Murder on Deck!* were also chosen to represent a variety of crimes. The high crime of mutiny and its aftermath is the subject of Sir Arthur Conan Doyle's "The 'Gloria Scott.'" Inadvertent betrayal of military secrets is depicted in Ellery Queen's "The Adventure of the Murdered Ship," a radio play written at the height of World War II as a lesson in keeping confidential information out of enemy hands.

While the shipboard setting offers the greatest advantages to mystery writers in the classic tradition, Lester Dent's "Sail" proves that it is possible for a hard-boiled writer to manipulate the milieu effectively. In fact, although "Sail" was only one of two Dent stories to appear in *Black Mask* magazine, it was so highly regarded that today it is considered representative of the hard-boiled *Black Mask* school of writing at its best. If Dent's prose is hard-boiled, Richard Deming's might be characterized as hardfrozen. In his sexy "Honeymoon Cruise" an essential iciness underlies a new bride's apparently sultry activities.

Finally, and also first of all, the stories in this volume were chosen to entertain. Each author deftly manipulates the reader's mood: Mortimer and Aird tickle the funny bone; Ely, van de Wetering, and Rippen inspire frisson; Simenon arouses pity; and Susan Moody, in "Oh, Who Hath Done This Deed?," leaves one wondering—and close to tears.

The editor of this volume invites you to enjoy a privileged society, tour a rich variety of settings, and indulge yourself in a wealth of moods. But remain alert to the tempests of jealousy, the titter of gossips, the howling of fate, and the delicate sound of champagne glasses smashing, for *Murder on Deck!* is a cruise through exciting international waters, which also plumbs the depths of human emotions.

—Rosemary Herbert

ACKNOWLEDGMENTS

The editor would like to express warm appreciation to the following men of mystery who generously gave of their libraries, time, expertise, and impeccable taste as this volume was put together:

Edward D. Hoch
Robert H. Morehouse
Dan Posnansky

This volume could not have been assembled without the magnificent resources of the Harry Elkins Widener Memorial Library and the Houghton Library at Harvard University. The author would like to thank Joe Bourneuf, Lorraine Clairmont, Edward Doctoroff, and Sarah Phillips at Widener Library for their help and Peter X. Accardo at the Houghton Library for his expertise in chasing down literary ghosts. The reference librarians and Joan Nordell at the Boston Athenaeum made the resources of that splendid institution available as well.

Others who supported this effort include Linda Halvorson Morse and Karen Murphy at Oxford University Press; Sonia Turek, Kevin Convey, Mark Chapman, Eric Norment, Dana Bisbee, and more friends in the newsroom at the *Boston Herald*; and Jean C. Behnke, Margaret Byer, Justine du Hoffmann, Carol El-Shihibi, Darie Enriquez, Margaret Gorenstein, Jeremiah Healy, Jiro Kimura, Kate Mattes, Elaine M. Ober, Richard M. Olken, Diana O'Neill, Susan and Stephen Moody, Wilma Solomon, Bridget Thompson and the Winser family, Joyce Williams, and Scott Williamson.

The editor wishes to acknowledge her grandfather, the late Harry Fransen, for sharing his love of Long Island Sound; and to thank her father, Robert D. Herbert, for wonderful hours in the Old Town canoe; her mother, Barbara F. Herbert, for her loving support; her daughter Daisy Partington for piano accompaniment; and her daughter Juliet Partington for her boundless, cheerful encouragement.

MURDER ON DECK!

SIR ARTHUR CONAN DOYLE

(1859–1930)

It seems appropriate to launch a volume of shipboard and shoreline mystery stories with a tale of murder, mayhem, and mutiny on deck. This also happens to be the account of the first case undertaken by the world's great consulting detective, Sherlock Holmes. Although Holmes was introduced in Sir Arthur Conan Doyle's "A Study in Scarlet" in 1887, "The 'Gloria Scott,' " published six years later, holds a special place in the canon of Holmes stories. Here Holmes recounts the case that revealed to him that his extraordinary skills at observation might serve him—and others in need—as more than the "hobby" of a restless intellect.

Doyle wrote his first Holmes stories to pass the time when his own medical practice in Southsea, England, was less than lively. He based Holmes in part on his medical professor, Dr. Joseph Bell, who amazed Doyle and other students with his use of physical clues in order to gain insight into the habits and character of patients. In "The 'Gloria Scott,' " the usual role of the awestruck Dr. John H. Watson is played by Trevor and his father. One of the clues in this story, the flattened ears of a pugilist, would be familiar to Doyle from his own experience as a boxer. Doyle was also no stranger to shipboard settings, since he served as a ship's doctor on voyages to West Africa and the Arctic before setting up his Southsea medical practice.

In "The 'Gloria Scott,' " it is not insignificant that Holmes recalls himself as a young man from a more mature perspective. Narrated in the past tense by Holmes to Watson, this story shows Holmes openly describing himself as alternately astonished and vulnerable, as a person who cared enough to help out his only schoolfriend, Trevor, and that friend's father, in a perplexing and threatening situation. Along with "A Scandal in Bohemia," in which Holmes's emotional reserve is challenged by the beautiful Irene Adler, "The 'Gloria Scott' " succeeds at revealing a personal side of the omniscient sleuth. This is also one of the more adventurous of the Holmes stories. Here past action on the high seas is narrated with an immediacy derived from the fact that an old secret still has the power to destroy all that a man has accomplished in his life.

The "Gloria Scott"

1893

"I have some papers here," said my friend Sherlock Holmes as we sat one winter's night on either side of the fire, "which I really think, Watson, that it would be worth your while to glance over. These are the documents in the extraordinary case of the *Gloria Scott*, and this is the message which struck Justice of the Peace Trevor dead with horror when he read it."

He had picked from a drawer a little tarnished cylinder, and, undoing the tape, he handed me a short note scrawled upon a half-sheet of slate-gray paper.

The supply of game for London is going steadily up [it ran]. Head-keeper Hudson, we believe, has been now told to receive all orders for fly-paper and for preservation of your hen-pheasant's life.

As I glanced up from reading this enigmatical message, I saw Holmes chuckling at the expression upon my face.

"You look a little bewildered," said he.

"I cannot see how such a message as this could inspire horror. It seems to me to be rather grotesque than otherwise."

"Very likely. Yet the fact remains that the reader, who was a fine, robust old man, was knocked clean down by it as if it had been the butt end of a pistol."

"You arouse my curiosity," said I. "But why did you say just now that there were very particular reasons why I should study this case?"

"Because it was the first in which I was ever engaged."

I had often endeavoured to elicit from my companion what had first turned his mind in the direction of criminal research, but had never caught him before in a communicative humour. Now he sat forward in his armchair and spread out the documents upon his knees. Then he lit his pipe and sat for some time smoking and turning them over.

"You never heard me talk of Victor Trevor?" he asked. "He was the only friend I made during the two years I was at college. I was never a very sociable fellow, Watson, always rather fond of moping in my rooms and working out my own little methods of thought, so that I never mixed much with the men of my year. Bar fencing and boxing I had few athletic tastes, and then my line of study was quite distinct from that of the other fellows, so that we had no points of contact at all. Trevor was the only man I knew, and that only through the accident of his bull terrier freezing on to my ankle one morning as I went down to chapel.

"It was a prosaic way of forming a friendship, but it was effective. I was laid by the heels for ten days, and Trevor used to come in to inquire after me. At first it was only a minute's chat, but soon his visits lengthened, and before the end of the term we were close friends. He was a hearty, full-blooded fellow, full of spirits and energy, the very opposite to me in most respects, but we had some subjects in common, and it was a bond of union when I found that he was as friendless as I. Finally he invited me down to his father's place at Donnithorpe, in Norfolk, and I accepted his hospitality for a month of the long vacation.

"Old Trevor was evidently a man of some wealth and consideration, a J.P., and a landed proprietor. Donnithorpe is a little hamlet just to the north of Langmere, in the country of the Broads. The house was an old-fashioned, widespread, oak-beamed brick building, with a fine lime-lined avenue leading up to it. There was excellent wild-duck shooting in the fens, remarkably good fishing, a small but select library, taken over, as I understood, from a former occupant, and a tolerable cook, so that he would be a fastidious man who could not put in a pleasant month there.

"Trevor senior was a widower, and my friend his only son.

"There had been a daughter, I heard, but she had died of diphtheria while on a visit to Birmingham. The father interested me extremely. He was a man of little culture, but with a considerable amount of rude strength, both physically and mentally. He knew hardly any books, but he had travelled far, had seen much of the world, and had remembered all that he had learned. In person he was a thick-set, burly man with a shock of grizzled hair, a brown, weather-beaten face, and blue eyes which were keen to the verge of fierceness. Yet he had a reputation for kindness and charity in the countryside, and was noted for the leniency of his sentences from the bench.

"One evening, shortly after my arrival, we were sitting over a glass of port after dinner, when young Trevor began to talk about those habits of observation and inference which I had already formed into a system, although I had not yet appreciated the part which they were to play in my life. The old man evidently thought that his son was exaggerating in his description of one or two trivial feats which I had performed.

" 'Come, now, Mr. Holmes,' said he, laughing good-humouredly. 'I'm an excellent subject, if you can deduce anything from me.'

" 'I fear there is not very much,' I answered. 'I might suggest that you have gone about in fear of some personal attack within the last twelve-month.'

"The laugh faded from his lips, and he stared at me in great surprise.

" 'Well, that's true enough,' said he. 'You know, Victor,' turning to his son, 'when we broke up that poaching gang they swore to knife us, and Sir Edward Holly has actually been attacked. I've always been on my guard since then, though I have no idea how you know it.'

" 'You have a very handsome stick,' I answered. 'By the inscription I observed that you had not had it more than a year. But you have taken some pains to bore the head of it and pour melted lead into the hole so as to make it a formidable weapon. I argued that you would not take such precautions unless you had some danger to fear.'

" 'Anything else?' he asked, smiling.

" 'You have boxed a good deal in your youth.'

" 'Right again. How did you know it? Is my nose knocked a little out of the straight?'

" 'No,' said I. 'It is your ears. They have the peculiar flattening and thickening which marks the boxing man.'

" 'Anything else?'

" 'You have done a good deal of digging by your callosities.'

" 'Made all my money at the gold fields.'

" 'You have been in New Zealand.'

" 'Right again.'

" 'You have visited Japan.'

" 'Quite true.'

" 'And you have been most intimately associated with someone whose initials were J. A., and whom you afterwards were eager to entirely forget.'

"Mr. Trevor stood slowly up, fixed his large blue eyes upon me with a strange wild stare, and then pitched forward, with his face among the nutshells which strewed the cloth, in a dead faint.

"You can imagine, Watson, how shocked both his son and I were. His attack did not last long, however, for when we undid his collar and sprinkled the water from one of the finger-glasses over his face, he gave a gasp or two and sat up.

" 'Ah, boys,' said he, forcing a smile, 'I hope I haven't frightened you. Strong as I look, there is a weak place in my heart, and it does not take much to knock me over. I don't know how you manage this, Mr. Holmes, but it seems to me that all the detectives of fact and of fancy would be children in your hands. That's your line of life, sir, and you may take the word of a man who has seen something of the world.'

"And that recommendation, with the exaggerated estimate of my ability with which he prefaced it, was, if you will believe me, Watson, the very first thing which ever made me feel that a profession might be made out of what had up to that time been the merest hobby. At the moment, however, I was too much concerned at the sudden illness of my host to think of anything else.

" 'I hope that I have said nothing to pain you?' said I.

" 'Well, you certainly touched upon rather a tender point. Might I ask how you know, and how much you know?' He spoke now in a half-jesting fashion, but a look of terror still lurked at the back of his eyes.

" 'It is simplicity itself,' said I. 'When you bared your arm to draw that fish into the boat I saw that J. A. had been tattooed in the bend of the elbow. The letters were still legible, but it was perfectly clear from their blurred appearance, and from the staining of the skin round them, that efforts had been made to obliterate them. It was obvious, then, that those initials had once been very familiar to you, and that you had afterwards wished to forget them.'

" 'What an eye you have!' he cried with a sigh of relief. 'It is just as you say. But we won't talk of it. Of all ghosts the ghosts of our old loves are the worst. Come into the billiard-room and have a quiet cigar.'

"From that day, amid all his cordiality, there was always a touch of suspicion in Mr. Trevor's manner towards me. Even his son remarked it.

'You've given the governor such a turn,' said he, 'that he'll never be sure again of what you know and what you don't know.' He did not mean to show it, I am sure, but it was so strongly in his mind that it peeped out at every action. At last I became so convinced that I was causing him uneasiness that I drew my visit to a close. On the very day, however, before I left, an incident occurred which proved in the sequel to be of importance.

"We were sitting out upon the lawn on garden chairs, the three of us, basking in the sun and admiring the view across the Broads, when a maid came out to say that there was a man at the door who wanted to see Mr. Trevor.

" 'What is his name?' asked my host.

" 'He would not give any.'

" 'What does he want, then?'

" 'He says that you know him, and that he only wants a moment's conversation.'

" 'Show him round here.' An instant afterwards there appeared a little wizened fellow with a cringing manner and a shambling style of walking. He wore an open jacket, with a splotch of tar on the sleeve, a red-and-black check shirt, dungaree trousers, and heavy boots badly worn. His face was thin and brown and crafty, with a perpetual smile upon it, which showed an irregular line of yellow teeth, and his crinkled hands were half closed in a way that is distinctive of sailors. As he came slouching across the lawn I heard Mr. Trevor make a sort of hiccoughing noise in his throat, and, jumping out of his chair, he ran into the house. He was back in a moment, and I smelt a strong reek of brandy as he passed me.

" 'Well, my man,' said he. 'What can I do for you?'

"The sailor stood looking at him with puckered eyes, and with the same loose-lipped smile upon his face.

" 'You don't know me?' he asked.

" 'Why, dear me, it is surely Hudson,' said Mr. Trevor in a tone of surprise.

" 'Hudson it is, sir,' said the seaman. 'Why, it's thirty year and more since I saw you last. Here you are in your house, and me still picking my salt meat out of the harness cask.'

" 'Tut, you will find that I have not forgotten old times," cried Mr. Trevor, and, walking towards the sailor, he said something in a low voice. 'Go into the kitchen,' he continued out loud, 'and you will get food and drink. I have no doubt that I shall find you a situation.'

" 'Thank you, sir,' said the seaman, touching his fore-lock. 'I'm just off a two-yearer in an eight-knot tramp, short-handed at that, and I wants a rest. I thought I'd get it either with Mr. Beddoes or with you.'

" 'Ah!' cried Mr. Trevor. 'You know where Mr. Beddoes is?'

" 'Bless you, sir, I know where all my old friends are,' said the fellow with a sinister smile, and he slouched off after the maid to the kitchen.

Mr. Trevor mumbled something to us about having been shipmate with the man when he was going back to the diggings, and then, leaving us on the lawn, he went indoors. An hour later, when we entered the house, we found him stretched dead drunk upon the dining-room sofa. The whole incident left a most ugly impression upon my mind, and I was not sorry next day to leave Donnithorpe behind me, for I felt that my presence must be a source of embarrassment to my friend.

"All this occurred during the first month of the long vacation. I went up to my London rooms, where I spent seven weeks working out a few experiments in organic chemistry. One day, however, when the autumn was far advanced and the vacation drawing to a close, I received a telegram from my friend imploring me to return to Donnithorpe, and saying that he was in great need of my advice and assistance. Of course I dropped everything and set out for the North once more.

"He met me with the dog-cart at the station, and I saw at a glance that the last two months had been very trying ones for him. He had grown thin and careworn, and had lost the loud, cheery manner for which he had been remarkable.

" 'The governor is dying,' were the first words he said.

" 'Impossible!' I cried. 'What is the matter?'

" 'Apoplexy. Nervous shock. He's been on the verge all day. I doubt if we shall find him alive.'

"I was, as you may think, Watson, horrified at this unexpected news.

" 'What has caused it?' I asked.

" 'Ah, that is the point. Jump in and we can talk it over while we drive. You remember that fellow who came upon the evening before you left us?'

" 'Perfectly.'

" 'Do you know who it was that we let into the house that day?'

" 'I have no idea.'

" 'It was the devil, Holmes,' he cried.

"I stared at him in astonishment.

" 'Yes, it was the devil himself. We have not had a peaceful hour since—not one. The governor has never held up his head from that evening, and now the life has been crushed out of him and his heart broken, all through this accursed Hudson.'

" 'What power had he, then?'

" 'Ah, that is what I would give so much to know. The kindly, charitable good old governor—how could he have fallen into the clutches of such a ruffian! But I am so glad that you have come, Holmes. I trust very much to your judgment and discretion, and I know that you will advise me for the best.'

"We were dashing along the smooth white country road, with the long stretch of the Broads in front of us glimmering in the red light of the setting sun. From a grove upon our left I could already see the high chimneys and the flag-staff which marked the squire's dwelling.

" 'My father made the fellow gardener,' said my companion, 'and then, as that did not satisfy him, he was promoted to be butler. The house seemed to be at his mercy, and he wandered about and did what he chose in it. The maids complained of his drunken habits and his vile language. The dad raised their wages all round to recompense them for the annoyance. The fellow would take the boat and my father's best gun and treat himself to little shooting trips. And all this with such a sneering, leering, insolent face that I would have knocked him down twenty times over if he had been a man of my own age. I tell you, Holmes, I have had to keep a tight hold upon myself all this time; and now I am asking myself whether, if I had let myself go a little more, I might not have been a wiser man.

" 'Well, matters went from bad to worse with us, and this animal Hudson became more and more intrusive, until at last, on his making some insolent reply to my father in my presence one day, I took him by the shoulders and turned him out of the room. He slunk away with a livid face and two venomous eyes which uttered more threats than his tongue could do. I don't know what passed between the poor dad and him after that, but the dad came to me next day and asked me whether I would mind apologizing to Hudson. I refused, as you can imagine, and asked my father how he could allow such a wretch to take such liberties with himself and his household.

" ' "Ah, my boy," said he, "it is all very well to talk, but you don't know how I am placed. But you shall know, Victor. I'll see that you shall know, come what may. You wouldn't believe harm of your poor old father, would you, lad?" He was very much moved and shut himself up in the study all day, where I could see through the window that he was writing busily.

" 'That evening there came what seemed to me to be a grand release, for Hudson told us that he was going to leave us. He walked into the dining-room as we sat after dinner and announced his intention in the thick voice of a half-drunken man.

" ' "I've had enough of Norfolk," said he. "I'll run down to Mr. Beddoes in Hampshire. He'll be as glad to see me as you were, I daresay."

" ' "You're not going away in an unkind spirit, Hudson, I hope," said my father with a tameness which made my blood boil.

" ' "I've not had my 'pology," said he sulkily, glancing in my direction.

" ' "Victor, you will acknowledge that you have used this worthy fellow rather roughly," said the dad, turning to me.

" ' "On the contrary, I think that we have both shown extraordinary patience towards him," I answered.

" ' "Oh, you do, do you?" he snarled. "Very good, mate. We'll see about that!"

" 'He slouched out of the room and half an hour afterwards left the house, leaving my father in a state of pitiable nervousness. Night after night I heard him pacing his room, and it was just as he was recovering his confidence that the blow did at last fall.'

" 'And how?' I asked eagerly.

" 'In a most extraordinary fashion. A letter arrived for my father yesterday evening, bearing the Fordingbridge postmark. My father read it, clapped both his hands to his head, and began running round the room in little circles like a man who has been driven out of his senses. When I at last drew him down on to the sofa, his mouth and eyelids were all puckered on one side, and I saw that he had had a stroke. Dr. Fordham came over at once. We put him to bed, but the paralysis has spread, he has shown no sign of returning consciousness, and I think that we shall hardly find him alive.'

" 'You horrify me, Trevor!' I cried. 'What then could have been in this letter to cause so dreadful a result?'

" 'Nothing. There lies the inexplicable part of it. The message was absurd and trivial. Ah, my God, it is as I feared!'

"As he spoke we came round the curve of the avenue and saw in the fading light that every blind in the house had been drawn down. As we dashed up to the door, my friend's face convulsed with grief, a gentleman in black emerged from it.

" 'When did it happen, doctor?' asked Trevor.

" 'Almost immediately after you left.'

" 'Did he recover consciousness?'

" 'For an instant before the end.'

" 'Any message for me?'

" 'Only that the papers were in the back drawer of the Japanese cabinet.'

"My friend ascended with the doctor to the chamber of death, while I remained in the study, turning the whole matter over and over in my head, and feeling as sombre as ever I had done in my life. What was the past of this Trevor, pugilist, traveller, and gold-digger, and how had he placed himself in the power of this acid-faced seaman? Why, too, should he faint at an allusion to the half-effaced initials upon his arm and die of fright when he had a letter from Fordingham? Then I remembered that Fordingham was in Hampshire, and that this Mr. Beddoes, whom the seaman had gone to visit and presumably to blackmail, had also been mentioned as living in Hampshire. The letter, then, might either come from Hudson, the seaman, saying that he had betrayed the guilty secret which appeared to exist, or it might come from Beddoes, warning an old confederate that such a betrayal was imminent. So far it seemed clear enough. But then how could this letter be trivial and grotesque, as de-

scribed by the son? He must have misread it. If so, it must have been one
of those ingenious secret codes which mean one thing while they seem to
mean another. I must see this letter. If there was a hidden meaning in it,
I was confident that I could pluck it forth. For an hour I sat pondering
over it in the gloom, until at last a weeping maid brought in a lamp, and
close at her heels came my friend Trevor, pale but composed, with these
very papers which lie upon my knee held in his grasp. He sat down
opposite to me, drew the lamp to the edge of the table, and handed me
a short note scribbled, as you see, upon a single sheet of gray paper. 'The
supply of game for London is going steadily up,' it ran. 'Head-keeper
Hudson, we believe, has been now told to receive all orders for fly-paper
and for preservation of your hen-pheasant's life.'

"I daresay my face looked as bewildered as yours did just now when
first I read this message. Then I reread it very carefully. It was evidently
as I had thought, and some secret meaning must lie buried in this strange
combination of words. Or could it be that there was a pre-arranged sig-
nificance to such phrases as 'fly-paper' and 'hen-pheasant'? Such a meaning would be arbitrary and could not be deduced in any way. And yet I
was loath to believe that this was the case, and the presence of the word
Hudson seemed to show that the subject of the message was as I had
guessed, and that it was from Beddoes rather than the sailor. I tried it
backward, but the combination 'life pheasant's hen' was not encouraging.
Then I tried alternate words, but neither 'the of for' nor 'supply game
London' promised to throw any light upon it.

"And then in an instant the key of the riddle was in my hands, and I
saw that every third word, beginning with the first, would give a message
which might well drive old Trevor to despair.

"It was short and terse, the warning, as I now read it to my companion:

" 'The game is up. Hudson has told all. Fly for your life.'

"Victor Trevor sank his face into his shaking hands. 'It must be that,
I suppose,' said he. 'This is worse than death, for it means disgrace as
well. But what is the meaning of these "head-keepers" and "hen-
pheasants"?'

" 'It means nothing to the message, but it might mean a good deal to
us if we had no other means of discovering the sender. You see that he
has begun by writing "The . . . game . . . is," and so on. Afterwards he had,
to fulfil the pre-arranged cipher, to fill in any two words in each space.
He would naturally use the first words which came to his mind, and if
there were so many which referred to sport among them, you may be
tolerably sure that he is either an ardent shot or interested in breeding.
Do you know anything of this Beddoes?'

" 'Why, now that you mention it,' said he, 'I remember that my poor
father used to have an invitation from him to shoot over his preserves
every autumn.'

" 'Then it is undoubtedly from him that the note comes,' said I. 'It only remains for us to find out what this secret was which the sailor Hudson seems to have held over the heads of these two wealthy and respected men.'

" 'Alas, Holmes, I fear that it is one of sin and shame!' cried my friend. 'But from you I shall have no secrets. Here is the statement which was drawn up by my father when he knew that the danger from Hudson had become imminent. I found it in the Japanese cabinet, as he told the doctor. Take it and read it to me, for I have neither the strength nor the courage to do it myself.'

"These are the very papers, Watson, which he handed to me, and I will read them to you, as I read them in the old study that night to him. They are endorsed outside, as you see, 'Some particulars of the voyage of the bark *Gloria Scott*, from her leaving Falmouth on the 8th October, 1855, to her destruction in N. Lat. 15° 20', W. Long. 25° 14', on Nov. 6th.' It is in the form of a letter, and runs in this way.

" 'My dear, dear son, now that approaching disgrace begins to darken the closing years of my life, I can write with all truth and honesty that it is not the terror of the law, it is not the loss of my position in the county, nor is it my fall in the eyes of all who have known me, which cuts me to the heart; but it is the thought that you should come to blush for me— you who love me and who have seldom, I hope, had reason to do other than respect me. But if the blow falls which is forever hanging over me, then I should wish you to read this, that you may know straight from me how far I have been to blame. On the other hand, if all should go well (which may kind God Almighty grant!), then, if by any chance this paper should be still undestroyed and should fall into your hands, I conjure you, by all you hold sacred, by the memory of your dear mother, and by the love which has been between us, to hurl it into the fire and to never give one thought to it again.

" 'If then your eye goes on to read this line, I know that I shall already have been exposed and dragged from my home, or, as is more likely, for you know that my heart is weak, be lying with my tongue sealed forever in death. In either case the time for suppression is past, and every word which I tell you is the naked truth, and this I swear as I hope for mercy.

" 'My name, dear lad, is not Trevor. I was James Armitage in my younger days, and you can understand now the shock that it was to me a few weeks ago when your college friend addressed me in words which seemed to imply that he had surprised my secret. As Armitage it was that I entered a London banking-house, and as Armitage I was convicted of breaking my country's laws, and was sentenced to transportation. Do not think very harshly of me, laddie. It was a debt of honour, so called, which I had to pay, and I used money which was not my own to do it, in the certainty that I could replace it before there could be any possibility of its being missed. But the most dreadful ill-luck pursued me. The money which I had reckoned upon never came to hand, and a premature examination of accounts exposed my deficit. The case might have been dealt leniently with, but the laws were more harshly administered thirty years ago than now, and on my twenty-third birthday I found myself chained as a felon with thirty-seven other convicts in the 'tween-decks of the bark *Gloria Scott*, bound for Australia.

" 'It was the year '55, when the Crimean War was at its height, and the old convict ships had been largely used as transports in the Black Sea. The government was compelled, therefore, to use smaller and less suitable vessels for sending out their prisoners. The *Gloria Scott* had been in the Chinese tea-trade, but she was an old-fashioned, heavy-bowed, broad-beamed craft, and the new clippers had cut her out. She was a five-hundred-ton boat; and besides her thirty-eight jail-birds, she carried twenty-six of a crew, eighteen soldiers, a captain, three mates, a doctor, a chaplain, and four warders. Nearly a hundred souls were in her, all told, when we set sail from Falmouth.

" 'The partitions between the cells of the convicts, instead of being of thick oak, as is usual in convict-ships, were quite thin and frail. The man next to me, upon the aft side, was one whom I had particularly noticed when we were led down the quay. He was a young man with a clear, hairless face, a long, thin nose, and rather nut-cracker jaws. He carried his head very jauntily in the air, had a swaggering style of walking, and was, above all else, remarkable for his extraordinary height. I don't think any of our heads would have come up to his shoulder, and I am sure that he could not have measured less than six and a half feet. It was strange among so many sad and weary faces to see one which was full of energy and resolution. The sight of it was to me like a fire in a snow-storm. I was glad, then, to find that he was my neighbour, and gladder still when, in the dead of the night, I heard a whisper close to my ear and found that he had managed to cut an opening in the board which separated us.

" ' "Hullo, chummy!" said he, "what's your name, and what are you here for?"

" 'I answered him, and asked in turn who I was talking with.

" ' "I'm Jack Prendergast," said he, "and by God! you'll learn to bless my name before you've done with me."

" 'I remembered hearing of his case, for it was one which had made an immense sensation throughout the country some time before my own arrest. He was a man of good family and of great ability, but of incurably vicious habits, who had by an ingenious system of fraud obtained huge sums of money from the leading London merchants.

" ' "Ha, ha! You remember my case!" said he proudly.

" ' "Very well, indeed."

" ' "Then maybe you remember something queer about it?"

" ' "What was that, then?"

" ' "I'd had nearly a quarter of a million, hadn't I?"

" ' "So it was said."

" ' "But none was recovered, eh?"

" ' "No."

" ' "Well, where d'ye suppose the balance is?" he asked.

" ' "I have no idea," said I.

" ' "Right between my finger and thumb," he cried. "By God! I've got more pounds to my name than you've hairs on your head. And if you've money, my son, and know how to handle it and spread it, you can do *anything*. Now, you don't think it likely that a man who could do anything is going to wear his breeches out sitting in the stinking hold of a rat-gutted, beetle-ridden, mouldy old coffin of a Chin China coaster. No, sir, such a man will look after himself and will look after his chums. You may lay to that! You hold on to him, and you may kiss the book that he'll haul you through."

" ' That was his style of talk, and at first I thought it meant nothing; but after a while, when he had tested me and sworn me in with all possible solemnity, he let me understand that there really was a plot to gain command of the vessel. A dozen of the prisoners had hatched it before they came aboard, Prendergast was the leader, and his money was the motive power.

" ' "I'd a partner," said he, "a rare good man, as true as a stock to a barrel. He's got the dibbs, he has, and where do you think he is at this moment? Why, he's the chaplain of this ship—the chaplain, no less! He came aboard with a black coat, and his papers right, and money enough in his box to buy the thing right up from keel to main-truck. The crew are his, body and soul. He could buy 'em at so much a gross with a cash discount, and he did it before ever they signed on. He's got two of the warders and Mereer, the second mate, and he'd get the captain himself, if he thought him worth it."

" ' "What are we to do, then?" I asked.

" ' "What do you think?" said he. "We'll make the coats of some of these soldiers redder than ever the tailor did."

" ' "But they are armed," said I.

" ' "And so shall we be, my boy. There's a brace of pistols for every mother's son of us; and if we can't carry this ship, with the crew at our back, it's time we were all sent to a young misses' boarding-school. You speak to your mate upon the left to-night, and see if he is to be trusted."

" ' I did so and found my other neighbour to be a young fellow in much the same position as myself, whose crime had been forgery. His name was Evans, but he afterwards changed it, like myself, and he is now a rich and prosperous man in the south of England. He was ready enough to join the conspiracy, as the only means of saving ourselves, and before we had crossed the bay there were only two of the prisoners who were not in the secret. One of these was of weak mind, and we did not dare to trust him, and the other was suffering from jaundice and could not be of any use to us.

" 'From the beginning there was really nothing to prevent us from taking possession of the ship. The crew were a set of ruffians, specially picked for the job. The sham chaplain came into our cells to exhort us, carrying a black bag, supposed to be full of tracts, and so often did he come that by the third day we had each stowed away at the foot of our beds a file, a brace of pistols, a pound of powder, and twenty slugs. Two of the warders were agents of Prendergast, and the second mate was his right-hand man. The captain, the two mates, two warders, Lieutenant Martin, his eighteen soldiers, and the doctor were all that we had against us. Yet, safe as it was, we determined to neglect no precaution, and to make our attack suddenly by night. It came, however, more quickly than we expected, and in this way.

" 'One evening, about the third week after our start, the doctor had come down to see one of the prisoners who was ill, and, putting his hand down on the bottom of his bunk, he felt the outline of the pistols. If he had been silent he might have blown the whole thing, but he was a nervous little chap, so he gave a cry of surprise and turned so pale that the man knew what was up in an instant and seized him. He was gagged before he could give the alarm and tied down upon the bed. He had unlocked the door that led to the deck, and we were through it in a rush. The two sentries were shot down, and so was a corporal who came running to see what was the matter. There were two more soldiers at the door of the stateroom, and their muskets seemed not to be loaded, for they never fired upon us, and they were shot while trying to fix their bayonets. Then we rushed on into the captain's cabin, but as we pushed open the door there was an explosion from within, and there he lay with his brains smeared over the chart of the Atlantic which was pinned upon the table, while the chaplain stood with a smoking pistol in his hand at his elbow. The two mates had both been seized by the crew, and the whole business seemed to be settled.

" 'The stateroom was next the cabin, and we flocked in there and flopped down on the settees, all speaking together, for we were just mad with the feeling that we were free once more. There were lockers all round, and Wilson, the sham chaplain, knocked one of them in, and pulled out a dozen of brown sherry. We cracked off the necks of the bottles, poured the stuff out into tumblers, and were just tossing them off when in an instant without warning there came the roar of muskets in our ears, and the saloon was so full of smoke that we could not see across the table. When it cleared again the place was a shambles. Wilson and eight others were wriggling on the top of each other on the floor, and the blood and the brown sherry on that table turn me sick now when I think of it. We were so cowed by the sight that I think we should have given the job up if it had not been for Prendergast. He bellowed like a bull and rushed for the door with all that were left alive at his heels. Out we ran, and there on the poop were the lieutenant and ten of his men. The swing skylights above the saloon table had been a bit open, and they had fired on us through the slit. We got on them before they could load, and they stood to it like men; but we had the upper hand of them, and in five minutes it was all over. My God! was there ever a slaughter-house like that ship! Prendergast was like a raging devil, and he picked the soldiers up as if they had been children and threw them overboard alive or dead. There was one sergeant that was horribly wounded and yet kept on swimming for a surprising time until someone in mercy blew out his brains. When the fighting was over there was no one left of our enemies except just the warders, the mates, and the doctor.

" 'It was over them that the great quarrel arose. There were many of us who were glad enough to win back our freedom, and yet who had no wish to have murder on our souls. It was one thing to knock the soldiers over with their muskets in their hands, and it was another to stand by while men were being killed in cold blood. Eight of us, five convicts and three sailors, said that we would not see it done. But there was no moving Prendergast and those who were with him. Our only chance of safety lay in making a clean job of it, said he, and he would not leave a tongue with power to wag in a witness-box. It nearly came to our sharing the fate of the prisoners, but at last he said that if we wished we might take a boat and go. We jumped at the offer, for we were already sick of these blood-thirsty doings, and we saw that there would be worse before it was done. We were given a suit of sailor togs each, a barrel of water, two casks, one of junk and one of biscuits, and a compass. Prendergast threw us over a chart, told us that we were shipwrecked mariners whose ship had foundered in Lat. 15° and Long. 25° west, and then cut the painter and let us go.

" 'And now I come to the most surprising part of my story, my dear son. The seamen had hauled the fore-yard aback during the rising, but now as we left them they brought it square again, and as there was a light wind from the north and east the bark began to draw slowly away from us. Our boat lay, rising and falling, upon the long, smooth rollers, and Evans and I, who were the most educated of the party, were sitting in the sheets working out our position and planning what coast we should make for. It was a nice question, for the Cape Verdes were about five hundred miles to the north of us, and the African coast about seven hundred to the east. On the whole, as the wind was coming round to the north, we thought that Sierra Leone might be best and turned our head in that direction, the bark being at that time nearly hull down on our starboard quarter. Suddenly as we looked at her we saw a dense black cloud of smoke shoot up from her, which hung like a monstrous tree upon the sky-line. A few seconds later a roar like thunder burst upon our ears, and as the smoke thinned away there was no sign left of the *Gloria Scott*.

In an instant we swept the boat's head round again and pulled with all our strength for the place where the haze still trailing over the water marked the scene of this catastrophe.

" 'It was a long hour before we reached it, and at first we feared that we had come too late to save anyone. A splintered boat and a number of crates and fragments of spars rising and falling on the waves showed us where the vessel had foundered; but there was no sign of life, and we had turned away in despair, when we heard a cry for help and saw at some distance a piece of wreckage with a man lying stretched across it. When we pulled him aboard the boat he proved to be a young seaman of the name of Hudson, who was so burned and exhausted that he could give us no account of what had happened until the following morning.

" 'It seemed that after we had left, Prendergast and his gang had proceeded to put to death the five remaining prisoners. The two warders had been shot and thrown overboard, and so also had the third mate. Prendergast then descended into the 'tween-decks and with his own hands cut the throat of the unfortunate surgeon. There only remained the first mate, who was a bold and active man. When he saw the convict approaching him with the bloody knife in his hand he kicked off his bonds, which he had somehow contrived to loosen, and rushing down the deck he plunged into the after-hold. A dozen convicts, who descended with their pistols in search of him, found him with a match-box in his hand seated beside an open powder-barrel, which was one of a hundred carried on board, and swearing that he would blow all hands up if he were in any way molested. An instant later the explosion occurred, though Hudson thought it was caused by the misdirected bullet of one of the convicts rather than the mate's match. Be the cause what it may, it was the end of the *Gloria Scott* and of the rabble who held command of her.

" 'Such, in a few words, my dear boy, is the history of this terrible business in which I was involved. Next day we were picked up by the brig *Hotspur*, bound for Australia, whose captain found no difficulty in believing that we were the survivors of a passenger ship which had foundered. The transport ship *Gloria Scott* was set down by the Admiralty as being lost at sea, and no word has ever leaked out as to her true fate. After an excellent voyage the *Hotspur* landed us at Sydney, where Evans and I changed our names and made our way to the diggings, where, among the crowds who were gathered from all nations, we had no difficulty in losing our former identities. The rest I need not relate. We prospered, we travelled, we came back as rich colonials to England, and we bought country estates. For more than twenty years we have led peaceful and useful lives, and we hoped that our past was forever buried. Imagine, then, my feelings when in the seaman who came to us I recognized instantly the man who had been picked off the wreck. He had tracked us down somehow and had set himself to live upon our fears. You will understand now how it was that I strove to keep the peace with him, and you will in some measure sympathize with me in the fears which fill me, now that he has gone from me to his other victim with threats upon his tongue.'

"Underneath is written in a hand so shaky as to be hardly legible, 'Beddoes writes in cipher to say H. has told all. Sweet Lord, have mercy on our souls!'

"That was the narrative which I read that night to young Trevor, and I think, Watson, that under the circumstances it was a dramatic one. The good fellow was heart-broken at it, and went out to the Terai tea planting, where I hear that he is doing well. As to the sailor and Beddoes, neither of them was ever heard of again after that day on which the letter of warning was written. They both disappeared utterly and completely. No complaint had been lodged with the police, so that Beddoes had mistaken a threat for a deed. Hudson had been seen lurking about, and it was believed by the police that he had done away with Beddoes and had fled. For myself I believe that the truth was exactly the opposite. I think that it is most probable that Beddoes, pushed to desperation and believing himself to have been already betrayed, had revenged himself upon Hudson, and had fled from the country with as much money as he could lay his hands on. Those are the facts of the case, Doctor, and if they are of any use to your collection, I am sure that they are very heartily at your service."

M. McDONNELL BODKIN

(1850–1933)

The steamship *Titanic* slides smoothly through the waves—setting out from New York as though it had survived its first fateful voyage to that city from Southampton, England—in this 1908 story written before the actual ship made its disastrous maiden voyage in 1912. M. McDonnell Bodkin may have read about plans for the luxury ship's construction, since he describes the vessel as "the largest and fastest passenger boat afloat." Unaware of the ship's doom, Bodkin wrote a story in which the only anxiety a passenger might entertain during a voyage is the fear of encountering cardsharpers.

Matthias McDonnell Bodkin was born in Ireland, where he received a Catholic education and later became a barrister, Queen's counsel, member of the Irish Bar, member of Parliament, and County Court Judge of Clare. He wrote comic fiction and historical romances before turning his hand to detective fiction in his late thirties. Bodkin continued to write detective fiction for about a decade and then produced mostly nonfiction works, including his memoirs, *Recollections of an Irish Judge: Press, Bar and Parliament* (1914).

Bodkin's first series detective, Paul Beck, was known as "the rule of thumb detective," since he relied upon ordinary common sense to "muddle and puzzle out" his cases. Like Arthur Morrison's Martin Hewitt, Beck is an example of the plain man or ordinary male sleuth created in reaction to the brilliant, omniscient consulting detective Sherlock Holmes and his scores of imitators. Bodkin later created a little-known early female sleuth, whom he introduced in *Dora Myrl, the Lady Detective* (1900). Beck and Myrl are hired by adversarial employers in *The Capture of Paul Beck* (1909) but before the novel is through, the two sleuths are married. Their son, introduced in 1911 in *Young Beck, a Chip of the Old Block,* also takes a commonsense approach to crime.

The Ship's Run

1908

It began this way. She dropped her purse and he caught it as it fell. Don't run away with the notion that this was the starting point of a romance, for though the lady was young and pretty there was a wedding ring on her finger, and the man was stout, sedate and middle-aged.

They were standing together on the upper promenade deck of the great ship *Titanic* as she slid in the grey dusk, a softly-moving island, in and out through the multitudinous shipping of New York harbour. A soft mist was over the sea and the sky, stealing away their colour. The huge Statue of Liberty stood up from the smooth floor of the sea like a fine grey etching against the fainter grey of the sky. High up in the lifted hand of the great figure the beacon flared red through the haze. The dawn grew slowly—the mist changed from grey to white, from dark to light. There was a luminous splash of brightness in the clouds to the east, and without warning the blood-red rim of the sun showed over the water.

It was at that instant that pretty Mrs. Eyre dropped her purse as she leant over the rail, and Mr. Rhondel, with a snap like a swooping hawk, caught it a yard from her hand.

"Cricket!" he explained, as he restored it to the fair owner.

"Thanks," she said; "you're real smart. There were five hundred dollars in that purse on their way to the bottom of the sea, when you chipped in and caught it. Say, isn't that just fine!"—she waved a small hand admiringly at the red sun—"guess he knows how to wake things up rather."

"Going over for the first time?" said Mr. Rhondel, ignoring the opportunity of discussing the sun's capabilities.

"First time, Bob and I, to the old country."

"You're Irish, then?"

It was a bold shot. The girl—she was hardly a woman—was typically American, tall, slim, graceful, carrying her head well: and her voice had a faint twang of the American drawl, which is pleasant from pretty lips. But the shot was straight, all the same, and went home. The eyes of forget-me-not blue deepened to violet.

"Am I Irish? Why, sure; and Bob, too. My grandfather by the mother's side came over in the forties. But Bob is Irish all the way through, from his toe-nails to his top-knot. There goes the bugle for breakfast. Come along; we'll get together, we three. I'll fix it all right with the steward; you'll like my boy."

She fixed it all right, and Mr. Rhondel sat beside her at the bounteous breakfast-table. Beyond her, on the other side, was her "boy"—a handsome, clean-shaven young fellow of twenty-five.

"Where have you been, Kitty? I've waited a minute and a half, and I'm as hungry as a hawk."

He dexterously peeled a big apple as he spoke.

"Seeing the sun up," Kitty exclaimed, "and carelessly dropping my purse over the rails."

"I'm sorry."

"It's all right; don't worry. Mr. Rhondel, here, caught it as it fell. This is Bob, Mr. Rhondel—Bob Eyre, my husband; you can shake hands behind my back."

She drew herself straight and close to the table, and they shook hands behind her back, Mr. Eyre with an admiring wink at the shapely little poll on which the coils of glossy, red-brown hair were piled.

"Try a kippered herring, Mr. Rhondel," said Bob, "with tenderloin steak to follow—best thing to begin breakfast with. Sole for you, Kitty?"

They chatted freely all through the long breakfast, and by the time it was over they were old friends. Mr. Rhondel manœuvred his deck chair close to Mrs. Eyre, making no secret of his admiration. Bob Eyre sauntered off to play deck quoits. There was quicksilver in the young fellow's blood. He could not sit still for a moment; brain and muscle were full of restless vitality that craved incessant exertion and excitement.

Life on board soon settled down to a routine. On the third day out the same hour found Mrs. Eyre and Mr. Rhondel seated on their deck chairs close together, and Mr. Eyre playing shuffle-board.

"May I smoke?" said Mr. Rhondel.

"Why, certainly. I love a cigar in another person's mouth; don't smoke myself, not a cigarette even; don't like it."

She carefully found her place in her book, and then set it face down on the rug that Mr. Rhondel had tucked cosily around her.

"You are the great South African millionaire, aren't you, Mr. Rhondel?"

"So they say."

"Oh, you need not get riled. I wanted to give you a word of warning; there's cardsharpers aboard. I coaxed it out of the doctor. They plucked so many pigeons the last few voyages that now the company has a detective to watch them. The doctor wouldn't or couldn't tell me which was the detective. I guess myself it is the curate, the Rev. Abel Lankin."

"Surely not!" said Mr. Rhondel.

"Well, I suspect him. He looks too innocent to be natural. Look at him now with the fool woman over there. Isn't he a pretty buttercup? Well, I hope he'll catch the cheats, anyway."

Mr. Rhondel hoped so, too, and then their talk drifted lazily from one subject to another as the great vessel—the largest and fastest passenger boat afloat—slid smoothly through the waves.

Mrs. Eyre was sudden and frank as a child in her friendship. She told him all about herself, and all she knew about her husband.

"I worked the 'phone in New York," she confided. "My folk could have kept me at home, but I wouldn't. Bob was a conductor on the street cars when I met him; he was an inspector when I married him. We went to Niagara for the honeymoon and concluded the celebration in the Manhattan Hotel till the dollars ran out. We had fixed it up to live in New York, and we were on the look-out for a flat when the news came that started us homewards."

"What news?" said Mr. Rhondel, as he lit a cigar carefully all round from the glowing stump which he tossed overboard into the froth of waves. This frank-spoken little woman interested him. It was not mere politeness that prompted the question.

"Oh, you have got the soft end of the talk this time. It is easy to say: 'Well, what's the news?' It's not so easy to answer you slick. I'm not clear about it myself; I doubt if Bob is. I had to get the story out of him in bits, like the kernel out of a walnut, and some stuck. He was a landlord once over in Ireland. But there wasn't a cent in the job. His income was considerably less than nothing a year when he started for the States, leaving his lawyer in charge of the mortgages.

"He often told me he was the first man of his breed that had ever earned a cent. Then the British Congress passed some Act or another to boom real property, and Bob's land came in on the top of the boom. I don't know what happened. The tenants bought the land, and the State paid for it, and they paid him a bonus for selling at a big price.

"Then the State Legislature, the Senate, House of Lords, or the King of England for all I know, bought Bob's castle and demesne lands, and sold them back to Bob for less than was paid for them, and made him a free gift of the balance. It was all set out in the lawyer's letter; and I couldn't understand a word of it, but the end was plain enough. Bob had fifty thousand pounds clear out of the deal, and the old castle was waiting for him on the other side.

" 'We'll take on the job, Kitty,' he said to me; 'you'll like it and I'll like it. I always got on well with the boys, though we had our little differences about rent. I reckon they'll be glad to have me back, and Mrs. Kitty Eyre will make the county folk sit up. Between us we'll set things humming. Fifty thousand pounds is a fortune in Ireland. I'll give the boys a lead in farming. There's money to be made out of land if one knows how to make it. We'll start a poultry farm and dairy farm. I'll give you your choice, Kitty, and I'll lay a hundred dollars I beat you on the year's return.' I took him up. I've backed the chicken coop against the milk pails, and I mean to win, sure."

Just then Bob Eyre in grey flannels and bright-yellow, rubber-soled shoes came sauntering up, flushed with his efforts at shuffle-board—a fine, shapely cut of a man, with a figure that showed breeding like a thoroughbred horse: light on his feet, and agile in his motions as a cat.

As he reached his wife he opened a shapely hand and showed a fistful of money, silver and gold.

"Won it with the shovel," he explained. "The other chap fancied himself more than a bit."

He dropped down on the deck close to his wife's feet, and pushed his tweed cap back from a tangle of crisp curls.

"I'll make another bit," he said, "before we touch land; you see if I don't. Play poker, sir?" he said, turning abruptly to Mr. Rhondel.

"Sometimes," said Mr. Rhondel, smiling at a pleasant reminiscence. "Do you?"

"Rather, only in a small way up to this—half-dollar rise and five-dollar limit. I take it a gentleman should never risk more than he can pay when the last hand is played. But I'd like to have a chance of a real game. I fancy I'd sweep the board."

"Why don't you?" asked Mr. Rhondel, carelessly.

"Cannot. The captain has forbidden big play. He's a sportsman all right himself—says he's very sorry, but company's orders must be carried out. There's a 'tec on board—a whipper-snapper chap, rigged out as a sky pilot, nosing round. Old Colonel Rollin pointed him out to me when I hinted at a game. 'No use, my boy, when that chap's around,' he said. 'Eyes like a ferret.' "

"I'm real glad, Bobsie," his wife interposed, "the big game is barred. I know you. You'd bet the fifty thousand pounds on a pair if you thought the man next you was bluffing, and you'd laugh when he raked in the pool on a straight flush."

"Give us a chance, little one, I'm not that sort. Besides, it's my last hope of a flutter. I have promised never to bet more than five dollars on any game after we touch Old Ireland, and you know I'm a man of my word."

Miss Phœbe Everly passed at this moment—a genuine Gibson girl, with superlative curves and restless activity.

"Lazy!" she threw the word back at Bob Eyre as she passed, and he leapt instantly to his feet at the challenge.

"Have a game of shuffle-board?" he retorted.

"No, come for a smart walk instead. I want to ask you something."

She nodded a gay little nod to Kitty and carried him off.

"Well?" he said when they were half up the promenade deck, "what's your question? If it is *the* question, I cannot—I'm married already."

"Don't trouble on my account. I'll never take a hand in that gamble. I want you to tell me what they mean by 'a bit on the run.' "

"Don't know."

"Then find out like a good boy. I heard old Colonel M'Clure talking to Pop at lunch a lot of stuff about the day's run and the auction of the numbers and the high field and the low field. But when I asked him what it meant he told me to run away and play, it wasn't good for little girls to know everything. So I want to find out just to spite him."

"Leave it to me," said Bob Eyre; "if it's a bit of a gamble, and it sounds like it, I'll be glad to find out on my own account."

Presently he accosted Colonel M'Clure with a diplomatic question or two, and found him most genial and freely communicative. His ruddy face and white hair and whiskers gave the old Colonel a benevolent, Father Christmassy appearance. But his was not the goody-goody order of benevolence, for he could drink his glass and tell a story with the best, and his jolly laugh was a pick-me-up to a man in low spirits.

"The run of the ship!" he cried in reply to Bob Eyre's frank question. "My dear boy"—he was of the kind that call all young men dear boys— "don't tell me you have never heard of the lottery on the run of the ship."

"Won't you let me tell the truth, Colonel, once in a while? Remember, I've had only one voyage before, and that was steerage."

"Well, you've come to the right shop for information. I've been auctioneer and general boss of the lottery a score of times. Couldn't live through the voyage without it. The trip takes considerably less than no time when you have the lottery going, you bet your bottom dollar on that. I tell you what, sir—"

"Easy there!" Bob Eyre broke in upon the enthusiast before he got into his stride. "First tell me, if you please, what the thing is, anyway."

The Colonel passed from enthusiasm to explanation.

"You know the little map hanging in the broad passage between the library and the smoking-room on the upper deck?"

Eyre nodded.

"Then you have seen the day's run of the vessel is drawn each day on that map in a red line across the blue sea, with the length marked in plain figures?"

"With the last voyage marked in full," added Eyre.

"Exactly, my boy. I see you have your eyes skinned. Perhaps you have noticed that the length of the day's run ranges from about four eighty-five to five twenty. The variation is twenty or thirty miles, and the average run about five hundred. Now, here is the way the lottery is worked. A score of us—more or less—have a pound each in the pool. We put numbers up to a certain limit in a hat—say from 490 to 510—and draw. Whichever number hits the ship's run for that day scoops the pool. See?"

"But I don't see—"

"Easy on, my boy. I know what you were going to say. Maybe none of the numbers would hit the ship's run. To meet that chance there is the 'high field'—all numbers over the highest number in that hat—and the 'low field'—all under the lowest.

"But that's not the whole game either. The best is to follow. The numbers, after they are drawn, are put up to general auction. A man may bid for his own number. If he buys it in he has only to pay half the price into the general pool. If an outsider buys, the owner gets half the price bid, and the pool takes the other half. The 'high field' and the 'low field' are not drawn for at all, but auctioned right away. The auction is the real fun—eh, what?"

"A bully game!" cried Bob Eyre with enthusiasm. "Is there room for one more inside?"

"We'll try to squeeze you in, my boy. The draw will be in half-an-hour's time. There are seventeen in already; you'll make eighteen."

Later on, when Bob, as in duty bound, tried to explain the mystery to Miss Phœbe, she cut him short midway without mercy. "It sounds like a conundrum, and I hate conundrums," she said.

But Bob found her father, Judge Everly, there when he came to draw his number that evening. Mr. Rhondel was also beguiled into taking a hand in the game. The bidding in the smoking-room ran its lively course amid a storm of good-humoured chaff to which Colonel M'Clure was the main contributor.

Bob Eyre persisted that it was a bully game, in which view he was confirmed when two days later he scooped the pool of £134 with the figure 505 which he had bought at the auction for £11, having sold his own figure 504 for £10.

He was intoxicated with his success, stood drinks all round, and strutted about next day, with his tail up, to where his wife sat on the deck chair reading placidly.

"I told you so, Kitty," he crowed. "I knew I could meet and beat the knowing ones at their own game. Just a little bit of head work, that's all. I took a note of the wind and the weather, and picked the right number out on my own judgment first try. It's a little bit of all right, my dear, and here's your share of the winnings." He poured a clinking stream of gold coins into her lap.

"I wish you would leave it at that, Bob; I'm afraid."

"Fear killed a cat, or was it care? It does not matter which; don't let either kill my mouse. Keep your eye on your hubby, he'll see you through. I only wish I could get these johnnies to pile it on a bit. I don't care for this game of chuck farthing."

That evening, when they were only one day out from Queenstown, Bob Eyre had his wish. The boat had been making great time of late, averaging 515 miles a day, and there was general surprise when Colonel M'Clure, to whom the arrangement of the figure was intrusted for the most part, fixed the range of the lottery from 485 to 510.

"It's a dead cert for the 'high field,' " objected one of the coterie.

"Don't you believe it," retorted the Colonel. "Fine weather cannot last for ever. I have crossed more times than you, my boy; there is generally a bit of a blow as we come close to the poor distressful country. I don't mind having a try at the 'low field' myself, I can tell you."

The majority were, however, of the other way of thinking. The sky was without a cloud, the wind behind them, the glass going up. "Shouldn't mind betting an even pony," said one languid youth in grey flannels, "that we do our 520 this run."

"Done," cried the Colonel so sharply that the languid youth's jaw fell, and he abandoned the opposition.

Then Colonel M'Clure developed an unexpected vein of obstinacy. He seemed hurt that his judgment was questioned, and the talk began to grow hot when Judge Everly, in the interests of peace, came round to the side of the Colonel.

"Easy with the pepper castor, gentlemen," he said, "let the Colonel have his way. It's as good for the goose as the gander. We can each back our own fancy in the lottery, and the laugh will be on him when the 'high field' romps in an easy winner."

Bob Eyre joined in on the same side, and the Colonel carried the day.

"I know the Colonel was all wrong, of course," Bob confided to Kitty, "but it was not my cue to tell him so. So I kept my eye on the 'high field' as a dead cert."

That night there was wild excitement in the smoking-room when the numbers were put up to auction. Colonel M'Clure, wielding a huge pipe-case for an auctioneer's hammer, was better fun than ever. His good-humoured jests were like oil on the troubled waters of the gamblers' feverish excitement. For the bidding ran high. By a chance, lucky or un-lucky, the Rev. Abel Lankin, whose protesting presence was always a check upon any kind of gambling, did not put in an appearance.

The high spirits of the company, excited at the thought of approaching their journey's end, found a vent in high betting. Number after number was bid close up to three figures. The bigger the number the bigger the bidding, but when the Colonel reached the "high field," which looked so like a certainty, the company threw their self-control completely away, and the bidding was fast and furious. All joined in at first, and three hundred was bid before the pack began to thin off.

When five hundred was reached three men had the bidding between them—Judge Everly, thin-lipped and determined; Colonel M'Clure, full of jovial good-humour; and Bob Eyre, more reckless than ever from a slight overdose of champagne. These three kept capping each other's bids with monotonous regularity, while the rest of the company sat silent with the secondary excitement which high gambling always begets amongst the onlookers. The bidding mounted up and up, five pounds at each jump, until it seemed it would never stop. At three thousand pounds Colonel M'Clure suddenly gave way.

"I'm out of it," he said, pausing to mop his red face with a big silk handkerchief, and sucking hard at a huge cherry cobbler crowned with small icebergs that stood beside him, "this is too hot for me! Any bidding after three thousand?"

"Three thousand and five," said the Judge, in a dogged voice.

"Guineas," shouted Bob Eyre, defiantly.

That settled it. There was a long, breathless silence. The Judge seemed to hesitate for a moment. A bid hung poised on the tip of his tongue; then with an angry movement he abruptly turned his back on the auctioneer.

"Three thousand one hundred and fifty bid," Colonel M'Clure went on imperturbably. "Any bid after that? Now's your time, gentlemen, to make your fortune; going for a trifle, the chance of a lifetime. You will be cursing to-morrow when our young friend here rakes in the pool. Going! going! gone! The 'high field' to Robert Eyre, Esq., for three thousand one hundred and fifty to be paid into the pool."

It was thought that the auction of the "low field" would be a very tame business after this. The "low field" seemed so plainly out of the running that it looked as if the Colonel could buy it for a song; but a surprise awaited the company.

Mr. Rhondel, who had been drinking silently and steadily while the auction was in progress, apparently impervious to the excitement around him, now suddenly took a hand in the game.

To all present it seemed a case of a born gambler suddenly breaking loose from the curb of self-restraint and letting himself go. He bid with mad recklessness. Bob Eyre had been cool and prudent by comparison.

The company looked on in amazement. It was a duel to the death between two men—Mr. Rhondel and the auctioneer. At first Colonel M'Clure was inclined to jest at his opponent while the bidding mounted rapidly.

"All the better for the pool, boys," he said with a side wink to Bob Eyre, who sat at his right exulting in his own "dead cert."

But when Mr. Rhondel took to piling it on fifty at a time the jovial Colonel's manner changed. His face hardened; he threw away his cigar, put aside his cherry cobbler, called for a brandy-and-soda, and went to work doggedly.

There was not a second's interval between the bids, and the total mounted with bewildering rapidity. It was a fierce contest, but a short one—the pace was too hot to last.

At four thousand and fifty Mr. Rhondel suddenly collapsed, and, after a long delay and many urgent appeals to the company to come in and make their fortunes—"It was just picking up money"—the jovial Colonel, his good-humour now completely restored, knocked the "low field" down to himself.

Then there was the reaction after the excitement. The high figures had sobered the company. Through the dead silence the clear, incisive voice of Judge Everly was heard:

"This is a big gamble, gentlemen," he said, "and a ready-money business, I take it. There should be about seven thousand three hundred all told in the pool. I vote that we settle up and appoint a stakeholder before we part."

There was a murmur of approval. "I'm agreeable," said Bob Eyre, "I will pay in at once spot cash. I beg to nominate Mr. Rhondel as stakeholder, as he is out of the gamble."

"I will be glad to have Mr. Rhondel if he has no objection," said Colonel M'Clure, cordially, "though he did push me to the pin of my collar that time. Another fiver and I would have knocked under. But I love a stout fighter."

Thereupon Mr. Rhondel, whose excitement seemed to have completely fallen away when he was knocked out of the bidding, declared his readiness to act.

Several of the men retired to their cabins for cheque-books or money.

Eventually the entire amount to the last penny was paid over to Mr. Rhondel.

There were several cheques, but Bob Eyre, Colonel M'Clure and Judge Everly, who between them contributed more than nine-tenths of the pool, plumped down spot cash.

Mr. Rhondel gave a receipt for the money and left the saloon, one pocket bulging with a huge roll of notes and cheques to the tune of seven thousand three hundred pounds, and the other with a heavy revolver of the latest pattern.

He had a few minutes' talk with Mrs. Eyre, who was seated in the starlight waiting for the news of the final gamble, and to whom he gave a brief and graphic description of the exciting scene in the smoking-room.

"Three thousand guineas!" said the little woman, dolefully. "How many dollars in that, I wonder?"

"Fifteen thousand seven fifty," replied Mr. Rhondel, promptly.

"That makes it sound a deal worse. Fifteen thousand seven fifty dollars gone in a snap of the fingers to the bottom of the sea!"

"Don't say that, young woman. See, I've got it here in this pocket-book, with a lot more of other people's money."

"I've a great mind to rob you."

"Better not." He showed the butt of a big revolver protruding from his pocket.

"Sit further away," she cried in affected fear, "the brute might go off; besides, I'm ashamed of your getting mixed up in things of this kind, and encouraging Bob to scatter his dollars. At your age, too!"

"What would you say if I handed the pocket-book and all its contents over to you to-morrow?"

"You don't mean it, of course, but I could almost kiss you if you did."

"I hate that word 'almost.' "

"And I hate that word 'if.' "

"If I drop out 'if,' will you drop out 'almost'?"

"Sure."

"Good-night, then, and mind I'll keep you to your word. I've an early start to-morrow morning. The parson chap has arranged with Anderson, the chief engineer, to show him over the engines and machinery at eight o'clock, and I'm going too. Halloa, Mr. Anderson!"

A stout, dark-bearded man with a clever, resolute face passed them, peering into the semi-darkness as if in search of somebody.

"Yes, I'm here and want a word with you," said Mr. Rhondel. "Good-night again, Mrs. Eyre, and don't forget your promise."

The two men walked up and down the full length of the deck half a dozen times at at least, talking earnestly.

"It's the only way," Mr. Rhondel said at last.

"And a dang good way too," retorted Sandy Anderson, "if you're right in the rest. I'm your man to the finish. You do your part, I'll do mine. See you to-morrow morning at eight; meanwhile take care of yourself."

An early party of five curious sightseers, including Mr. Rhondel and the parson, passed through a long passage to the steerage decks, where already a number of the early-rising Irish "boys" and "colleens" were strolling affectionately in couples, and talking, doubtless, of the old land.

"This way, gentlemen," said Mr. Anderson, and opened a door that led to a long iron staircase running down to the hollow womb of the big boat.

The chief engineer welcomed them heartily to his kingdom of steel and steam. Looking down through the open ironwork of the hardworking giants in the yawning cavern, they had only a vague, confused vision of rushing pistons and revolving cranks. But Mr. Anderson led them down the interminable iron steps to the very den of the monsters.

He answered all questions with the pride and delight of a fond father when his clever children show off before strangers. Because his admiration of those wonders was the most demonstrative of all, the Rev. Abel Lankin came in for most attention. The curate was like a child in his frank surprise and delight at the steel miracles around him.

He pointed to one of two huge columns of polished metal a hundred yards long that ran from the engine-room right through the stern of the steamer.

"That's the rod of the screw," said Mr. Anderson.

"Rod!" cried the Rev. Mr. Lankin, in amazement, "it's more like a church pillar. What does it do?"

"It pushes this big ship, twenty-three thousand tons of steel without the extras, through the sea, rough or smooth, it doesn't matter which, at the rate of twenty miles an hour. Takes it easy, doesn't it? Put your hand there."

Mr. Lankin touched the shiny steel with timid fingers.

"It doesn't seem to move at all," he said.

"Oh, it moves right enough, or this ship wouldn't move. The surface is so smooth you don't feel it. Easy on," he added laughingly, as Mr. Lankin stepped from the gangway down beside the revolving column, "easy there, or you will burst your way through. There's no more than three-quarters of an inch of steel between your foot and the ocean."

"Am I so near the surface?"

"You are twenty feet under the surface, sir, and that's as near as you want to go to land in that direction I'm thinking. Come along, there are other things worth seeing."

But Mr. Lankin wouldn't budge an inch.

"What are those little holes for?" he said.

"For oil," Mr. Anderson answered good-naturedly, as humouring a child.

"And if you don't put oil in?"

"The metal would get red-hot, maybe melt, and someone would have a wigging, you bet."

At last Mr. Lankin tore himself away, and followed with the exploring party through the great cavern lit with electric light, and fresh and cool with clean ocean air sent down through the ventilating shaft that captured the Atlantic breezes a hundred feet overhead. The fascination of the great propeller shaft, however, still held the curate's imagination amid all the mechanical marvels of this cave of mystery. The white-hot furnaces, the swinging cranks, the purring dynamos, could not capture his attention.

He crept quietly back for a last look before he returned with his party to the upper air. Mr. Anderson was plainly impatient at the delay.

"You should keep with the party, sir," he said sharply, when the meek little curate showed himself at last, "you might easily get hurt by the machinery."

Undeterred by this sharp rebuke, and with a muttered apology that he had forgotten his cigar-case, Mr. Rhondel bolted back into the hold.

The genial Mr. Anderson tugged at his short beard irritably, but he said no word. Mr. Rhondel was back again in a moment, his cigar-case ostentatiously in his hand. He muttered a few words of apparent apology to Mr. Anderson that were inaudible to the rest of the company.

But whatever he said failed to bring Mr. Anderson back to good-humour. The genial guide was suddenly transformed into the curt official.

"Kindly show these gentlemen their way back," he said sharply to one of his subordinates. "I've got my work to attend to."

Without a word more he turned his back on the party and again went swiftly down the long ladder to his own restless dominions.

The party had scarcely got safely up to the deck when a strange thing happened. The throbbing and heaving of the giants in the hold, which day and night sent an incessant tremor through the huge bulk of the vessel, suddenly ceased. Swiftly and smoothly at first, and then slowly and more slowly, the great ship slid forward over the smooth sea till at last she lay quite still:

"As idle as a painted ship upon a painted ocean."

Then a wild hubbub arose amongst the passengers.

In less than a moment the captain was down amongst them, cheerily assuring them that there was not the slightest danger. There had been some slight trouble with the machinery, which would be put right in less than no time.

Still the ship lay motionless for a long hour, and the excitement amongst the gamblers was every moment more intense. Colonel M'Clure puffed himself out triumphantly, taking all the credit of the hindering accident to his own sagacity.

"I knew the 'low field' could not lose," he said. "What have you chaps to say for yourselves now?"

"Luck, pure luck," grumbled Bob Eyre, who every moment saw his chance slipping away from him. "Bar accident the 'high field' was a sure thing; but there's no fighting against luck."

"Accidents will occur in the best-regulated ships," chuckled the Colonel.

He seemed a bit disappointed when, after about an hour, the big ship began again to slip through the waters, slowly at first, but with momentarily increasing speed. He took out his gold repeater.

"I reckon," he said, "she has lost a good twenty miles by her trouble, whatever it was. The pool is as good as mine."

At about half-past eleven Mr. Rhondel appeared on deck hastily, and gathered the Judge and the Colonel and the rest interested in the pool into the smoking-room. He seemed nervous and excited.

"I have found something out," he said, "from Anderson, which I want you all to hear—especially you, Judge; and you, Colonel, as you are the most interested. I want your advice."

"Get up on the table," cried the Colonel, good-humouredly. "Some of you chaps shut the door, and don't let anyone else in. We don't mind the ladies, bless 'em, but we don't want eavesdroppers. Now, my boy, fire away!"

Mrs. Kitty Eyre had come into the room with Miss Phœbe Everly and two or three other ladies. But there was no sign of the Rev. Mr. Lankin, and all knew whom the Colonel wished to keep out.

Mr. Rhondel, mounted on a table, looked round at the eager circle of listeners till his eyes rested on Colonel M'Clure and Judge Everly, who stood close to the table together. He startled them by his first words.

"There has been foul play," he said—"the machinery in the ship's hold has been tampered with. That's how the vessel was stopped."

The smile died out of the Colonel's frank blue eyes—the genial face set hard. As if by instinct his right hand went down to a hip pocket that held his weapon.

"Have a care, sir," he snapped out—"have a care. Do you accuse any gentleman here of foul play?"

But Mr. Rhondel went on, bland, conciliatory, unabashed.

"Certainly not, Colonel—most certainly not, Judge. I accuse no one, I only state the facts. After the chief engineer had shown a party of us over the hold this morning, this was found sticking in one of the holes for oiling the screw rod." He held up for all to see the half of an hour-glass, full of sand.

"How do you know it was found?" queried the Judge.

"Well, I, myself, found it. I went back for my cigar-case and found it. Only just in time—a minute more and the machinery would have been white-hot, and would have melted with the tremendous friction, and the vessel stopped for the day. As it was, there was an hour's delay to clean and oil."

"Well," said the Colonel, briskly, "assuming all this rigmarole is true—what have we got to say to it?"

"What about the stakes I hold?" queried Mr. Rhondel; "are the bets off? I wanted to make sure before the day's run is announced."

"Not likely," roared the Colonel. "I'm too old a campaigner to be diddled in that style. If 'low field' wins, I take the pool."

"Hear, hear!" cried two or three of the men who had got low figures and fancied their own chance. Then Judge Everly spoke out sharply.

"The gamble was unconditional," he said, "every man is entitled to his chance. I have no interest in the thing one way or the other."

"I say so too," chimed in Bob Eyre, "a bet is a bet, and I'm not the one to squeal if the luck goes against me."

That settled it. There was a general murmur of assent.

"Then the figure of the day's run takes the pool," said Mr. Rhondel. "I've no objection to that; I only want to know are you all agreed?"

"All!" they cried with one voice.

He looked at his watch, still standing on the table.

"In five minutes the captain will be here to tell us the day's run."

The five minutes seemed five hours, so intense was the excitement. A low buzz of talk was in the air, like the eager whispering of a swarm of bees. It ceased in dead silence when the captain's handsome face showed at the door.

"Ladies and gentlemen," he cried in a pleasant voice that filled the silent room, "I've good news for you. In spite of the little trouble this morning we've made the record of the voyage. The run is 521 miles. I will have the figure marked on the chart."

The door had closed on him before the amazement in the room had found its voice. The impossible had happened—the "high field" had won!

"Three cheers for Bob Eyre," someone cried suddenly, and the cheers were given with a will that showed how popular was the winner.

"Ladies and gentlemen," cried Mr. Rhondel again, and there was a new and dominant note in his voice that instantly captured attention. "You would like to know the answer to this riddle—perhaps I can help you to guess it. Don't go, Colonel, don't go, Judge, my remarks are particularly intended for you. Have you ever heard of a Mr. Beck?—Paul Beck at your service." He plucked off his brown beard as he spoke and whisked away a pair of bushy eyebrows, and his face seemed to change its expression, almost its features. Mr. Rhondel disappeared—Mr. Beck arrived.

"Ha! I thought so," he exclaimed—for the two men stared at him open-mouthed. "I have met the Judge and the Colonel before, and it's pleasant to be remembered by old friends. Well, the Blue Star Company were kind enough to think I would be useful on board. There had been too much professional gambling on their ships of late.

"Somehow, when I saw you so keen on the 'low field,' I thought it possible that something might happen to the machinery this morning—coincidences are always occurring. That's why I made you pay for your fancy. My good friend Anderson ran the ship at extra speed all night, in case by any chance there might be an accident in the morning. It was Mr. Lankin who left this pretty little toy behind him by accident in the engine-room. Lucky, wasn't it, that I found it before it had done much harm. You don't know Mr. Lankin, of course, Colonel; nor you, Judge? He just played this monkey trick off his own bat for the fun of the thing. Never had a thought about the 'low field' when he did it. No one would suggest such a thing as collusion. But we needn't go into that, need we? As Judge Everly said just now, it was an unconditional gamble. The stakes go by the figure, and the 'high field' scoops the pool."

There followed a shout of applause and laughter, for Mr. Beck's exposure was complete. The Colonel and the Judge cut very sorry figures, as, self-confessed swindlers, they sneaked out of the room. All were delighted at the neat way in which the tricksters had been caught in their own trap.

"There only remains," went on Mr. Beck, suavely, "to pay over the cash to Mr. Eyre—or rather, if he will allow me, to his wife, who has kindly promised me a receipt in full."

Kitty, who had listened delightedly to the rogues' discomfiture, started at the sound of her own name, looked up and met the challenge in his eyes, and remembered her promise of the night before.

Blushing and smiling, she flashed back her answer to the challenge, and said saucily, in her dainty drawl:

"Sure."

VIOLA BROTHERS SHORE
(1890–1970)

When Viola Brothers Shore died at the age of seventy-nine in 1970, her *New York Times* obituary did not mention that she was the creator of Gwynn Leith, the highly capable amateur sleuth who solves "The Mackenzie Case." Shore dropped out of high school to pursue her dream of becoming a violinist but became an office worker, wife, and mother before taking up writing. A multi-talented writer, Shore pursued journalism, wrote titles for silent movies and screenplays for early sound movies, and penned her own plays. She also authored a biography of the producer John Golden.

As a journalist, Shore worked as a freelance features writer for the syndicates. She was a frequent contributor of short stories to the *Saturday Evening Post, Colliers, College Humor,* and women's magazines. Some of these stories are collected in *The Heritage and Other Stories* (1921). She also taught short story writing at New York University. When she turned her hand to detective fiction, Shore proved that she could produce polished work in which she competently manipulates the genre's conventions. She authored two novels, *The Beauty-Mask Murder* (1930) and *Murder on the Glass Floor* (1933), the latter of which is set on board ship. Both feature Leith and her husband, Colin Keats.

Shore's mystery writing was enriched by the dramatist's ear for dialogue, which keeps her characters' conversational exchanges lively and, in "The Mackenzie Case," also provides a clue. Set on both shipboard and the Cuban shore, "The Mackenzie Case" shows Leith quietly outsmarting her sophisticated social set by refusing to accept anything at face value and acting on her "hunches." Until now largely forgotten by fans and chroniclers of the literary history of detective fiction, her work was admired by Ellery Queen, who selected "The Mackenzie Case" as "one of three great short stories about women sleuths" published in the definitive anthology *101 Years' Entertainment* (1941). Shore anticipated trends in detective fiction today by writing work dependent upon dialogue and creating a female sleuth with a spouse sidekick. Leith refers to her husband, who chronicles her work and shows suitable amazement at her deductions, as her "perfect straight man" and her "Watson."

The Mackenzie Case

1934

"So you had a dull trip down," laughed Clarence Cobb, our host, after some sally by my wife about our recent fellow passengers.

Five of us were sipping *frappés* on the terrace, while Mrs. Cobb showed Erik Schroeder her tropical gardens by moonlight. The Cobbs have a beautiful home outside Havana and at their request we had brought with us three dinner guests—Dr. Whitmore, the ship's surgeon; Erik Schroeder; and Leni Dill, a pretty girl in whom Schroeder had shown some interest during the trip. None of us, except Schroeder and my wife, had anything to do with the Mackenzie case.

"So dull that a man jumped overboard the first night out of New York," replied my wife.

"The first night out!" Clarence Cobb is a lawyer. "That's unusual. Ordinarily they wait a little longer."

"That's what struck me, too," commented my wife, lightly.

"Are you in earnest?" demanded Leni Dill. "You mean a man really jumped off our boat?"

"Ask the doctor," replied Gwynn. "I don't suppose there's any reason for keeping it secret any longer."

Dr. Whitmore regarded my wife curiously. "How did you know, Mrs. Keats?"

"Trust Gwynn," chuckled Clarence Cobb. "Don't you know she's the famous Gwynn Leith? And her husband there is Colin Keats, who Dr. Watsons her."

The doctor, it seems, recalled my book on the Hanaford murder. Gwynn laughed off his awe. "I just happened to have a lucky hunch. But Mr. Schroeder is a *real* detective."

Leni Dill almost jumped out of her chair. "Erik Schroeder—? He told me he was a big game hunter!"

Everybody laughed. "He's solved more crimes than any man in the country," said Gwynn. "But he doesn't happen to have a husband to write him up."

"I didn't hear any mention of a suicide," remarked Clarence Cobb.

"It was kept very quiet," explained the ship's surgeon. "The Captain didn't want the other passengers distressed. He was somebody utterly unknown—secretary to a wealthy man on board."

"How do you know Mackenzie is wealthy?" inquired Gwynn.

"Well, a man who travels with a secretary—" argued the doctor.

"Oh. . . . I see. . . ." said Gwynn with that look of complete innocence which immediately made me demand:

"What makes you think he isn't?"

"Well—for one thing, he didn't tip his steward."

"Perhaps that was the Scotch in him," I suggested, a little annoyed that my wife had not taken me into her confidence.

"But that first night—up in the bar—he insisted on treating everybody in sight—"

"Maybe that was the rye in him."

"Tell us about it," coaxed Leni Dill. Gwynn referred the question to the doctor.

"All I know is that Schmidt went overboard some time Wednesday night, and nobody knows why or how."

"Oh, come," protested Gwynn. "I saw you talking earnestly to Mackenzie in the bar after dinner."

"He was merely complaining of not feeling well and I told him there are people who become ill as soon as they get on a boat. He said his secretary must be of that type, because he had gone to bed as soon as the engines started. He had had the man out on the deck for a while, but he was so ill Mackenzie had had to put him back in bed. However, Mackenzie himself had crossed a dozen times and never felt sick. So I inquired what they had eaten for lunch. And when I heard tuna fish salad, I decided they were both suffering from ptomaine poisoning and suggested having a look at the secretary.

"But he asked me not to. 'He's just dropped off to sleep,' he told me. 'He wouldn't let me send for you. Ardent Scientist, you know. But I'm not, so if there's anything you can recommend for me—' And that's all I know except that Mackenzie was quite sick for the balance of the trip."

"But why did Schmidt commit suicide?" insisted Leni.

"Nobody knows. Nobody had ever spoken to the man. Even Mackenzie didn't know anything about his private life. Schmidt had been in his employ only a few days."

"Well, but how did you know he committed suicide?"

"He wasn't anywhere on the boat."

"But how did you discover he wasn't?" persisted Leni.

"From the stewards. When Mackenzie became ill he took another room on A deck and sent down a steward for his bag, cautioning him not to disturb Mr. Schmidt. The steward reported that Mr. Schmidt wasn't in the room. Later the C deck steward reported that he couldn't find him. Well, after a boat has been searched, there's only one thing to think, isn't there?"

"Except, of course, why he did it," suggested Gwynn. "What else did the steward on C deck have to report?"

"He only verified what Mackenzie had said. Soon after they came on board the one man went to bed. Later the other man—that was Mackenzie—rang and asked him to carry a chair out to C deck. Together they helped the sick man out. He was very sick. When the steward had freshened up the berth, he was slumped over the railing, his head on his arms, and his face looked ghastly. The steward suggested getting me. But although the man was so sick that Mackenzie had to bend down to get his answer, he wouldn't have me.

"Some time during dinner the steward went to 361 in answer to the bell. Mackenzie met him in the companionway and told him Schmidt had dropped off to sleep. 'But you might look in,' he said, 'in a couple of hours and see if he wants anything. I'm going up on deck. Feeling a little rocky myself.' And according to the steward, he *did* look rocky."

"I thought he did, too," said Gwynn, "but he insisted on buying more and more drinks. When he got the color of ashes of split-pea soup, I took him out on deck and heard all about how he came from Alberta; had been in the States only for short visits; how Schmidt had told him a hard-luck story, but was evidently incompetent, having selected doubtful tuna and an inferior room, to which Mackenzie couldn't bear to return—particularly as he had given Schmidt the lower. So I suggested that he get another room."

"I noticed you were taking quite an interest in him," I remarked, in the immemorial manner of husbands.

"Oh," laughed my wife, "I'm just a child at heart and I was fascinated by his wrist watch."

"Were you in his room the morning I couldn't find you?"

"You bet. But his passion for my company seemed to have waned."

"Serves you right. You just went in there to snoop around. Did you find anything?"

"Two things," replied my wife. "A faint odor of ipecac and a mirror that swung with the boat."

"And what did they tell the Great Mind?"

"The mirror told me that the handsome Mr. Mackenzie didn't like my visit—in fact, if I'm not reading too much into a mere look, he was fairly terrified. And the ipecac—well, it's what you give croupy babies to make them vomit, isn't it, Doctor?"

"Why, Gwynn!" exclaimed Helen Cobb from the doorway, where she had been standing with Schroeder. "You haven't been sleuthing in competition with the Real Thing?"

Erik Schroeder looked at my wife out of shrewd blue eyes. He has white hair and the hawklike features of the Conan Doyle tradition.

Leni Dill eyed him accusingly. "Erik! You never told me there was a suicide. And Mrs. Keats knew all about it!"

"That was because I had the luck to be in the next room to Mr. Mackenzie," said Gwynn.

I snickered. "I don't suppose you were the one who saw the Purser about getting him that room—?"

"Well, but I had the luck to see the Captain and the First Officer go in there and to hear the doctor tell them Mr. Mackenzie was too ill to be questioned. And considering that somebody had been inquiring after Mr.

Schmidt—and the engines had been reversed—I couldn't help inferring *something*. But I daresay Mr. Schroeder knows all about it, since he went in there with the Captain."

"I wasn't there officially," smiled Schroeder. "The Captain merely asked me to step in while he questioned Mackenzie. And I went over Schmidt's belongings to see if we could discover his identity. But there wasn't a scrap of paper—nothing that would give a clue."

"That wasn't what I gathered from our steward," said Gwynn.

"What did you gather from your steward?"

"That you had found some handkerchiefs and things monogrammed *P.S.*—of fine quality, but not new—which led to the belief that Mr. Schmidt had once had money. All the other things—the newer ones— were of very inferior quality."

"Well, that's true," admitted Schroeder. "I thought it might supply a motive—a man who had come down in the world and couldn't take it."

"But on the other hand," suggested Clarence Cobb, "he had a job—" Schroeder shrugged. "And don't you think it strange that he carried *nothing* to identify him?"

"As if somebody had gone through his things and removed anything that *might*—" supplemented my wife.

"Look here, Mrs. Keats," said Schroeder, "just what have you in mind?"

"What I bet you also had in mind, Mr. Schroeder . . . that Mr. Mackenzie murdered his secretary."

"Gwynn!" I cried. The others looked at her in various degrees of amazement. When the doctor recovered his voice he was thoroughly outraged. Mackenzie was an exceptionally charming man. Schmidt had simply gone overboard.

"But *why*?"

"Violently seasick people often contemplate suicide. The man was probably a neurotic."

"Ardent Scientists are never neurotics," reproved Gwynn. "Mr. Mackenzie must have overlooked that when he talked it over with you."

The doctor looked irritated. "I imagine sometimes Scientists go out of their minds. Even the steward said how terribly sick he was."

"So sick that two of them had to help him out on deck."

Schroeder had not taken his eyes from my wife's face—troubled eyes. "What makes you think it wasn't suicide, Mrs. Keats?"

"Just a hunch," replied Gwynn.

Schroeder continued to look grave. "And what else?"

"Well—there was one thing, at least, that should have been in Schmidt's bag."

"And what was that?"

"Mrs. Eddy's book. Don't you think an ardent Scientist would have had it with him on the trip?"

The ghost of a smile narrowed Erik Schroeder's eyes. "I commented on that, but the Captain seemed satisfied—and I'm on a holiday. Besides, there doesn't seem to be much motive for a man to murder his secretary."

"You have only Mackenzie's word that Schmidt *was* his secretary—"

"He's listed that way," protested the doctor. "*Wm. R. Mackenzie and Secretary.*"

"Suppose a man had found his secretary making love to his wife," suggested Leni.

"Hardly likely," said Schroeder. "Mackenzie is a handsome, engaging young man and according to the steward, Schmidt was middle-aged and plain."

"Tell me," asked Gwynn. "Was Schmidt a bigger man than Mackenzie?"

"No, smaller. Why?"

"Did you happen to notice Mackenzie's wrist watch?"

"An ordinary silver watch with a leather strap. I've seen them in Canada for a pound sterling."

"And it didn't strike you as odd—?"

"Many rich men wear cheap watches while traveling. Particularly a Scotchman might—"

"But I mean about the leather strap."

"It was apparently much worn—"

"What does it mean when one eyelet is badly worn, the others not at all?"

"The worn one has been used," volunteered Clarence.

"Well, the eyelet that fastened the strap firmly around Mackenzie's wrist wasn't the used one. It was three farther down. So it looked as though the watch had been worn for a long time by somebody with a smaller wrist than Mr. Mackenzie and had only recently been taken over by Mr. M."

"May I use your phone?" asked Schroeder. Clarence went with him and I strained my ears, but the conversation was in Spanish.

Helen Cobb's eyes widened. "My gracious, Gwynn, you've started something. He's speaking to the Commissioner of Police!"

"I know—he's suggesting holding Mackenzie for further questioning. They naturally asked him to stay in Havana for the routine investigation. But he hasn't stirred out of his room since we landed."

"I suppose that's what you were discussing with the chambermaid this morning?"

"It was," replied Gwynn, utterly unabashed. "I was trying to figure out some excuse for calling on him. I'd like to ask him how he came to hire a secretary—without references."

Gwynn certainly plays in luck. When we reached the Nacional, there was a message from Mackenzie asking us to call him. We stopped at his room instead. William Mackenzie could not have been over twenty-six, with a fine athletic frame and a lot of curly hair and gray-blue eyes in which there was something helplessly worried as he begged us to come in.

He told us the Commissioner had been there, wearing him down with questions about Schmidt. "I think Schroeder put him up to it. He's darned clever, Schroeder. Of course I stuck to what I told them all along."

"Why not, if it's true?"

"But it isn't," said Mackenzie. I hoped he didn't see the look Gwynn shot me out of those absurdly expressive brown eyes. "We had sailed as Mackenzie and Secretary and I didn't see why certain things should be dragged in that I was anxious to keep quiet. But this Cuban chap put the screws on me pretty hard. And I'm anxious to get away. You're the only people I know in this part of the world, and I'd like to ask your advice."

I did not look at my wife although, in case I have not mentioned it, she is very easy to look at, with dark hair going off one ear and towards the other in a natural swirl, and clothes that always make other women look either overdressed or undergroomed.

"Last Thursday," began Mackenzie, "I arrived in New York with my wife. We went to the Wendham Hotel. Saturday morning, a little before ten, I went out to keep a business engagement. When I came back, my wife was not there. And she was not in the dining room, or anywhere in the hotel. I opened her closet and it was bare. The bureau was empty, too. Everything belonging to my wife had been cleaned out of the place!

"While I was trying to grasp what could have happened, there was a knock at the door. A strange man stepped into the room.

" 'Look here, Mr. Mackenzie,' he said, 'my name is Schmidt. I'm the house detective. I was next to the operator when you called down to ask about Mrs. Mackenzie.' And he told me he had seen my wife drive off with her bags, but had thought it better to say nothing downstairs in case there was anything in the nature of a scandal. Because there had been a man in the cab—also with bags.

"You have to understand the relationship between my wife and myself to realize my state of mind. Three years ago I took a trip to Hollywood and met my wife, who was working in pictures. In ten days we were married. Since then we had never been separated for a day—hardly an hour. And now she was gone . . . with another man! I was utterly stunned and grateful for this stranger's help. Alone I would not have known where to turn.

"I hadn't the faintest notion of who this other man could be. We had been in New York only two days, and together all the time. She hadn't known until the day we left that she was coming. How could she have arranged an elopement? And up on the farm we lived a very secluded life. The few people who visited us were old friends of mine.

"Schmidt went out to make some inquiries. The more I thought, the more I was baffled. I admit I have a jealous nature and I had always been watchful. I could recall nothing—no absence—no letters—no mysterious phone calls that should have made me suspicious at the time, or that offered any clue as I paced my room, waiting for Schmidt."

"And being a suspicious man, you hadn't asked Schmidt anything about himself?" inquired Gwynn.

"Why, no. He was the house detective—and besides I was too upset to think about him. And of course I didn't know he was going to jump off a boat and get me in a mess."

"Of course not. I suppose he asked you for money."

"I gave him a little for immediate expenses. Later, of course, I furnished money for cables and bribes and all sorts of things—a lot of money," he concluded ruefully.

"He came back to say that the starter recalled it was a Yellow Cab, and also the man in the cab, but not his appearance. We agreed not to mention anything to anybody, since I was eager to avoid scandal and the hotel people might resent his conduct. But he was sick of his job and eager to start off as a private investigator.

"Finally he found a driver who had been picked up by a man with a gladstone bag and stopped at the Wendham for a lady answering the description of Mrs. Mackenzie. He had driven them to the Ward Line pier. The *Orizaba* had sailed that Saturday. And Schmidt's next report was that a tall blonde in a black coat with a Persian collar and a man with a gladstone bag had sailed on the *Orizaba*.

"Schmidt offered to trail them. Of course I wanted to go, too. He made all the arrangements. I was too stunned to do more than follow his instructions. I swear to God that's all I know about Philip Schmidt. But you can see why I didn't immediately blurt it out when I was questioned."

"Of course," said Gwynn. "You certainly seem to be having hard luck. And now that you're eager to be after your wife, they hold you here. Have you made any inquiries at all?"

"No. I didn't think it wise—feeling that I was under surveillance."

"There!" said I to my wife as we were getting ready for bed. "What do you think of your murder case now?"

"I admit I have an entirely different slant on it. Let's talk to Schroeder tomorrow. . . . But doesn't it seem funny that Schmidt, having secured the kind of job he wanted, should take himself off so mysteriously?" And she began to sing: " 'Just for a handful of ptomaine he left us—' "

I turned out the light.

The next day we called at Schroeder's hotel. He had already seen Mackenzie, who, on Gwynn's advice, had told him the story. Schroeder was surprised that Mackenzie had confided in us.

"It's because I wore my Girl Scout badge," said Gwynn. "Matter of fact, I don't know whether he wanted our advice half so much as our money. He was dying to get us into a game."

"What kind of game?"

"Any kind—as soon as he heard we were bad money players."

I am always amazed at how mean and suspicious Gwynn can be when she doesn't like a person.

"I don't like him, either," admitted Schroeder, "but I've checked his story. Mackenzie and wife registered at the Wendham from Edmonton. She left two days later. However, the starter couldn't recall whether she left alone, and denied having given any information about a Yellow Cab. In fact, Schmidt was unknown at the Wendham and they employed no house detective.

"So any deception seems to have been on the part of Schmidt. I haven't the faintest idea what his game was. But since he's gone, why bother? We have also had word from Edmonton that a William R. Mackenzie lives there, and that he left last week for New York with his wife. So there seems no further reason for holding Mackenzie and I understand the Cuban police have told him he may go."

"May I make a suggestion?" said Gwynn. "Before he checks out, ask him what his business was in New York, and what his wife's name is. Perhaps, if he is so anxious to trace her, he will show you a picture."

"But why? What have you in mind?"

"Nothing," replied Gwynn, "only I'd like to see the type of woman who would run out on a man like Mackenzie. Of course, it may have been his stinginess. But then, there was that lavish display in the bar. If a tight man loosens up to that extent, there must be some reason. The reason is missing. A lot of things are missing. Principally why Schmidt killed himself."

The following morning Mackenzie tapped on our door to ask us whether we wouldn't care for a chukker of backgammon—which we wouldn't—and to tell us he had been released by the authorities.

"That's fine," said Gwynn. "I suppose you can't wait to start looking for your wife. How are you going about it?"

He gestured helplessly. "I don't know where to begin."

"How about the Commissioner?" I suggested.

"How about Erik Schroeder?" suggested Gwynn. "If anybody can find her, Schroeder can."

"But he'll want too much money. And besides, I don't like him. What concern is it of his what my business was in New York? Matter of fact, I wouldn't mind telling it to you. If you're writers, you might be able to use it. It would make a great yarn."

My wife and I exchanged that certain look. Everybody has a story that would make a great yarn. And everybody is so generous in the manner of telling it!

"I've been working on an invention in Canada. I needn't tell you what it is—but it has to do with film. It should be worth a fortune if properly marketed. Of course it's tough dealing with those big corporations and the proper approach is as important as the invention.

"Well, one day I got a letter from a man named Paul Stone outlining a scheme for promoting my patent. And the details of the scheme were exactly as I had dreamed them. I don't know how he got wind of my invention, because I kept it very quiet. I have my own laboratory. My wife helped me and not another soul knew about it. Naturally I wrote back to Stone and he suggested that I come to New York and talk it over. He wanted me to come alone, but at the last minute I decided to take my wife. I felt she was entitled to a trip."

"Also, wives get into trouble if they're left alone."

"I thought of that. So she came along."

"Eagerly, I'll bet?"

"Well, of course, she claimed she had no clothes, but—This fellow Stone had reserved a room for me at the Wendham and we went there. I found a wire saying he had been called out of town, but would be back Saturday. So my wife and I went sightseeing and Saturday morning Stone phoned and asked me to meet him in the lobby of the Alamac."

"Up on 71st Street?"

"That's it. Well, I waited awhile, and then had him paged, and then waited some more. Then I inquired at the desk whether he was in his room. They told me there was no Paul Stone registered at the Alamac! I didn't know what to make of it, because I had always written him there. However, he had brought me all the way from Alberta for that appointment and I was sure he meant to keep it. But at one o'clock I went back to my own hotel. And would you believe it—I never heard another word from Stone? What do you make of that?"

"I make that Mr. Stone was very eager to get Mr. Mackenzie out of the way so that Mrs. Mackenzie could get out of the Wendham. I make also that Mrs. Mackenzie prompted Mr. Stone's entire correspondence. There is always an accommodating laundress to receive mail, or a farmer's wife who brings around fresh eggs. . . . The decision to take Mrs. Mackenzie to New York probably upset the original plan. If Mr. Mackenzie had gone alone, he would perhaps not have heard from Mr. Stone at all. Nor found Mrs. Mackenzie back on the farm in Edmonton."

Mackenzie looked stupefied, then furious. "What a fool I've been! I'll put Schroeder on her track—no matter what it costs! Where is Schroeder? I want to see him!"

We offered to take him to Schroeder's hotel. On the way out we stopped for the mail. Mackenzie tore open a letter and read it, a puzzled frown between his brows.

"What do you make of this?" he demanded, holding it out to me.

" 'Darling Philip—' " it began.

I looked up. "For Schmidt?"

He held out the envelope. It was addressed to *Philip Schmidt, Care William R. Mackenzie, Hotel Nacional,* and bore a Cuban stamp.

"Perhaps I shouldn't have opened it, but—you understand. Read it," he urged.

When I sent that wire to the boat I really meant to patch things up with Emilio and never see you again. But last night he was drunk again—terribly—Oh my darling this time I mean it. I will go away with you—Come at once. I need you. Love—love—love—

C—

It seemed plain enough then. Schmidt had wanted to get to Havana. In some way he got wind of Mrs. Mackenzie's flight and played on Mackenzie's credulity and distress to work the trip. On the boat he received a cable from his *Señora* calling the deal off. Curtain for Mr. Schmidt.

I was so pleased with my perspicuity that I blurted it out, not thinking of the effect on Mackenzie. I suppose subconsciously I felt I was doing him a good turn. I didn't realize that all along he had been buoyed up by the hope and excitement of the chase. With the prop removed he was in a bad way. No use now in seeing Schroeder. No use in anything.

He seemed on the point of collapse and I did what I could for him. It was pitiful the way he clung to us. By nightfall Gwynn had a headache, but I went in and played cards with him. And the next morning, as the headache persisted, we started off without her for Morro Castle. He looked wretched and there was a feverish light in his eyes. As I look back now I can understand it. His manner became more and more curious. He carried a Panama hat; but although the sun was doing its tropical best, he refused to put it on. And under his arm he clutched a package as though it contained rubies. I remember, before we left, Gwynn moved the package and he jumped and took it away from her and held it on his lap until I was ready to go.

Clarence Cobb had sent us a Captain of the Militia to act as guide. As he walked around the outside of the fortress, Mackenzie kept asking about sharks. The Captain told us stories. Vivid stories. They seemed to have a horrible effect on Mackenzie, who kept peering into the water and insisting he saw sharks. I couldn't get him away from those rocks. And he asked me whether I thought there had been sharks when Schmidt went overboard. I assured him there were none.

"I hate to think—maybe there were sharks—" He shut his eyes and swayed. I begged him to put on his hat. I thought the sun was affecting him. But he continued to spot sharks and mumble about Schmidt—once excusing him: "I can understand him. Why go on living without the one thing you want most?" and the next time cursing him: "I had no reason for loving the ——— but if I had thought that there were sharks—"

That sentence stuck in my mind until I realized it was because of the tense. If he didn't know until yesterday . . .

The Captain was telling us about the dungeons where tradition has embroidered fantastic tales of cruelty to prisoners. Mackenzie shuddered and swayed again.

"Look here," I said, "if you'd rather not go in . . . ?"

"Why shouldn't I?" He bridled. "Why shouldn't I look at dungeons?"

I wanted to get away. An idea had occurred to me. Since Mackenzie had opened Schmidt's letter, perhaps he had also opened that wire on the boat and read it. . . . Fury at Schmidt would supply a motive. . . . I wanted to talk it over with Gwynn.

There is nothing in those dungeons except what imagination paints into them. But we had no sooner stepped inside than Mackenzie had to go out again. We waited for him to return and then went in search of him. Back on the rocks where we had watched for sharks I saw something. I picked it up. It was a wallet monogrammed *W. R. M.* It had not fallen there. It had been wedged between the rocks—conspicuously—where searchers would not fail to find it.

I looked down at the graying water. A Panama hat floated on a wave. Was it imagination or did I see a dark fin cutting the surface of the water? . . . Suddenly the hat disappeared. I became violently ill.

The papers gave the story a great play. Suicide of Wealthy Canadian in Waters off Morro Castle . . . Eyewitness Sees Sharks Attack Hat . . . Wm. R. Mackenzie, despondent over the loss of his wife, ended his life etc. . . . etc. . . . And they gave plenty of space to the wallet, which contained travelers' checks and a farewell note addressed to Mrs. Mackenzie.

"So I guess Mrs. Keats had the right hunch," said Schroeder, "and Mackenzie did finish Schmidt before he went up to the bar."

"Quite a while before," said Gwynn, and outlined what she thought had taken place. "I figure he got him out on deck and possibly hit him over the head while he was leaning over the rail. The steward said the man was lying with his head on his arms and looked ghastly. Our boy friend may only have pretended to get an answer about the doctor. Maybe there was no answer. Watching his chance, he dropped him overboard. Then he went into the stateroom and fixed up Schmidt's suitcase—messed up the bed—rang for the steward and met him in the companionway to register that Schmidt was asleep. Then he went to the bar and began that wild orgy of treating, during which he proceeded to get so sick that he wouldn't have to go back into that cabin, or have anything to do with discovering Schmidt's absence. Or answer too many questions. And I daresay, when I dropped in, he was a little sorry he had been so friendly the night before."

"Poor guy," said I. "Out of a boatload of people, he just had to pick on *you*. Author of Perfect Crime Makes One Fatal Error."

"Author of *this* perfect crime made several. And something tells me
it will eventually make good telling."

"Eventually! Why not now?"

"I should say not! Think of my sense of drama. By the way, Mr.
Schroeder, did you ever find out his wife's name?"

"Temple Mackenzie."

"Temple—" said Gwynn musingly.

"Why?"

"It might be a good thing to remember."

Back in New York, we received a phone call from Erik Schroeder. He was
working on a big case and wanted Gwynn's hunch on it—the well-known
woman's angle. At his apartment the talk naturally drifted to Mackenzie.
Schroeder had followed up certain threads. "You never can tell," he
jeered, "I may want to write it up for the magazines."

Gwynn laughed. "Without the final chapter?"

"I think I have a tag—"

"Then you saw that bit in yesterday's paper?"

"What bit—?"

"From Hollywood?"

"What has Hollywood to do—"

"Pardon me, I spoke out of turn. What's your tag?"

"Well, far from being a rich man, the only estate Mackenzie left was
his expectations from that patent which, unfortunately, isn't worth a
damn. One of the G.E. men told me everything in it is covered by better
patents of their own. You questioned his being a rich man. In fact, you
called all the turns. Having read some of your fiction detectives, I should
say Lady Novelist takes Great Detective for a ride all along the line—and
that makes our last chapter."

"Next to the last," corrected Gwynn. "You haven't by any chance seen
'Wild Eagle' at the Paramount this week?"

"Don't change the subject," said I. "Stick to the Mackenzie tale."

"That's it."

"The picture you saw this afternoon? Don't be so damn' cryptic."

"Can't a girl have her simple pleasures? Knowing we were going to
see Mr. Schroeder I couldn't resist a sort of coup. My dramatic instinct,
you know. I'll sit through the picture again for the pleasure of watching
your faces. And then I'll tell you *my* final chapter."

For two reels nothing happened. And then Schroeder straightened up
in his seat and I exclaimed aloud. . . . There on the screen in riding
breeches was Wm. R. Mackenzie!

"The son-of-a-gun!" said Schroeder, when we were back in his apartment.
"I'll bet you got a shock when he walked on this afternoon."

"Not exactly. I went there expressly to see him. But maybe I'd better go back and 'tell all'?" inquired my wife brightly.

"Maybe you'd better," replied her husband grimly.

"Remember the night you went to Philadelphia, Colin?" I did, of course. "Well, it's a good thing you didn't call me because I wasn't home. I was out all night."

I refrained from comment.

"I was at the Wendham. Took a room on the same floor on which the Mackenzies had stayed and got clubby with Helen, the chambermaid. She remembered Mrs. Mackenzie—a tall, pretty blonde. It seems she had got clubby with Helen, too, and complained about Mackenzie . . . he had plenty of money but was terribly tight . . . kept her cooped up on a farm like a prisoner. 'Of course,' said Helen, 'if she left him she wouldn't get a cent and he left her everything in his will. He made it before they were married. But she said to me, she said, "What the hell! Money isn't everything." '

"I'd been wondering how Temple managed to communicate with her lover."

"How did you know she had a lover?" demanded Schroeder. "Schmidt may have made up that whole business."

"Oh—she had to have a lover, for my hunch. Anyway, the bathroom of the Mackenzie suite has a door into the next suite. Temple goes in, turns on a tub, and has ready communion with the gentleman in the next suite, whom, by the way, you saw tonight—the tall, curly-headed young man in breeches."

"Hold everything! That one was Mackenzie—"

"The billing says Pat Salisbury," Gwynn pointed out.

"Yes, but I thought Mackenzie had taken the name of Salisbury—"

"No—the other way round. Salisbury took the name of Mackenzie. After he murdered him and dropped him overboard."

"By God!" Schroeder brought his fist down.

"Wait a minute!" I cried. "I don't get you—"

"Take your time," replied Gwynn. "Or—I'll tell it to you by easy stages. I'd better begin three years ago—in Hollywood with a couple of young people named Temple Drury and Pat Salisbury—both working in pictures—and the going pretty rough for the girl. Along comes Mackenzie—poses as a millionaire—even making out a will leaving her his fortune. Poor man thought he would have one, some day! She marries him and he takes her to Canada and keeps her cooped up while he monkeys with his invention. Having had a taste of starvation, maybe for a while she is grateful for the security of a roof and three squares. But eventually she gets restless and manages to communicate with the old boy-friend, Salisbury.

"At last she decides to run away. But Mackenzie watches her like a hawk. So Salisbury, in New York on a little spree, writes the husband exactly the kind of letter that would interest him, signing it Paul Stone, and lures him to New York. But something about Temple's manner at the last minute worries Mackenzie and he decides to take her with him.

"Salisbury, who has been staying at the Wendham, and only picking up mail addressed to 'Stone' at the Alamac, gets him a suite next to his. Temple and he perfect their plans through the bathroom door and he phones Mackenzie, as Paul Stone, of course, and sends him on a wild-goose chase up to the Alamac.

"He puts Temple in another hotel and, knocking later at Mackenzie's door, introduces himself as Philip Schmidt, a detective. And he gets expense money from Mackenzie, which he turned over to Temple . . . I trust.

"Maybe his first idea was only to get a few thousand dollars from Mackenzie—string him along—and blow. But Mackenzie wasn't easy to pluck. And it probably seemed a pity that he and Temple should be broke—when that will left her all that money! If only Mackenzie were out of the way. . . .

"Salisbury worked out a pretty neat scheme. On a boat nobody knows who anybody is for the first day. The steward only knows that the two gentlemen in 361 are Mr. Mackenzie and Mr. Schmidt. And if one jumped overboard and the other claimed that Schmidt was missing—who would think it was Mackenzie who was gone? Whereas, if a wealthy man were to disappear under mysterious circumstances, investigation might involve his secretary. And certainly the wife would be questioned and her connection with Mr. Salisbury uncovered. But when Schmidt was missing even Mr. Schroeder asked: 'What motive would a man have for murdering his secretary?'

"Probably the ipecac which made the young man too sick for questioning also made Mackenzie too sick for talking. As soon as the boat starts, Salisbury-Stone-Schmidt puts Mackenzie to bed and does all the talking for the team—making out the poor man is a Scientist, so even the doctor won't be brought in.

"Then while the steward is freshening up the room, Salisbury gets the real Mackenzie on deck and finishes him. And from then on he has a fourth identity. He is now known as Wm. R. Mackenzie. And nobody questions that identity. Still, everything doesn't go as smoothly as Mr. Salisbury-Mackenzie would have liked. There is a snoopy detective on board and a very snoopy woman. They keep wanting a reason for Schmidt's suicide. So the young man supplies a reason—in a letter from a non-existent lady in Havana—without any address.

"When he went out to post that letter, by the way, was the only time he left the Nacional. You see, he didn't have any money. Unfortunately, all the real Mackenzie's money was in travelers' checks which he couldn't cash!

"Of course that letter from 'C' also provided a motive for a fit of despondency in which he could make it seem that Mackenzie had killed himself. Because for Temple to inherit Mackenzie's money, Mackenzie had to be legally dead. So Mackenzie apparently jumps into shark-infested waters—after a fine piece of acting by Mr. Salisbury-Mackenzie. Which suicide, incidentally, took care of the bill at the Nacional. On the waves floats the Panama hat which he never could wear because it was too small! On the rocks lie the travelers' checks, which will revert to Temple and be of *some* use—and a note to remove any possible doubt of his suicide.

"But there doesn't seem to have been any doubt. Only the package worried me. What could there have been in a package that a man would want to have with him when he set out to kill himself—with a suicide note all typed in his pocket? . . . And what had become of it? Had he taken it with him?

"You know how those flashes come to you. Of course he had taken it with him . . . out of the fortress . . . a coat and a cap! Suppose Colin and the Captain had asked the guard—which they didn't, once they saw the note—about a blond hatless man in a Palm Beach suit? Would they have connected him with a young man in, say, a blue serge coat, a cap pulled down over his hair, and perhaps dark glasses?"

Schroeder smoked in thoughtful silence. But I insisted on knowing, step by step, how she had hit on it.

"Oh, darling, you *are* such a perfect straight man! Sometimes you just smell a phony and begin to reason from the smell."

"Or maybe you note little things," smiled Schroeder, "and then begin to sniff."

"Maybe. . . . I knew I wouldn't get anything out of Schroeder by asking, so I brought the talk around to it at Cobb's, and then we began to make a little headway. But a couple of times Salisbury threw me off—like when he told that long circumstantial story of Mrs. Mackenzie's elopement which Mr. Schroeder could check . . . and did."

"Why do you suppose he told all that?" I demanded foggily.

"I think he was secretly proud of his scenario and was having fun with Schroeder and me. And I'm sure he was vain of his acting."

"Not bad acting," admitted Schroeder grudgingly. He smiled again, however.

"Excellent . . . only somebody else should have written his lines and left out the American slang. That was the first whiff I got . . . pure American idiom from a man who had only been in the States twice—on short visits!

"Anybody could have found out what I did at the Wendham . . . that Mackenzie was a middle-aged, darkish man . . . that when the Mackenzies had Suite 805, 806 was occupied by a Pat Salisbury, registered from Hollywood . . . and anybody would have been impressed by the similarity of the initials . . . Pat Salisbury—Paul Stone—Philip Schmidt.

"And anybody would have written to Hollywood and found out that Wm. R. Mackenzie had married Temple Drury in June 1930 . . . that Temple Drury was listed at Central Casting among the extras . . . that she had one bit in a Fox picture and that Pat Salisbury had a part in the same opus . . . that his last rôle was a small one in 'Wild Eagle,' after which he left for New York. It was all there to put together—except where he got the money to get out of Havana and back to Temple."

"A man as resourceful as Mr. Salisbury probably found a way," suggested Schroeder.

"Not probably—actually. They even got out to Hollywood—although it must have been a blow to find that Mackenzie hadn't left any fortune."

"How do you know he got to Hollywood?" asked Schroeder. "That picture was made before he left for New York."

"That," said Gwynn, "is the pay-off. I asked you whether you'd seen an item in the papers. I brought the clipping with me."

ACTOR AND WIFE KILLED

Mr. and Mrs. Pat Salisbury were instantly killed when their car crashed through a railing on a sharp turn of Topanga Pass. The car had been rented by the young couple for the day. Pat Salisbury was last seen in "Wild Eagle"—a Paramount Picture. Mrs. Salisbury was formerly Temple Drury. The couple had not found work since their recent return to Hollywood. Police are investigating the theory of a suicide pact.

AGATHA CHRISTIE
(1890–1976)

When the locked-room mystery occurs on board ship, it is more accurately termed a locked-cabin crime. Agatha Christie presents one such puzzle to Hercule Poirot in "Problem at Sea," a story concerning the death of a rich and disagreeable woman who belittles her apparently devoted husband, leaving everyone wondering why he doesn't "take a hatchet to her."

In most puzzle-centered mysteries, in both short stories and novels, the corpse is discovered early on. The rest of the story concerns the sleuth's activities in solving the mystery. In "Problem at Sea," Christie spends more time setting up the trick than in solving it. Behaving like a good conjurer, she presents all that is needed to see the solution while causing observers to look upon the evidence in a misleading manner. Once the solution is revealed, the clues that the audience has already seen suddenly form a new pattern requiring little explanation.

Christie was born Agatha Mary Clarissa Miller in Torquay, on the south coast of Devon, England. She was educated privately, mostly at home, and attended finishing school in Paris. A talented pianist, she could not achieve her dream of becoming a performer since she was unable to overcome a shyness so extreme that she could hardly bear for her family to observe her practicing. In 1914 she married the dashing Archibald Christie. While he served in the Royal Flying Corps during the First World War, she became a volunteer nurse and dispenser of drugs, acquiring knowledge and experience that would later be invaluable when constructing her mysteries. In 1919, she gave birth to her only child, Rosalind. A devoted daughter herself, Christie was devastated by the death of her own mother in 1926, the same year that her husband demanded a divorce. Christie's ten-day disappearance—never explained—also occurred that year. In 1930 she married Max Mallowan, an archeologist. She accompanied him on digs that provided background details for her mysteries as well as an outlet for her photographic talent.

Christie wrote 66 novels, 144 collected short stories, several plays, a travel book, two volumes of verse, and her own autobiography. Her most memorable detective series characters are Hercule Poirot, Miss Jane Marple, Tommy and Tuppence Beresford, and Parker Pyne, Detective. She also wrote six novels under the pen name Mary Westmacott.

In "Problem at Sea," Christie proves that she feels at home in the shipboard setting, where the circle of suspects is easily limited and accounted for. Poirot, however, is malcontent there, suffering from *mal de mer*.

Problem at Sea

1936

"Colonel Clapperton!" said General Forbes. He said it with an effect midway between a snort and a sniff.

Miss Ellie Henderson leaned forward, a strand of her soft gray hair blowing across her face. Her eyes, dark and snapping, gleamed with a wicked pleasure.

"Such a *soldierly*-looking man!" she said with malicious intent, and smoothed back the lock of hair to await the result.

"Soldierly!" exploded General Forbes. He tugged at his military mustache and his face became bright red.

"In the Guards, wasn't he?" murmured Miss Henderson, completing her work.

"Guards? Guards? Pack of nonsense. Fellow was on the music hall stage! Fact! Joined up and was out in France counting tins of plum and apple. Huns dropped a stray bomb and he went home with a flesh wound in the arm. Somehow or other got into Lady Carrington's hospital."

"So that's how they met."

"Fact! Fellow played the wounded hero. Lady Carrington had no sense and oceans of money. Old Carrington had been in munitions. She'd been a widow only six months. This fellow snaps her up in no time. She wangled him a job at the War Office. *Colonel* Clapperton! Pah!" he snorted.

"And before the war he was on the music hall stage," mused Miss Henderson, trying to reconcile the distinguished gray-haired Colonel Clapperton with a red-nosed comedian singing mirth-provoking songs.

"Fact!" said General Forbes. "Heard it from old Bassington-ffrench. And he heard it from old Badger Cotterill who'd got it from Snooks Parker."

Miss Henderson nodded brightly. "That does seem to settle it!" she said.

A fleeting smile showed for a minute on the face of a small man sitting near them. Miss Henderson noticed the smile. She was observant. It had shown appreciation of the irony underlying her last remark—irony which the General never for a moment suspected.

The General himself did not notice the smiles. He glanced at his watch, rose and remarked: "Exercise. Got to keep oneself fit on a boat," and passed out through the open door onto the deck.

Miss Henderson glanced at the man who had smiled. It was a well-bred glance indicating that she was ready to enter into conversation with a fellow traveler.

"He is energetic—yes?" said the little man.

"He goes round the deck forty-eight times exactly," said Miss Henderson. "What an old gossip! And they say *we* are the scandal-loving sex."

"What an impoliteness!"

"Frenchmen are always polite." said Miss Henderson—there was the nuance of a question in her voice.

The little man responded promptly. "Belgian, Mademoiselle."

"Oh! Belgian."

"Hercule Poirot. At your service."

The name aroused some memory. Surely she had heard it before—?

"Are you enjoying this trip, M. Poirot?"

"Frankly, no. It was an imbecility to allow myself to be persuaded to come. I detest *la mer*. Never does it remain tranquil—no, not for a little minute."

"Well, you admit it's quite calm now."

M. Poirot admitted this grudgingly. "*À ce moment*, yes. That is why I revive. I once more interest myself in what passes around me—your very adept handling of the General Forbes, for instance."

"You mean—" Miss Henderson paused.

Hercule Poirot bowed. "Your methods of extracting the scandalous matter. Admirable!"

Miss Henderson laughed in an unashamed manner. "That touch about the Guards? I knew that would bring the old boy up spluttering and gasping." She leaned forward confidentially. "I admit I *like* scandal—the more ill-natured, the better!"

Poirot looked thoughtfully at her—her slim well-preserved figure, her keen dark eyes, her gray hair; a woman of forty-five who was content to look her age.

Ellie said abruptly: "I have it! Aren't you the great detective?"

Poirot bowed. "You are too amiable, Mademoiselle." But he made no disclaimer.

"How thrilling," said Miss Henderson. "Are you 'hot on the trail' as they say in books? Have we a criminal secretly in our midst? Or am I being indiscreet?"

"Not at all. Not at all. It pains me to disappoint your expectations, but I am simply here, like everyone else, to amuse myself."

He said it in such a gloomy voice that Miss Henderson laughed.

"Oh! Well, you will be able to get ashore tomorrow at Alexandria. You have been to Egypt before?"

"Never, Mademoiselle."

Miss Henderson rose somewhat abruptly.

"I think I shall join the General on his constitutional," she announced.

Poirot sprang politely to his feet.

She gave him a little nod and passed out onto the deck.

A faint puzzled look showed for a moment in Poirot's eyes, then, a little smile creasing his lips, he rose, put his head through the door and glanced down the deck. Miss Henderson was leaning against the rail talking to a tall, soldierly-looking man.

Poirot's smile deepened. He drew himself back into the smoking-room with the same exaggerated care with which a tortoise withdraws itself into its shell. For the moment he had the smoking-room to himself, though he rightly conjectured that that would not last long.

It did not. Mrs. Clapperton, her carefully waved platinum head protected with a net, her massaged and dieted form dressed in a smart sports suit, came through the door from the bar with the purposeful air of a woman who has always been able to pay top price for anything she needed.

She said: "John—? Oh! Good-morning, M. Poirot—have you seen John?"

"He's on the starboard deck, Madame. Shall I—?"

She arrested him with a gesture. "I'll sit here a minute." She sat down in a regal fashion in the chair opposite him. From the distance she had looked a possible twenty-eight. Now, in spite of her exquisitely made-up face, her delicately plucked eyebrows, she looked not her actual forty-nine years, but a possible fifty-five. Her eyes were a hard pale blue with tiny pupils.

"I was sorry not to have seen you at dinner last night," she said. "It was just a shade choppy, of course—"

"*Précisément,*" said Poirot with feeling.

"Luckily, I am an excellent sailor," said Mrs. Clapperton. "I say luckily, because, with my weak heart, seasickness would probably be the death of me."

"You have the weak heart, Madame?"

"Yes, I have to be *most* careful. I must *not* overtire myself! *All* the specialists say so!" Mrs. Clapperton had embarked on the—to her—ever-fascinating topic of her health. "John, poor darling, wears himself out trying to prevent me from doing too much. I live so intensely, if you know what I mean, M. Poirot?"

"Yes, yes."

"He always says to me: 'Try to be more of a vegetable, Adeline.' But I can't. Life was meant to be *lived*, I feel. As a matter of fact I wore myself out as a girl in the war. My hospital—you've heard of my hospital? Of course I had nurses and matrons and all that—but *I* actually ran it." She sighed.

"Your vitality is marvelous, dear lady," said Poirot, with the slightly mechanical air of one responding to his cue.

Mrs. Clapperton gave a girlish laugh.

"Everyone tells me how young I am! It's absurd. I never try to pretend I'm a day less than forty-three," she continued with slightly mendacious candor, "but a lot of people find it hard to believe. 'You're so *alive*, Adeline,' they say to me. But really, M. Poirot, what would one *be* if one wasn't alive?"

"Dead," said Poirot.

Mrs. Clapperton frowned. The reply was not to her liking. The man, she decided, was trying to be funny. She got up and said coldly: "I must find John."

As she stepped through the door she dropped her handbag. It opened and the contents flew far and wide. Poirot rushed gallantly to the rescue. It was some few minutes before the lipsticks, vanity boxes, cigarette case and lighter and other odds and ends were collected. Mrs. Clapperton thanked him politely, then she swept down the deck and said, "John—"

Colonel Clapperton was still deep in conversation with Miss Henderson. He swung round and came quickly to meet his wife. He bent over her protectively. Her deck chair—was it in the right place? Wouldn't it be better—? His manner was courteous—full of gentle consideration. Clearly an adored wife spoilt by an adoring husband.

Miss Ellie Henderson looked out at the horizon as though something about it rather disgusted her.

Standing in the smoking-room door, Poirot looked on.

A hoarse quavering voice behind him said:

"I'd take a hatchet to that woman if I were her husband." The old gentleman known disrespectfully among the Younger Set on board as the Grandfather of All the Tea Planters had just shuffled in. "Boy!" he called. "Get me a whisky peg."

Poirot stooped to retrieve a torn scrap of notepaper, an overlooked item from the contents of Mrs. Clapperton's bag. Part of a prescription, he noted, containing digitalin. He put it in his pocket, meaning to restore it to Mrs. Clapperton later.

"Yes," went on the aged passenger. "Poisonous woman. I remember a woman like that in Poona. In '87 that was."

"Did anyone take a hatchet to her?" inquired Poirot.

The old gentleman shook his head sadly.

"Worried her husband into his grave within the year. Clapperton ought to assert himself. Gives his wife her head too much."

"She holds the purse strings," said Poirot gravely.

"Ha ha!" chuckled the old gentleman. "You've put the matter in a nutshell. Holds the purse strings. Ha ha!"

Two girls burst into the smoking-room. One had a round face with freckles and dark hair streaming out in a windswept confusion, the other had freckles and curly chestnut hair.

"A rescue—a rescue!" cried Kitty Mooney. "Pam and I are going to rescue Colonel Clapperton."

"From his wife," gasped Pamela Cregan.

"We think he's a *pet*. . . ."

"And she's just awful—she won't let him do *anything*," the two girls exclaimed.

"And if he isn't with her, he's usually grabbed by the Henderson woman. . . ."

"Who's quite nice. But terribly *old*. . . ."

They ran out, gasping in between giggles:

"A rescue—a rescue . . ."

That the rescue of Colonel Clapperton was no isolated sally, but a fixed project, was made clear that same evening when the eighteen-year-old Pam Cregan came up to Hercule Poirot, and murmured: "Watch us, M. Poirot. He's going to be cut out from under her nose and taken to walk in the moonlight on the boat deck."

It was just at that moment that Colonel Clapperton was saying: "I grant you the price of a Rolls Royce. But it's practically good for a lifetime. Now my car—"

"*My* car, I think, John." Mrs. Clapperton's voice was shrill and penetrating.

He showed no annoyance at her ungraciousness. Either he was used to it by this time, or else—

"Or else?" thought Poirot and let himself speculate.

"Certainly, my dear, *your* car," Clapperton bowed to his wife and finished what he had been saying, perfectly unruffled.

"*Voilà ce qu'on appelle le pukka sahib*," thought Poirot. "But the General Forbes says that Clapperton is no gentleman at all. I wonder now."

There was a suggestion of bridge. Mrs. Clapperton, General Forbes and a hawk-eyed couple sat down to it. Miss Henderson had excused herself and gone out on deck.

"What about your husband?" asked General Forbes, hesitating.

"John won't play," said Mrs. Clapperton. "Most tiresome of him."

The four bridge players began shuffling the cards.

Pam and Kitty advanced on Colonel Clapperton. Each one took an arm.

"You're coming with us!" said Pam. "To the boat deck. There's a moon."

"Don't be foolish, John," said Mrs. Clapperton. "You'll catch a chill."

"Not with us, he won't," said Kitty. "We're hot stuff!"

He went with them, laughing.

Poirot noticed that Mrs. Clapperton said No Bid to her initial bid of Two Clubs.

He strolled out onto the promenade deck. Miss Henderson was standing by the rail. She looked round expectantly as he came to stand beside her and he saw the drop in her expression.

They chatted for a while. Then presently as he fell silent she asked: "What are you thinking about?"

Poirot replied: "I am wondering about my knowledge of English. Mrs. Clapperton said: 'John won't play bridge.' Is not 'can't play' the usual term?"

"She takes it as a personal insult that he doesn't, I suppose," said Ellie drily. "The man was a fool ever to have married her."

In the darkness Poirot smiled. "You don't think it's just possible that the marriage may be a success?" he asked diffidently.

"With a woman like that?"

Poirot shrugged his shoulders. "Many odious women have devoted husbands. An enigma of Nature. You will admit that nothing she says or does appears to gall him."

Miss Henderson was considering her reply when Mrs. Clapperton's voice floated out through the smoking-room window.

"No—I don't think I will play another rubber. So stuffy. I think I'll go up and get some air on the boat deck."

"Good-night," said Miss Henderson. "I'm going to bed." She disappeared abruptly.

Poirot strolled forward to the lounge—deserted save for Colonel Clapperton and the two girls. He was doing card tricks for them, and noting the dexterity of his shuffling and handling of the cards, Poirot remembered the General's story of a career on the music hall stage.

"I see you enjoy the cards even though you do not play bridge," he remarked.

"I've my reasons for not playing bridge," said Clapperton, his charming smile breaking out. "I'll show you. We'll play one hand."

He dealt the cards rapidly. "Pick up your hands. Well, what about it?" He laughed at the bewildered expression on Kitty's face. He laid down his hand and the others followed suit. Kitty held the entire club suit, M. Poirot the hearts, Pam the diamonds and Colonel Clapperton the spades.

"You see?" he said. "A man who can deal his partner and his adversaries any hand he pleases had better stand aloof from a friendly game! If the luck goes too much his way, ill-natured things might be said."

"Oh!" gasped Kitty. "How *could* you do that? It all looked perfectly ordinary."

"The quickness of the hand deceives the eye," said Poirot sententiously—and caught the sudden change in the Colonel's expression.

It was as though he realized that he had been off his guard for a moment or two.

Poirot smiled. The conjuror had shown himself through the mask of the *pukka sahib*.

The ship reached Alexandria at dawn the following morning.

As Poirot came up from breakfast he found the two girls all ready to go on shore. They were talking to Colonel Clapperton.

"We ought to get off now," urged Kitty. "The passport people will be going off the ship presently. You'll come with us, won't you? You wouldn't let us go ashore all by ourselves? Awful things might happen to us."

"I certainly don't think you ought to go by yourselves," said Clapperton, smiling. "But I'm not sure my wife feels up to it."

"That's too bad," said Pam. "But she can have a nice long rest."

Colonel Clapperton looked a little irresolute. Evidently the desire to play truant was strong upon him. He noticed Poirot.

"Hullo, M. Poirot—you going ashore?"

"No, I think not," M. Poirot replied.

"I'll—I'll—just have a word with Adeline," decided Colonel Clapperton.

"We'll come with you," said Pam. She flashed a wink at Poirot. "Perhaps we can persuade her to come too," she added gravely.

Colonel Clapperton seemed to welcome this suggestion. He looked decidedly relieved.

"Come along then, the pair of you," he said lightly. They all three went along the passage of B deck together.

Poirot, whose cabin was just opposite the Clappertons', followed them out of curiosity.

Colonel Clapperton rapped a little nervously at the cabin door.

"Adeline, my dear, are you up?"

The sleepy voice of Mrs. Clapperton from within replied: "Oh, bother—what is it?"

"It's John. What about going ashore?"

"Certainly not." The voice was shrill and decisive. "I've had a very bad night. I shall stay in bed most of the day."

Pam nipped in quickly, "Oh, Mrs. Clapperton, I'm so sorry. We did so want you to come with us. Are you sure you're not up to it?"

"I'm quite certain." Mrs. Clapperton's voice sounded even shriller.

The Colonel was turning the door-handle without result.

"What is it, John? The door's locked. I don't want to be disturbed by the stewards."

"Sorry, my dear, sorry. Just wanted my Baedeker."

"Well, you can't have it," snapped Mrs. Clapperton. "I'm not going to get out of bed. Do go away, John, and let me have a little peace."

"Certainly, certainly, my dear." The Colonel backed away from the door. Pam and Kitty closed in on him.

"Let's start at once. Thank goodness your hat's on your head. Oh! gracious—your passport isn't in the cabin, is it?"

"As a matter of fact it's in my pocket—" began the Colonel.

Kitty squeezed his arm. "Glory be!" she exclaimed. "Now, come on."

Leaning over the rail, Poirot watched the three of them leave the ship.

He heard a faint intake of breath beside him and turned his head to see Miss Henderson. Her eyes were fastened on the three retreating figures.

"So they've gone ashore," she said flatly.

"Yes. Are you going?"

She had a shade hat, he noticed, and a smart bag and shoes. There was a shore-going appearance about her. Nevertheless, after the most infinitesimal of pauses, she shook her head.

"No," she said. "I think I'll stay on board. I have a lot of letters to write."

She turned and left him.

Puffing after his morning tour of forty-eight rounds of the deck, General Forbes took her place. "Aha!" he exclaimed as his eyes noted the retreating figures of the Colonel and the two girls. "So *that's* the game! Where's the Madam?"

Poirot explained that Mrs. Clapperton was having a quiet day in bed.

"Don't you believe it!" The old warrior closed one knowing eye. "She'll be up for tiffin—and if the poor devil's found to be absent without leave, there'll be ructions."

But the General's prognostications were not fulfilled. Mrs. Clapperton did not appear at lunch and by the time the Colonel and his attendant damsels returned to the ship at four o'clock, she had not shown herself.

Poirot was in his cabin and heard the husband's slightly guilty knock on his cabin door. Heard the knock repeated, the cabin door tried, and finally heard the Colonel's call to a steward.

"Look here, I can't get an answer. Have you a key?"

Poirot rose quickly from his bunk and came out into the passage.

The news went like wildfire round the ship. With horrified incredulity people heard that Mrs. Clapperton had been found dead in her bunk—a native dagger driven through her heart. A string of amber beads was found on the floor of her cabin.

Rumor succeeded rumor. All bead sellers who had been allowed on board that day were being rounded up and questioned! A large sum in cash had disappeared from a drawer in the cabin! The notes had been traced! They had not been traced! Jewelry worth a fortune had been taken! No jewelry had been taken at all! A steward had been arrested and had confessed to the murder!

"What is the truth of it all?" demanded Miss Ellie Henderson, waylaying Poirot. Her face was pale and troubled.

"My dear lady, how should I know?"

"Of course you know," said Miss Henderson.

It was late in the evening. Most people had retired to their cabins. Miss Henderson led Poirot to a couple of deck chairs on the sheltered side of the ship. "Now tell me," she commanded.

Poirot surveyed her thoughtfully. "It's an interesting case," he said.

"Is it true that she had some very valuable jewelry stolen?"

Poirot shook his head. "No. No jewelry was taken. A small amount of loose cash that was in a drawer has disappeared, though."

"I'll never feel safe on a ship again," said Miss Henderson with a shiver. "Any clue as to which of those coffee-colored brutes did it?"

"No," said Hercule Poirot. "The whole thing is rather—strange."

"What do you mean?" asked Ellie sharply.

Poirot spread out his hands. "*Eh bien*—take the facts. Mrs. Clapperton had been dead at least five hours when she was found. Some money had disappeared. A string of beads was on the floor by her bed. The door was locked and the key was missing. The window—*window*, not port-hole— gives on the deck and was open."

"Well?" asked the woman impatiently.

"Do you not think it is curious for a murder to be committed under those particular circumstances? Remember that the postcard sellers, money changers and bead sellers who are allowed on board are all well known to the police."

"The stewards usually lock your cabin, all the same," Ellie pointed out.

"Yes, to prevent any chance of petty pilfering. But this—was murder."

"What exactly are you thinking of, M. Poirot?" Her voice sounded a little breathless.

"I am thinking of the *locked door*."

Miss Henderson considered this. "I don't see anything in that. The man left by the door, locked it and took the key with him so as to avoid having the murder discovered too soon. Quite intelligent of him, for it wasn't discovered until four o'clock in the afternoon."

"No, no, Mademoiselle, you don't appreciate the point I'm trying to make. I'm not worried as to how he got *out*, but as to how he got *in*."

"The window of course."

"*C'est possible.* But it would be a very narrow fit—and there were people passing up and down the deck all the time, remember."

"Then through the door," said Miss Henderson impatiently.

"But you forget, Mademoiselle. *Mrs. Clapperton had locked the door on the inside.* She had done so before Colonel Clapperton left the boat this morning. He actually tried it—so we *know* that is so."

"Nonsense. It probably stuck—or he didn't turn the handle properly."

"But it does not rest on his word. We actually heard *Mrs. Clapperton herself say so.*"

"We?"

"Miss Mooney, Miss Cregan, Colonel Clapperton and myself."

Ellie Henderson tapped a neatly shod foot. She did not speak for a moment or two. Then she said in a slightly irritable tone:

"Well—what exactly do you deduce from that? If Mrs. Clapperton could lock the door she could unlock it too, I suppose."

"Precisely, precisely." Poirot turned a beaming face upon her. "And you see where that leads us. *Mrs. Clapperton unlocked the door and let the murderer in.* Now would she be likely to do that for a bead seller?"

Ellie objected: "She might not have known who it was. He may have knocked—she got up and opened the door—and he forced his way in and killed her."

Poirot shook his head. "*Au contraire.* She was lying peacefully in bed when she was stabbed."

Miss Henderson stared at him. "What's your idea?" she asked abruptly.

Poirot smiled. "Well, it looks, does it not, as though she *knew* the person she admitted. . . ."

"You mean," said Miss Henderson and her voice sounded a little harsh, "*that the murderer is a passenger on the ship?*"

Poirot nodded. "It seems indicated."

"And the string of beads left on the floor was a blind?"

"Precisely."

"The theft of the money also?"

"Exactly."

There was a pause, then Miss Henderson said slowly: "I thought Mrs. Clapperton a very unpleasant woman and I don't think anyone on board really liked her—but there wasn't anyone who had any reason to kill her."

"Except her husband, perhaps," said Poirot.

"You don't really think—" She stopped.

"It is the opinion of every person on this ship that Colonel Clapperton would have been quite justified in 'taking a hatchet to her.' That was, I think, the expression used."

Ellie Henderson looked at him—waiting.

"But I am bound to say," went on Poirot, "that I myself have not noted any signs of exasperation on the good Colonel's part. Also, what is more important, he had an alibi. He was with those two girls all day and did not return to the ship till four o'clock. By then, Mrs. Clapperton had been dead many hours."

There was another minute of silence. Ellie Henderson said softly: "But you still think—a passenger on the ship?"

Poirot bowed his head.

Ellie Henderson laughed suddenly—a reckless defiant laugh. "Your theory may be difficult to prove, M. Poirot. There are a good many passengers on this ship."

Poirot bowed to her. "I will use a phrase from one of your detective story writers. 'I have my methods, Watson.' "

The following evening, at dinner, every passenger found a typewritten slip by his plate requesting him to be in the main lounge at 8:30. When the company were assembled, the Captain stepped onto the raised platform where the orchestra usually played and addressed them.

"Ladies and Gentlemen, you all know of the tragedy which took place yesterday. I am sure you all wish to co-operate in bringing the perpetrator of that foul crime to justice." He paused and cleared his throat. "We have on board with us M. Hercule Poirot, who is probably known to you all as a man who has had wide experience in—er—such matters. I hope you will listen carefully to what he has to say."

It was at this minute that Colonel Clapperton, who had not been at dinner, came in and sat down next to General Forbes. He looked like a man bewildered by sorrow—not at all like a man conscious of great relief. Either he was a very good actor or else he had been genuinely fond of his disagreeable wife.

"M. Hercule Poirot," said the Captain and stepped down. Poirot took his place. He looked comically self-important as he beamed on his audience.

"*Messieurs, Mesdames,*" he began. "It is most kind of you to be so indulgent as to listen to me. M. *le Capitaine* has told you that I have had a certain experience in these matters. I have, it is true, a little idea of my own about how to get to the bottom of this particular case." He made a sign and a steward pushed forward and passed up to him a bulky, shapeless object wrapped in a sheet.

"What I am about to do may surprise you a little," Poirot warned them. "It may occur to you that I am eccentric, perhaps mad. Nevertheless I assure you that behind my madness there is—as you English say—a method."

His eyes met those of Miss Henderson for just a minute. He began unwrapping the bulky object.

"I have here, *Messieurs* and *Mesdames*, an important witness to the truth of who killed Mrs. Clapperton." With a deft hand he whisked away the last enveloping cloth, and the object it concealed was revealed —an almost life-sized wooden doll, dressed in a velvet suit and lace collar.

"Now, Arthur," said Poirot and his voice changed subtly—it was no longer foreign—it had instead a confident English, a slightly Cockney inflection. "Can you tell me—I repeat—can you tell me—anything at all about the death of Mrs. Clapperton?"

The doll's neck oscillated a little, its wooden lower jaw dropped and wavered and a shrill high-pitched woman's voice spoke:

"*What is it, John? The door's locked. I don't want to be disturbed by the stewards. . . .*"

There was a cry—an overturned chair—a man stood swaying, his hand to his throat—trying to speak—trying. . . . Then suddenly, his figure seemed to crumple up. He pitched headlong.

It was Colonel Clapperton.

Poirot and the ship's doctor rose from their knees by the prostrate figure.

"All over, I'm afraid. Heart," said the doctor briefly.

Poirot nodded. "The shock of having his trick seen through," he said.

He turned to General Forbes. "It was you, General, who gave me a valuable hint with your mention of the music hall stage. I puzzle—I think—and then it comes to me. Supposing that before the war Clapperton was a *ventriloquist*. In that case, it would be perfectly possible for three people to hear Mrs. Clapperton speak from inside her cabin *when she was already dead*. . . ."

Ellie Henderson was beside him. Her eyes were dark and full of pain. "Did you know his heart was weak?" she asked.

"I guessed it. . . . Mrs. Clapperton talked of her own heart being affected, but she struck me as the type of woman who likes to be thought ill. Then I picked up a torn prescription with a very strong dose of digitalin in it. Digitalin is a heart medicine but it couldn't be Mrs. Clapperton's because digitalin dilates the pupils of the eyes. I had never noticed such a phenomenon with her—but when I looked at his eyes I saw the signs at once."

Ellie murmured: "So you thought—it might end—this way?"

"The best way, don't you think, Mademoiselle?" he said gently.

He saw the tears rise in her eyes. She said: "You've known. You've known all along. . . . That I cared. . . . But he didn't do it for *me*. . . . It was those girls—youth—it made him feel his slavery. He wanted to be free before it was too late. . . . Yes, I'm sure that's how it was. . . . When did you guess—that it was he?"

"His self-control was too perfect," said Poirot simply. "No matter how galling his wife's conduct, it never seemed to touch him. That meant either that he was so used to it that it no longer stung him, or else—*eh bien*—I decided on the latter alternative. . . . And I was right. . . .

"And then there was his insistence on his conjuring ability—the evening before the crime. He pretended to give himself away. But a man like Clapperton doesn't give himself away. There must be a reason. So long as people thought he had been a *conjuror* they weren't likely to think of his having been a *ventriloquist*."

"And the voice we heard—Mrs. Clapperton's voice?"

"One of the stewardesses had a voice not unlike hers. I induced her to hide behind the stage and taught her the words to say."

"It was a trick—a cruel trick," cried out Ellie.

"I do not approve of murder," said Hercule Poirot.

LESTER DENT
(1905–1959)

It seems fitting that Lester Dent made a living as a night-shift telegrapher in Tulsa, Oklahoma, sending out words at high speeds for the Associated Press, when he decided to try his hand at writing. A coworker had sold a story to a magazine for handsome pay, and Dent, who at age twenty had given up his notion of becoming a banker when he learned that telegraphers earned more, was attracted to writing when he saw money in it.

Telegraphing by night and writing rapidly by day for pay-by-the-word pulp magazines, Dent wrote up to 140,000 words a month during his next, most energetic decade, the 1930s. He swiftly honed a style that relied on quick dialogue sparked with wisecracks. Within three years of picking up a pen, he was able to leave the Associated Press and make his way to New York, where he became a house writer for Dell Publishing and contributed to a variety of pulp magazines. He created the immensely successful Doc Savage series under the pseudonym Kenneth Robeson in 1935 and continued the series to more than 160 novels. The Doc Savage series brought him financial success, enabling him to return to LaPlata, Missouri, where he was born and had spent the latter part of his childhood on a dairy farm. He had spent his earliest years on a ranch in Wyoming.

Additional series characters Dent invented are Chance Malloy; Click Rush, the Gadget Man; Foster Fade, the Crime Spectacularist; Lee Nace, the Blond Adder; a scientific sleuth called Lynn Lash; and a reluctant private eye known as Ed Stone. All of these heroes were literally larger than life, standing very tall. They enjoyed employing disguises and amazing gadgets in their efforts to nab criminals.

Dent is remembered as both a pulp writer whose quantity of words sometimes exceeded their quality and an author whose most accomplished work, published in *Black Mask* magazine, represents the best of the Black Mask school of writing. Dent, however, did not confine his energies to writing. He also acquired plumbing and electrician's certificates and radio operator's and pilot's licenses. In addition, he took up aerial photography, mountain-climbing, deep-sea fishing, sailing, and swimming. He and his wife cruised the Caribbean for two years on their own boat, where, no doubt, the midwestern author picked up the shipboard and shoreline details included in two of his most successful stories, "Angelfish" and "Sail."

Sail

1936

The fish shook its tail as the knife cut off its head. Red ran out of the two parts and the fluid spread enough to cover the wet red marks where two human hands had failed to hold to the dock edge.

Oscar Sail wet the palm of his own left hand in the puddle.

The small policeman kept coming out on the dock, tramping in the rear edge of glare from his flashlight.

Sail split the fish belly, shook it over the edge of the yacht dock and there were some splashes below in the water. The stuff from the fish made the red stain in the water a little larger.

When the small policeman reached Sail, he stopped and gave his cap a cock. He looked down at Sail's feet and up at Sail's head.

The cop said, "Damned if you ain't a long drink of water."

Sail said nothing.

The cop asked, "That you give that yell a minute ago?"

Sail showed plenty of teeth so that his grin would be seen in the moonlight. He picked up the fishhook and held it close to his red-wetted left palm.

"Little accident," he said.

When the cop put light on the hand, Sail tightened the thumb down and made a wrinkle in the palm. Red was squeezed out of the wrinkle and two or three drops fell on the dock. It was enough like seepage from a cut the fishhook might have torn that Sail went on breathing.

"Hook, eh?" the cop said vaguely.

He put the toe of his right shoe into the fish head's open mouthful of snake-fang teeth.

"Barracuda," he added, not sounding as if that was on his mind. "They don't eat 'em in Miami. Not when you catch the damn things in the harbor, anyhow."

Sail's laugh did not go off so well and he turned it into a throat clearing.

He said, "People get hot ideas."

The policeman did not say anything and began spearing around with his flashlight beam. He poked it over the edge of the dock at one of the fish organs floating on the stained water. He held it there for what seemed a year.

After he finally began pointing the beam at other places, the light located the bugeye. The bugeye was tied at the end of the dock with springlines. Sloping masts were shiny and black and black canvas covers were on the sails. The hull looked black, neat, new.

The cop dabbed his light up and down each of the two bugeye masts and asked, "Yours?"

Sail said, "Yep."

"What you call that kind of a boat?"

Sail began talking heartily about the boat.

He said, "Chesapeake Bay five-log bugeye. She is thirty-four feet long at the waterline and forty-five overall. Her bottom is made out of five logs drifted together with Swedish iron rods. She has twelve foot beam and only draws a little over two feet of water with the centerboard up. A bugeye has sloping masts. You tell 'em by that, and the clipper bow they always put on them. They're made—"

"Yeah," the cop said. "Uh-huh."

He splashed light on Sail.

Sail would have been all right if he had been a foot or two shorter. His face would never wear a serious look successfully. Too much mouth. Sun and salt water was on its way to ruining his hair. Some of the black had been scrubbed out of his black polo shirt and black dungarees. Bare feet had long toes. Weather had gotten to all of the man a lot.

The policeman switched off his light.

"That was a hell of a funny yell," he said. "And damned if you aren't the tallest thing I ever saw."

He stamped his feet as he walked away.

Sail shut and opened his eyes slowly and by the time he got rid of the effects of the flashlight, the officer was out of sight on shore.

Sail held both hands out about a foot from his eyes. There was enough moonlight for him to see them. A slight breeze made coolness against one side of his face. Loud music came from the Take-a-Sail-in-the-Moonlight-for-a-Dollar-a-Couple boat at the far end of the City Yacht Basin, but a barker spoiled the effect of the music. Two slot machines chugged along-side the lunch stand at Pier Six.

After he had watched his hands tremble for a while, Sail picked up hook, line, fish, knife, and got aboard the bugeye.

Sail, name of the bugeye, was in white letters on the black life pre-servers tied to the main stays.

Sail grasped a line, took half hitches off a cleat, and pulled a live-box made of laths partly out of the water. Some crawfish, crabs and two more live barracuda were in the live-box. He cut the line close to the live-box and let the weighted box sink.

The tiny cabin of the bugeye had headroom below for a man of or-dinary height. Sail had to stoop. The usual gear was neatly, in places cleverly, stowed in the cabin.

Sail popped the fish into a kettle in the galley, hurrying.

With the point of the fishhook, he gouged a small place in his left palm, making faces over the job.

He straightened out the stuff in the tackle locker enough to get rid of signs that a hook and line had been grabbed out in haste.

After he had washed and held the mouth of a mercurochrome bottle against the gouge, he looked out of the hatch.

The young policeman was back where the fish had bled and was using his flashlight. He squatted and picked up the fish head. He squeezed it and got fresh blood out of it. After a while, he stood up and approached the dock end. When his flashlight brightened the bugeye's dark sloping masts and black sail covers, Sail was at the galley, making enough noise cutting up the fish to let the cop know where he was and what he was doing.

Sail let four or five minutes pass before he put his head out of the hatch and looked. Perspiration had made the back of his polo shirt moist by then.

The cop had gone somewhere else.

Sail was still looking and listening for the policeman when he heard a man yell and a woman curse.

The woman said, "Dam' stinker!" and more that was worse.

The man's yell was just a yell.

The sounds came out of Bayfront Park, which lay between the yacht basin and Biscayne Boulevard.

Sail got out on deck and stretched his neck around. He saw a man run among the palms in the park. The man was alone.

Then the small policeman and his flashlight appeared among the palms. During the next five minutes, the policeman and his flashlight were not motionless long enough for him to have found anything.

Sail dropped into the bugeye cabin and stripped naked, working fast. His body looked better without clothes. The hair on it was golden and long, but not thick. He put on black jersey swim trunks.

Standing in the companion and looking around, his right hand absently scratched his chest. No one was in sight.

He got over the side without being conspicuous.

The water had odor and its normal quota of floating things. The tide was high slack, almost, but still coming in a little. Sail swam under the dock.

The dock had been built strongly because of the hurricanes. There was a net of cross timbers underneath, and anything falling off the south side of the dock would be carried against them by the tide.

Sail counted pilings until he knew he was under the place on the dock where he had used the fish. He began diving and groping around underwater. He was quiet about that.

He found what he was seeking on the sixth or seventh dive. He kept in the dark places as he swam away with it.

One of the little islands in the harbor seemed to be the only place that offered privacy. He made for it.

The island—an artificial half acre put there when they dredged the City Yacht Basin—was a heap of dark silence when Sail swam tiredly to it. Pine trees on the island had been bent by the hurricanes, some uprooted. The weeds did not seem to have been affected.

Sail tried not to splash coming out of the shallows onto the sand beach. He towed the Greek under water as long as possible.

Two stubborn crabs and some seaweed hung to the Greek when Sail carried him into the pines and weeds. The knife sticking in the Greek, and what it had done, did not help. Weeds mashed under the body when Sail laid it down.

Pulpy skins in the Greek's billfold were probably greenbacks, and stiffer, smaller rectangles, business cards. Silver coins, a pocket knife, two clips for an automatic. The gun was in a clip holster under the left armpit of the corpse.

Inside the Greek's coat lining was a panel, four inches wide, five times as long, a quarter of an inch thick, hard and rigid.

The Greek's wristwatch ticked.

Sail put the business cards and the panel from the coat lining inside his swim trunks, and was down on his knees cleaning his hands with sand when the situation got the best of his stomach. By the time he finished with that, he had sweated profusely and had a headache over the eyes.

He left the Greek on the island.

The water felt cold as he swam back towards the bugeye, keeping in what dark places he could find. The water chill helped the headache.

Having reached the bugeye with the stuff still in his swim trunks, he clung to the bobstay, the chain brace which ran from the bow waterline to the end of the long bowsprit. He blew the brackish bay water off his lips quietly and listened.

There was no sign anywhere that he had been seen or heard.

He made himself sink and began feeling over the parts of the dock which would still be under water at low tide. Everything under water was inches thick with barnacles and oysters.

He found a niche that would do, took the stuff out of his trunks and wedged it there tightly enough so that there was not much danger of it working out.

Sail clung to the bugeye's bobstay until all the water ran off him that wanted to run, then scrambled aboard and ducked into the cabin.

He had started to shed the bathing suit when the woman said, "Puh-lease!"

Sail came up straight and his head thumped a ceiling carling.

She swung her legs off the forward bunk. Even then, light from the kerosene gimbal lamp did not reach more than her legs. The feet were small in dark blue sandals which showed red enameled toenails. Her legs had not been shaved recently, and were nice.

Sail chewed an imaginary something between two eye-teeth while he squinted at the girl. He felt of his head where it had hit the ceiling. Two or three times, he seemed about to say something, but didn't and went forward into one of the pair of small single staterooms. The shadow-embedded rest of her did not look bad as he passed.

He shut the stateroom door and got out of the swim trunks. He tied a three-pound fish sinker to the trunks and dropped them through a port-hole into the bay, which was dredged three fathoms deep there. He put on his scrubbed dark polo and dungarees.

The girl had moved into the light when he opened the door and entered the cabin. The rest of her was interesting. Twenty something, he judged.

She smiled and said, "You don't act as if you remember me, Wesley."

Sail batted his eyes at her.

"Gosh," she said, "but you're tall!"

Sail scratched behind his right ear, changed his eyebrows around at her, gave the top of his head three hard rubs, then leaned back against the galley sink. This upset a round bottle. He caught it, looked at it, and seemed to get an idea.

He asked, "Drink?"

She had crossed her legs. Her skirt was split. "That would be nice," she smiled.

Sail, his back to her, made more noise than necessary in rattling bottles and glasses and pinking an opener into a can of condensed milk. He mixed two parts of gin, one of creme de cocoa, one of condensed milk. He put four drops from a small green bottle in one drink and gave that one to the girl, holding it out a full arm length, as if bashful.

They sipped.

"It's not bad without ice, Wesley," she murmured.

Sail said, "Thanks, lady," politely.

Her blue handbag started to slip out of the hollow of her crossed legs and she caught it quickly.

"For a husband, you're a darn polite cuss," she said.

Sail swallowed with a distinctly pigeon noise. "Eh?"

"My Gawd, don't you *remember*?"

"What?"

"If this isn't something! Two weeks ago Tuesday. Four o'clock in the morning. We were pretty tight, but we found a justice of the peace in Cocoanut Grove. You had to hock the engagement ring with the jeep for his fee and twenty dollars, and we all went out and had some drinks, and I kind of lost track of things, including you."

"I'll be—" Sail said vaguely.

The girl put her head back and laughed. The mirth did not sound just right.

"I didn't know what to do," she said. "I remembered you said you were a jewelry drummer out of Cincinnati. I sat around the hotel. Then I began to get a mad up."

An unnaturalness was growing in her voice. She pinched her eyes shut and shook her head. Her blue purse slid to the floor.

"I'm here to tell you I had a time locating you," she said. "I might have known you would be a sailor. Gawd, imagine! Anyway, Mama is right on deck now, Mister, and I want something done about it. If you think you're not the man, you're going to have to prove it in a big way."

"You want me to prove my name, business and recent whereabouts? Is that it?"

"You bet."

Sail said, "That's what I figured."

She peered at him, winking both eyes. Then fright grabbed her face.

"You ain't so damn' smart!" she said through her teeth.

She started to get up, but something was wrong with her knee joints by now, and she slid off the bench and sat hard on the black battleship linoleum.

Sail moved fast and got his long fingers on the blue purse as she clawed it open. A small bright revolver fell out of the purse as they had a tug-o'-war over it.

"Blick!" the girl gasped.

Blick and a revolver came out of the oilskin locker. The gun was a small bright twin to the girl's. Blick's Panama fell off slick mahogany hair, and disarranged oilskins fell down in the locker behind him. Blick had his lips rolled in until he seemed to have no lips. He looked about old enough to have fought in the last war.

"Want it shot off?" he gritted.

Sail jerked his hand away from the girl's purse as if a bullet were already heading for it. He put his hands up as high as the cabin carlings and ceiling would allow. The upper part of his stomach jumped slightly with each beat of his heart, moving the polo shirt fabric.

The girl started to get up, couldn't. She said, "Blick!" weakly.

Blick, watching Sail, threw at her, "You hadda be a sucker and try that married-when-you-were-tight gag to find out who he is!"

The girl's lips worked with some words before they got out as sounds. "... was—I—know he—doped drink."

Blick gritted at Sail, "Bud, she's my sis, and if she don't come out of that, I wouldn't wanta be you!"

Sail watched the bright gun. Sweat had come out on his forehead enough to start running.

"She'll be all right," he said.

"What'd you give her?"

"Truth serum."

"You louse! Fat lot of good it'll do you."

Sail said nothing.

Blick ran his eyes up and down Sail, then said, "They sure left the faucet on too long when they poured you, didn't they, bud?"

Sail got his grin to operate. He said, "Let's see if some words will clear this any."

Blick said, "That's an idea, bud. I think I got you figured. You're some guy Andopolis rung in. It was like Andopolis to get himself some help."

"Andopolis was the one who got knifed?" Sail asked.

"You ain't that dumb."

"Was he?"

"Naw. That was Sam, my pal."

Sail rubbed the top of his head. "I'm sort of confused."

"You and us both," Blick said. "We're confused by you. We ain't seen you around before today. But me and Nola and Sam are watching Andopolis, and he starts out on this dock. You're the only boat out here, so it's a cinch he wanted to see you."

"He only made it about half way out the dock," Sail said dryly.

"Sure. Sam headed him off. Sam wanted to talk to Andopolis was all—"

"It wasn't all," Sail drawled. "What Sam really wanted was to make Andopolis tell him something. Andopolis had some information. Sam wanted it. Sam told Andopolis that if he didn't cough up on the spot he would get his entrails shot out, or words to such effect. Sam reached for his gun. But he had made the mistake of not unbuttoning his coat before he started the argument. Andopolis knew exactly where to put a knife. Sam went off the dock after he gave just one yell."

"And that brought the cop."

Sail squinted one eye. Perspiration was stinging it. He echoed, "And that brought the cop."

Blick was holding the gun steady. He said, "Andopolis ran before the cop got here. He hid in the park and Nola and I tried to get him later, but he broke away and ran."

"Then you came here."

Blick grinned thinly. "Let's get back to the time between the knifing of Sam and the arrival of the cop. You, bud, done some fast work. You were sweet, what I mean. You got a hook and line, grabbed a live fish out of your live-box, jumped on the dock and butchered the fish to hide the marks where Sam got it. You even got the insides of the fish into the water to hide any bloodstains where Sam sank. Then you fed the cop a line when he got there."

"You sure had your eyes open," Sail said.

"Did the cop go for your story?"

"I'm still wondering," Sail said thoughtfully.

Blick watched Sail. "How much do you know?"

Sail got rid of his made grin. "I'll bite. How much?"

"So you're going to start that," Blick said.

Nola was breathing noisily. Blick pointed at her, said, "Help me get her going!"

Sail grasped the girl and lifted her.

"Stay that way," Blick ordered, then searched Sail, found no weapon, and said, "Out."

Sail walked the girl up the companionway and on to the dock, then started to let go the girl and get back aboard.

"Along with us," Blick ordered. "It'd be swell if Andopolis has told you what we're trying to find out, wouldn't it?"

Sail said nothing. His breathing was as audible as the girl's. Blick got on the other side of the girl and helped hold her up. "We're tight," Blick said. "Stagger."

They staggered along the dock to the sidewalk, and along that.

Yacht sailors stood in a knot at the end of the Pier Six lunch stand, and out of the knot came the chug of the slot machines. Blick put his hand and small revolver into a coat pocket. They turned to the right, away from the lunch stand.

Sail said, "You might have the wrong idea about me."

"We'll go into that, bud," Blick said. "We'll go into that in a nice place I know about."

They scuffed over the sidewalk and Blick, walking as if he did not feel as if he weighed more than a ton, seemed to think of a possibility which pleased him.

"Hell, Nola! This guy covered up that knifing for Andopolis, so he's got to be with Andopolis all the way."

Nola did not answer. She was almost sound asleep. Blick pinched her, slapped her, and that awakened her somewhat.

A police radio car was parked at the corner of Biscayne Boulevard and the street they were traveling. Blick did not see it in time. When he did discover it, he took his breath in with a sharp noise.

"We're drunk," Blick warned. "Taking each other home."

Sail shoved a little to steer the girl to the side of the walk farthest from the prowl car. Blick shoved back to straighten them up. He also got mad.

Blick's gun was in his coat pocket, and if shooting started, it was no time for a gun to be in a pocket. Blick started to take it out, probably intending to hold it at his side where it could not be seen from the police car.

Sail watched the gun start out of the pocket. It had a high front sight and there was an even chance of it hanging on the pocket lining. It did.

Sail shoved Blick and Nola as hard as he could. Force of the effort bounced him toward the police car. He grabbed the spare tire at the back of the machine and used it to help himself around.

A policeman in the car yelled, "What the hell's this?" He wasn't excited.

Blick did not shoot. He got Nola over a shoulder and ran. A taxicab was on its stand at the corner. Blick made it.

Sail shouted, "Kidnapers!"

One of the cops leaned out, looked at him, said, "Huh?"

Blick leaped into the taxi with his sister. An instant later, the hack driver fell out of his own machine, holding his head. The taxi took off.

"They stole my heap!" the taxi driver shrieked.

The police car starter began whining. It whined and whined and nothing happened, one cop wailed, "It never done this before!"

"Try turning on the switch!" Sail yelled.

The motor started.

An officer stuck his head out of the car, said, "You stick around here, wise guy!" and the machine left in pursuit of the cab.

Sail, who had the legs for it, ran away from there very fast.

Sail, when he reached the Pier Six lunch stand, planted his hip against the counter, and caught up with his breathing. A young man who looked as youths in lunch stands somehow always look came over, swiped at the counter with his towel, got a look at Sail, blinked and wanted to know, "How's the weather up there?"

"Dry," Sail said. "What you got in cans?"

Sail drank the first and second cans of beer in gulps, but did some pondering over the third. When it was down, he absent-mindedly put three dimes on the counter.

"Forty-five," the youth corrected. "Cans is fifteen."

Sail substituted a half dollar and put the nickel change in one of the slot machines, still involved with his thoughts. The one-armed bandit gave him a lemon and two bars, another bar just showing.

"Almost a jackpot," someone said.

"History," Sail said, "repeating itself."

A telephone booth was housed at the end of Pier Four. Sail dialed the 0 and asked for Police Headquarters.

The slot machines chugged at the lunch stand while he waited. A card on the phone box told how to report a fire, get the police or call an ambulance. He read part of it, and Headquarters answered.

Sail said, "I want to report an attempted robbery. This is Captain Oscar Sail of the yacht *Sail*. A few minutes ago, a man and a woman boarded my boat and marched me away at the point of a gun. I do not know why. I feel they intended to kill me. There was a police car parked at the corner of Biscayne, and I broke away. The man and woman fled in a taxi. The officers chased them. I do not know whether the officers have reported yet."

"They have."

"Did they catch the pair?"

"No."

Sail almost said that was what he had called to find out, but caught himself in time.

"It might help if you described the pair," the police voice said.

Sail described an imaginary couple that were not like Blick and Nola in any particular except that they were man and woman.

"Thanks," said the voice at Headquarters. "When you get aboard your boat, tell Patrolman Joey Cripp to give us a ring. I'm Captain Rader. You'll probably find Patrolman Cripp on your boat."

Sail was wearing a startled look as he hung up and felt for a nickel in the coin return cup of the telephone.

Three men were waiting in the cabin of *Sail* when Sail got there. Two wore police uniforms, the other had civilian clothes.

One policeman was using his tongue to lather a new cigar with saliva. The tongue was coated. His neck had some loose red skin on it. He was shaking, not very much, but shaking.

The second officer was the young small patrolman. He still had his flashlight.

The man in civilian clothes was putting bottles and test tubes in a scuffed leather bag which held more of the same stuff and a microscope off which much of the enamel had been worn. His suit was fuzzy gray, rimless spectacles were pinched tight on his nose, and he had chewed half of the cigar in his mouth without lighting it. The cigar was the same kind the policeman with the shakes was licking.

Sail said, "Captain Rader wants Patrolman Joey Cripp to call him."

"That's me," the young patrolman said, and started for the companionway.

"Wait a minute," Sail said. "You didn't happen to get a look at a man and a woman who left here with me a while ago?"

"I sure did. I was behind a bush in the park." The young officer went out.

The shaking policeman got up slowly, holding his damp cigar and looking miserable. He took a full breath and started words coming.

"Gracious but you're a tall man," he said. "I'm Captain Cripp and Joey is my son. This is Mister Waterman. You have a wonderful boat here. Some day I am going to get me a boat like this and go to the South Seas. I want to thank you for reporting your trouble to Captain Rader, which

I presume you have just done. And I want to congratulate you on your narrow escape from those two. But next time, don't take such chances. Never fool with a man with a gun. We'll let you know as soon as we hear anything of your attacker and his companion. They got away from the radio car. I hope you have a good time in Miami, and no more trouble. We have a wonderful city, a wonderful climate." He shook with his chill.

Captain Cripp pulled out another cigar and a shiny cylindrical metal lighter. He took another breath.

"Smoke? Of course you do. Better light it yourself. I shake like a leaf. I've got the damned malaria, and every other day, I shake. That's an excellent cigar, if I do say so myself. One of our native products. Made right here in Miami, and as mild as an old maid's kiss. There! Didn't I tell you it was a good cigar?"

He took back his lighter. He did not touch the bright metal where Sail had held it and made fingerprints.

"Isn't admission charged to this?"

"Eh? Oh, yes, you are naturally puzzled by our presence here. Forget it. It means nothing at all. It's just an idea Captain Rader got after talking to Joey about a yell and a fish."

Patrolman Joey Cripp jumped aboard and came below.

"Captain Rader offers his apologies for sending us aboard your boat in your absence," Joey said. "And he wonders if you have anything you would like to say to us."

Sail, his scowl getting blacker and blacker, gritted, "I'm making an effort not to say it!"

Joey said, "Well, Mister Sail, if you will excuse me, we will be going."

The rabbity man, Waterman, finished putting things in his bag and picked up a camera with a photoflash attachment, pointed the camera at Sail. The outfit clicked and flashed.

"Thank you," he said, not very politely.

They left.

Sail threw the cigar overboard, then examined the cabin. Almost everything had been put back in place carefully. But in one spot, he found fingerprint powder enough to show they had printed the place.

Sail tried to sleep the rest of the night. He did get a little. The rest of the time he spent at the companion with a mirror which he had rigged on the tip joint of a fishing rod so as to look around without showing himself.

Boats at a slip do not usually have an anchor watch. But on a big Matthews at the opposite slip, somebody seemed to be standing at anchor. The watcher did not smoke, did not otherwise allow any light to get to his features. He might have been tall or short, wide or narrow. The small things he did were what any man would do during a long tiresome job.

There was one exception. The watcher frequently put a finger deep in his mouth and felt around.

Sail took a shower with the dock hose. It gave him a chance to get a better look at the Matthews. The watcher of the night was not in evidence.

The *Sail*'s dinghy rode in stern davits, bugeye fashion, at enough of a tilt not to hold spray. Sail lowered it. He got a brush and the dock hose and washed down the black topsides, taking off dried salt which sea water had deposited. He dropped his brush in the water at different times. In each case, it sank, and he had to reach under for it.

The fourth time he reached under for the brush, he retrieved the stuff which he had taken off the Greek. The articles had not worked out of the niche between the dock cross braces under water, where he had jammed them.

Sail finished washing down, hauled the dink up on the davits, and during the business of coiling the dock hose around its faucet, looked around. Any of a dozen persons in sight might have been the watcher off the Matthews. The others would be tourists down for a gawk at the yachts.

He spirited the Greek's stuff below with the scrub brush.

One of the cards said Captain Santorin Gura Andopolis of the yacht *Athens Girl* chartered for Gulf Stream fishing, nobody catching more fish. The address was Pier Five.

The other twenty-six cards said Captain Sam Dokomos owned the Lignum Vitae Towing Company. An address and a telephone number for day calls only.

There was also a piece of board four by twenty inches, a quarter of an inch thick, mahogany, with screw holes in four corners. The varnish was peeled, rather than worn, as was some of the gold leaf. The gold leaf formed a letter, four figures.

K 9420

Sail burned everything in the galley Shipmate.

There was no one in the telephone booth at the end of the pier. He looked up the number of Pier Five, which was no more than two hundred feet distant, and dialed it.

"Captain Andopolis," he requested.

Through the window, he could see them go looking for Captain Andopolis. It took them almost five minutes to decide they couldn't find him.

"Maybe he went to the dentist, somebody thought," the one who had hunted suggested.

"Yeah?"

"Yeah. He's been having a toothache, somebody said."

Sail went back to the bugeye and put on a dark suit, tropical weight, a black polo shirt and black shoes. His shore cruising rig.

The cafeteria was overdone in chromium. The waiters who carried the trays were dressed in the same red that was on the walls. There were a score of customers and a boy who wandered among the tables selling newspapers and racing dope sheets. He sold more dope sheets than papers.

One man eating near the door did not put syrup on his pancakes or sugar in his coffee. When he finished, he put a finger in the back of his mouth to feel.

Sail finished his beer and doughnuts and strolled around the corner to a U-Drive-It.

The only car on which they did not want a deposit was a little six-cylinder sedan, not new. Sail drove it around, sticking his head out frequently to look for a tall building. He found it and parked in front of it.

He made a false start into the building, then came back to take another look at an upright dingus. Then he went inside.

He told the elevator operator loudly, "Five!" before they started up.

The fifth floor corridor was empty.

When the man who had felt of his tooth in the cafeteria came sneaking up the stairs, Sail was set. He had his belt strapped tight around his fist. The man got down on all fours to mew his pain. Sail hit again, then unwrapped the belt, blew on his fist, worked the fingers.

He had the senseless man in his arms when the elevator answered his signal.

"Quick! I gotta rush my friend to a place for a treatment!" he explained.

He drove five or six miles on a side road off the Tamiami Trail before he found a lonesome spot and got out. He hauled the man out.

The man began big at the top and tapered. His small hands were calloused, dirt was ground into the callouses, the nails broken. His face was darker than his hair.

A leather envelope purse held three hundred in old and new bills. There was a dollar sixty-one in change and the cashier's slip for his cafeteria breakfast in his trousers.

A knife was in a holster against the small of his back. It was flat and supported by a high belt. Sail threw it in the canal at the roadside. It was not the one with which he had knifed Sam. He had left that one in his victim.

Handfuls of water from the canal did not speed his revival much. When he finally came around, he groaned, squirmed, and started feeling of his bad tooth.

Sail stood back and showed him a fat blue revolver. "Just try to be nonchalant, Andopolis," he advised.

Andopolis immediately stood up.

"Sit down!" Sail directed sharply.

Andopolis walked towards him.

Sail shoved the gun out, gritting desperately, "This thing is loaded, you fool!"

Andopolis leaped. Sail dodged, but hardly enough. Andopolis hit him with a shoulder. The impact spun him. Since he didn't want to shoot, the gun was a handicap. It tied up his fists. Andopolis hit him on the belt buckle. Numbness grabbed the whole front of his body. Something suddenly against his back was the ground.

"Yah!" Andopolis screeched. "Yah!"

He jumped, feet together, at Sail's middle. Sail was too numb to move clear. The feet hit his chest, everything seemed to break, and red-hot pain knocked the numbness out. Sail got Andopolis' legs, jerked. Andopolis windmilled his arms, but fell.

Sail clamped on to one of the man's feet and began doing things to it and the leg. Andopolis, turning over and over, raised a dust cloud. He moaned and bellowed and made dog noises. When he judged Andopolis was dizzy enough, Sail pounced on the dust cloud. He hit, variously, an arm, the ground, a hip, and other places which he could not identify.

Andopolis, bewildered and with dirt in his eyes, failed to get his jaw out of the way.

Sail straightened, put back his head and started to take a full breath. He began coughing. Hacking, gagging, holding his chest, he sat down in the road. He began to sweat profusely. After a while, he unbuttoned his pants and pulled up his shirt. There was one purple print of the entire bottom of both of Andopolis' feet, and the chest was skinned, the loose skin mixed with the long golden hair. There was not much blood.

Andopolis got his eyes open and snarled, "Yah! I stomp you good if you don't lay off me!"

Sail coughed and got up. He kept his feet far apart, but did not teeter much.

He said thickly, "My Macedonian friend, you stood anchor watch on me all night and you were still trailing me this morning. Where do you get that lay off stuff?"

"Before that, I'm talk about," Andopolis growled.

"Eh?"

Andopolis took a breath and blew words out. "For two week now, you been follow me like dog. I go to Bimini two day, and you and that black bugeye in Bimini before long. I make the run from Bimini here yesterday. You make him too. Vat you take me for? One blind owl, huh?"

Sail asked, "Do you think you're bulletproof, too?"

Andopolis snorted. "Me, I don't theenk you shoot."

"What gave you that idea?"

"Go jump in hell," Andopolis said.

Sail coughed some, deep and low, trying to keep it from moving his ribs.

He said, "All right, now that we're being honest with each other, I'll tell you a true story about a yacht named *Lady Luck*. That's just so there won't be any misunderstanding about who knows what."

Andopolis crowded his lips into a bunch and pushed the bunch out as far as he could, but didn't say anything.

Sail began:

"The *Lady Luck*, Department of Commerce registration number K 9420, was as neat a little yacht as ever kedged off Featherbed Bank. She belonged to Bill Lord of Tulsa. Oil. Out in Tulsa, they call Bill the Osage Ogre, on account of he's got what it seems to take to find oil. Missus Bill likes jewelry, and Bill likes her, so he buys her plenty. Because Missus Bill really likes her rocks, she carries them around with her. You following me?"

Andopolis was. He still had his lips pursed.

"Bill Lord had his *Lady Luck* anchored off the vet camp on Lower Matecumbe last November," Sail continued. "Bill and the Missus were ashore, looking over the camp. Bill was in the trenches himself, back when, and is some kind of a shot in the American Legion or the Democrats, so he was interested in the camp. The Missus left her pretties on the yacht. Remember that. Everybody has read about the hurricane that hit that afternoon, and maybe some noticed that Bill and his Missus were among those who hung on behind that tank car. But the *Lady Luck* wasn't so lucky, and she dragged her picks off somewhere and sank. For a while, nobody knew where."

Sail stopped to cough. He had to lay down on his back before he could stop, and he was very careful about getting erect again. Perspiration had wet most of him.

He said, "A couple of weeks ago, a guy asked the Department of Commerce lads to check and give him the name of the boat, and the name of the owner, that carried the number K 9420. That was the mistake."

"Pooey," Andopolis said, "on your story."

"The word got to me," Sail continued. "Never mind how. And it was easy to find you were the lad asking for the dope on K 9420. Inquiry brought out that you had had a fishing party down around Matecumbe and Long Key a few days before you suddenly got curious about K 9420. It was a little harder to locate the parties who had your boat hired at the time. Two Pan-American pilots. They said you anchored off Lower Matecumbe to bottom fish, and your anchor fouled something, and you had a time, and finally, when you got the anchor up, you brought aboard some bow planking off a sunken boat. From the strain as it was torn loose, it was apparent the anchor had pulled the planking off the rest of the boat, which was still down there. You checked up as a matter of course to learn what boat you had found."

Andopolis looked as if something besides his tooth hurt him.

"Tough you didn't get in touch with the insurance people instead of contacting Captain Sam Dokomas, a countryman of yours who had a towing and salvage outfit, and a bad reputation."

Andopolis growled, "Damn! You said somethin' then!"

Sail kept his voice lower to decrease the motion of his ribs in, expelling air for words. "You needed help to get the *Lady Luck*. But Captain Sam Dokomas tried to make you cough up the exact location. Then you smelled a double cross, got scared and lit for Bimini.

"I had been hanging around all this time, and not doing a good job of it, so you got wise to me. That scared you back to Miami. You had decided on a showdown, and were headed for my boat when Captain Sam collared you on the dock. You took care of part of your troubles with a knife right there. But that left Captain Sam's girl friend and her brother, Blick and Nola, or whatever their names are. They were in the know. They tried to grab you in the park after you fixed Sam up, but you outran them.

"Now, that's a very complete story, don't you think? Oh, yes. You got reckless and jumped me a minute ago because you figured I wouldn't shoot you because nobody but you knows the exact location of the *Lady Luck*. The two Pan-American boys fishing down there with you when you found the ship forgot to take bearings and didn't have a smell of an idea where they were at the time."

Andopolis was a man who did his thinking with the help of his face, and there was more disgust than anything else on his features.

"You trying to cut in?" he snarled finally.

"Not trying. Have."

Andopolis thought that over. The sun was comfortable, but mosquitoes were coming out of the swamp around the road to investigate, hungrier than land sharks.

"Yeah," Andopolis muttered finally. "I guess you have, at that."

"Let's get this straight, Andy. You and I, and nobody else." Andopolis nodded. "Okey."

"Now just who is this Blick?"

"Nola's brother."

"Now, hell, Andy—"

"And Nola was married to that double-crosser, Sam."

Sail made a whistling mouth. "So it was Nola's husband you dirked. She'll like you for that."

"So what? She didn't go for him much."

"No?"

"Naw. That dame—"

"Skip it," Sail said suddenly. He put his shirt on, favoring his chest. "Dang, feller, you sure busted up my ribs. We've got to watch the insurance company. They paid off on Missus Bill's stuff. Over a hundred thousand. They'll have wires out."

Andopolis nodded. "What about stuff for diving?"

"There's sponger equipment aboard my bugeye," Sail said. "I tried that racket over in Tarpon Springs, but you can't compete with those Greeks over there."

"Let's go," Andopolis said.

He was feeling of his tooth when he got in the car. Sail drove slowly. The road, nothing more than a high dike built up with material scooped out to make the drainage canal, was rough. It hurt his ribs.

Sail had driven no more than half a mile when both front tires let go their air. Maybe the car would still have remained on the road. But bullets also knocked holes in the windshield. The car was in the canal before anything could be done about it.

The car broke most of its windows going down the canal bank. The canal must have been six feet deep. Its tea-colored water filled the machine at once. Sail's middle hurt, and he had lost his air, and had to breathe in, and there was nothing but water.

After the water had filled the car, it seemed to rush around inside. Sail tried the doors, but they wouldn't open. He did not touch Andopolis in his struggles. Andopolis did not seem to be in the car. Sail couldn't remember him having been thrown out.

The first window Sail found was too small. He pummeled the car roof, but hardly had strength enough to knock himself away from what he was hitting. Then he was suddenly out of the car. He didn't know just how he had managed it. He reached the top, but sank twice before he clutched a weed on shore, after which an attack of the spasms kept him at first from hearing the shots.

Yells were mixed in the shot noise. Sail squeezed water off his eyeballs with the lids, looked, and saw Andopolis on the canal bank. Andopolis was some distance away and running madly.

Blick and his sister Nola were running after Andopolis. They were shooting at Andopolis' legs, it seemed.

They all three ran out of sight, but the sounds told Sail they had winged Andopolis and grabbed him.

Sail had wrenched some of the water out of his lungs by now. He swam to a bush which hung down into the water and got under it. He managed to get his coughing stopped.

Andopolis was sobbing at the top of his voice when Blick and Nola dragged him up.

"Shoot his other leg off if he acts up, Nola," Blick said. "I'll get out tall bud."

Sail began to want to cough. He desired the cough until it was almost worth getting shot for.

"He must be a submarine," Blick said. He got a stick and poked around. "Hell, Nola, this water is eight feet deep here anyhow."

Andopolis bubbled something in Greek.

"Shut up," Blick said, "or we'll put bullets into you like we put 'em into the tires of your car."

Andopolis went on bubbling.

"His leg is bleeding bad, Blick," Nola said.

"Hell I care! He knifed your husband, didn't he?"

Air kept coming up in big bubbles from the submerged car. Sail tried to keep his mind off the cough. Blick stood for a century on the bank with his bright little pistol.

"He musta drowned," Blick said.

Andopolis moaned.

"Didn't you know we had been shaggin' you all night and mornin'?" Blick asked him. "Hell, if you hadn't been so occupied with that long lean punk, you'd have got wise, maybe."

Nola said, "We better get his leg fixed."

"If he ain't free with his information, he won't need his leg any more," Blick said. "Let's get the hell away from here."

Andopolis whimpered as they hazed him away. They apparently had a car in the bushes beside the canal some distance down the road. Its noise went away. Sail crawled out and had a good cough.

Captain Cripp looked wide-eyed and hearty and without a sign of a chill as he exclaimed, "Well, well, good morning, good morning. You know, we began to think something had happened to you."

Sail looked at him with eyes that appeared to be drained of everything but the will to carry on, then stumbled down the remaining three steps into the main cabin of *Sail*. He let himself down on the starboard seat. Pads of cotton under gauze thickened his neck and wrists. He had discovered the car windows had cut him. Iodine had run from under one of the pads and dried. He had just come from the hospital.

Young bony Patrolman Joey Cripp looked at Sail. His grin took the looseness out of the corner of his mouth.

"Tsk, tsk," he said. "Now that's terrible. You look a sight. By God, it's a wonder you're alive. I hope that didn't happen in Miami."

Sail gave them a look of bile. "This is a private boat, in case you forgot."

"Now, now, I hope we can keep things on an amiable footing," Captain Cripp murmured.

Sail said, "Drag it!" His face was more cream than any other color. He reached behind himself in the tackle locker and got a gaff hook. A four-foot shaft of varnished oak with a tempered bright steel hook of needle point. He showed them the hook and his front teeth. "I've got a

six-aspirin headache, and things to go with it! You two polite public servants get out of here before I go fishing for kidneys!"

Patrolman Joey Cripp stood up. "I didn't think we'd have any trouble with you, Mister Sail. I hoped we wouldn't, on account of you acted like a gentleman last night."

"Sit the hell down, Joey," Captain Cripp put in. "Mister Sail, you're under arrest, I'm sorry to say."

Sail said, "Arrest?" He scowled. "Is this on the level?"

"It sure is."

"Pop said it," agreed young Joey.

Captain Cripp shook a finger at Sail. He said:

"Listen. Waterman found human blood in that fish mess on the dock last night. The harbor squad's diver went down this morning. He found a bathing suit with a sinker tied to it. He also found a live-box with some live barracuda in it. It was a barracuda you butchered on the dock. Your fishline you had in your hand when Joey got there was wet, but it don't take a minute to wet a line. You described a man and a woman that looked a lot different from the pair Joey saw you with. We been doing some arithmetic, and we figure you were covering up."

"Now," Sail said, "I guess I'm supposed to get scared?"

"I don't know," Captain Cripp said, "but a dead Greek was found over on the island this morning. And in your bathing suit which the diver got was some island sand, and some stickers off the pine trees like grow on the island."

"I guess," Joey said, "it does look kinda funny."

"I regret that it does," Captain Cripp agreed. "After all, eviden[ce] evidence, and while Miami has a wonderful hospitality, we do draw li[ne] and when our visitors go so far as to use knives on—"

"Let's get this straight!" Sail put in. "Pine tree stickers and san[d] just about alike here and in Key West, and points between."

"You may be assured—"

Sail sprang up gripping the hook. He began to yell.

"What's the idea of this clowning? I know two lug cops wh[o] 'em. If you got something to say, get it off your chests."

Joey sighed. "I guess courtesy is somethin' you can't acquir[e] say, Pop? Hell with the chief's courtesy campaign, huh?"

"Now that you mention it, Joey, okey." Captain Cripp pu[lled] cles out of his hip pocket. "We're gonna fan you into the can[and] gonna work you over until we get the straight of this."

Sail slammed the gaff into a corner.

"That's more like. If you hadn't tried to fancy pants arou[nd] I'd have showed you something then."

Sail shuffled into the galley and got the rearmost can[from] the icebox. It gurgled when he shook it, but that was beca[use]

sealed jar of water which fitted inside it. Stuffed around the jar were some sheets of paper. He held the documents out to the two policemen.

Joey raked his eyes over the print and penned signatures, then spelled them out, lips moving.

"Aw, this don't make no difference," he said. "Or does it?"

Captain Cripp complained, "My glasses fell off yesterday when I was having one of my infernal chills. What does it say, Joey?"

"He's a private dick commissioned to locate some stuff that sank on a yacht called the *Lady Luck*. The insurance people hired him."

Captain Cripp buttoned his coat, squared it over his hips, set his cap with a pat on the top. "Who signed the papers, Joey?"

Joey said, "They're all right, Pop. From what it says, I guess this private op is the head of something called Marine Investigations. Reckon that's an agency, huh?"

Captain Cripp sighed and ambled over to the companionway. "Beauty before age, Joey."

Joey bristled. "Shamus or no shamus, I say it don't make no difference!"

"Let the next guy have the honor, Joey."

"Look, Pop, damn it—"

"The last private op I worked over got me two years in the sticks. He said something about me chiseling in on the reward, and the skipper believed him. It was a damned lie, except—well—out, Joey."

"But Pop, this stinker—"

"Out!" Captain Cripp barked. "You're as big a fool as your maw!"

Joey licked his lips, raking Sail with malevolent eyes. Then he turned and climbed the companion steps.

Captain Cripp looked at Sail. He felt for the bottom step with one foot without looking down. As if he didn't expect it to do any good, he asked, "You wouldn't want to cooperate?"

"I wouldn't."

"Why not?"

"I've done it before."

Captain Cripp grinned slightly. "Just as you say. But if you get yourelf in a sling, it'd be better if you had a reason for refusing to help the olice."

"All I get out of this is ten per cent for recovering the stuff. I can't see split. I need the dough."

"And you with a boat like this."

"Maybe I like boats and maybe it keeps me broke."

"The only reason you're not in the can right now is that any shyster ild make this circumstantial evidence look funny as hell. Forget the it."

"Thanks," Sail said. "Now I'm going to sound off. It just might be

that you lads think you can let me finish it out, then step in, and maybe find the location of that boat for yourselves. Then, while I was in your bastile, trying to explain things you could think to ask me, the stuff might disappear off the boat."

"That's kind of plain talk."

"I feel kind of plain right now."

Captain Cripp's ears moved up a little with the tightening of his jaw muscles. He took his foot off the companion step. He gave his cap an angry adjustment. Then he put the foot back again.

"This malaria is sure something. I feel like a lark today, only I keep thinking about the chills tomorrow."

"Try whiskey and quinine," Sail said.

"I think the whiskey part gave it to me."

The two cops went away with Joey kicking his feet down hard at the dock planks.

Sail took rye and aspirin for what ailed him, changed clothes, took a taxi uptown and entered what looked like the largest hardware store. He asked where they kept their marine charts.

The nervous old salesman in the chart department had a rip in his canvas apron. He mixed his talk in with waving gestures of a pipe off which most of the stem had been chewed.

"Mister, you must have some funny things happen to you, you being so tall," he said. "Right now, you look as if you had had an accident."

Sail steadied himself by holding to the counter edge. "Who sells government charts here, Dad?"

"Well, there's one other store besides us. Hopkins Carter. But if you're going down in the Keys, we got everything you need here. If you go inside, you'll want charts thirty-two-sixty and sixty-one. They're the strip charts. But if you take Hawk Channel, you'll need harbor chart five-eighty-three, and charts twelve-forty-nine, fifty and fifty-one. Here, I'll show—"

Sail squinted his eyes, swallowed, and said, "I don't want to buy a chart. I want you to slip out and telephone me if either of a certain two persons comes in here and asks for chart twelve-fifty, the one which covers Lower Matecumbe."

"Huh?"

Sail said patiently, "It's easy, Dad. You just tell the party you got to get the chart, and go telephone me. Then stall around three or four minutes as if you were getting the chart out of the stock room. That will give me time to get over here and pick up their trail."

The nervous old man put his pipe in his mouth and immediately took it out again. "What kind of shenanygin is this?"

Sail showed him a license to operate in Florida.

"One of them fellers, huh?" The old man did not seem impressed.

Sail put a five-dollar bill on the counter. "That one's got a twin. How about it?"

The old man picked up the bill, squinted at it. "You mean this is a counterfeit or something. What—"

"No, no, control your imagination, Dad. The five is good, and it's yours, and another one like it, if you help me."

"You mean I keep this whether they show up or not?"

"That's the idea."

"Go ahead, Mister, and describe them people."

Sail made a word picture of Blick and Nola. Not trusting Dad's memory, he put the salient points down on a piece of paper. He added a telephone number. "That phone is a booth in a cigar store on the next corner. How far is this Hopkins Carter store?"

" 'Bout two blocks, reckon."

"I'll be there for the next ten minutes. Then I'll be in the cigar store. Ask for Chief Steward Johnson, when you call."

"That you?"

"Uh-huh."

Sail, walking off, was not as pale as he had been on the boat. He had put on a serge suit with more black than blue and a new black polo. When he was standing in front of the elevator, taking a pull at a flat amber bottle which had a crown and a figure on the label, the old man yelled, "Mister!"

Sail lowered the bottle, started coughing.

"Lemme look at this again and see if you said anything about the way he talked," the old man said.

Sail moved back to where he could see the old fellow peering at the paper which held the descriptions. The old man took his pipe out of his teeth. "Mister, what does that feller talk like?"

"Well, about like the rest of these crackers. No, wait. He'll call you bud two or three times."

The old man waved his pipe. "I already sold that man a twelve-fifty."

"The hell!"

"Around half an hour ago, I reckon."

"That's swell!" Sail pumped air out of his lungs in a short laugh which had no sound except such noise as the air made going past his teeth and out of his nostrils. "There was this one chance. They would probably want a late chart for their X-marks-the-spot. And now they've got it, so they'll be off to the wars." He kissed a palm sneeringly. "That for the whole works!"

He weaved around, a lot more unsteady than he had been a minute before. He put the flat flask between his teeth and looked at the spinning ceiling fan. By the time the bottle was empty, his head and eyes were screwing around in time with the fan blades. He got his feet tracking in the general direction of the door.

The old man said, "That there chart was delivered."

Sail maneuvered a turn and halt. "Eh?"

"He ordered it over the telephone, and we delivered. I got the address somewhere." The old man thumbed his order book, stopping to point at each name with his pipe stem.

"*Whileaway*," he said finally. "A houseboat on the Miami River below the Twelfth Street Causeway."

Sail cocked the empty bottle in a wastebasket, put five dollars in front of the old man and headed for the elevator. He was a lot steadier.

The houseboat *Whileaway* was built for rivers, and not very wide ones. Sixty feet or thereabouts waterline, she had three decks that put her up like a skyscraper. She was white, or had been. A man who loved boats would have said she should never have been built.

Scattered on shore near was a gravel pile, two trucks with nobody near them, a shed, junk from the hurricane, a trailer with both tires flat and windows broken, and two rowboats in as bad shape as the trailer.

Sail was behind most of the junk at one time or another on his way to the river bank. The river ran between wooden bulkheads at this point. Between Sail and *Whileaway*, two tugs, a yawl, a cruiser and another houseboat were tied to dolphins along the bulkhead. Nobody seemed to be on any of the boats.

Sail stripped to dark blue silk underwear shorts. He hid everything else under the junk. The water had a little more smell and floating things than in the harbor. After he had eased down into it, he kept behind the moored boats, next to the bulkhead. The tide carried him. He was just coming under the bow of *Whileaway* when one of the square window ports of the houseboat opened.

Sail sank suddenly. He thought somebody was going to shoot, or use a harpoon.

Something heavy—evidently it fell out of the porthole—hit the water. It sank quickly. Touching Sail, it pushed him aside. It went on sinking. Sail got the idea that a navy anchor was at the lowermost part of the sinking object.

He swam down after it. The river had only two fathoms here. He did not have much trouble finding it. When he clung to the object, the tide stretched his legs out behind.

Whoever had tied the knots was a sailor. Sailor knots, while they hold, are made to be easily untied. Sail got them loose. He began to think he wouldn't make the top with his burden. He was out of air.

His head came out of the water with eyes open, fixed in the direction of the square port. Nobody's head was there. No weapon appeared.

Sail looked around, then threw an arm up. He missed the first spring-line which held the houseboat to the bulkhead. He grasped the next one. He held Nola's head out.

Water leaked from Nola's nose and mouth.

Some of the rope which had tied her to the heavy navy anchor was still wrapped around her. Sail used it to tie her to the springline, so that her head was out of the water.

Then he had to try twice before he could get up the springline to the houseboat deck. Nola began gagging and coughing. It made a racket.

Sail stumbled through the handiest door. Waves of pain jumped from his ribs to his toes, from ribs to hair. The bandages had turned red, and it was not from mercurochrome.

The houseboat furnishings must have been something fifteen years ago. Most of the varnish had alligatored. Sail got into the galley by accident. Rust, dirt, smell. He grabbed the only things in sight, a quart brass fire extinguisher and a rusted ice pick.

He found a dining salon beyond the galley. He was half across it when Andopolis came in the opposite door.

Andopolis had a rusty butcher knife in one hand. He was using the other hand to handle a chair for a crutch, riding it with the knee of the leg which Blick and Nola had put a bullet through.

Clustered around Andopolis' eyes—more on the lids than elsewhere— were puffy gray blisters. They were about the size burning cigarettes would make. Two fingernails were off one of his hands, the one which held the butcher knife. Red ran from the mutilated fingertips down over the rusty knife.

Sail threw the fire extinguisher. He was weaker even than he had thought. The best he could do was bounce the extinguisher off the bulk-head behind Andopolis.

Andopolis said thickly, "I feex you up this time, fran!" and reversed the knife for throwing.

Sail threw his ice pick. It was a good shot. The pick stuck into An-dopolis' chest over his heart. But it did not go in deep enough to trouble Andopolis. He never bothered to jerk it out. He already had enough pain elsewhere not to know it was there.

Feet banged through the boat behind Sail. They approached.

Andopolis threw. Sail dropped. His weakness seemed to help. The knife went over his head.

A uniformed cop had appeared in the door. Bad luck put him in the path of the knife. He made a bleating sound, took spraddling steps and leaned against a bulkhead, his hands trying to cover the handle of the butcher knife and his left shoulder. He made a poor job of it.

Sail got up and lurched around Andopolis. The chair crutch made Andopolis clumsy.

Once through the door behind Andopolis, Sail found himself in what had once been the main cabin, and pretended to be, still.

Blick sat on the cabin floor, his face a mess. His visage was smeared with blue ink. The ink bottle was upside down under a table on which a new marine chart was spread open. A common writing pen lay on the chart.

Andopolis came in after Sail, banging on the chair crutch. The ice pick still stuck in his chest by its point. He came at Sail, hopped on one leg, and swung his chair with the other.

Sail, coughing, hurting all over, tried to dodge. He made it, but fell down. Andopolis swung the chair. Sail rolled, and the chair went to pieces on the floor.

Nola was still screaming. Men were swearing outside. More men were running around on the houseboat, trying to find the way below. A police siren was whining.

Andopolis held a leg of his chair still. It was heavy enough to knock the brains out of an ox. He hopped for Sail.

Sail, looking about wildly, saw the fire extinguisher on the floor. It must have bounced in here. Maybe somebody had kicked it in accidentally. He rolled to it.

Andopolis lifted the chair leg.

The extinguisher made sickly noises as Sail pumped it. No tetrachloride came out. Nothing happened to indicate it ever would. Then a first squirt ran out about a foot. The second was longer. The third wet Andopolis' chest. Sail aimed and pumped. The tetrachloride got into Andopolis' eyes.

Andopolis made snarling sounds and couldn't see any more.

Sail got up and weaved to the table.

The chart on the table had two inked lines forming a V with arms that ran to landmarks on Lower Matecumbe island in the Florida Keys. Compass bearings were printed beside each arm, and the point where the lines came together was ringed.

Several times, Sail's lips moved, repeating the bearings, the landmarks.

Then Sail picked up the pen. He made a NE into a NNE and a SSE out of an E.

His letters looked enough like the others that nobody would guess the difference. And the lines of the V were wavy. They had not been laid out with a protractor from the compass roses. Therefore, they did not indicate an exact spot. Probably they varied as much as a mile, for the *Lady Luck* seemed to lie well off Matecumbe. Nobody would locate any sunken boat from that chart now.

Sail was repeating the true bearings to fix them in his memory when Andopolis came hopping in. Andopolis was still blind, still had his chair leg.

Blick, on the floor, called, "Nola—kid—what's wrong?" He didn't seem to know where he was or what was happening.

Andopolis weaved for Blick's mumbling voice.

"Blick!" Sail yelled thickly. "Jump!"

Blick said foolishly, "Was that—you—Nola?"

Sail was stumbling towards him, fully aware he would not make it in time. He didn't. He woke up nights for quite a while hearing the sound Andopolis' chair leg and Blick's head made.

Andopolis hopped around, still quite blind, and made for Sail. He had his chair leg raised. Hair, blood and brains stuck to the hickory chair leg. Sail got out of the way.

Andopolis stopped, stood perfectly still, and listened. Sail did not move. He was pale, swaying. He squatted, got his hands on the floor, sure he was going to fall if he didn't. He tried not to breathe loudly enough for Andopolis to hear.

Captain Cripp, Patrolman Joey Cripp and the old man from the hardware store came in together looking around.

The old man pointed at Sail and began, "There's the man who asked about the feller that got the chart. I told you I told him the chart was delivered here, and he probably had come right—"

Andopolis rushed the voice, holding his chair leg up.

"Look out!" Sail croaked.

Andopolis instantly veered for where he thought Sail's voice had come from. He was a little wrong. It was hard for him to maintain a direction hopping on one leg. He hopped against a wall. Hard.

Andopolis sighed, leaned over backward and hit the floor. He had a fit. A brief fit, ending by Andopolis straightening out and relaxing. Hitting the wall had driven the ice pick the rest of the way into his chest.

Sail remained on all fours on the floor. He felt, except for the pain, as if he were very drunk on bad liquor. He must have remained on his hands and knees a long time, for he was vaguely aware that Captain Cripp and Joey had walked around and around him, but without speaking. Then they went over to the table and found the chart.

They divided their looking between the chart and each other.

"It's it," Joey said.

"Yeah." Captain Cripp sounded thoughtful. "What about it, Joey?"

"You're the boss, Pop."

Captain Cripp turned the corners of his mouth down. He folded the chart, stuck it inside his clothing, under his belt. Then he straightened his uniform.

A doctor came in at last. He seemed to be a very silent doctor. He picked up Andopolis' wrist, held it a while, then put it back on the floor carefully. The wrist and arm were more flexible than that much rubber would have been. The doctor did not speak.

Sail was still on all fours. The doctor upset him gently. Sail had his tongue between his teeth. The doctor explored with his hands; when he came to Sail's chest, a small amount of sound escaped between Sail's tongue and teeth.

"My God!" the doctor said.

Four men helped with the stretcher as far as the ambulance, but only two when it came to getting the stretcher into the ambulance. Two could manage it better, using a system which they had. The ambulance motor started.

Captain Cripp got into the ambulance with Sail. He was holding his right hand to his nose.

"About Joey," he said. "I been wondering if Joey believed in something on the side, when he could get it. You know, kinda the modern idea."

He took his hand from his nose and quickly put a handkerchief in its place. The handkerchief got red at once.

Then he put the folded marine chart under Sail's head.

"Joey," he chuckled, "is as old-fashioned as angels, only he about busted my beak before I could explain."

WILLIAM FAULKNER
(1897–1962)

A Nobel laureate in literature, the southern-born William Faulkner became one of the foremost American novelists of his generation. His work, set in the fictional Yoknapatawpha County, Mississippi, mapped the territory in both a physical and moral sense. He knew his southern scene well. Born William Cuthbert Falkner (he later changed the spelling of the family name), he grew up in Oxford, Mississippi, where he did not complete high school. He joined Canada's Royal Air Force, then attended the University of Mississippi, where he served as the university postmaster. He also produced a privately printed book of poetry before living briefly in New Orleans and writing sketches for newspapers there. He traveled to Europe and later returned to Oxford, where he married, had one daughter, and embarked upon his career as a full-time writer.

Particularly during the 1930s, Faulkner wrote a number of stories that fall into the crime and mystery genre. "Hand upon the Waters" is typical of these in its use of local color, biblical references, and a puzzle plot interpreted by Uncle Gavin Stevens. Although Stevens is a character who graduated Phi Beta Kappa from Harvard, he does not rely on academic prowess to solve crimes. Instead he applies his powers of observation and his longtime acquaintance-ship with the denizens of small-town and backwoods Mississippi to help him understand what has occurred. In "Hand upon the Waters," Faulkner places the essential clue right before the readers' eyes yet still achieves a surprise ending. However, as is often the case with a superior author, the more memorable aspect of the work is likely to lie in his skilled development of characters. This is particularly true of the poignantly portrayed Joe, who can neither hear nor speak, but whose actions address the despair that violent crime can leave in its wake.

Hand upon the Waters

1939

The two men followed the path where it ran between the river and the dense wall of cypress and cane and gum and brier. One of them carried a gunny sack which had been washed and looked as if it had been ironed too. The other was a youth, less than twenty, by his face. The river was low, at mid-July level.

"He ought to been catching fish in this water," the youth said.

"If he happened to feel like fishing," the one with the sack said. "Him and Joe run that line when Lonnie feels like it, not when the fish are biting."

"They'll be on the line, anyway," the youth said. "I don't reckon Lonnie cares who takes them off for him."

Presently the ground rose to a cleared point almost like a headland. Upon it sat a conical hut with a pointed roof, built partly of mildewed canvas and odd-shaped boards and partly of oil tins hammered out flat. A rusted stove pipe projected crazily above it, there was a meager woodpile and an ax, and a bunch of cane poles leaned against it. Then they saw, on the earth before the open door, a dozen or so short lengths of cord just cut from a spool near by, and a rusted can half full of heavy fishhooks, some of which had already been bent onto the cords. But there was nobody there.

"The boat's gone," the man with the sack said. "So he ain't gone to the store." Then he discovered that the youth had gone on, and he drew in his breath and was just about to shout when suddenly a man rushed out of the undergrowth and stopped, facing him and making an urgent whimpering sound—a man not large, but with tremendous arms and shoulders; an adult, yet with something childlike about him, about the way he moved, barefoot, in battered overalls and with the urgent eyes of the deaf and dumb.

"Hi, Joe," the man with the sack said, raising his voice as people will with those who they know cannot understand them. "Where's Lonnie?" He held up the sack. "Got some fish?"

But the other only stared at him, making that rapid whimpering. Then he turned and scuttled on up the path where the youth had disappeared, who, at that moment, shouted: "Just look at this line!"

The older one followed. The youth was leaning eagerly out over the water beside a tree from which a light cotton rope slanted tautly downward into the water. The deaf-and-dumb man stood just behind him, still whimpering and lifting his feet rapidly in turn, though before the older man reached him he turned and scuttled back past him, toward the hut. At this stage of the river the line should have been clear of the water, stretching from bank to bank, between the two trees, with only the hooks on the dependent cords submerged. But now it slanted into the water from either end, with a heavy downstream sag, and even the older man could feel movement on it. "It's big as a man!" the youth cried.

"Yonder's his boat," the older man said. The youth saw it, too—across the stream and below them, floated into a willow clump inside a point. "Cross and get it, and we'll see how big this fish is."

The youth stepped out of his shoes and overalls and removed his shirt and waded out and began to swim, holding straight across to let the current carry him down to the skiff and got the skiff and paddled back, standing erect in it and staring eagerly upstream toward the heavy sag of the line, near the center of which the water, from time to time, roiled heavily with submerged movement. He brought the skiff in below the older man, who, at that moment, discovered the deaf-and-dumb man just behind him again, still making the rapid and urgent sound and trying to enter the skiff.

"Get back!" the older man said, pushing the other back with his arm. "Get back, Joe!"

"Hurry up!" the youth said, staring eagerly toward the submerged line, where, as he watched, something rolled sluggishly to the surface, then sank again. "There's something on there, or there ain't a hog in Georgia. It's big as a man too!"

The older one stepped into the skiff. He still held the rope, and he drew the skiff, hand over hand, along the line itself.

Suddenly, from the bank of the river behind them, the deaf-and-dumb man began to make an actual sound. It was quite loud.

2

"Inquest?" Stevens said.

"Lonnie Grinnup." The coroner was an old country doctor. "Two fellows found him drowned on his own trotline this morning."

"No!" Stevens said. "Poor damned feeb. I'll come out." As county attorney he had no business there, even if it had not been an accident. He knew it. He was going to look at the dead man's face for a sentimental reason. What was now Yoknapatawpha County had been founded not by one pioneer but by three simultaneous ones. They came together on horseback, through the Cumberland Gap from the Carolinas, when Jefferson was still a Chickasaw Agency post, and bought land in the Indian patent and established families and flourished and vanished, so that now, a hundred years afterward, there was in all the county they helped to found but one representative of the three names.

This was Stevens, because the last of the Holston family had died before the end of the last century, and the Louis Grenier, whose dead face Stevens was driving eight miles in the heat of a July afternoon to look at, had never even known he was Louis Grenier. He could not even spell the Lonnie Grinnup he called himself—an orphan, too, like Stevens, a man a little under the medium size and somewhere in his middle thirties, whom the whole county knew—the face which was almost delicate when you looked at it again, equable, constant, always cheerful, with an invariable fuzz of soft golden beard which had never known a razor, and light-colored peaceful eyes—"touched," they said, but whatever it was had touched him lightly, taking not very much away that need be missed—living, year in and year out, in the hovel he had built himself of an old tent and a few mismatched boards and flattened oil tins, with the deaf-and-dumb orphan he had taken into his hut ten years ago and clothed and fed and raised, and who had not even grown mentally as far as he himself had.

Actually his hut and trotline and fish trap were in almost the exact center of the thousand and more acres his ancestors had once owned. But he never knew it.

Stevens believed he would not have cared, would have declined to accept the idea that any one man could or should own that much of the earth which belongs to all, to every man for his use and pleasure—in his own case, that thirty or forty square feet where his hut sat and the span of river across which his trotline stretched where anyone was welcome at any time, whether he was there or not, to use his gear and eat his food as long as there was food.

And at times he would wedge his door shut against prowling animals and with his deaf-and-dumb companion he would appear without warning or invitation at houses or cabins ten and fifteen miles away, where he would remain for weeks, pleasant, equable, demanding nothing and without servility, sleeping wherever it was convenient for his hosts to have him sleep—in the hay of lofts, or in beds in family or company rooms, while the deaf-and-dumb youth lay on the porch or the ground just outside, where he could hear him who was brother and father both, breathing. It was his one sound out of all the voiceless earth. He was infallibly aware of it.

It was early afternoon. The distances were blue with heat. Then, across the long flat where the highway began to parallel the river bottom, Stevens saw the store. By ordinary it would have been deserted, but now he could already see clotted about it the topless and battered cars, the saddled horses and mules and the wagons, the riders and drivers of which he knew by name. Better still, they knew him, voting for him year after year and calling him by his given name even though they did not quite understand him, just as they did not understand the Harvard Phi Beta Kappa key on his watch chain. He drew in beside the coroner's car.

Apparently it was not to be in the store, but in the grist mill beside it, before the open door of which the clean Saturday overalls and shirts and the bared heads and the sunburned necks striped with the white razor lines of Saturday neck shaves were densest and quietest. They made way for him to enter. There was a table and three chairs where the coroner and two witnesses sat.

Stevens noticed a man of about forty holding a clean gunny sack, folded and refolded until it resembled a book, and a youth whose face wore an expression of weary yet indomitable amazement. The body lay under a quilt on the low platform to which the silent mill was bolted. He crossed to it and raised the corner of the quilt and looked at the face and lowered the quilt and turned, already on his way back to town, and then he did not go back to town. He moved over among the men who stood along the wall, their hats in their hands, and listened to the two witnesses—it was the youth telling it in his amazed, spent, incredulous voice—finish describing the finding of the body. He watched the coroner

sign the certificate and return the pen to his pocket, and he knew he was
not going back to town.

"I reckon that's all," the coroner said. He glanced toward the door.
"All right, Ike," he said. "You can take him now."

Stevens moved aside with the others and watched the four men cross
toward the quilt. "You going to take him, Ike?" he said.

The eldest of the four glanced back at him for a moment. "Yes. He
had his burying money with Mitchell at the store."

"You, and Pose, and Matthew, and Jim Blake," Stevens said.

This time the other glanced back at him almost with surprise, almost
impatiently.

"We can make up the difference," he said.

"I'll help," Stevens said.

"I thank you," the other said. "We got enough."

Then the coroner was among them, speaking testily: "All right, boys.
Give them room."

With the others, Stevens moved out into the air, the afternoon again.
There was a wagon backed up to the door now which had not been there
before. Its tail gate was open, the bed was filled with straw, and with the
others Stevens stood bareheaded and watched the four men emerge from
the shed, carrying the quilt-wrapped bundle, and approach the wagon.
Three or four others moved forward to help, and Stevens moved, too, and
touched the youth's shoulder, seeing again that expression of spent and
incredulous wild amazement.

"You went and got the boat before you knew anything was wrong,"
he said.

"That's right," the youth said. He spoke quietly enough at first. "I
swum over and got the boat and rowed back. I knowed something was
on the line. I could see it swagged—"

"You mean you swam the boat back," Stevens said.

"—down into the—Sir?"

"You swam the boat back. You swam over and got it and swam it
back."

"No, sir! I rowed the boat back. I rowed it straight back across! I never
suspected nothing! I could see them fish—"

"What with?" Stevens said. The youth glared at him. "What did you
row it back with?"

"With the oar! I picked up the oar and rowed it right back, and all
the time I could see them flopping around in the water. They didn't want
to let go! They held on to him even after we hauled him up, still eating
him! Fish were! I knowed turtles would, but these were fish! Eating him!
Of course it was fish we thought was there! It was! I won't never eat
another one! Never!"

It had not seemed long, yet the afternoon had gone somewhere, taking some of the heat with it. Again in his car, his hand on the switch, Stevens sat looking at the wagon, now about to depart. *And it's not right,* he thought. *It don't add. Something more that I missed, didn't see. Or something that hasn't happened yet.*

The wagon was now moving, crossing the dusty banquette toward the highroad, with two men on the seat and the other two on saddled mules beside it. Stevens' hand turned the switch; the car was already in gear. It passed the wagon, already going fast.

A mile down the road he turned into a dirt lane, back toward the hills. It began to rise, the sun intermittent now, for in places among the ridges sunset had already come. Presently the road forked. In the V of the fork stood a church, white-painted and steepleless, beside an unfenced straggle of cheap marble headstones and other graves outlined only by rows of inverted glass jars and crockery and broken brick.

He did not hesitate. He drove up beside the church and turned and stopped the car facing the fork and the road over which he had just come where it curved away and vanished. Because of the curve, he could hear the wagon for some time before he saw it, then he heard the truck. It was coming down out of the hills behind him, fast, sweeping into sight, already slowing—a cab, a shallow bed with a tarpaulin spread over it.

It drew out of the road at the fork and stopped; then he could hear the wagon again, and then he saw it and the two riders come around the curve in the dusk, and there was a man standing in the road beside the truck now, and Stevens recognized him: Tyler Ballenbaugh—a farmer, married and with a family and a reputation for self-sufficiency and violence, who had been born in the county and went out West and returned, bringing with him, like an effluvium, rumors of sums he had won gambling, who had married and bought land and no longer gambled at cards, but on certain years would mortgage, his own crop and buy or sell cotton futures with the money—standing in the road beside the wagon, tall in the dusk, talking to the men in the wagon without raising his voice or making any gesture. Then there was another man beside him, in a white shirt, whom Stevens did not recognize or look at again.

His hand dropped to the switch; again the car was in motion with the sound of the engine. He turned the headlights on and dropped rapidly down out of the churchyard and into the road and up behind the wagon as the man in the white shirt leaped onto the running board, shouting at him, and Stevens recognized him too: A younger brother of Ballenbaugh's, who had gone to Memphis years ago, where it was understood he had been a hired armed guard during a textile strike, but who, for the last two or three years, had been at his brother's, hiding, it was said, not from the police but from some of his Memphis friends or later business associates. From time to time his name made one in reported brawls and fights at country dances and picnics. He was subdued and thrown into

jail once by two officers in Jefferson, where, on Saturdays, drunk, he
would brag about his past exploits or curse his present luck and the older
brother who made him work about the farm.

"Who in hell you spying on?" he shouted.

"Boyd," the other Ballenbaugh said. He did not even raise his voice.
"Get back in the truck." He had not moved—a big somber-faced man
who stared at Stevens out of pale, cold, absolutely expressionless eyes.
"Howdy, Gavin," he said.

"Howdy, Tyler," Stevens said. "You going to take Lonnie?"

"Does anybody here object?"

"I don't," Stevens said, getting out of the car. "I'll help you swamp
him."

Then he got back into the car. The wagon moved on. The truck backed
and turned, already gaining speed; the two faces fled past—the one which
Stevens saw now was not truculent, but frightened; the other, in which
there was nothing at all save the still, cold, pale eyes. The cracked tail
lamp vanished over the hill. *That was an Okatoba County license number*, he
thought.

Lonnie Grinnup was buried the next afternoon, from Tyler Ballenbaugh's house.

Stevens was not there. "Joe wasn't there, either, I suppose," he said.
"Lonnie's dummy."

"No. He wasn't there, either. The folks that went in to Lonnie's camp
on Sunday morning to look at that trotline said that he was still there,
hunting for Lonnie. But he wasn't at the burying. When he finds Lonnie
this time, he can lie down by him, but he won't hear him breathing."

3

"No," Stevens said.

He was in Mottstown, the seat of Okatoba County, on that afternoon.
And although it was Sunday, and although he would not know until he
found it just what he was looking for, he found it before dark—the agent
for the company which, eleven years ago, had issued to Lonnie Grinnup
a five-thousand-dollar policy, with double indemnity for accidental death,
on his life, with Tyler Ballenbaugh as beneficiary.

It was quite correct. The examining doctor had never seen Lonnie
Grinnup before, but he had known Tyler Ballenbaugh for years, and Lonnie had made his mark on the application and Ballenbaugh had paid the
first premium and kept them up ever since.

There had been no particular secrecy about it other than transacting
the business in another town, and Stevens realized that even that was not
unduly strange.

Okatoba County was just across the river, three miles from where
Ballenbaugh lived, and Stevens knew of more men than Ballenbaugh who
owned land in one county and bought their cars and trucks and banked

their money in another, obeying the country-bred man's inherent, possibly atavistic, faint distrust, perhaps, not of men in white collars but of paving and electricity.

"Then I'm not to notify the company yet?" the agent asked.

"No. I want you to accept the claim when he comes in to file it, explain to him it will take a week or so to settle it, wait three days and send him word to come in to your office to see you at nine o'clock or ten o'clock the next morning; don't tell him why, what for. Then telephone me at Jefferson when you know he has got the message."

Early the next morning, about daybreak, the heat wave broke. He lay in bed watching and listening to the crash and glare of lightning and the rain's loud fury, thinking of the drumming of it and the fierce channeling of clay-colored water across Lonnie Grinnup's raw and kinless grave in the barren hill beside the steepleless church, and of the sound it would make, above the turmoil of the rising river, on the tin-and-canvas hut where the deaf-and-dumb youth probably still waited for him to come home, knowing that something had happened, but not how, not why. *Not how*, Stevens thought. *They fooled him someway. They didn't even bother to tie him up. They just fooled him.*

On Wednesday night he received a telephone message from the Mottstown agent that Tyler Ballenbaugh had filed his claim.

"All right," Stevens said. "Send him the message Monday, to come in Tuesday. And let me know when you know he has gotten it." He put the phone down. *I am playing stud poker with a man who has proved himself a gambler, which I have not*, he thought. *But at least I have forced him to draw a card. And he knows who is in the pot with him.*

So when the second message came, on the following Monday afternoon, he knew only what he himself was going to do. He had thought once of asking the sheriff for a deputy, or of taking some friend with him. *But even a friend would not believe that what I have is a hold card*, he told himself, *even though I do: That one man, even an amateur at murder, might be satisfied that he had cleaned up after himself. But when there are two of them, neither one is going to be satisfied that the other has left no ravelings.*

So he went alone. He owned a pistol. He looked at it and put it back into its drawer. *At least nobody is going to shoot me with that*, he told himself. He left town just after dusk.

This time he passed the store, dark at the roadside. When he reached the lane into which he had turned nine days ago, this time he turned to the right and drove on for a quarter of a mile and turned into a littered yard, his headlights full upon a dark cabin. He did not turn them off. He walked full in the yellow beam, toward the cabin, shouting: "Nate! Nate!"

After a moment a Negro voice answered, though no light showed.

"I'm going in to Mr. Lonnie Grinnup's camp. If I'm not back by daylight, you better go up to the store and tell them."

There was no answer. Then a woman's voice said: "You come on away from that door!" The man's voice murmured something.

"I can't help it!" the woman cried. "You come away and let them white folks alone!"

So there are others besides me, Stevens thought, thinking how quite often, almost always, there is in Negroes an instinct not for evil but to recognize evil at once when it exists. He went back to the car and snapped off the lights and took his flashlight from the seat.

He found the truck. In the close-held beam of the light he read again the license number which he had watched nine days ago flee over the hill. He snapped off the light and put it into his pocket.

Twenty minutes later he realized he need not have worried about the light. He was in the path, between the black wall of jungle and the river, he saw the faint glow inside the canvas wall of the hut and he could already hear the two voices—the one cold, level and steady, the other harsh and high. He stumbled over the woodpile and then over something else and found the door and flung it back and entered the devastation of the dead man's house—the shuck mattresses dragged out of the wooden bunks, the overturned stove and scattered cooking vessels—where Tyler Ballenbaugh stood facing him with a pistol and the younger one stood half-crouched above an overturned box.

"Stand back, Gavin," Ballenbaugh said.

"Stand back yourself, Tyler," Stevens said. "You're too late."

The younger one stood up. Stevens saw recognition come into his face. "Well, by—" he said.

"Is it all up, Gavin?" Ballenbaugh said. "Don't lie to me."

"I reckon it is," Stevens said. "Put your pistol down."

"Who else is with you?"

"Enough," Stevens said. "Put your pistol down, Tyler."

"Hell," the younger one said. He began to move; Stevens saw his eyes go swiftly from him to the door behind him. "He's lying. There ain't anybody with him. He's just spying around like he was the other day, putting his nose into business he's going to wish he had kept it out of. Because this time it's going to get bit off."

He was moving towards Stevens, stooping a little, his arms held slightly away from his sides.

"Boyd!" Tyler said. The other continued to approach Stevens, not smiling, but with a queer light, a glitter, in his face. "Boyd!" Tyler said. Then he moved, too, with astonishing speed, and overtook the younger and with one sweep of his arm hurled him back into the bunk. They faced each other—the one cold, still, expressionless, the pistol held before him aimed at nothing, the other half-crouched, snarling.

"What the hell you going to do? Let him take us back to town like two damn sheep?"

"That's for me to decide," Tyler said. He looked at Stevens. "I never intended this, Gavin. I insured his life, kept the premiums paid—yes. But it was good business: If he had outlived me, I wouldn't have had any use for the money, and if I had outlived him, I would have collected on my judgment. There was no secret about it. It was done in open daylight. Anybody could have found out about it. Maybe he told about it. I never told him not to. And who's to say against it anyway? I always fed him when he came to my house, he always stayed as long as he wanted to, come when he wanted to. But I never intended this."

Suddenly the younger one began to laugh, half-crouched against the bunk where the other had flung him. "So that's the tune," he said. "That's the way it's going." Then it was not laughter any more, though the transition was so slight or perhaps so swift as to be imperceptible. He was standing now, leaning forward a little, facing his brother. "I never insured him for five thousand dollars! I wasn't going to get—"

"Hush," Tyler said.

"—five thousand dollars when they found him dead on that—"

Tyler walked steadily to the other and slapped him in two motions, palm and back, of the same hand, the pistol still held before him in the other.

"I said, hush, Boyd," he said. He looked at Stevens again. "I never intended this. I don't want that money now, even if they were going to pay it, because this is not the way I aimed for it to be. Not the way I bet. What are you going to do?"

"Do you need to ask that? I want an indictment for murder."

"And then prove it!" the younger one snarled. "Try and prove it! I never insured his life for—"

"Hush," Tyler said. He spoke almost gently, looking at Stevens with the pale eyes in which there was absolutely nothing. "You can't do that. It's a good name. Has been. Maybe nobody's done much for it yet, but nobody's hurt it bad yet, up to now. I have owed no man, I have taken nothing that was not mine. You mustn't do that, Gavin."

"I mustn't do anything else, Tyler."

The other looked at him. Stevens heard him draw a long breath and expel it. But his face did not change at all. "You want your eye for an eye and tooth for a tooth."

"Justice wants it. Maybe Lonnie Grinnup wants it. Wouldn't you?"

For a moment longer the other looked at him. Then Ballenbaugh turned and made a quiet gesture at his brother and another toward Stevens, quiet and peremptory.

Then they were out of the hut, standing in the light from the door; a breeze came up from somewhere and rustled in the leaves overhead and died away, ceased.

At first Stevens did not know what Ballenbaugh was about. He watched in mounting surprise as Ballenbaugh turned to face his brother, his hand extended, speaking in a voice which was actually harsh now:

"This is the end of the row. I was afraid from that night when you came home and told me. I should have raised you better, but I didn't. Here. Stand up and finish it."

"Look out, Tyler!" Stevens said. "Don't do that!"

"Keep out of this, Gavin. If it's meat for meat you want, you will get it." He still faced his brother, he did not even glance at Stevens. "Here," he said. "Take it and stand up."

Then it was too late. Stevens saw the younger one spring back. He saw Tyler take a step forward and he seemed to hear in the other's voice the surprise, the disbelief, then the realization of the mistake. "Drop the pistol, Boyd," he said. "Drop it."

"So you want it back, do you?" the younger said. "I come to you that night and told you you were worth five thousand dollars as soon as some-body happened to look on that trotline, and asked you to give me ten dollars, and you turned me down. Ten dollars, and you wouldn't. Sure you can have it. Take it." It flashed, low against his side; the orange fire lanced downward again as the other fell.

Now it's my turn, Stevens thought. They faced each other; he heard again that brief wind come from somewhere and shake the leaves over-head and fall still.

"Run while you can, Boyd," he said. "You've done enough. Run, now."

"Sure I'll run. You do all your worrying about me now, because in a minute you won't have any worries. I'll run all right, after I've said a word to smart guys that come sticking their noses where they'll wish to hell they hadn't—"

Now he's going to shoot, Stevens thought, and he sprang. For an instant he had the illusion of watching himself springing, reflected somehow by the faint light from the river, that luminousness which water gives back to the dark, in the air above Boyd Ballenbaugh's head. Then he knew it was not himself he saw, it had not been wind he heard, as the creature, the shape which had no tongue and needed none, which had been waiting nine days now for Lonnie Grinnup to come home, dropped toward the murderer's back with its hands already extended and its body curved and rigid with silent and deadly purpose.

He was in the tree, Stevens thought. The pistol glared. He saw the flash, but he heard no sound.

4

He was sitting on the veranda with his neat surgeon's bandage after sup-per when the sheriff of the county came up the walk—a big man, too, pleasant, affable, with eyes even paler and colder and more expressionless than Tyler Ballenbaugh's. "It won't take but a minute," he said, "or I wouldn't have bothered you."

"How bothered me?" Stevens said.

The sheriff lowered one thigh to the veranda rail. "Head feel all right?"

"Feels all right," Stevens said.

"That's good, I reckon you heard where we found Boyd."

Stevens looked back at him just as blankly. "I may have," he said pleasantly. "Haven't remembered much today but a headache."

"You told us where to look. You were conscious when I got there. You were trying to give Tyler water. You told us to look on that trotline."

"Did I? Well, well, what won't a man say, drunk or out of his head? Sometimes he's right too."

"You were. We looked on the line, and there was Boyd hung on one of the hooks, dead, just like Lonnie Grinnup was. And Tyler Ballenbaugh with a broken leg and another bullet in his shoulder, and you with a crease in your skull you could hide a cigar in. How did he get on that trotline, Gavin?"

"I don't know," Stevens said.

"All right. I'm not sheriff now. How did Boyd get on that trotline?"

"I don't know."

The sheriff looked at him; they looked at each other. "Is that what you answer any friend that asks?"

"Yes. Because I was shot, you see. I don't know."

The sheriff took a cigar from his pocket and looked at it for a time. "Joe—that deaf-and-dumb boy Lonnie raised—seems to have gone away at last. He was still around there last Sunday, but nobody has seen him since. He could have stayed. Nobody would have bothered him."

"Maybe he missed Lonnie too much to stay," Stevens said.

"Maybe he missed Lonnie." The sheriff rose. He bit the end from the cigar and lit it. "Did that bullet cause you to forget this too? Just what made you suspect something was wrong? What was it the rest of us seem to have missed?"

"It was that paddle," Stevens said.

"Paddle?"

"Didn't you ever run a trotline, a trotline right at your camp? You don't paddle, you pull the boat hand over hand along the line itself from one hook to the next. Lonnie never did use his paddle; he even kept the skiff tied to the same tree his trotline was fastened to, and the paddle stayed in his house. If you had ever been there, you would have seen it. But the paddle was in the skiff when that boy found it."

DAVID WINSER
(1915–1944)

It is the joy of the anthologist to introduce readers to a writer of quality who has receded from public attention. David (Michael de Reuda) Winser is a case in point. Neglected by chroniclers of the literary history of crime and mystery writing, Winser nonetheless produced a story that was regarded by Ellery Queen as "the only short story we know of that involves boating as a true sport." Winser's foray into crime writing was but one of the many accomplishments that he achieved during his brief life. He had earned distinction as a sportsman, writer, doctor, and military man before he was tragically killed at the age of twenty-nine during World War II.

Winser was educated at Winchester College, where he demonstrated his sporting skills as a champion marksman and as a member of the rowing team. At Winchester, Winser also won the King's Gold Medal for Latin Verse and earned a scholarship to Oxford's Corpus Christi College.

At Oxford, he again distinguished himself as a poet and sportsman. He won the Newdigate Prize for modern verse in 1936, for five linked poems in which he foresees his own death in battle. He employed his rowing skills to help Oxford prevail over Cambridge in the race between the two in 1937, the same year in which Winser took his degree and earned a Commonwealth Scholarship to Yale University. Winser studied medicine at Yale and did his clinical training at Charing Cross Hospital, London. He was also a stretcher-bearer during the London blitz, and then served the Royal Army Medical Corps, attached to the 48th Royal Marine Commandos, where he earned a Military Cross for gallantry.

Winser's intimate knowledge of the world of rowing enriches his story, "The Boat Race Murder." Written in a man-to-man, confidential tone, the tale is narrated by the coxswain or "cox" of the Oxford crew team and focuses on the last part of the crew's training period for their famous annual boat race. The success of this period piece comes from Winser's depiction of the activities of the crew—including a neat description of "fizz night," when the crew releases tension along with champagne corks. As the narrator describes it, "You have to realize that ten or eleven men think of practically nothing else, for twelve whole weeks of training, than getting into the crew and seeing Oxford win." Winser sees the crew as emotionally fragile, superstitious, and obsessed with winning to the point that each would stop at nothing—including murder—to ensure a victory.

The Boat Race Murder

1940

For the three weeks before the Boat Race the Oxford crew generally lives at Ranelagh. This costs quite a penny, though it is conveniently close to the boat houses, but the question of money doesn't much worry the rowing authorities. The reason for this is that rowing, like every other Oxford sport, is more or less entirely supported by the gate receipts of the Rugger Club. So there we lived, in Edwardian comfort, and played croquet on the immaculate croquet lawns in the special croquet galoshes they give you and admired the birds and the ruins. They also fed us remarkably well considering we were in training.

All kinds of things occurred. There was one peacock, an amorous bird, which had a crush on the president, who rowed two. It used to come and display its tail in front of him and wait for him to submit. He never did, though.

But at Ranelagh, in spite of the way they'd sometimes put our names in the papers, we led a completely reporterless life, if that's the word I want. We didn't like the sort of stories that got told about rowing, such as the one which held that the crew that won after Barnes all died in the next five years (they're actually mostly alive still). So what with the O.U.B.C. and Ranelagh, and the fact that all the rowing reporters were friends of ours and of rowing, you didn't hear much. But, now, I think this story needs telling. In fact I more or less have to tell it.

You must try and picture a fizz night at Ranelagh. Someone, the coach or some other old Blue, has suddenly produced a dozen bottles of champagne and the coach has said that the crew's been going so well that it damn well deserves the filthy stuff. Actually, as he and everyone else knows, the main purpose of fizz is to stop the crew getting stale. But the tradition's always the same: it's supposed to be a reward for hard work. On this particular night the coach and an old Blue between them had produced *two* dozen bottles, because the second crew, the *Isis*, was coming over to dinner from Richmond.

Perhaps you can imagine the rest already. Solly Johnstone leaning back in his chair and laughing so hard at his own jokes that everyone else is laughing. Once I saw the president try to stop him making jokes because it was hurting him terribly to go on laughing so hard, but Solly didn't stop. And then, after dinner, two crews milling about in the big games room, the president taking cine-camera pictures with an enormous searchlight affair, the *Isis* crew taking on the varsity at billiards and ping-pong, Ronnie playing the piano and someone singing, the gramophone playing "The Donkey Serenade," Solly still making his incredible jokes,

and somewhere over in the corner Melvin Green talking about rowing to
Dr. Jeffreys, who coached the crew for the first part of training. The noise,
and the general tohu-bohu, as Solly said, were both considerable.

I was watching this with a benevolent and yet slightly mildewed eye,
because I had a feeling that I didn't deserve to be quite as cheerful as the
rest of them. I was the cox, and furthermore I had had some very bad
news. And again, when people like Jon Peters and Harry Whitteredge
were slightly out of control, their fourteen stone made walking dangerous
for coxes. No one who saw them that night would have credited them
with the dignity, the dignity which only their genius stopped short of
ponderousness, with which they sent that boat along in the race. They
looked about as dignified as a bull on skates. But I happened to know
that they were going to get as bad a shock as I had, nearly as bad a shock
as Jim Matthews. Jim Matthews was the stroke, and he was going to find
himself out of the crew.

Now this may not sound especially serious. Jim Matthews never had
the reputation of Brocklebank, or Lawrie, or Sutcliffe, or Bryan Hodgson.
You didn't read in the papers that he was going to pull off the race all
by himself. And in a way he wasn't. But I heard a conversation once
between Jon and Harry, who were wonderful oarsmen in their day, and
it was rather significant.

"That fellow Matthews," Jon said, or words to this effect, "doesn't
look much, and he doesn't do much, and doesn't talk much. Also I don't
like him particularly. But I'm damned if there's anyone else who gives
me time to come forward."

"The trouble with us, Jon," Harry said, "is that we need such a hell
of a lot of time."

"Yes, but Jim gives it to us. If we have Jim we'll win this race."

"Don't you think we will anyway?"

"Not without Jim."

"I know. Nor do I."

I don't suppose it matters much to you who wins the Boat Race. But, for
the purposes of this story, to get the record straight, you have to realize
that ten or eleven men think of practically nothing else, for twelve whole
weeks of training, than getting into the crew and seeing Oxford win. It
becomes an obsession, a continual idea at the back of one's mind. Jon had
a baby car, and once, when the crew was travelling by car from Oxford
to Henley, Jon and Harry took an omen. If they could pass and *touch with
their hands* every other O.U.B.C. car, Oxford would win the Boat Race. So,
at considerable risk to their lives (and Oxford wouldn't have won without
them), they touched every car. It was that sort of thing every day. And
now the coaches were going to drop Jim Matthews, and those two
wouldn't have time to come forward. When that happened all their dignity and poise over the stretcher went with the wind and they became

more of a hindrance than a help, charging backwards and forwards in the boat. So, not for you or Oxford perhaps, but for those men who rowed in the crew, Jim's going was a real tragedy. Everyone knew that once they'd put in Davis, the dark-haired short-built *Isis* stroke, they'd leave him there. And Davis, who had plenty of guts and rowed as hard as he could, was hopelessly short in the water. There'd be hell to pay.

As for Jim, I knew a bit how he felt. I'd been in and out of the crew myself, because the *Isis* cox was at least as good as I was and knew the river even better. I wouldn't have been a bit surprised at anything Jim had done. But, as soon as the coaches told him, he'd frozen up completely. He hadn't said anything to them, which was stupid of him. They hadn't wanted to make the change; his own carelessness, which we knew was designed to save himself for one of those terrific races he'd row, looked sloppy. The coaches were worried, and the rowing correspondents started saying Oxford was stale. Hence the fizz, and hence Davis.

And all Jim said, in front of the coaches, he said to me. "Come on, Peter," he said. "I'm going to scare the Alacrity bird."

So Jon and I took him back to Ranelagh in my small M.G. and dropped him near the Alacrity bird's usual haunt; the bird was a crane which flew when you chased it. Then I let Jon drive the car into its garage. He wasn't allowed his car or his pipe during the last six weeks of training, and he needed a few luxuries like that. He joined me again before I reached the main house and we walked in together.

"Your petrol's low," he said. He didn't know about Jim yet but he sounded depressed, as if he knew something of the sort was afoot.

"There's enough for to-morrow, isn't there?"

"Provided the gauge is right, you've got half a gallon."

"That's all right then. Don't worry about the outing, Jon. Fizz night to-night."

Somewhere outside in the garden poor Jim Matthews was walking. I think the Alacrity bird was only an excuse because he wanted to be by himself. I was sorry for Jim. He'd have one more outing, with Davis rowing two, and then he'd go.

Next day, as might be expected after a fizz night, everything went wrong. To begin with I left it too late to get down to the river in time, thinking I'd take my car. I was the only one of the crew allowed to go into shops, because the others were thought to be especially susceptible to flu at that stage of training, so I used to take my car with me and go out shopping after the outing. But that morning I found there wasn't any petrol after all, so I had to run all the way across the polo grounds. They were just getting the boat out when I came, with a little boy doing my work. I pushed him aside without saying thanks, and behaved in a thoroughly bad manner. And then Davis, who was pardonably nervous, paddled on hard when I told him to touch her gently and the boat just missed drifting on to a buoy. Jim Matthews, like everyone else, sat there doing nothing, while I swore. The only incident of interest was that Jon and Harry swore back, being apparently by now aware that Davis was coming up to stroke. Davis rowed too fast. They got tired, and the coaches would accuse them of bucketing, and the boat would start stopping. I didn't blame them for swearing. I swore too.

The coach picked up his megaphone. "Ready, cox?" he asked. He didn't ask it out of kindness.

I said Yes.

"Paddle on down to the Eyot," he said. "Jim, make them work it up a bit once or twice."

Now the Eyot is a good fifteen minutes' paddle from the boat houses, and Jim, I suppose because it was his last time at stroke, took them along really hard. When he worked it up he worked it right up, nearly to forty, and he kept it there for a full minute. Then, not so long afterwards, he did it again. And to end up with he put in a terrific burst of rowing. All the time he was steady, swinging them easily along. I could see the great green holes in the water Jon and Harry made. The boat travelled. I wondered whether the coaches were going to change their mind. No one will know that now, not even Jim. I'd noticed Davis' blade wasn't coming through very well at the end of the paddle, but I hadn't thought anything else about it. When we'd easied he leant forward over his oar and stayed there, but again this wasn't very unusual; it had been about as hard work as a paddle like that can be. After a rest I gave the order to come half forward, because we were going to do a rowing start. But Davis didn't move.

"Half forward, two!" I said, still angrily.

Then apparently bow leant forward and touched him, because his body slumped forward, slid over the gunnel, and went into the water. I don't know when he died, but he was dead when the launch reached him. Luckily Dr. Jeffreys was on the spot, waiting to see what difference the change would make. Well, he'd seen.

If I'd ever doubted whether the coaches deserved their positions, and during training you doubt most things, I was all wrong. They took the launch on up to the London University boat house, where no one ever went during the mornings, got Solly's car round there, put Davis' body in it, brought it to Ranelagh without either the crew or the press or the secretary of Ranelagh seeing, and before lunch they'd got the whole crew together, and Dr. Joe Jeffreys was talking to them. One of the chief duties of the coaches was to keep the crew feeling happy.

"Well," said Joe, "you all saw what happened. Poor young Davis died of heart failure. I know how you feel, and you know how I feel. But there's one thing you ought to understand clearly. The reason he died was that his heart was dicky before he started. I never tested it, but I know it was, because your heart doesn't fail at the end of a paddle unless it *is* dicky. And I know all your hearts are damn sound, because I *did* test them. Just to make sure I'm going to test them again to-day."

And he did, and he was quite right; there was nothing wrong with any of the toughs.

But in the middle, when Jon had just gone out and Solly, Joe and I were alone in the room, Joe suddenly stopped.

"I *did* test Davis' heart," he said.

Well, Solly made a rather typical crack about the value of tests, but apparently this was a pretty sound test. Anyway we went and rang up the police.

"That kid was murdered," said Joe. I suppose Solly thought he was just humouring him. Another of the duties of coaches is to keep the other coaches feeling happy. Those last weeks of training are the devil all round.

It was rather typical of the way the Boat Race gets a grip on people that the crew went out that afternoon. Solly insisted he was only doing it to allay any suspicion about Davis in the minds of the press. But anyway the boat went out, and, with Jim stroking beautifully, they rowed the best two minutes they'd ever done, clearing their wash by yards at thirty-six. When Jim was there, that was as good a crew as any.

The police were around when we got back, but that didn't bother us much. You see, we all knew each other pretty well; you don't have murderers rowing with you. Murderers are professionals, probably, as they've worked with their hands. Anyway, you don't.

Well, they found out what had killed Davis. We'll call it diphenyl tyrosine; Jim and I knew what its real name was because we happened to be medical students. Joe Jeffreys knew it too, of course. The odd thing about it is that it's a component of quite a common patent medicine. That's all right, because it only quickens up your heart for a day or so; but when you start with a quickened heart and then row hard in a Boat Race crew your heart gets very quick indeed, so quick that it doesn't really function adequately. It starts to jump about a bit, and then it starts to fibrillate, to quiver all over in rather a useless way. Then, if it's the ventricle fibrillating, you die. Davis had plenty of guts; he went on just as long as his heart did. He had the guts of a good stroke, but he wasn't Jim Matthews. I was sorry for Davis, but, for the crew's sake, I was glad Jim was safe. The funny thing was that whoever killed Davis must have known that he'd got guts.

Now they started in on a long investigation of the crew's movements during the day before. It had to be the day before because they'd got a very interesting bit of evidence. A man had come into a chemist's in

Putney and he'd asked for this patent medicine, as no doubt men did every day. He'd worn a mackintosh and an old hat.

But underneath the mackintosh the chemist had noticed he was wearing those queer white blanket trousers the crews wear out of the boat.

The policeman who was doing the detective work then had two very frustrating conversations which he described to us with fair relish.

He'd asked the chemist if the purchaser in the white trousers had been a big man. The chemist said Yes.

"Bigger than me?"

"Well, maybe."

"Sure he wasn't fairly small?"

The chemist considered. "Well," he said, "you might call him small."

"Could you draw a line against the wall showing just his height?"

The chemist stepped forward confidently, stopped, tried to think, and then said:—

"No. Not exactly, somehow."

"What colour was his hair then?"

"Oh," said the chemist, "if I noticed the colour of all my customers' hair I'd be in a pretty state." He became a little irritable. "All I know is," he said, "he had white trousers on."

The other conversation was the sequel to the discovery that Jon and I brought my car back when the rest of the crew came in. They wanted to find if anyone went *out* of Ranelagh in a car like mine.

The detective people went to the porters at the two gates. "Did you see a small black sports car go out of the grounds?" they asked. "After 5.30."

Those were the days when Hornets and M.G.'s were as common as sneezing. One porter said he'd seen four, colour unnoticed; the other had seen seven, three of them black or dark-brown.

"Well," said the fellows, "did you see any coming back again?"

"Those seven," said the porter, who wasn't colour-blind, "was going both ways." He wasn't shaken from this peculiar belief. In short they didn't get any change out of porters or chemists. Someone in the crew *did* buy this patent medicine and someone *could* have gone out in my car. They never found the bottle, of course. There were hundreds of ways to get rid of it—you might put it down the lavatory and pull the plug, for instance. It was one of those small bottles. You'll be guessing its name in a minute but, luckily, you'll guess wrong.

Then, also in front of me, someone realized that if the chemist had been at all an efficient man he'd have made the fellow in the mackintosh sign for the medicine, simply because, technically, it was poison if you had a whole bottleful. So one of them went off to find out if the chemist was as efficient as all that, and the other started to find out where we'd all been.

Now the curious thing about all this investigation was that it had taken a very short time. It was still only the day after the murder. As soon as they knew it was murder they'd started thinking about heart drugs, the sort you might mix up in someone's milk as they went to bed, or drop in a glass of fizz; so they thought of diphenyl tyrosine and, sure enough, there it was when they did an autopsy on Davis. No one knew when he'd taken it; but they'd decided it must have been in the fizz. Personally the mechanism of this seems pretty difficult to me, but that's what they said. I suppose they'd had experience of that sort of thing. Anyway he'd certainly not have been looking out for it; very few people expect to be poisoned in the middle of a fizz night. They seemed so certain about it all, quite rightly as it turned out, that we didn't like to doubt their word. So we were all terribly efficient when it came to describing our movements.

They only wanted to know about the time between 5.30, when we all came back from the outing, and six. The chemist said the purchaser in the white trousers had come in at about 5.45, and the reason he knew was that it was a quarter of an hour before he closed at six, and the fact that no other customers had come in afterwards had made him think he'd been a sap not to close quarter of an hour earlier. This looked pretty good evidence to me, and the detective fellows liked it a lot.

Most of the crew had been together from 5.30 till six, all in the big games room. Jon, Jim and I hadn't been there at first. We knew where Jim was, outside with the Alacrity bird. The three of us got back from the outing a little later than the rest of them because of that talk with the coaches, and Jim had come into the house again at ten to six. We were sure of that, or very nearly sure, because by six o'clock, when the news came on, he'd played a complete game of ping-pong with Ronnie. That left quarter of an hour of Jim unaccounted for.

Jon said he'd been in his room all the time till six, when he came down for the news.

I said I hadn't been in the games room at all. First of all I'd done the crossword and then I'd been signing autographs for the crew.

"How do you mean 'for the crew'?" one of them asked.

I told him that the rest of them could never be bothered to sign autograph books. All the coxes after Peter Bryan's time had had to forge the signatures of everyone else; it was one of their duties. So long as you had two or three different nibs and patience you could make a very good job of it indeed.

"Oh," they said, laughing. "That's dangerous."

I said not so dangerous as they thought.

Well, one of the detectives walked to the chemist's and back. It took twenty-five minutes, walking hard. That meant that Jon or I could have gone on our feet or by car, while Jim could only have gone by car. On his way there he met the detective who'd been to see if anyone signed.

Someone had, all right, but it was probably not his name. *A. G. Gallimage,* someone had written.

They went to work on this clue, rather ingeniously. The detective said he wanted a genuine autograph, and went round to each member of the crew with some sentimental story about his daughter being ill in bed and only needing a genuine autograph to recover. It's wonderful what rowing men will swallow. Jim was the only one who made a fuss. He was playing ping-pong again and he said, as rudely as usual:—

"The cox can forge mine."

The detective said he knew that. His daughter wanted a real one. After that Jim signed, a bit grudgingly; and went on playing.

He signed in a writing very like Gallimage's.

This more or less meant Jim or me. I forgot to say that they'd checked up on Jon and found that a maid had seen him in his room between 5.40 and 5.50. She didn't say so, but I expect he went up there for a smoke. He thought it improved *his* rowing but nobody else's. So Jim and I were left, and the signature did very well for either of us. It was typical of the effect of the Boat Race atmosphere that the detectives came and asked Solly if they could arrest both of us. I know they did because I was in the room at the time.

"Would you mind if we arrested Matthews and your cox?" they asked.

"Yes, old chap," said Solly. "We can get another cox, but we haven't any more strokes. Leave them both if you can."

The detective looked serious. "Evidence is bad," he said.

Solly leant back in his chair. "Trot it out," he said. "The cox and I will spoil it. The cox does the crossword in half an hour every morning."

"Twenty-five minutes with Jon," I said. "That was two days ago."

Then I shut up.

The detective trotted out the evidence. At the end I pointed out a flaw. It wasn't half as hard as the *Times* crossword, let alone Torquemada.

"But if Jim went," I said, "he must have used the car."

"Yes."

"But there wasn't any petrol in the car."

"Sure?"

"Quite sure. You see Jon and I both saw the gauge reading half a gallon. Only next morning it still read half a gallon and there wasn't any petrol in her. It foxed me completely."

"It certainly did," said Solly.

"You realize what you're saying?" asked the detective.

"No," I said.

"If Jim Matthews didn't take your car, then someone walked to the shop. That means you walked, because Jim didn't have time."

"He could have run," I said.

"Ah," said the detective. "That's where you're wrong. *He wasn't out of breath.*"

I suppose I looked pretty shaken by this bit of information, because Solly patted me on the back in a very kindly way. "That's all right," he said. "It'll turn out not to have been either of you. Glad you remembered about the petrol."

I was a good deal comforted by this. "Well," I said, "that fellow who coxes the *Isis* is a damn fine cox, and I've got one Blue already. I know we'll win. But I wish they had wireless sets in prison."

"We'll try and let you know all about it," said the detective. This seemed to me a pretty decent way to speak to a murderer.

That isn't all, and it won't be all either. Oxford won, of course, with one of Jim's beautifully timed spurts. He couldn't have made it without Harry and Jon and they couldn't have made it if he hadn't been there, swinging them along so steadily and easily that you'd have thought they were paddling. That is, until you saw how the boat moved.

Furthermore those detectives forgot one thing. Perhaps you saw what it was. Of course my petrol gauge is a bit odd; they can easily test it and show *that it sticks on the half-gallon mark.*

I'm sorry for Jim. I wish it hadn't happened. To be honest, I don't see any other way we could have won; but even Jim, who was a casual ambitious fellow, didn't mean to pay that price for it. He thought Davis would feel ill and give up in the middle of the paddle. But Davis went on rowing till his heart stopped.

ELLERY QUEEN

The most unusual piece in this volume is a radio play created at the height of World War II by the Ellery Queen writing team at the request of the United States Office of War Information. While "The Adventure of the Murdered Ship" has been both praised as a patriotic effort and denigrated as propaganda, there is no doubt that this drama, first broadcast in January 1943, remains an important piece of documentary evidence about the time in which it was written and the ways in which writers of popular fiction were asked to use their talents.

Beginning with an "urgent summons from an extremely important official of the government," Ellery Queen the sleuth is asked to discover how the Japanese were able to ambush an American convoy despite its movements being classified top secret. Furthermore, he is asked to explain why the name "Ellery Q" was found on a captured enemy commander. Thus the stage is set for the Queen character—and indeed the Queen writing team—to respond to Uncle Sam's summons to aid the nation.

At this time, cousins Frederic Dannay (Daniel Nathan, 1905–1982) and Manfred Bennington Lee (Manfred Lepofsky, 1905–1971) had been collaborating on mystery writing for fifteen years. The Brooklyn-born pair were educated at Boys' High School and pursued careers in Manhattan before creating the character who bore the same name as the cousins' pseudonym. Their Ellery Queen character was a young mystery writer and amateur sleuth endowed with sophistication and with a very useful father, Inspector Richard Queen of the New York City Police Department. The Ellery Queen series was so successful that by the time of Dannay's death, 150 million Queen books had been sold worldwide and *Ellery Queen Mystery Magazine* was well established, providing a showcase for the mystery short story, as it still does today.

While Dannay wrote many of the introductions and notes in the Queen anthologies and in the *Ellery Queen* magazine, it was Lee who wrote a letter to Leslie Charteris explaining the creation of "The Adventure of the Murdered Ship." Charteris published Lee's letter along with the radio play in *The Saint's Choice, Vol. 7: Radio Thrillers* (1946). It stated, "This was a 'command performance,' so to speak, by the OWI, with whom we co-operated in the 'loose talk' campaign. As a special assignment from Washington, it represents—we think—something superior in radio propaganda, inasmuch as it doesn't bat its audience over the head, but approaches the lesson through entertainment."

The Adventure of the Murdered Ship

1943

The Characters

ELLERY QUEEN............................... *the detective*
NIKKI PORTER............................... *his secretary*
INSPECTOR QUEEN........................... *his father, of Police Headquarters*
SERGEANT VELIE .... *of Inspector Queen's staff*
WASHINGTON OFFICIAL...................... *an extremely important official of the Government, who must remain anonymous*
MRS. BROWN .... *an American mother from Richmond, Virginia*
REVEREND JONES........................... *an American father, a clergyman, from Minneapolis, Minnesota*
MRS. SMITH................................. *a young American bride, from Los Angeles, California*

Scene

Private Office of Washington Official—The Queen
Apartment in New York City—Mrs. Brown's
House in Richmond—Rev. Jones's
Vestry in Minneapolis—An
Airplane Factory Near Los Angeles

SCENE 1: *Private Office of High Official in Washington (Ellery Queen and his father, Inspector Queen, are ushered into the Official's office. Both men seem puzzled, anxious, and apprehensive.)*

OFFICIAL: Sit down, gentlemen. (*Ellery and the Inspector take chairs timidly.*) Mr. Queen, I suppose you're wondering why I asked you to come to Washington.

ELLERY QUEEN: (*Very respectfully*) Yes, Sir. An urgent summons from such a distinguished Government official as yourself, Sir—I can't imagine why I should be so honored.

INSPECTOR QUEEN: Sir, I hope you don't mind my coming along with my son. I was—well, a little nervous—

OFFICIAL: I quite understand, Inspector Queen; glad you came. Mr. Queen, I've summoned you to Washington to lay a very important case before you—(*Quietly*) the most important case you'll ever be called upon to investigate.

ELLERY: I'm completely at your service, Sir.

OFFICIAL: (*Gravely*) On a certain date—recently—a certain armed vessel of the United States was waylaid by a swarm of enemy submarines on the high seas. At exactly 5 P.M. three torpedoes crashed into our ship, and it sank almost immediately. The loss of American lives was considerable.

ELLERY: (*Low*) I'm sorry to learn that, Sir.

OFFICIAL: This ship was involved in an extremely important operation, gentlemen. Its loss through surprise submarine attack not only caused the deaths of a large number of American fighting men, but a war plan closely integrated with the all-over Allied strategy was licked before it got started.

ELLERY: But the plan must have been a strict War Department secret, Sir!

OFFICIAL: (*Dryly*) It was even stricter than usual, Mr. Queen. Only six people knew it—and their integrity cannot possibly be questioned. Yet—that nest of enemy subs was lying in wait.

INSPECTOR: Mightn't they have been there by pure accident, Sir?

OFFICIAL: No, Inspector. In the naval action which followed the attack, one of the enemy subs was captured by our forces. The enemy commander has been thoroughly interrogated, his effects examined. There's no doubt but that those subs had positive information.

ELLERY: But if total secrecy was maintained, Sir, how did the enemy *get* its information?

OFFICIAL: That, Mr. Queen, is why you're in Washington today. In the first place, the investigating agencies of the Government are short-handed—we can use all the expert help we can get—

INSPECTOR: And I suppose my son's

reputation for solving tough problems qualifies him—eh, Sir?

OFFICIAL: Very much so, Inspector. But there's still another reason I called you, Mr. Queen.

ELLERY: What's that, Sir?

OFFICIAL: You're involved.

ELLERY: (*Blankly*) I beg your pardon, Sir?

INSPECTOR: (*Aghast*) My son's involved . . . in the sinking of one of our ships by the enemy? I don't get it, Sir.

OFFICIAL: Neither do we, Inspector—we haven't had time to work on it. The clue reached Washington only this morning.

ELLERY: (*Slowly*) A clue linking *me* with the torpedoing of an American warship? May I see it, Sir?

OFFICIAL: Certainly. (*He hands Ellery a piece of paper.*) This scrap of paper, Mr. Queen, was found on the captured enemy sub commander.

ELLERY: Thank you, Sir. (*He examines it.*) But—this is fantastic!

INSPECTOR: For Pete's sake, son, what's on that paper?

ELLERY: Just two words, dad—or rather a word and an initial. (*He reads aloud slowly.*) "Ellery Q."

INSPECTOR: "Ellery Q!" But—how in time did your name get on a memo in the possession of an enemy sub commander, son?

ELLERY: (*Grimly*) I'd certainly like to find out.

OFFICIAL: (*Dryly amused*) I take it, then, Mr. Queen, you'd welcome the opportunity to investigate this case?

ELLERY: Try me, Sir!

OFFICIAL: Very well. Effective immediately, consider yourself a

Special Investigator for the United States Government.

ELLERY: (*Crisply*) Thank you, Sir. To whom am I to report?

OFFICIAL: You're accountable directly to me. . . . Inspector, it's been a pleasure. (*Inspector ad lib.*) Mr. Queen—good luck.

ELLERY: Thank you, Sir. I'll find out how those enemy subs knew about that ship if I never solve another case in my life!

INSPECTOR: (*Grimly*) And what "Ellery Q" was doing on an Axis submarine!

ELLERY: Right, dad. Come on— we've got a man-sized mystery to solve *this* time!

SCENE 2: *The Queen Apartment in New York, Next Day*

NIKKI PORTER: Do you suppose the Inspector and Sergeant Velie will get a leave of absence from the Police Department, Ellery?

ELLERY: (*Chuckling*) I've deputized them as assistant Special Investigators, haven't I, Nikki? They won't have any trouble. But where are they, blast it? I can't do a thing till I get those lists!

NIKKI: What lists, Ellery? (*They hear the Inspector and Sergeant Velie enter the apartment.*)

ELLERY: Dad! Velie! (*Their responses off.*) Did you get it?

INSPECTOR: (*Fading on*) Here it is, son.

SERGEANT VELIE: (*Fading on*) Just came by special courier from the War Department, Ellery. (*He waves a sheaf of papers.*)

NIKKI: (*Sniffing*) A lot of papers!

Don't tell me we have to go through a batch of stuffy reports.

VELIE: (*Grimly*) They ain't "stuffy reports," Miss Porter.

NIKKI: Then what are they?

INSPECTOR: A list of the names and home addresses of the survivors, the missing . . . and the dead of that torpedoed American ship, Nikki. (*Sneak chord.*)

NIKKI: The . . . *dead?* I'm sorry.

ELLERY: (*Crisply*) All right, dad, now we can get to work. We've got to question the families of every man on this list.

INSPECTOR: (*Heavily*) Yes, son.

VELIE: But Maestro, there are thousands of names here. They stretch all the way from Maine and Florida to Oregon an' California.

ELLERY: There's no other way, Sergeant. Nikki! (*Nikki's crisp ad lib.*) Your job is to take these lists and arrange them by states and cities. Dad, you and Velie work out a practical traveling schedule for the four of us. We'll cover the entire country, working our way West.

NIKKI: But Ellery, what do you expect to find by questioning the families of the victims?

ELLERY: Clues, Nikki—clues that will tell us how the enemy knew about our warship and where to lie in wait for it! Somewhere in these names and addresses are our suspects and the solution to the crime.

VELIE: And maybe the answer to that "Ellery Q" on that piece of Axis paper. That one gets *me*.

ELLERY: Never mind that now, Sergeant. Let's get to work!

SCENE 3: *Mrs. Brown's House in Richmond, Virginia, Some Weeks Later (The Queens, Nikki, and Sergeant Velie are walking up the path of a shabby little frame house. Nikki is consulting a list.)*

NIKKI: Mrs. Mary-Jane Brown. . . . It's this house, all right.

ELLERY: Mrs. Brown. Widow. One son. Richmond, Virginia—

VELIE: We sure are coverin' territory! How many visits does this make, Miss Porter?

NIKKI: Five hundred and forty-one, Sergeant.

VELIE: And we're still on the Eastern seaboard.

INSPECTOR: I hope we have some luck with this Mrs. Brown, Ellery. I can't see that we're getting anywhere at all. Not a clue so far.

ELLERY: *(Grimly)* I told you it would be a big job, dad. *(They mount to the porch.)* Well, Sergeant, rouse Mrs. Brown. *(Velie wearily rings the doorbell.)* Mother of Harry Brown, Seaman Third Class, U.S. Navy—*(The door opens.)* Mrs. Brown?

MRS. BROWN: *(Fading on)* I'm Miz Brown. *(She is a faded woman of Southern stock, middle-aged and work-worn.)*

ELLERY: Mrs. Brown, we're special investigators from Washington.

MRS. BROWN: Gover'ment people! Come in. *(They go in and she leads the way to a dim parlor.)* Ain't nothin' wrong with my son, Harry?

NIKKI: No, Mrs. Brown. Your son's getting along fine in the naval hospital.

MRS. BROWN: Thank goodness! Gave me a start. . . . Mah parlor's

a little messy—Won't y'all set? *(They thank her and sit down.)*

ELLERY: Your son, Harry, was wounded in a recent naval engagement, Mrs. Brown—was quite a hero—

MRS. BROWN: *(Proudly)* I know, suh. He's a real American.

INSPECTOR: So we're just here to talk to a hero's mother—

MRS. BROWN: Harry's a wonderful boy, suh. Enlisted right off in the Wah. Proud? Why, suh, he thinks bein' an American sailuh is the finest thing theah is!

VELIE: Ain't nothin' finer, Mrs. Brown.

MRS. BROWN: Why, my Harry's so proud of *The Manila Bay*—that's his ship—*he* says it's the best ship in the Navy.

INSPECTOR: *(Chuckling)* That's what all the boys say, Mrs. Brown.

MRS. BROWN: Well, suh, it's a fact I got into an argument with Mistuh Williams a couple weeks before Christmas—

ELLERY: Who is Mr. Williams, Mrs. Brown?

MRS. BROWN: *(Sniffing)* Yankee storekeeper—keeps the groc'ry and meat market half mile into town. He's got a boy in the Navy, too. And *he* says his *son's* ship, *The Buffalo*, is the finest in the Navy. Izzat so? I says. Mah Harry's ship, *The Manila Bay*, is! Almost came to throwin' things. Theah was a crowd aroun' the counter laughin' their heads off, that ol' fool Williams was so mad. *(Softening)* But then we sort o' patched it up, an' Mistuh Williams give me a specially fine mess o' chitlins to show there was no hard feelin's.

NIKKI: Mrs. Brown, did you ever hear your son, Harry, mention the name "Ellery Queen," or "Ellery Q"?

MRS. BROWN: Beg pahdon, ma'am? I don't think so . . .

ELLERY: (*Smoothly*) We needn't take up any more of Mrs. Brown's time, Nikki. (*Nikki: "But Ellery—!"*) Thank you, Mrs. Brown. (*Quietly*) Dad. Sergeant—

MRS. BROWN: But suh, I could tell y'all lots more 'bout mah Harry—

ELLERY: I'm sure you could, Mrs. Brown. (*They bid Mrs. Brown goodbye as they go to the door.*)

MRS. BROWN: Tell Harry his mom's prayin' he'll get better quick, suh. (*They reassure her, and go down the path*).

INSPECTOR: I don't blame you for cutting that one short, son.

VELIE: Another washout.

NIKKI: Hasn't heard of Ellery Queen! We'll *never* solve the mystery of that "Ellery Q."

ELLERY: Nevertheless, gentlemen and Miss Porter, Mrs. Brown has given us *our first clue* in 541 visits. (*They look blank*). Nikki, you took notes?

NIKKI: Yes, Ellery, of everything she said, but—

VELIE: But *what* clue, Maestro?

ELLERY: Didn't you spot it, Sergeant? It's not an important clue—it doesn't tell us much—but it encourages me to keep going. We're on the right track! Dad, who's next on our list?

INSPECTOR: Somebody in Lexington, Kentucky. Clue Number 1, uh? Too much for me!

ELLERY: Let's hurry, or we'll miss our train connection. Who knows? We may find Clue Number 2 in the State of Kentucky!

SCENE 4: *Rev. Jones's Vestry in Minneapolis, Two Weeks Later (The Queen group is sitting tiredly, waiting. Organ church music is playing off, audible from the church.*)

ELLERY: Tired, Nikki?

NIKKI: (*Wearily*) Oh, I'm fine, Ellery.

INSPECTOR: She is not! I'm pretty pooped myself, son.

ELLERY: I know, dad.—Sergeant! Wake up.

VELIE: Huh! . . . Oh. (*He yawns.*) We still waitin' for this Reverend Whatzisname? This vestry is a nice place for a snooze.

ELLERY: Reverend Jones will be out in a minute, Velie.

INSPECTOR: Nikki, how do we stand now? (*He yawns.*)

NIKKI: No luck in Kentucky, Inspector. Or in Ohio. Or in Indiana, Illinois, Wisconsin. Number of States covered: 20. People visited: 'way over 1000. (*She yawns.*) So we find ourselves in Minneapolis, Minnesota, about to question the father of Lieutenant Thomas L. Jones, U.S. Army— (*Change of tone*)—deceased.

INSPECTOR: Not even killed in action. Drowned on that ship the subs sank. (*He frowns.*)

VELIE: If y'ask me, it's hopeless. 1265 visits—and one clue. In Richmond, Virginia. *He says.* (*The door from the church opens, and Rev. Jones appears.*) Uh-uh. Here's the Reverend. (*Rev. Jones is a fragile gentleman of 60, looking as if he has recently suffered a great shock.*)

REV. JONES: (*Fading on*) Mr. Queen? Forgive me for having kept you waiting. But my duties in the church—

ELLERY: It's quite all right, Reverend Jones. You know why we're here?

REV. JONES: My sexton's told me. Won't you all sit down? (*He sighs.*) It's about my son . . . and how he died in the service of his country.

VELIE: (*Muttering*) Drowned without a rat's chance.

INSPECTOR: I'm a father myself, Reverend—

NIKKI: We know how you feel.

REV. JONES: Thank you. . . . We were very close—Tom and I. He was so full of life—I'm afraid sometimes my parish thought Tommy was a bit *too* full of life! (*Tremulously*) God bless him.

ELLERY: (*Gently*) He wrote to you frequently, Reverend?

REV. JONES: (*Brightening*) Oh, yes, Mr. Queen, every day! My wife is bedridden, you know. Tom knew how anxious his mother was about his daily welfare—how much his letters meant to us. (*He opens a drawer of his desk.*) As a matter of fact, I . . . happened to keep the very last letter he ever wrote us. From camp. Dated Christmas Eve. If you wouldn't be bored—(*They protest.*)

ELLERY: I assure you, Reverend, we're very much interested in Lieutenant Jones's last letter to his parents.

REV. JONES: That's kind of you, Mr. Queen. I . . . (*He stops, turning the pages of a letter slowly, suddenly. He chuckles.*) For example, listen to this—it's a part of the letter I've repeated to many of my friends

and parishioners.—You're sure I'm not boring you?

ELLERY: (*Gently*) Quite sure, Reverend Jones.

REV. JONES: (*Clearing his throat*) "You especially will appreciate this, dad. Just today one of the boys brought out an autographed photo of Dorothy Lamour and Shavetail Billy Green said he'd swiped it from *him,* and the other contestant—one of my special buddies in the company, Frank Winters—Frank said the h—— he had, and they almost had a brawl about it." (*All chuckle*) "So finally I said: 'You both claim it—why not put it up to Old Grouchy?' (our C.O.). They said okay, and I had a hard time keeping a straight face, because our C.O. is full of surprises. Well, Old Grouchy heard the case, and without batting an eye, he says: 'Gentlemen,' he says, 'you each claim possession of the autographed photo of this comely and estimable young woman,' he says, 'and since there are no other facts, I'll decide the case with absolute justice, to wit: I'll tear the photo in half—like this!'—and he rips poor Lamour right down the middle—'and give *each* of you one half. Now scram,' the C.O. snarls, 'and start thinking about the War, or you'll find yourselves with a couple of desk jobs while the rest of us are having fun!' You should have seen Frank's and Billy's faces . . ." (*His voice breaks.*) . . . "dad." (*Pause*)

ELLERY: (*Low*) Dad. Velie. Nikki. Let's go.

REV. JONES: (*Muffled*) Oh, but really. I'm sorry. It—all came back. If you'll give me just a moment, please . . .

ELLERY: Thank you, Reverend Jones. We shan't intrude any further. (*They make their adieus, leaving him at his desk, a broken old man.*)

NIKKI: (*Sniffling*) That was . . . such a sad letter. Ellery, you didn't even give me a chance to ask about "Ellery Q." You *never* do.

ELLERY: Never mind "Ellery Q" now, Nikki. Dad, we're in luck!

INSPECTOR: What luck?

VELIE: Yeah. So we meet Reverend Jones in Minneapolis, so he reads us Lieutenant Jones's last letter, so what have we got? The usual nothin'.

ELLERY: On the contrary, Sergeant. *We've got Clue Number 2.*

INSPECTOR: Now wait a minute, son. You mean to say that somehow the enemy got hold of that boy's yarn to his father about Dorothy Lamour's photograph?

ELLERY: (*Grimly*) I mean just that.

VELIE: But suppose they did, Maestro? So what?

ELLERY: Never mind now, Sergeant. Dad, we're really beginning to get somewhere! Nikki, who's next on our list?

NIKKI: (*Wearily*) Somebody in Laramie, Wyoming.

INSPECTOR: (*Wearily*) Westward ho!

SCENE 5: *An Airplane Factory near Los Angeles (The Queens are ushered into the executive office of the factory. The din is deafening—they can scarcely hear one another. They all look tired and discouraged).*

MAN: Wait in this office, Mr. Queen. I'll get her off the assem-

bly line. (*He goes out and shuts the door. The noise of production comes through faintly.*)

VELIE: So how do we stand now, Miss Porter?

NIKKI: We're scraping the bottom of the barrel, Sergeant.

VELIE: East, South, Middle West, Far West—Oregon, Washin'ton, now Los Angeles, Cal.—and whatta we got? Sore pups.

INSPECTOR: And two clues I don't understand.

NIKKI: Are you sure you weren't *dreaming* of clues in Richmond and Minneapolis, Ellery?

ELLERY: (*Impatiently*) No, no, Nikki, they were clear as crystal. But there *must* be another clue somewhere! Perhaps more than one.

INSPECTOR: Who's this we're investigating in this airplane factory, Nikki?

NIKKI: A Mrs. Richard K. Smith of Los Angeles. She works here, Inspector—(*The door opens, letting in the din again. Mrs. Smith enters—a bitter-looking girl with a smudge on her cheek.*)

VELIE: Here she is. (*The door closes, and the din is a whisper again.*)

NIKKI: Why, she's no older than I am. In overalls!

MRS. SMITH: (*Fading on abruptly*) Who's Mr. Queen?

ELLERY: I am, Mrs. Smith. Special Investigator for the—

MRS. SMITH: (*Curtly*) Yeah, I know— the foreman told me. I don't know what I can tell you. My husband's dead—died on a ship. So I got myself this job helpin' to make planes.

ELLERY: That's courageous of you, Mrs. Smith.

MRS. SMITH: Courageous? Hooey. I wish they'd let me shoot a machine gun. Make it snappy, please. Every minute I'm away from my bench means I'm holdin' up a plane.

INSPECTOR: Your husband was Private Richard K. Smith?

MRS. SMITH: Yeah. A draftee. We met while he was in camp near San Francisco. We . . . fell for each other. (*Tensely*) Why do I have to go over all this? I wanna get back to my work!

ELLERY: I assure you it's necessary, Mrs. Smith.

NIKKI: I know how you feel, Mrs. Smith.

MRS. SMITH: (*Bitterly*) Yeah? (*Low*) Dick didn't get leaves more'n once in a blue moon, and I couldn't afford to make the trip up to Frisco to visit him. It was . . . tough. Then—all of a sudden Dick shows up in L.A.—December 24th. Unexpected one-day leave, he says. I bawled like a fool. Dick said there was a rumor in camp they were shovin' off, and that's why the boys got leave. . . . (*She begins to cry.*)

NIKKI: (*Low*) Do you want my handkerchief, Mrs. Smith?

MRS. SMITH: Th-thanks. (*Sniffs*) I had a feelin' in my bones I'd never see my Dick again. So I said: Dick, let's get married. Now. Right away! . . . He—he kissed me. But he said we ain't got no time—he's supposed to report back to camp in Frisco, and he just had time to make it. . . .

INSPECTOR: But you did manage it, didn't you, Mrs. Smith?

VELIE: You must of, since you're a Missus.

MRS. SMITH: (*Raptly*) Yeah. It was like a miracle. The last minute Dick gets a phone call from some officer in his camp, sayin' he was not to report back to camp but somewheres else. . . .

ELLERY: Just where was he to report, Mrs. Smith?

MRS. SMITH: I don't know. All I know is the switch in plan gave my Dick 7 hours extra leave. So we got a lot of my friends together and told 'em all about it, and—and we got married, and then . . . Dick went away. (*Cries*) I never even got a letter from him. . . .

ELLERY: (*Gently*) We're terribly sorry, Mrs. Smith.

MRS. SMITH: (*Fiercely*) What am I cryin' for? I got a date with a bomber! And I hope it gets the dirty rat that got my husband! (*She strides out.*) I gotta get back. . . . (*She disappears in the maw of the factory, a forlorn, gallant little figure.*)

NIKKI: (*Sniffling*) I don't like this job, Ellery. I—I want to go back home to New York. (*Ellery soothes her.*)

INSPECTOR: We can't go home, Nikki. Not till we finish with this list of survivors and casualties from that torpedoed ship.

VELIE: (*Heavily*) Who's next, Inspector?

INSPECTOR: Relative of some missing boy from Santa Ana, Velie.

ELLERY: Never mind that list, dad. We're through with it.

NIKKI: Through with it!

VELIE: *Through* with it?

ELLERY: (*Crisply*) Yes. *We've just found the third—and most important—clue.* We don't need any more.

INSPECTOR: Don't need any more? But Ellery, that means—

ELLERY: Yes, dad, now I know how the enemy found out when and where to ambush that American ship!

VELIE: I'll never understand nothin', I guess.

NIKKI: But how about the "Ellery Q," Ellery? That scrap of paper with your name on it that was found on the enemy submarine commander?

INSPECTOR: You know what that means, too, son?

ELLERY: Oh, I knew the answer to that, dad, a long time ago. Let's go back to Washington—and report a successful solution of the case!

And so ELLERY QUEEN *now knows the answer to the mystery of the Murdered Ship. Do you?*

The many millions who listen to "The Adventures of ELLERY QUEEN" *on the air, from Maine and Florida to Seattle and Los Angeles, not only enjoy the drama of these unique mystery dramas but the battle of wits which is waged weekly between themselves and* ELLERY—*a friendly and exciting battle. They try to figure out the answer to the broadcast mystery problem before* ELLERY *reveals it in his solution. This same enjoyment can be reaped by you, here, in these special adaptations of* ELLERY'S *radio adventures for readers of "*ELLERY QUEEN'S *Mystery Magazine."*

In The Adventure of the Murdered Ship, you should be able to answer three questions correctly: (1) What were the three clues ELLERY *spotted? (2) What did they mean to the enemy? (3) What did "*ELLERY Q" *mean?*

And now, if you think you've figured out the answer, read ELLERY QUEEN'S *own answer below.*

The Solution

SCENE 6: *The Washington Official's Office, Two Days Later*

OFFICIAL: So you also solved the mystery of that "Ellery Q" on the enemy sub commander's scrap of paper, Mr. Queen? (*Ellery laughs.*)

INSPECTOR: What *did* your name on that memo mean, son?

ELLERY: It wasn't my name, dad. It isn't a name at all—the appearance of a name was a coincidence. It's a *code*. (*They exclaim*) Let's take the "Q" part first. Which letter of the alphabet is "Q"?

VELIE: (*Muttering rapidly*) A, b, c, d, e, f, g, h . . .

NIKKI: The 17th letter, Ellery.

ELLERY: Remember that. Now one of our facts was that the ship was torpedoed at 5 P.M. In one international system of figuring time, A.M. and P.M. are not used—the hours are numbered from 1 to 24. By this system, the letter "Q" in the code-phrase "Ellery Q" would stand for *the 17th hour.* What *is* the 17th hour in terms of A.M. or P.M.?

INSPECTOR: 5 P.M.—the time of the torpedoing!

ELLERY: So we know "Q" is the

time-instruction given to the commander of the enemy submarine.

NIKKI: But what does the "Ellery" stand for?

ELLERY: Obviously, Nikki, for a word which, when grouped with "Q," or "5 P.M.," gives a clear message. Think of it as a group of letters—E, L, L, E, R, Y. Now note that the 1st and 4th letters are the same, and the 2nd and 3rd. Can you think of *another* word with a similar construction?

VELIE: (*Hastily*) Who, me, Maestro?

ELLERY: Well, Sergeant, what *happened* at 5 P.M.? There was an *attack* on the ship. "Attack"—A, T, T, A, C, K!

INSPECTOR: "Ellery"—the code word for "Attack"!

ELLERY: Yes, dad. "Ellery Q" simply meant to the sub commander: "Attack at 5 P.M.," which, combined with his other information, gave him all he had to know.

OFFICIAL: Exactly what the F.B.I. figured out, Mr. Queen, the day after you took this assignment. But how did the enemy know about the ship—that it was sailing, when, from where, and all about it?

ELLERY: I found three clues, Sir, that told me the whole tragic story. Dad, what did Mrs. Brown of Richmond, Virginia, tell us about her son, Seaman Harry Brown?

INSPECTOR: Why, Mrs. Brown said he claimed his ship, *The Manila Bay*, was the finest in the Navy—

ELLERY: Clue Number 1! *The name of the ship—The Manila Bay*. Ships in the United States Navy are named by a system. One type of

American warship is named after famous American battles. Manila Bay was a famous American battle of the Spanish-American War. What type of ship is *named* after famous battles?

VELIE: *Aircraft carriers!*

ELLERY: An enemy agent overheard Mrs. Brown's thoughtless remark that morning two weeks before Christmas—in a crowded store. When the enemy's intelligence headquarters in the United States fitted *The Manila Bay* into its other information, it was able to say: An aircraft carrier never sails alone. It is always accompanied by many other fighting craft, to protect it. *Therefore a large naval force is involved.*

NIKKI: But Ellery, I still don't see—

ELLERY: Ah, but what little bit of information did Reverend Jones of Minneapolis unconsciously reveal? Dad?

INSPECTOR: He read us that letter from his son Tom—

VELIE: That joke about the argument in camp over Dorothy Lamour's photo and how their C.O. settled it—

ELLERY: That yarn came from Lieutenant Jones's *last letter*—written, therefore, just before he was shipped out of camp. Reverend Jones's son knew he might never come back, so on the eve of departure he tried to give his father an important piece of information by *inventing* a bit of apparently innocent camp gossip.

NIKKI: Information that was censorable!

ELLERY: Right. Can we figure out what Tom was trying to say? Oh, yes. Consider that the letter was written to *a minister of the gospel on Christmas Eve.* Consider that it was the story of two people claiming the same cherished object and a wise arbiter who said: *Cut it in half.*

INSPECTOR: Tom was writing a parallel to the *Bible* story! Of the wise king who ordered an infant cut in half when two women claimed it!

ELLERY: And who was that wise king? King *Solomon.*

NIKKI: *The Solomon Islands!*

VELIE: Tom was tryin' to tell his father he was bein' shipped off to the Solomons!

ELLERY: Precisely. Reverend Jones thoughtlessly repeated it to his friends and parishioners—

OFFICIAL: (*Grimly*) And eventually it reached a spy's ears, or some Axis sympathizer, and was sent along to enemy H.Q. to be added to the other bits of information about *The Manila Bay* and its accompanying naval force. And the third clue, Mr. Queen?

ELLERY: We picked that one up from a woman war-worker in Los Angeles, Sir. Nikki, what did Mrs. Smith say?

NIKKI: Well, that there was a rumor Dick Smith's outfit was going overseas. The day before Christmas, when he was on unexpected leave, at the last minute he got an extra 7 hours' leave.

ELLERY: Or put it this way. Private Dick Smith, on unexpected leave in Los Angeles, was supposed to return to his camp near San Francisco. This trip normally takes 10 hours. But because Private Smith was notified at the last minute to report to a *different* place, he found himself with 7 hours' extra leave. In other words, his outfit had suddenly been moved from a place 10 hours' travel from Los Angeles to a place only 3 hours' travel from Los Angeles! (*They look startled.*) What important troop-embarkation point *is* 3 hours' travel from Los Angeles?

INSPECTOR: San Diego!

NIKKI: And everybody at the Smiths' last-minute wedding was told about it by Mrs. Smith!

OFFICIAL: (*Grimly*) That little tid-bit reached an enemy agent's ears very quickly. It must have got to enemy intelligence within a matter of hours.

ELLERY: Yes, Sir, and when the enemy put all the bits and pieces together, along with other information that clearly tied them into a single operation, he knew:

1st, that a large naval force of fighting ships was involved.

2nd, this naval force was bound for the Solomons—and not only that, but *troops* were involved, because Tom Jones was an *Army* officer, and Private Smith was a draftee. But this meant the fighting ships were convoying *troop transports.* And to warrant such a large naval escort, it must involve a great *number* of transports—so it was an *important troop movement.*

3rd, the convoy was sailing from San Diego, California. When? Lieutenant Jones wrote on Christmas Eve—Private Smith got his unexpected leave the same day, December 24th—so the *time* of the sailing was the next day, Christmas Day!

The enemy relayed to its subs operating in the South Pacific these facts, and they merely lay in wait along the easily estimated route until the convoy appeared—a simple nautical calculation. There it is, Sir—the whole picture, from three little bits of loose talk!

OFFICIAL: A whole convoy endangered—an important military operation spiked—the lives of hundreds of patriotic American fighting men uselessly sacrificed—all because three people didn't stop to think before they talked.

ELLERY: Mrs. Brown loves her boy Harry, but I wonder if she realizes that she's responsible for his lying wounded in that naval hospital.

INSPECTOR: Just as Reverend Jones is responsible for his son Tom's death.

NIKKI: And Mrs. Smith is at least an accomplice in the murder of Dick, the husband she never had a chance to be happy with.

OFFICIAL: Yes, if people would only remember not to talk about anything but what they hear over the radio or read in their newspapers!

INSPECTOR: (*Quietly*) We're all prone to be offenders once in a while, Sir. But we mustn't be—ever.

NIKKI: I'll make the resolution to keep my mouth shut—right now!

VELIE: That goes double.

ELLERY: Amen.

(*The music comes up.*)

GEORGES SIMENON

(1903–1989)

Belgian-born Georges (Joseph Christian) Simenon was the son of an account-ant and a frustrated social climber. Throughout his writing career, he used the tensions that he saw in his parents' marriage as a foundation for a view that prized the solid values of the petite bourgeoisie and denigrated social preten-sions as ultimately leading to disillusionment. When he was sixteen years old, with his father seriously ill, Simenon left school in order to support his strug-gling family. He tried his hand at two jobs before he found success in news-paper work. Within a year he published his first novel, *Au pont des arches* (1921), and his fantastically prolific career was launched. In 1929 he wrote his first work centering on Chief Inspector of the Police Judicaire, Jules Mai-gret, "Pietr-le-Letton" (1931; *The Strange Case of Peter the Lett*, 1933), and wrote nineteen more between 1930 and 1934. He is said to have written one romance novel in a single morning and a thousand stories in a three-year period. Typically, he spent three to five days writing a novel. Simenon re-counted his writing and living habits in *Memoires intimes* (1981; *Intimate Memoirs*, 1984), a controversial book that discusses his two failed mar-riages, boasts about his sexual exploits, and speculates about the suicide of his daughter.

Simenon's fiction often shows Maigret reaching a solution by identifying with key characters in order to understand their crimes. Maigret frequently finds that murderers have misled themselves into literally fatal disappoint-ments. Simenon makes this less-than-concrete approach to crime solving seem convincing in large part because he grounds these psychological inves-tigations in a descriptive prose anchored in French realism and enhanced by romantic atmospheric touches. In "Two Bodies on a Barge," for instance, Simenon demonstrates his ability to make material items, like the dog's chain and sheet used to hang two bodies, and atmosphere, here embodied in gloomy drizzle, into tactile experiences for the reader.

Two Bodies on a Barge

1944

The lock keeper of Le Coudray was a lean, depressed-looking fellow in a corduroy suit, with drooping moustaches and a suspicious eye, like a typical estate bailiff. He made no distinction between Maigret and the fifty other people—gendarmes, journalists, policemen from Corbeil and representatives of the Department of Public Prosecution—to whom he had told his story over the past two days. And as he spoke he kept a watchful eye, upstream and downstream, over the grey-green surface of the Seine.

It was November. The weather was cold and a bleak pale sky was reflected in the water.

"I had to get up at six this morning to look after my wife," (and Maigret reflected that these decent, sad-eyed men are always the ones who have sick wives to look after) . . . "While I was lighting the fire I thought I heard something. But it was only later, while I was up on the first floor preparing her poultice, that I realized somebody was calling . . . I came downstairs . . . I went out on to the lock, and there I could vaguely make out a dark mass against the weir . . .

" 'What's up?' I shouted.

" 'Help!' somebody called out hoarsely.

" 'What are you doing there?' I asked.

"And he went on shouting: 'Help!'

"I took my wherry to go after him. I could see it was the *Astrolabe*. As it was beginning to get light at last, I made out old Claessens on deck. I could take my oath that he was still tight and that he had no idea what his barge was doing up against the lock. The dog was loose, and indeed I asked him to hold on to it. And that's it . . ."

The important thing, from his point of view, was that a barge had run into his lock and might have damaged it if the current had been stronger. He seemed totally unconcerned by the fact that, apart from the drunken old carter and a big Alsatian dog, there had been nobody on board but two corpses, a man and a woman, both hanged.

The *Astrolabe* had been released and was now moored a hundred and fifty metres away, guarded by a constable who kept himself warm pacing up and down the tow-path. It was an old barge without a motor, a "stable-boat" as they call those barges that travel along canals with their horses on board. Passing cyclists turned to stare at this greyish hull, about which all the papers had been talking for the past two days.

As usual, when Superintendent Maigret had been brought in, it was because there were no fresh clues to be noted. Everybody had gone into the case, and the witnesses had already been questioned fifty times, first by the local gendarmerie, then by the Corbeil police, by magistrates and by reporters.

"You'll see it was Emile Gradut who committed the crime," he had been told.

And Maigret, after spending two hours questioning Gradut, was back on the scene of the incident, his hands in the pockets of his heavy over-coat, looking cross and staring at the gloomy landscape as though he was considering buying a plot of land there.

The interest lay not in the lock at Coudray into which the barge had crashed, but at the other end of the reach, eight kilometres higher upstream at the lock of La Citanguette.

The setting here was much the same as lower down. The villages of Morsang and Seine-Port were on the opposite bank, a longish way off; so that there was nothing to be seen but the quiet water with copses beside it and the occasional scar of an old gravel pit.

But at La Citanguette there was a bistro, and boats did their utmost to spend the night there. It was a real boatmen's bistro where they sold bread, canned goods, sausage, tackle, and oats for the horses.

And that was really where Maigret conducted his inquiry, without appearing to do so, taking a drink from time to time, sitting down by the stove or taking a turn outside while the *patronne*, who was so fair as to be almost an albino, watched him with a slightly ironical respect.

About that Wednesday evening the following facts were known. When it was beginning to get dark, the *Aiglon VII*, a small tug from the Upper Seine, had brought her six lighters, like a brood of ducklings, up to the Citanguette lock. It was drizzling at the time. When the boats were moored the men forgathered as usual in the bistro for a drink, while the lock keeper took in his cranks.

The *Astrolabe* came round the river bend only half an hour later, by which time darkness had fallen. Old Arthur Aerts, the skipper, was at the wheel, while Claessens walked along the tow-path in front of his horses with his whip over his shoulder.

Then the *Astrolabe* had moored behind the string of boats, and Claessens had taken his horses on board. At that point nobody had paid attention to them.

It was seven o'clock at least and everyone had finished eating when Aerts and Claessens came into the bistro and sat down by the stove. The skipper of *Aiglon VII* was doing most of the talking and the two old men did not speak. The white-haired *patronne*, with a baby in her arms, served them with four or five glasses of marc, but she had taken little notice of them.

That was how it had been, Maigret now realized. All these people were more or less acquainted with one another. They would come in with a brief gesture of greeting and sit down without a word. Sometimes a woman would come in, just to buy provisions for next day and then to warn her husband, as he sat there drinking: "Don't be too late back . . ."

That had been the case with Aerts's wife Emma, who had bought bread, eggs and a rabbit.

From that point onwards every detail acquired crucial importance, every piece of evidence became extremely valuable. And so Maigret persisted.

"You're sure that when he left about ten o'clock Arthur Aerts was drunk?"

"Quite tight as usual . . ." the proprietress replied. "He was a Belgian, a good fellow on the whole, who always sat in his corner saying nothing and went on drinking till he'd just got strength enough left to go back to his boat."

"And Claessens the carter?"

"He could take a bit more. He stayed about a quarter of an hour longer, then he went off, after coming back for his whip which he'd forgotten."

So far, so good. It was easy to picture the banks of the Seine at night, below the lock, the tug with its six lighters behind it, then Aerts's barge, with a lamp hanging over each boat and the steady drizzle pouring down over it all.

About half past nine Emma had gone back on board the barge with her provisions. At ten, Aerts had gone back himself, quite tight, as the *patronne* had said. And at a quarter past the carter had at last made his way back to the *Astrolabe*.

"I was only waiting for him to leave to close down, because boatmen go to bed early and there was nobody else left."

So much was reliable evidence and could be confirmed; but it was all. After that, not the smallest piece of exact information. At six in the morning the skipper of the tug had been surprised not to see the *Astrolabe* behind his lighters, and a little later he had noticed that the moorings had been cut.

At the same moment the lock keeper at Le Coudray, who was looking after his sick wife, had heard the shouts of the old carter, and soon afterwards had discovered that the barge had run into his weir.

The dog was running loose on the deck. The carter, woken up by the collision, knew nothing and declared that he had been asleep all night in his stable as usual.

Only, in the cabin at the back of the boat, Aerts's body was discovered; he had been hanged, not with a rope but with the dog's chain. Then, behind a curtain that concealed the wash-basin, his wife Emma was found hanging too; she had been hanged with a sheet taken from the bed.

And that was not all, since just before setting forth, the skipper of the *Aiglon VII*, after vainly calling for his stoker Emile Gradut, discovered that the man had disappeared.

"Gradut was the murderer . . ."

Everybody was convinced of it, and that very evening the newspapers were full of such headlines as: "Gradut seen prowling round Seine-Port," "Man-hunt in forest of Rougeau," "Aerts's hoard still not found . . ."

For all evidence went to prove that old Aerts had had a hoard, and indeed everyone agreed on the sum: 100,000 francs. It was a long yet quite simple story. Aerts, who was sixty and had two grown-up, married sons, had married as his second wife Emma, a tough Strasbourgeoise twenty years his junior.

Things were not going at all well between the couple. At every lock they stopped at, Emma would grumble about the miserliness of the old man, who scarcely gave her enough to eat.

"I don't even know where he keeps his money," she would say. "He wants his sons to have it when he dies . . . And meanwhile I have to kill myself looking after him and steering the boat; not to mention . . ."

She would add crude details, sometimes in front of Aerts himself, while he just shook his head stubbornly; then, after she had left, he would mutter:

"She only married me for my hundred thousand francs, but she's going to be disappointed . . ."

Emma would comment, furthermore:

"As though his sons needed it to live on!"

In fact the elder son, Joseph, was the skipper of a tugboat at Antwerp, while Théodore, with his father's help, had bought a fine self-propelled barge, the *Marie-France*; he had been notified of his father's death while passing through Maestricht, in Holland.

"But I'm going to find those hundred thousand francs of his . . ."

She would tell you all this out of the blue, when she'd only known you five minutes, giving the most intimate details about her old husband, and adding cynically:

"He surely can't suppose that it was out of love that a young woman like myself . . ."

And she was unfaithful to him. The evidence was indisputable. Even the skipper of the *Aiglon VII* knew about it.

"I can only tell you what I know . . . But it's a fact that during the fortnight we were lying idle at Alfortville and the *Astrolabe* was being loaded, Emile Gradut often went to meet her, even in broad daylight . . ."

So what next?

Emile Gradut, twenty-three years of age, was a bad character, that was obvious. He had, in fact, been caught after twenty-four hours, half starved, in the forest of Rougeau, less than five kilometres from La Citanguette.

"I've done nothing!" he yelled at the policemen, as he tried to ward off their blows.

A nasty little ruffian with whom Maigret had been closeted for two hours in his office and who kept stubbornly repeating:

"I've done nothing . . ."

"Then why did you run away?"

"That's my business!"

As for the examining magistrate, convinced that Gradut had hidden the hoard in the forest, he had fresh searches made there in vain.

There was something infinitely dreary about it all, as dreary as the river which reflected the same sky from morning till night, or those strings of boats that announced their arrival with a blast from a hooter (one blast for each barge being towed) as they threaded their way into the lock in an endless stream. Then, while the women stayed on deck to look after the children and keep an eye on the movements of the boat, the men went up to the bistro for a drink and then walked slowly back.

"It's plain sailing," one of his colleagues had said to Maigret.

And yet Maigret, as sullen as the Seine itself, as sullen as a canal in the rain, had returned to his lock and could not bring himself to leave it.

It's always the same story: when a case seems too clear-cut, nobody bothers to probe it in detail. Everybody agreed that Gradut was the criminal, and he had such a villainous look about him that it seemed self-evident.

Nonetheless, the results of the post mortem had now come in and they led to some curious conclusions. Thus in the case of Arthur Aerts, Dr. Paul said:

"... *Slight bruising at the base of the chin* ... *From the state of rigor mortis and the contents of the stomach it can be specified that death by strangulation occurred between 10 and 10:30 p.m.*"

Now Aerts had gone back on board at ten o'clock. According to the white-haired *patronne*, Claessens had followed him a quarter of an hour later, and Claessens declared that he had gone straight into his cabin.

"Was there a light in the Aertses' cabin?"

"I don't know . . ."

"Was the dog tied up?"

The poor old fellow had thought for a long time, but had finally made a helpless gesture. No, he didn't know. He hadn't noticed . . . How could he have foretold that it would matter so much what he did that particular evening? He had been drowsy with drink as usual; he slept in his clothes, on the straw, lying cosily beside his horse and his mare.

"You heard no noise?"

He didn't know! He couldn't have known! He had gone to sleep and when he woke up he had found himself in midstream, up against the weir.

At this point, however, there was a piece of evidence. But could it be taken seriously? It came from Madame Couturier, the wife of the skipper of the *Aiglon VII*. The head of the Corbeil police had questioned her like everyone else before letting the train of boats carry on its journey towards the Loing canal. Maigret had the report in his pocket.

Q. *Did you hear anything during the night?*

A. *I wouldn't swear to it.*

Q. *Tell us what you heard.*

A. *It's so uncertain . . . I woke up at one point and looked at the time on my alarm clock . . . It was a quarter to eleven . . . I thought I heard people speaking near the boat . . .*

Q. *Did you recognize the voices?*

A. No. But I thought it must be Gradut meeting Emma . . . I must have fallen asleep immediately after . . .

Could one rely on this? And even if it was true, what did it prove?

Below the lock, the tugboat and its six lighters and the *Astrolabe* had been lying quiet that night and . . .

As regards Aerts, the report was definite: he had died of strangulation between 10 and 10:30 p.m.

But things became more complicated when it came to the second report, the one about Emma.

". . . The left cheek shows contusions produced either by a blunt instrument or by a violent blow with someone's fist . . . Death, due to asphyxia by hanging, must have taken place at about 1 a.m."

And Maigret became ever more deeply absorbed in the slow, ponderous life of La Citanguette, as though only there was he capable of thought. A self-propelled barge flying a Belgian flag reminded him of Théodore, Aerts's son, who must by now have reached Paris.

At the same time, the Belgian flag suggested the thought of gin. For on the table in the cabin there had been found a bottle of gin, more than half empty. Somebody had made a thorough search of the cabin itself and even tore open the mattress covers, scattering the flock stuffing.

Obviously, in an attempt to find the hidden hoard of 100,000 francs!

The first investigators had declared: "It's quite simple! Emile Gradut killed Aerts and Emma. Then he got drunk and hunted for the treasure, which he hid in the forest." Only . . . Yes! Only Dr. Paul, in his post mortem on Emma's body, had found in her stomach all the gin that was missing from the bottle!

Clearly, since Emma had drunk the gin, it couldn't have been Gradut!

"Sure!" the investigators had replied. "Gradut, after killing Aerts, had made the woman tipsy in order to overcome her more easily, for she was a strong creature, don't forget . . ."

So that if they were right, Gradut and his mistress must have stayed on board from 10 or 10:30 p.m., the time of Aerts's death, until midnight or 1 a.m., the time of Emma's.

It was possible, of course . . . Everything was possible . . . Only, Maigret wanted, somehow or other, to get to understand the bargees' way of thinking.

He had been as harsh as the rest with Emile Gradut. For two hours he had grilled him thoroughly. To begin with he had tried the wheedling method, *la chansonnette* as they said at the Quai des Orfèvres.

"Listen, old fellow . . . You're involved, that's clear . . . But to be frank with you, I don't believe you killed the pair of them . . ."

"I've done nothing!"

"You didn't kill them, that's for sure . . . But admit that you knocked

the old fellow about a bit . . . It was his own fault, of course . . . He caught
you together, and so in self-defence . . ."

"I've done nothing!"

"As for Emma, of course you didn't touch her, since she was your
woman . . ."

"You're wasting your time! I've done nothing . . ."

Afterwards Maigret had become harsher, even threatening.

"Oh, so that's how it is . . . Well, we shall see if, once you're on that
boat with the two bodies . . ."

But Gradut had not even flinched at the prospect of a reconstruction
of the crime.

"Whenever you like . . . I've done nothing . . ."

"All the same when we find the money you've put away somewhere . . ."

Then Emile Gradut gave a smile . . . a smile of pity . . . an infinitely
superior smile . . .

That evening the only vessels moored at La Citanguette were one motor-
ized barge and a "stable-boat." By the lower lock, a policeman was still
on duty on the deck of the *Astrolabe*, and he was greatly surprised when
Maigret, climbing up on board, announced:

"I haven't time to go back to Paris . . . I shall sleep here . . ."

The soft lapping of water could be heard against the hull, and the
footsteps of the policeman as he paced the deck for fear of going to sleep.
The poor man began to wonder whether Maigret was not going out of
his mind, for he was making as much noise, all alone inside the boat, as
if the two horses had been let loose in the hold.

"Excuse me, officer . . ." Maigret emerged from the hatchway, "could
you possibly get hold of a pickaxe for me?"

Get hold of a pickaxe at ten o'clock at night, in such a spot? However,
the policeman woke up the sad-looking lock keeper, who, being a gardener, owned a pickaxe.

"What does your Super want to do with it?"

"Blessed if I know . . ."

And they exchanged significant glances. As for Maigret, he went back
into the cabin with his pickaxe, and for an hour after that the policeman
heard muffled blows.

"Look here, officer . . ."

It was Maigret again, sweating and out of breath, thrusting his head
through the hatchway.

"Go and put through a phone call for me . . . I'd like the examining
magistrate to come as early as possible tomorrow morning and have
Emile Gradut brought along . . ."

The lock keeper had never looked so lugubrious as when he guided the examining magistrate to the barge, while Gradut followed, flanked by a couple of policemen.

"No . . . I swear I don't know anything!"

Maigret was asleep on the Aertses' bed. He did not even apologize, and seemed unaware of the magistrate's stupefaction at the sight of the cabin.

The floorboards had been lifted. Underneath there was a layer of cement, but this had been smashed with the pickaxe, and the mess was indescribable.

"Come in, *Monsieur le juge* . . . I was very late getting to bed and I haven't had time to tidy myself up yet . . ."

He lit a pipe. He had found some bottles of beer somewhere and he poured himself a drink.

"Come in, Gradut . . . And now . . ."

"Yes, now?" asked the magistrate.

"It's quite simple," Maigret declared, puffing at his pipe. "I'll explain to you what happened the other night. You see, there was one thing that struck me from the first: old Aerts had been hanged *with a chain* and his wife *with a sheet*.

"You'll soon understand. Study police records and I'll swear you'll never find a single case of a man hanging himself with a wire or a chain. It may be odd, but it's so . . . Suicides are sensitive people and the thought of those links bruising their throats and pinching the skin of their necks . . ."

"So Arthur Aerts was murdered?"

"That's my conclusion, yes, particularly since the bruise that was noticed on his chin seems to prove that the chain, having been slipped round his neck from behind while he was drunk, struck his face first . . ."

"I don't see . . ."

"Wait a minute! Now note that his wife, on the other hand, had been hanged with a twisted sheet . . . Not even a rope, whereas there are plenty of them on board a boat . . . No, a sheet off a bed, which is the gentlest way of hanging oneself, so to speak . . ."

"And that means?"

'That she hanged herself . . . She even had to swallow half a litre of gin to get up courage, whereas normally she never drank . . . Remember the forensic report . . ."

"I remember it . . ."

"So we have one murder and one suicide, the murder committed at about a quarter past ten, the suicide at midnight or 1 a.m. And that makes everything as clear as daylight . . . "

The magistrate was watching him somewhat suspiciously, and Emile Gradut with ironical curiosity.

"For a long time now," Maigret went on, "Emma, who had not got what she hoped for from her marriage to old Aerts and who was in love with Emile Gradut, had been obsessed by one idea: to get hold of the hoard and run away with her lover. Suddenly an opportunity arose. Aerts came home dead drunk. Gradut was close by, on board the tug. She'd already noticed, when she went to buy her provisions in the bistro, that her husband was pretty tipsy. So she unfastened the dog and waited, with the chain all ready to be slipped round the man's neck . . ."

"But . . ." the magistrate objected.

"Presently! Let me finish . . . Now, Aerts is dead. Emma, elated with her triumph, runs to fetch Gradut; don't forget, at this point, that the wife of the tugboat skipper had heard voices close to her boat at a quarter to eleven . . . Isn't that true, Gradut?"

"It's true!"

"The couple come on board to look for the treasure, search everywhere, even inside the mattress, but fail to find those hundred thousand francs. Is that true, Gradut?"

"It's true!"

"Time passes and Gradut grows impatient. He even wonders, I'd be willing to bet, if he's not been had, if those hundred thousand francs really exist. Emma swears they do . . . But what use are they if they can't be found? . . . So they keep on searching. Then Gradut gets fed up . . . He knows he'll be accused of the crime. He wants to clear off. Emma wants to go with him . . ."

"Excuse me . . ." the magistrate tried to put in.

"Presently! . . . I tell you she wants to go off with him and, since he has no desire to be burdened with a woman who hasn't even any money, he solves the problem by knocking her out with his fist. Having floored her, he cuts the moorings of the barge . . . Is that true, Gradut?"

This time Gradut seemed reluctant to reply.

"That's about all!" Maigret concluded. "If they had discovered the treasure they'd have gone off together, or else they'd have tried to make the old man's death look like suicide . . . Since they've failed to find it, Gradut takes fright, and roams through the countryside trying to take cover . . . Emma, when she comes round, finds the boat drifting downstream and the hanged man swinging by her side. No hope left for her, not even the hope of escape. It would mean waking Claessens to guide the barge with the boathook . . . In short, the whole thing has been a fiasco. And she decides to kill herself . . . Only as her courage fails her, she drinks first and then takes a soft sheet from the bed . . ."

"Is this true, Gradut?" asked the magistrate, watching the young thug.

"Since the Super says so . . ."

"But . . . wait a minute . . ." the magistrate objected. "What is to prove that he didn't find the treasure and, in order to keep it . . ."

Then Maigret merely kicked aside some pieces of cement and disclosed a hiding-place in which lay Belgian and French gold coins.

"Do you understand now?"

"More or less . . ." the magistrate muttered, without much conviction.

And Maigret, filling a fresh pipe, growled:

"One had to know, in the first place, that they use a cement foundation for repairing old barges. Nobody had told me that . . ."

Then, with a sudden change of tone:

"The oddest thing about it is that I've counted, and there really are a hundred thousand francs . . . A peculiar household, don't you think?"

JOHN DICKSON CARR
(1905–1977)

This anthology would not be complete without a story involving a corpse completely surrounded by sand—with no footprints leading to or from the murder site. The master of the impossible crime, John Dickson Carr, creates and solves this classic puzzle in "Invisible Hands," which tells a tale of a strangling—usually a hands-on crime—that has taken place on an armchair-shaped rock isolated on an untouched stretch of sand, indicating that no one has approached the victim close enough to get a grip on her.

Carr's stature as the creator of puzzling mysteries cannot be overestimated. His inventiveness was equaled only by the volume of his work. Critics agree that he was unsurpassed as a creator of "locked-room mysteries," in which a murder has occurred within a locked room, thus preventing the entry or exit of a murderer. In fact, Carr articulated his thinking on the topic in a classic locked-room novel, *The Three Coffins* (1935), published in England as *The Hollow Man*, in a section of that book that is known to fans as the "Locked-Room Lecture."

Carr was born in Uniontown, Pennsylvania, to a prominent family. His father had been a United States Congressman. He was educated at a preparatory school and at Haverford College in Pennsylvania. Two years after his graduation from college, he wrote for the British Broadcasting Corporation in London, where he began his love affair with the English way of life. Carr wrote for the BBC from 1939 to 1948 and again in 1955. He took up residence in England but returned to the United States periodically when the Labour Party was in power in England.

Carr turned out seventy mystery novels, most of which fall into three series. Under his own name, he wrote about the series characters Henri Bencolin, a Parisian *juge d'instruction*; and about Dr. Gideon Fell, an obese and omniscient sleuth whom he claimed to have modeled on the author G. K. Chesterton. Using the pseudonym Carter Dickson, he created Sir Henry Merrivale, who uses legal and medical expertise to solve apparently impossible crimes. Carr also wrote historical mysteries and numerous short stories, including nine stories written under the Carter Dickson pseudonym recounting the adventures of Colonel March of the Department of Queen Complaints, another expert in impossible crimes. Carr's nonfiction includes the notable authorized biography *The Life of Sir Arthur Conan Doyle* (1949).

Invisible Hands

1958

He could never understand afterward why he felt uneasiness, even to the point of fear, before he saw the beach at all.

Night and fancies? But how far can fancies go?

It was a steep track down to the beach. The road, however, was good, and he could rely on his car. And yet, halfway down, before he could even taste the sea-wind or hear the rustle of the sea, Dan Fraser felt sweat on his forehead. A nerve jerked in the calf of his leg over the foot brake.

"Look, this is damn silly!" he thought to himself. He thought it with a kind of surprise, as when he had first known fear in wartime long ago. But the fear had been real enough, no matter how well he concealed it, and they believed he never felt it.

A dazzle of lightning lifted ahead of him. The night was too hot. This enclosed road, bumping the springs of his car, seemed pressed down in an airless hollow.

After all, Dan Fraser decided, he had everything to be thankful for. He was going to see Brenda; he was the luckiest man in London. If she chose to spend weekends as far away as North Cornwall, he was glad to drag himself there—even a day late.

Brenda's image rose before him, as clearly as the flash of lightning. He always seemed to see her half laughing, half pouting, with light on her yellow hair. She was beautiful; she was desirable. It would only be disloyalty to think any trickiness underlay her intense, naïve ways.

Brenda Lestrange always got what she wanted. And she had wanted him, though God alone knew why: he was no prize package at all. Again, in imagination, he saw her against the beat and shuffle of music in a night club. Brenda's shoulders rose from a low-cut silver gown, her eyes as blue and wide-spaced as the eternal Eve's.

You'd have thought she would have preferred a dasher, a roaring bloke like Toby Curtis, who had all the women after him. But that, as Joyce had intimated, might be the trouble. Toby Curtis couldn't see Brenda for all the rest of the crowd. And so Brenda preferred—

Well, then, what was the matter with him?

He would see Brenda in a few minutes. There ought to have been joy bells in the tower, not bats in the—

Easy!

He was out in the open now, at sea level. Dan Fraser drove bumpingly along scrub grass, at the head of a few shallow terraces leading down to the private beach. Ahead of him, facing seaward, stood the overlarge, overdecorated bungalow which Brenda had rather grandly named "The King's House."

And there wasn't a light in it—not a light showing at only a quarter past ten.

Dan cut the engine, switched off the lights, and got out of the car. In the darkness he could hear the sea charge the beach as an army might have charged it.

Twisting open the handle of the car's trunk, he dragged out his suitcase. He closed the compartment with a slam which echoed out above the swirl of water. This part of the Cornish coast was too lonely, too desolate, but it was the first time such a thought had ever occurred to him.

He went to the house, round the side and toward the front. His footsteps clacked loudly on the crazy-paved path on the side. And even in a kind of luminous darkness from the white of the breakers ahead, he saw why the bungalow showed no lights.

All the curtains were drawn on the windows—on this side, at least.

When Dan hurried round to the front door, he was almost running. He banged the iron knocker on the door, then hammered it again. As he glanced over his shoulder, another flash of lightning paled the sky to the west.

It showed him the sweep of gray sand. It showed black water snakily edged with foam. In the middle of the beach, unearthly, stood the small natural rock formation—shaped like a low-backed armchair, eternally facing out to sea—which for centuries had been known as King Arthur's Chair.

The white eye of the lightning closed. Distantly there was a shock of thunder.

This whole bungalow couldn't be deserted! Even if Edmund Ireton and Toby Curtis were at the former's house some distance along the coast, Brenda herself must be here. And Joyce Ray. And the two maids.

Dan stopped hammering the knocker. He groped for and found the knob of the door.

The door was unlocked.

He opened it on brightness. In the hall, rather overdecorated like so many of Brenda's possessions, several lamps shone on gaudy furniture and a polished floor. But the hall was empty too.

With the wind whisking and whistling at his back Dan went in and kicked the door shut behind him. He had no time to give a hail. At the back of the hall a door opened. Joyce Ray, Brenda's cousin, walked toward him, her arms hanging limply at her sides and her enormous eyes like a sleepwalker's.

"Then you did get here," said Joyce, moistening dry lips. "You did get here, after all."

"I—"

Dan stopped. The sight of her brought a new realization. It didn't explain his uneasiness or his fear—but it did explain much.

Joyce was the quiet one, the dark one, the unobtrusive one, with her glossy black hair and her subdued elegance. But she was the poor relation, and Brenda never let her forget it. Dan merely stood and stared at her. Suddenly Joyce's eyes lost their sleepwalker's look. They were gray eyes, with very black lashes; they grew alive and vivid, as if she could read his mind.

"Joyce," he blurted, "I've just understood something. And I never understood it before. But I've got to tell—"

"Stop!" Joyce cried.

Her mouth twisted. She put up a hand as if to shade her eyes.

"I know what you want to say," she went on. "But you're not to say it! Do you hear me?"

"Joyce, I don't know why we're standing here yelling at each other. Anyway, I—I didn't mean to tell you. Not yet, anyway. I mean, I must tell Brenda—"

"You can't tell Brenda!" Joyce cried.

"What's that?"

"You can't tell her anything, ever again," said Joyce. "Brenda's dead."

There are some words which at first do not even shock or stun. You just don't believe them. They can't be true. Very carefully Dan Fraser put his suitcase down on the floor and straightened up again.

"The police," said Joyce, swallowing hard, "have been here since early this morning. They're not here now. They've taken her away to the mortuary. That's where she'll sleep tonight."

Still Dan said nothing.

"Mr.—Mr. Edmund Ireton," Joyce went on, "has been here ever since it happened. So has Toby Curtis. So, fortunately, has a man named Dr. Gideon Fell. Dr. Fell's a bumbling old duffer, a very learned man or something. He's a friend of the police; he's kind; he's helped soften things. All the same, Dan, if *you'd* been here last night—"

"I couldn't get away. I told Brenda so."

"Yes, I know all that talk about hard-working journalists. But if you'd only been here, Dan, it might not have happened at all."

"Joyce, for God's sake!"

Then there was a silence in the bright, quiet room. A stricken look crept into Joyce's eyes.

"Dan, I'm sorry. I'm terribly sorry. I was feeling dreadful and so, I suppose, I had to take it out on the first person handy."

"That's all right. But how did she die?" Then desperately he began to surmise. "Wait, I've got it! She went out to swim early this morning, just as usual? She's been diving off those rocks on the headland again? And—"

"No," said Joyce. "She was strangled."

"*Strangled?*"

What Joyce tried to say was "murdered." Her mouth shook and faltered round the syllables; she couldn't say them; her thoughts, it seemed, shied back and ran from the very word. But she looked at Dan steadily.

"Brenda went out to swim early this morning, yes."

"Well?"

"At least, she must have. I didn't see her. I was still asleep in that back bedroom she always gives me. Anyway, she went down there in a red swim suit and a white beach robe."

Automatically Dan's eyes moved over to an oil painting above the fireplace. Painted by a famous R.A., it showed a scene from classical antiquity; it was called *The Lovers*, and left little to the imagination. It had always been Brenda's favorite because the female figure in the picture looked so much like her.

"Well!" said Joyce, throwing out her hands. "You know what Brenda always does. She takes off her beach robe and spreads it out over King Arthur's Chair. She sits down in the chair and smokes a cigarette and looks out at the sea before she goes into the water.

"The beach robe was still in that rock chair," Joyce continued with an effort, "when I came downstairs at half-past seven. But Brenda wasn't. She hadn't even put on her bathing cap. Somebody had strangled her with that silk scarf she wore with the beach robe. It was twisted so tightly into her neck they couldn't get it out. She was lying on the sand in front of the chair, on her back, in the red swim suit, with her face black and swollen. You could see her clearly from the terrace."

Dan glanced at the flesh tints of *The Lovers*, then quickly looked away.

Joyce, the cool and competent, was holding herself under restraint.

"I can only thank my lucky stars," she burst out, "I didn't run out there. I mean, from the flagstones of the lowest terrace out across the sand. They stopped me."

" 'They' stopped you? Who?"

"Mr. Ireton and Toby. Or, rather, Mr. Ireton did; Toby wouldn't have thought of it."

"But—"

"Toby, you see, had come over here a little earlier. But he was at the back of the bungalow, practising with a .22 target rifle. I heard him once. Mr. Ireton had just got there. All three of us walked out on the terrace at once. And saw her."

"Listen, Joyce. What difference does it make whether or not you ran out across the sand? Why were you so lucky they stopped you?"

"Because if they hadn't, the police might have said I did it."

"Did it?"

"Killed Brenda," Joyce answered clearly. "In all that stretch of sand, Dan, there weren't any footprints except Brenda's own."

"Now hold on!" he protested. "She—she *was* killed with that scarf of hers?"

"Oh, yes. The police and even Dr. Fell don't doubt that."

"Then how could anybody, anybody at all, go out across the sand and come back without leaving a footprint?"

"That's just it. The police don't know and they can't guess. That's why they're in a flat spin, and Dr. Fell will be here again tonight."

In her desperate attempt to speak lightly, as if all this didn't matter, Joyce failed. Her face was white. But again the expression of the dark-fringed eyes changed, and she hesitated.

"Dan—"

"Yes?"

"You do understand, don't you, why I was so upset when you came charging in and said what you did?"

"Yes, of course."

"Whatever you had to tell me, or thought you had to tell me—"

"About—us?"

"About anything! You do see that you must forget it and not mention it again? Not ever?"

"I see why I can't mention it now. With Brenda dead, it wouldn't even be decent to think of it." He could not keep his eyes off that mocking picture. "But is the future dead too? If I happened to have been an idiot and thought I was head over heels gone on Brenda when all the time it was really—"

"Dan!"

There were five doors opening into the gaudy hall, which had too many mirrors. Joyce whirled round to look at every door, as if she feared an ambush behind each.

"For heaven's sake keep your voice down," she begged. "Practically every word that's said can be heard all over the house. I said never, and I meant it. If you'd spoken a week ago, even twenty-four hours ago, it might have been different. Do you think I didn't want you to? But now it's too late!"

"Why?"

"May I answer that question?" interrupted a new, dry, rather quizzical voice.

Dan had taken a step toward her, intensely conscious of her attractiveness. He stopped, burned with embarrassment, as one of the five doors opened.

Mr. Edmund Ireton, shortish and thin and dandified in his middle fifties, emerged with his usual briskness. There was not much gray in his polished black hair. His face was a benevolent satyr's.

"Forgive me," he said.

Behind him towered Toby Curtis, heavy and handsome and fair-haired, in a bulky tweed jacket. Toby began to speak, but Mr. Ireton's gesture silenced him before he could utter a sound.

"Forgive me," he repeated. "But what Joyce says is quite true. Every word can be overheard here, even with the rain pouring down. If you go on shouting and Dr. Fell hears it, you will land that girl in serious danger."

"Danger?" demanded Toby Curtis. He had to clear his throat. "What danger could *Dan* get her into?"

Mr. Ireton, immaculate in flannels and shirt and thin pullover, stalked to the mantelpiece. He stared up hard at *The Lovers* before turning round.

"The Psalmist tells us," he said dryly, "that all is vanity. Has none of you ever noticed—God forgive me for saying so—that Brenda's most outstanding trait was her vanity?"

His glance flashed toward Joyce, who abruptly turned away and pressed her hands over her face.

"Appalling vanity. Scratch that vanity deeply enough and our dearest Brenda would have committed murder."

"Aren't you getting this backwards?" asked Dan. "Brenda didn't commit any murder. It was Brenda—"

"Ah!" Mr. Ireton pounced. "And there might be a lesson in that, don't you think?"

"Look here, you're not saying she strangled herself with her own scarf?"

"No—but hear what I do say. Our Brenda, no doubt, had many passions and many fancies. But there was only one man she loved or ever wanted to marry. It was not Mr. Dan Fraser."

"Then who was it?" asked Toby.

"You."

Toby's amazement was too genuine to be assumed. The color drained out of his face. Once more he had to clear his throat.

"So help me," he said, "I never knew it! I never imagined—"

"No, of course you didn't," Mr. Ireton said even more dryly. A goatish amusement flashed across his face and was gone. "Brenda, as a rule, could get any man she chose. So she turned Mr. Fraser's head and became engaged to him. It was to sting you, Mr. Curtis, to make you jealous. And you never noticed. While all the time Joyce Ray and Dan Fraser were eating their hearts out for each other; and *he* never noticed either."

Edmund Ireton wheeled round.

"You may lament my bluntness, Mr. Fraser. You may want to wring my neck, as I see you do. But can you deny one word I say?"

"No." In honesty Dan could not deny it.

"Well! Then be very careful when you face the police, both of you, or they will see it too. Joyce already has a strong motive. She is Brenda's only relative, and inherits Brenda's money. If they learn she wanted Brenda's *fiancé*, they will have her in the dock for murder."

"That's enough!" blurted Dan, who dared not look at Joyce. "You've made it clear. All right, stop there!"

"Oh, I had intended to stop. If you are such fools that you won't help yourselves, I must help you. That's all."

It was Toby Curtis who strode forward.

"Dan, don't let him bluff you!" Toby said. "In the first place, they can't arrest anybody for this. You weren't here. I know—"

"I've heard about it, Toby."

"Look," insisted Toby. "When the police finished measuring and photographing and taking casts of Brenda's footprints, I did some measuring myself."

Edmund Ireton smiled. "Are you attempting to solve this mystery, Mr. Curtis?"

"I didn't say that." Toby spoke coolly. "But I might have a question or two for you. Why have you had your knife into me all day?"

"Frankly, Mr. Curtis, because I envy you."

"You—what?"

"So far as women are concerned, young man, I have not your advantages. I had no romantic boyhood on a veldt-farm in South Africa. I never learned to drive a span of oxen and flick a fly off the leader's ear with my whip. I was never taught to be a spectacular horseman and rifle shot."

"Oh, turn it up!"

" 'Turn it up?' Ah, I see. And was that the sinister question you had for me?"

"No. Not yet. You're too tricky."

"My profoundest thanks."

"Look, Dan," Toby insisted. "You've seen that rock formation they call King Arthur's Chair?"

"Toby, I've seen it fifty times," Dan said. "But I still don't understand—"

"And I don't understand," suddenly interrupted Joyce, without turning round, "why they made me sit there where Brenda had been sitting. It was horrible."

"Oh, they were only reconstructing the crime." Toby spoke rather grandly. "But the question, Dan, is how anybody came near that chair without leaving a footprint?"

"Quite."

"Nobody could have," Toby said just as grandly. "The murderer, for instance, couldn't have come from the direction of the sea. Why? Because the highest point at high tide, where the water might have blotted out footprints, is more than twenty feet in front of the chair. More than twenty feet!"

"Er—one moment," said Mr. Ireton, twitching up a finger. "Surely Inspector Tregellis said the murderer must have crept up and caught her from the back? Before she knew it?"

"That won't do either. From the flagstones of the terrace to the back of the chair is at least twenty feet, too. Well, Dan? Do you see any way out of that one?''

Dan, not normally slow-witted, was so concentrating on Joyce that he could think of little else. She was cut off from him, drifting away from him, forever out of reach just when he had found her. But he tried to think.

"Well... could somebody have jumped there?''

"Ho!" scoffed Toby, who was himself a broad jumper and knew better. "That was the first thing they thought of.''

"And that's out, too?''

"Definitely. An Olympic champion in good form might have done it, if he'd had any place for a running start and any place to land. But he hadn't. There was *no* mark in the sand. He couldn't have landed on the chair, strangled Brenda at his leisure, and then hopped back like a jumping bean. Now could he?''

"But somebody did it, Toby! It happened!''

"How?''

"I don't know.''

"You seem rather proud of this, Mr. Curtis,'' Edmund Ireton said smoothly.

"Proud?'' exclaimed Toby, losing color again.

"These romantic boyhoods—''

Toby did not lose his temper. But he had declared war.

"All right, gaffer. I've been very grateful for your hospitality, at that bungalow of yours, when we've come down here for weekends. All the same, you've been going on for hours about who I am and what I am. Who are *you?*''

"I beg your pardon?''

"For two or three years,'' Toby said, "you've been hanging about with us. Especially with Brenda and Joyce. Who are you? What are you?''

"I am an observer of life,'' Mr. Ireton answered tranquilly. "A student of human nature. And—shall I say?—a courtesy uncle to both young ladies.''

"Is that all you were? To either of them?''

"Toby!'' exclaimed Joyce, shocked out of her fear.

She whirled round, her gaze going instinctively to Dan, then back to Toby.

"Don't worry, old girl,'' said Toby, waving his hand at her. "This is no reflection on you.'' He kept looking steadily at Mr. Ireton.

"Continue,'' Mr. Ireton said politely.

"You claim Joyce is in danger. She isn't in any danger at all,'' said Toby, "as long as the police don't know how Brenda was strangled.''

"They will discover it, Mr. Curtis. Be sure they will discover it!''

"You're trying to protect Joyce?''

"Naturally.''

on, at ease again, matched the other's courtesy. "May I ask
reasons were?"

I wished to question the two maids. They have a room at the
Miss Ray has; and this afternoon, you may remember, they were
r hysterical."

that is all?"

f. Well, no." Dr. Fell scowled. "Second, I wanted to detain all of
e for an hour or two. Third, I must make sure of the motive for
me. And I am happy to say that I have made very sure."

ce could not control herself. "Then you did overhear everything!"

h?"

Every word that man said!"

espite Dan's signals, Joyce nodded toward Mr. Ireton and poured
he words. "But I swear I hadn't anything to do with Brenda's death.
t I told you today was perfectly true: I don't want her money and I
n't touch it. As for my—my private affairs," and Joyce's face flamed,
verybody seems to know all about them except Dan and me. Please,
ease pay no attention to what that man has been saying."

Dr. Fell blinked at her in an astonishment which changed to vast dis-
ess.

"But, my dear young lady!" he rumbled. "We never for a moment
believed you did. No, no! Archons of Athens, no!" exclaimed Dr. Fell, as
though at incredible absurdity. "As for what your friend Mr. Ireton may
have been saying, I did not hear it. I suspect it was only what he told me
today, and it did supply the motive. But it was not your motive."

"Please, is this true? You're not trying to trap me?"

"Do I really strike you," Dr. Fell asked gently, "as being that sort of
person? Nothing was more unlikely than that you killed your cousin,
especially in the way she was killed."

"Do you know how she was killed?"

"Oh, that," grunted Dr. Fell, waving the point away too. "That was
the simplest part of the whole business."

He lumbered over, reflected in the mirrors, and put down stick and
shovel-hat on a table. Afterward he faced them with a mixture of distress
and apology.

"It may surprise you," he said, "that an old scatterbrain like myself
can observe anything at all. But I have an unfair advantage over the police. I began life as a schoolmaster: I have had more experience with habitual liars. Hang it all, think!"

"Of what?"

"The facts!" said Dr. Fell, making a hideous face. "According to the
maids, Sonia and Dolly, Miss Brenda Lestrange went down to swim at
ten minutes to seven this morning. Both Dolly and Sonia were awake, but
did not get up. Some eight or ten minutes later, Mr. Toby Curtis began
practising with a target rifle some distance away behind the bungalow."

"And that's why you warned Da⌐
her?''

"Of course. What else?''

Toby straightened up, his hand inside

"Then why didn't you take him outside
the quiet? Why did *you* shout out that Dan
she was in love with him, and give 'em a mo
hear?''

Edmund Ireton opened his mouth, and shut

It was a blow under the guard, all the more
came from Toby Curtis.

Mr. Ireton stood motionless under the painting
pression of the pictured Brenda, elusive and mocking
his own. Whereupon, while nerves were strained and
Dan Fraser realized that there was a dead silence bec
stopped.

Small night-noises, the creak of woodwork or a drip o⌐
eaves, intensified the stillness. Then they heard footstep⌐
those of an elephant, slowly approaching behind another
The footfalls, heavy and slow and creaking, brought a note ⌐

Into the room, wheezing and leaning on a stick, lumbere⌐
enormous that he had to maneuver himself sideways through

His big mop of gray-streaked hair had tumbled over one
eyeglasses, with a broad black ribbon, were stuck askew on his n⌐
big face would ordinarily have been red and beaming, with chuck⌐
imating several chins. Now it was only absentminded, his bandit's ⌐
tache outthrust.

"Aha!" he said in a rumbling voice. He blinked at Dan with an ai⌐
refreshed interest. "I think you must be Mr. Fraser, the last of this rath⌐
curious weekend party? H'm. Yes. Your obedient servant, sir. I am Gideo⌐
Fell."

Dr. Fell wore a black cloak as big as a tent and carried a shovel-hat
in his other hand. He tried to bow and make a flourish with his stick,
endangering all the furniture near him.

The others stood very still. Fear was as palpable as the scent after rain.

"Yes, I've heard of you," said Dan. His voice rose in spite of himself.
"But you're rather far from home, aren't you? I suppose you had some—
er—antiquarian interest in King Arthur's Chair?"

Still Dr. Fell blinked at him. For a second it seemed that chuckles
would jiggle his chins and waistcoat, but he only shook his head.

"Antiquarian interest? My dear sir!" Dr. Fell wheezed gently. "If there
were any association with a semi-legendary King Arthur, it would be at
Tintagel much farther south. No, I was here on holiday. This morning
Inspector Tregellis fascinated me with the story of a fantastic murder. I
returned tonight for my own reasons."

"Don't look at me!" exclaimed Toby. "That rifle has nothing to do with it. Brenda wasn't shot."

"Sir," said Dr. Fell with much patience, "I am aware of that."

"Then what are you hinting at?"

"Sir," said Dr. Fell, "you will oblige me if you too don't regard every question as a trap. I have a trap for the murderer, and the murderer alone. You fired a number of shots—the maids heard you and saw you." He turned to Joyce. "I believe you heard too?"

"I heard one shot," answered the bewildered Joyce, "as I told Dan. About seven o'clock, when I got up and dressed."

"Did you look out of the windows?"

"No."

"What happened to that rifle afterwards? Is it here now?"

"No," Toby almost yelled. "I took it back to Ireton's after we found Brenda. But if the rifle had nothing to do with it, and I had nothing to do with it, then what the hell's the point?"

Dr. Fell did not reply for a moment. Then he made another hideous face. "We know," he rumbled, "that Brenda Lestrange wore a beach robe, a bathing suit, and a heavy silk scarf knotted round her neck. Miss Ray?"

"Y-yes?"

"I am not precisely an authority on women's clothes," said Dr. Fell. "As a rule I should notice nothing odd unless I passed Madge Wildfire or Lady Godiva. I have seen men wear a scarf with a beach robe, but is it customary for women to wear a scarf as well?"

There was a pause.

"No, of course it isn't," said Joyce. "I can't speak for everybody, but I never do. It was just one of Brenda's fancies. She always did."

"Aha!" said Dr. Fell. "The murderer was counting on that."

"On what?"

"On her known conduct. Let me show you rather a grisly picture of a murder."

Dr. Fell's eyes were squeezed shut. From inside his cloak and pocket he fished out an immense meerschaum pipe. Firmly under the impression that he had filled and lighted the pipe, he put the stem in his mouth and drew at it.

"Miss Lestrange," he said, "goes down to the beach. She takes off her robe. Remember that, it's very important. She spreads out the robe in King Arthur's Chair and sits down. She is still wearing the scarf, knotted tightly in a broad band round her neck. She is about the same height as you, Miss Ray. She is held there, at the height of her shoulders, by a curving rock formation deeply bedded in sand."

Dr. Fell paused and opened his eyes.

"The murderer, we believe, catches her from the back. She sees and hears nothing until she is seized. Intense pressure on the carotid arteries, here at either side of the neck under the chin, will strike her unconscious within seconds and dead within minutes. When her body is released, it should fall straight forward. Instead, what happens?"

To Dan, full of relief ever since danger had seemed to leave Joyce, it was as if a shutter had flown open in his brain.

"She was lying on her back," Dan said. "Joyce told me so. Brenda was lying flat on her back with her head towards the sea. And that means—"

"Yes?"

"It means she was twisted or spun round in some way when she fell. It has something to do with that infernal scarf—I've thought so from the first. Dr. Fell! Was Brenda killed with the scarf?"

"In one sense, yes. In another sense, no."

"You can't have it both ways! Either she was killed with the scarf, or she wasn't."

"Not necessarily," said Dr. Fell.

"Then let's all retire to a loony bin," Dan suggested, "because nothing makes any sense at all. The murderer still couldn't have walked out there without leaving tracks. Finally, I agree with Toby: what's the point of the rifle? How does a .22 rifle figure in all this?"

"Because of its sound."

Dr. Fell took the pipe out of his mouth. Dan wondered why he had ever thought the learned doctor's eyes were vague. Magnified behind the glasses on the broad black ribbon, they were not vague at all.

"A .22 rifle," he went on in his big voice, "has a distinctive noise. Fired in the open air or anywhere else, it sounds exactly like the noise made by the real instrument used in this crime."

"Real instrument? What noise?"

"The crack of a blacksnake whip," replied Dr. Fell.

Edmund Ireton, looking very tired and ten years older, went over and sat down in an easy chair. Toby Curtis took one step backward, then another.

"In South Africa," said Dr. Fell, "I have never seen the very long whip which drivers of long ox spans use. But in America I have seen the black-snake whip, and it can be twenty-four feet long. You yourselves must have watched it used in a variety turn on the stage."

Dr. Fell pointed his pipe at them.

"Remember?" he asked. "The user of the whip stands some distance away facing his girl-assistant. There is a vicious crack. The end of the whip coils two or three times round the girl's neck. She is not hurt. But she would be in difficulties if he pulled the whip towards him. She would be in grave danger if she were held back and could not move.

"Somebody planned a murder with a whip like that. He came here early in the morning. The whip, coiled round his waist, was hidden by a loose and bulky tweed jacket. Please observe the jacket Toby Curtis is wearing now."

Toby's voice went high when he screeched out one word. It may have been protest, defiance, a jeer, or all three.

"Stop this!" cried Joyce, who had again turned away.

"Continue, I beg," Mr. Ireton said.

"In the dead hush of morning," said Dr. Fell, "he could not hide the loud crack of the whip. But what could he do?"

"He could mask it," said Edmund Ireton.

"Just that! He was always practising with a .22 rifle. So he fired several shots, behind the bungalow, to establish his presence. Afterwards nobody would notice when the crack of the whip—that single, isolated 'shot' heard by Miss Ray—only seemed to come from behind the house."

"Then, actually, he was—?"

"On the terrace, twenty feet behind a victim held immovable in the curve of a stone chair. The end of the whip coiled round the scarf. Miss Lestrange's breath was cut off instantly. Under the pull of a powerful arm she died in seconds.

"On the stage, you recall, a lift and twist dislodges the whip from the girl-assistant's neck. Toby Curtis had a harder task; the scarf was so embedded in her neck that she seemed to have been strangled with it. He *could* dislodge it. But only with a powerful whirl and lift of the arm which spun her up and round, to fall face upwards. The whip snaked back to him with no trace in the sand. Afterwards he had only to take the whip back to Mr. Ireton's house, under pretext of returning the rifle. He had committed a murder which, in his vanity, he thought undetectable. That's all."

"But it can't be all!" said Dan. "Why should Toby have killed her? His motive—"

"His motive was offended vanity. Mr. Edmund Ireton as good as told you so, I fancy. He had certainly hinted as much to me."

Edmund Ireton rose shakily from the chair.

"I am no judge or executioner," he said. "I—I am detached from life. I only observe. If I guessed why this was done—"

"You could never speak straight out?" Dr. Fell asked sardonically.

"No!"

"And yet that was the tragic irony of the whole affair. Miss Lestrange wanted Toby Curtis, as he wanted her. But, being a woman, her pretense of indifference and contempt was too good. He believed it. Scratch her vanity deeply enough and she would have committed murder. Scratch *his* vanity deeply enough—"

"Lies!" said Toby.

"Look at him, all of you!" said Dr. Fell. "Even when he's accused of murder, he can't take his eyes off a mirror."

"*Lies!*"

"She laughed at him," the big voice went on, "and so she had to die.

Brutally and senselessly he killed a girl who would have been his for the asking. That is what I meant by tragic irony."

Toby had retreated across the room until his back bumped against a wall. Startled, he looked behind him; he had banged against another mirror.

"Lies!" he kept repeating. "You can talk and talk and talk. But there's not a single damned thing you can prove!"

"Sir," inquired Dr. Fell, "are you sure?"

"Yes!"

"I warned you," said Dr. Fell, "that I returned tonight partly to detain all of you for an hour or so. It gave Inspector Tregellis time to search Mr. Ireton's house, and the Inspector has since returned. I further warned you that I questioned the maids, Sonia and Dolly, who today were only incoherent. My dear sir, you underestimate your personal attractions."

Now it was Joyce who seemed to understand. But she did not speak.

"Sonia, it seems," and Dr. Fell looked hard at Toby, "has quite a fondness for you. When she heard that last isolated 'shot' this morning, she looked out of the window again. You weren't there. This was so strange that she ran out to the front terrace to discover where you were. She saw you."

The door by which Dr. Fell had entered was still open. His voice lifted and echoed through the hall.

"Come in, Sonia!" he called. "After all, you are a witness to the murder. You, Inspector, had better come in too."

Toby Curtis blundered back, but there was no way out. There was only a brief glimpse of Sonia's swollen, tear-stained face. Past her marched a massive figure in uniform, carrying what he had found hidden in the other house.

Inspector Tregellis was reflected everywhere in the mirrors, with the long coils of the whip over his arm. And he seemed to be carrying not a whip but a coil of rope—gallows rope.

DAVID ELY

(1927–)

David Eli Lilienthal, Jr., under the pseudonym David Ely, produced a body of fiction fueled by the author's fascination with men of power and influence who are suddenly driven to test and understand themselves in a quest to discover their true character. In a half-dozen novels, Ely places his protagonists in various challenging situations, such as the Paris underground of World War II, a Central American jungle, and the surveillance industry. In Ely's best-known novel, *Seconds* (1963), a successful businessman known only as Wilson is approached by a mysterious corporation and offered an attractive new life. Wilson soon discovers that he is lost when given too much freedom.

Ely said, "I have always been interested in corporate power, the effects of competition, and the male urge to succeed at all costs." In "The Sailing Club," Ely works out this preoccupation in prose. Here the aptly named John Goforth finds himself emotionally restless after an illness brings on an unexpected lethargy in the formerly vigorous business magnate. Just then, he is approached by a member of the mysterious and exclusive Sailing Club. Only at sea have the members found their answer to a similar lethargy. Ely said " 'The Sailing Club' came out of my acquaintanceship with someone who did sail and was also a ruthless business person. The story is about the thrill of danger and competition in corporate life taken to the extreme that provides my ending."

Born in Chicago, Ely spent a year at the University of North Carolina before transferring to Harvard University, where he earned a B.A. He was a Fulbright Scholar at Oxford University, then served in two branches of the military; the United States Navy in 1945–1946 and the United States Army in 1950–1952. In between his stints of military service, he was a reporter for the St. Louis *Post-Dispatch*. He married, had four children, and was an administrative assistant for the Development and Resources Corporation in New York. Later he became a full-time writer, supplementing his income with ghostwriting and penning corporate reports and speeches. He lives in a coastal community on Cape Cod, Massachusetts, where he is not a member of any sailing club.

The Sailing Club

1962

Of all the important social clubs in the city, the most exclusive was also the most casual and the least known to outsiders. This was a small group of venerable origin but without formal organization. Indeed, it was without a name, although it was generally referred to as the Sailing Club, for its sole apparent activity was a short sailing cruise each summer. There were no meetings, no banquets, no other functions—in fact, no club building existed, so that it was difficult even to classify it as a club.

Nevertheless, the Sailing Club represented the zenith of a successful businessman's social ambitions, for its handful of members included the most influential men in the city, and many a top executive would have traded all his other hard-won attainments for an opportunity to join. Even those who had no interest in sailing would willingly have sweated through long practice hours to learn, if the Club had beckoned. Few were invited, however. The Club held its membership to the minimum necessary for the operation of its schooner, and not until death or debility created a vacancy was a new man admitted.

Who were the members of this select group? It was almost impossible to be absolutely certain. For one thing, since the Club had no legal existence, the members did not list it in their *Who's Who* paragraphs or in any other catalogue of their honors. Furthermore, they appeared reluctant to discuss it in public. At luncheons or parties, for example, the Club might be mentioned, but those who brought up the name did not seem to be members, and as for those distinguished gentlemen who carefully refrained at such times from commenting on the subject—who could tell? They might be members, or they might deliberately be assuming an air of significant detachment in hopes of being mistaken for members.

Naturally, the hint of secrecy which was thus attached to the Sailing Club made it all the more desirable in the eyes of the rising business leaders who yearned for the day when they might be tapped for membership. They realized that the goal was remote and their chances not too likely, but each still treasured in his heart the hope that in time this greatest of all distinctions would reward a lifetime of struggle and success.

One of these executives, a man named John Goforth, could without immodesty consider himself unusually eligible for the Club. He was, first of all, a brilliant success in the business world. Although he was not yet fifty, he was president of a dynamic corporation which had become preeminent in several fields through a series of mergers he himself had expertly negotiated. Each year, under his ambitious direction, the corporation expanded into new areas, snapping up less nimble competitors and spurring the others into furious battles for survival.

Early in his career Goforth had been cautious, even anxious, but year by year his confidence had increased, so that now he welcomed new responsibilities, just as he welcomed the recurrent business crises where one serious mistake in judgment might cause a large enterprise to founder and to sink. His quick rise had not dulled this sense of excitement, but rather had sharpened it. More and more, he put routine matters into the hands of subordinates, while he zestfully attacked those problems that forced from him the fullest measure of daring and skill. He found himself not merely successful, but powerful, a man whose passage through the halls of a club left a wake of murmurs, admiring and envious.

This was the life he loved, and his mastery of it was his chief claim to recognition by the most influential social group of all, the Sailing Club. There was another factor which he thought might count in his favor: his lifelong attachment to the sea and to sailing.

As a boy, he had stood in fascination at the ocean's edge, staring out beyond the breakers to the distant sails, sometimes imagining himself to be the captain of a great ship; at those times, the toy bucket in his hand had become a long spyglass, or a pirate's cutlass, and the strip of reed that fluttered from his fingers had been transformed into a gallant pennant, or a black and wicked skull-and-bones.

At the age of ten, he had been taught to sail at his family's summer place on the shore; later, he was allowed to take his father's boat out alone—and later still, when he was almost of college age, he was chosen for the crew of one of the yacht club entries in the big regatta. By that time, he had come to regard the sea as a resourceful antagonist in a struggle all the more absorbing because of the danger, and a danger that was far from theoretical, for every summer at least one venturesome sailor would be lost forever, far from land, and even a sizable boat might fail to return from some holiday excursion.

Now, in his middle years, John Goforth knew the sea as something more than an invigorating physical challenge. It was that still, but he recognized that it was also an inexhaustible source of renewal for him. The harsh sting of blown spray was a climate in which he thrived, and the erratic thrusts of strength that swayed his little boat evoked a passionate response of answering strength within himself. In those moments—like the supreme moments of business crisis—he felt almost godlike, limitless, as he shared the ocean's solitude, its fierce and fitful communion with the wind, the sun, and the sky.

As time passed, membership in the Sailing Club became the single remaining honor which Goforth coveted but did not have. He told himself: not a member—no, not yet! But of course he realized that this prize would not necessarily fall to him at all, despite his most strenuous efforts to seize it. He sought to put the matter out of his mind; then, failing that, he decided to learn more about the Club, to satisfy his curiosity, at least.

It was no easy task. But he was a resourceful and determined man, and before long he had obtained a fairly accurate idea of the real membership of the Sailing Club. All these men were prominent in business or financial circles, but Goforth found it strange that they seemed to lack any other common characteristic of background or attainments. Most were university men, but a few were not. There was, similarly, a variety of ethnic strains represented among them. Some were foreign-born, even, and one or two were still foreign citizens. Moreover, while some members had a long association with sailing, others seemed to have no interest whatever in the sea.

Yet just as Goforth was prepared to shrug away the matter and conclude that there was no unifying element among the members of the Sailing Club, he became aware of some subtle element that resisted analysis. Did it actually exist, or did he merely imagine it? He studied the features of the supposed Club members more closely. They were casual, yes, and somewhat aloof—even bored, it seemed. And yet there was something else, something buried: a kind of suppressed exhilaration that winked out briefly, at odd moments, as though they shared some monumental private joke.

As his perplexing survey of the Club members continued, Goforth became conscious of a quite different sensation. He could not be sure, but he began to suspect that while he was quietly inspecting them, they in turn were examining him.

The most suggestive indication was his recent friendship with an older man named Marshall, who was almost certainly a Club member. Marshall, the chairman of a giant corporation, had taken the lead in their acquaintanceship, which had developed to the point where they lunched together at least once a week. Their conversation was ordinary enough—of business matters, usually, and sometimes of sailing, for both were ardent seamen—but each time, Goforth had a stronger impression that he was undergoing some delicate kind of interrogation which was connected with the Sailing Club.

He sought to subdue his excitement. But he often found that his palms were moist, and as he wiped them he disciplined his nervousness, telling himself angrily that he was reacting like a college freshman being examined by the president of some desirable fraternity.

At first he tried to moderate his personality, as well. He sensed that his aggressive attitude toward his work, for example, was not in harmony with the blasé manner of the Club members. He attempted a show of nonchalance, of indifference—and all at once he became annoyed. He had nothing to be ashamed of. Why should he try to imitate what was false to his nature? He was *not* bored or indifferent, he was *not* disengaged from the competitive battle of life, and he would not pretend otherwise. The Club could elect him or not, as it chose.

At his next session with Marshall he went out of his way to make clear how fully he enjoyed the daily combat of business. He spoke, in fact, more emphatically than he had intended to, for he was irritated by what seemed to be the other man's ironic amusement.

Once Marshall broke in, wryly, "So you really find the press of business life to be thoroughly satisfying and exciting?"

"Yes, I do," said Goforth. He repressed the desire to add, "And don't you, too?" He decided that if the Sailing Club was nothing but a refuge for burned-out men, bored by life and by themselves, then he wanted no part of it.

At the same time he was disturbed by the thought that he had failed. The Sailing Club might be a worthless objective for a man of his temperament—still he did not like to feel that it might be beyond his grasp.

After he had parted none too cordially from Marshall, he paced along the narrow streets toward the harbor, hoping that the ocean winds would blow away his discontent. As he reached the water's edge, he saw a customs launch bounce by across the widening wake of a huge liner. A veil of spray blew softly toward him. Greedily he awaited the familiar reassurance of its bitter scent. But when it came, it was not quite what he had expected.

He frowned out at the water. No, it was not at all the same.

That winter Goforth became ill for the first time in years. It was influenza, and not a serious case, but the convalescent period stretched on and on, and before he was well enough to do any work, it was spring.

His troubles dated from that illness, he decided; not business troubles, for he had a fine executive staff, and the company did not suffer. The troubles were within himself.

First, he went through a mild depression (the doctors had of course cautioned him of this as an aftereffect), and then an uncharacteristic lassitude, broken by intermittent self-doubts. He noted, for example, that his executive vice-president was doing a good job of filling in the presidency—and then subsequently realized that this fact had no particular meaning for him. He became uneasy. He should have felt impatient to get back in harness, to show them that old Goforth still was on top.

But he had felt no emotion. It was this that disturbed him. Was it simply a delayed result of illness, or was it some inevitable process of aging which the illness had accelerated?

He tested himself grimly. He made an analysis of a stock program proposal worked out by one of the economists. He did a masterly job; he knew it himself, with a rush of familiar pride. In its way, his study was as good as anything he had ever done. No, he was not growing feeble—not yet. The malaise that possessed him was something else, undoubtedly not permanent.

That summer he spent with his family at their place on the shore. He did not feel up to sailing; he watched others sail as he lay on the beach, and was again mildly surprised by his reaction. He did not envy them at all.

In the fall he was back at his desk, in full charge once more. But he was careful to follow the advice of the doctors and the urgings of his wife, and kept his schedule light. He avoided the rush-hour trains by going to work late and leaving early, and two or three times a month he remained at home, resting.

He knew that he once would have chafed impatiently at such a regimen, but now he thought it sensible and had no sensation of loss. As always, he passed the routine problems down to his staff; but now, it seemed, so many things appeared routine that there was not much left on his desk.

The shock came late in winter, when he realized that he had actually turned over to his staff a question of vital importance. It had been well handled, true enough, and he had kept in touch with its progress, but he should have attended to it personally. Why hadn't he? Was he going through some kind of metamorphosis that would end by his becoming a semiactive Chairman of the Board? Perhaps he should consider early retirement . . .

It was in his new condition of uncertainty that he had another encounter with Marshall, this time at a private university club to which they both belonged. Marshall offered to stand him a drink, and commented that he seemed to have recovered splendidly from his illness.

Goforth glanced at him, suspecting irony. He felt fully Marshall's age now, and looked, he thought, even older. But he accepted the drink, and they began to talk.

As they chatted, it occurred to him that he had nothing to lose by speaking frankly of his present perplexities. Marshall *was* older, in point of fact; possibly the man could offer some advice.

And so Goforth spoke of his illness, his slow convalescence, his disinclination to resume his old working pace, even his unthinkable transfer of responsibility to his staff—and strangest of all, his own feeling that it did not really matter, none of it.

Marshall listened attentively, nodding his head in quiet understanding, as if he had heard scores of similar accounts.

At length Goforth's voice trailed off. He glanced at Marshall in mild embarrassment.

"So," said Marshall calmly, "you don't find business life so exciting any more?"

Goforth stirred in irritation at this echo of their previous conversation. "No," he replied, shortly.

Marshall gave him a sharp, amused look. He seemed almost triumphant, and Goforth was sorry he had spoken at all.

Then Marshall leaned forward and said, "What would you say to an invitation to join the Sailing Club?"

Goforth stared at him. "Are you serious?"

"Quite so."

It was Goforth's turn to be amused. "You know, if you'd suggested this two years ago, I'd have jumped at the chance. But now—"

"Yes?" Marshall seemed not at all taken aback.

"But now, it seems of little importance. No offense, mind you."

"I completely understand."

"To put it with absolute frankness, I don't honestly care."

Marshall smiled. "Excellent!" he declared. "That's precisely what makes you eligible!" He winked at Goforth in a conspiratorial way. "We're all of that frame of mind, my friend. We're all suffering from that same disease—"

"But I'm well now."

Marshall chuckled. "So the doctors may say. But you know otherwise, eh?" He laughed. "The only cure, my friend, is to cast your lot with fellow sufferers—the Sailing Club!"

He continued with the same heartiness to speak of the Club. Most of it Goforth already had heard. There were sixteen members, enough to provide the entire crew for the Club's schooner during its annual summer cruise. One of the sixteen had recently died, and Goforth would be nominated immediately to fill the vacancy; one word of assent from him would be enough to assure his election.

Goforth listened politely; but he had reservations. Marshall did not say exactly what the Club did on its cruises, and Goforth moodily assumed it was not worth mentioning. Probably the members simply drank too much and sang old college songs—hardly an enviable prospect.

Marshall interrupted his musing. "I promise you one thing," he said, more seriously. "You won't be bored."

There was a peculiar intensity in the way he spoke; Goforth wondered at it, then gave up and shrugged. Why not? He sighed and smiled. "All right. Of course. I'm honored, Marshall."

The cruise was scheduled to begin on the last day of July. The evening before, Goforth was driven by Marshall far out along the shore to the estate of another member, who kept the schooner at his private dock. By the time they arrived, all the others were there, and Goforth was duly introduced as the new crewman.

He knew them already, either as acquaintances or by reputation. They included men so eminent that they were better known than the companies or banking houses they headed. There were a few less prominent, but none below Goforth's own rank, and certainly none was in any sense obscure. He was glad to note that all of them had fought their way through the hard competitive years, just as he had done, and then in the course of the evening he slowly came to realize a further fact—that not one of these men had achieved any major triumph in recent years.

He took some comfort from this. If he had fallen into a strange lassitude, then so perhaps had they. Marshall had evidently been right. He was among "fellow sufferers." This thought cheered him, and he moved more easily from group to group, chatting with as much self-possession as if he had been a member of the Club for years.

He had already been told that the ship was in full readiness and that the group was to sail before dawn, and so he was not surprised when the host, a gigantic old man named Teacher, suggested at nine o'clock that they all retire.

"Has the new member signed on?" someone inquired.

"Not yet," said Teacher. He beckoned to Goforth with one huge hairless hand. "This way, my friend," he said.

He led Goforth into an adjoining room, with several of the others following, and after unlocking a wall safe, withdrew a large black volume so worn with age that bits of the binding flaked off in his fingers.

He laid it on a table, thumbed through its pages, and at length called Goforth over and handed him a pen. Goforth noticed the old man had covered the top portion of the page with a blank sheet of paper; all that showed beneath were signatures, those of the other members.

"Sign the articles, seaman," said Teacher gruffly, in imitation of an old-time sea captain.

Goforth grinned and bent over the page, although at the same time he felt a constitutional reluctance to sign something he could not first examine. He glanced at the faces surrounding him. A voice in the background said, "You can read the whole thing, if you like—after the cruise."

There was nothing to do but sign, so he signed boldly, with a flourish, and then turned to shake the hands thrust out to him. "Well done!" someone exclaimed. They all crowded around then to initial his signature as witnesses, and Teacher insisted that they toast the new member with brandy, which they did cheerfully enough, and then went off to bed.

Goforth told himself that the ceremony had been a juvenile bit of foolishness, but somehow it had warmed him with the feeling of fellowship.

His sense of well-being persisted the next morning when in the predawn darkness he was awakened and hurriedly got dressed to join the others for breakfast.

It was still dark when they went down to the ship, each man carrying his sea bag. As he climbed aboard, Goforth was just able to make out the name painted in white letters on the bow: *Freedom IV*.

Since he was experienced, he was assigned a deck hand's job, and as he worked alongside the others to ready sails for hoisting, he sensed a marked change in their attitude.

The Club had its reputation for being casual, and certainly the night before, the members had seemed relaxed to the point of indolence; but there was a difference now. Each man carried out his tasks swiftly, in dead seriousness and without wasted motion, so that in a short time the *Freedom IV* was skimming eastward along the Sound toward the heart of the red rising sun.

Goforth was surprised and pleased. There was seamanship and discipline and sober purpose on this ship, and he gladly discarded his earlier notion that they would wallow about with no program beyond liquor and cards.

With satisfaction, he made a leisurely tour of the ship. Everything was smart and sharp, on deck and below, in the sleeping quarters and galley. Teacher, who seemed to be the captain, had a small cabin forward and it, too, was a model of neatness.

Goforth poked his head inside to admire it further. Teacher was not there, but in a moment the old man stepped through a narrow door on the opposite bulkhead, leading to some compartment below, followed by two other members. They greeted Goforth pleasantly, but closed and locked the door behind them, and did not offer to show him the compartment. He, for his part, refrained from asking, but later in the day he inspected the deck above it and saw that what had seemed earlier to be merely a somewhat unorthodox arrangement of crisscross deck planking was actually a hatchway, cleverly concealed.

He crouched and ran his fingers along the hidden edges of the hatch, then glanced up guiltily to meet Marshall's eyes. Marshall seemed amused, but all he said was, "Ready for chow?"

In the next few days Goforth occasionally wondered what the forward compartment contained. Then he all but forgot about it, for his enjoyment of the voyage was too deep-felt to permit even the smallest question to trouble him. He was more content now than he had been in many months. It was not because he was sailing again, but rather, he believed, because he was actively sharing with others like himself a vigorous and demanding experience. It seemed, indeed, that they formed a little corporation there on the *Freedom IV*—and what a corporation! Even the member who occupied the lowly post of cook's helper was a man accustomed to deal in terms of millions.

Yes, what a crew it was! Now Goforth began to understand the suppressed excitement he had long ago detected as a subtle mark identifying members of the Sailing Club. Theirs was no ordinary cruise, but a grand exercise of seamanship, as if they had decided to pit their collective will against the force and cunning of the ocean, to retrieve through a challenge to that most brutal of antagonists the sense of daring which they once had found in their work . . .

They were searching for something. For a week they sailed a zigzag course, always out of sight of land, but Goforth had not the faintest notion of their whereabouts, nor did he judge that it would be proper for him to inquire. Were they pursuing a storm to provide them with some ultimate test with the sea? He could not be sure. And yet he was quite willing to wait, for there was happiness enough in each waking moment aboard the *Freedom IV*.

On the eighth day he perceived an abrupt change. There was an almost tangible mood of expectancy among the members, a quickening of pace and movement, a tightening of smiles and laughter that reminded him oddly of the atmosphere in a corporation board room, when the final crisis of some serious negotiation approaches. He guessed that some word had been passed among the crew, save for himself, the neophyte.

The men were tense, but it was the invigorating tensity of trained athletes waiting in confidence for a test worthy of their skills. The mood was infectious; without having any idea of what lay ahead, Goforth began to share the exhilaration and to scan the horizon eagerly.

For what? He did not care now. Whatever it might be, he felt an elemental stirring of pride and strength and knew that he would meet whatever ultimate trial impended with all the nerve and daring that his life had stamped into his being.

The *Freedom IV* changed course and plunged due east toward a haze that lay beneath heavier clouds. Goforth thought perhaps the storm lay that way and keenly watched for its signs. There were none, but he took some heart at the sight of another yacht coming toward them, and hopefully imagined that it was retreating from the combat which the *Freedom IV* seemed so ardently to seek.

He studied the sky. The clouds drifted aimlessly, then broke apart for a moment to disclose a regular expanse of blue. He sighed as he saw it, and glanced around at the other crewmen to share his feeling of frustration.

But there was no disappointment on those faces. Instead, the mood of tension seemed heightened to an almost unbearable degree. The men stood strained and stiff, their features set rigidly, their eyes quick and piercing as they stared across the water.

Goforth searched their faces desperately for comprehension, and as it slowly came to him—when at last he *knew*—he felt the revelation grip him physically with a wild penetrating excitement.

He *knew*, and so he watched with fierce absorption but without surprise as the forward hatch swung open to permit what was below to rise to the surface of the deck, and watched still more intently as the crew leaped smartly forward to prepare it with the speed born of long hours of practice.

He stood aside then, for he knew he would need training, too, before he could learn his part; but after the first shot from the sleek little cannon had smashed a great hole in the side of the other yacht, he sprang forward as readily as the others to seize the rifles which were being passed around. And as the *Freedom IV* swooped swiftly in toward the floundering survivors, his cries of delight were mixed with those of his comrades, and their weapons cracked out sharply, gaily, across the wild echoing sea.

RICHARD DEMING
(1915–1983)

Richard Deming's tale of seduction and murder during a honeymoon cruise is a fine example of post–pulp magazine fiction that uses sexual tension to hook the reader. When Deming wrote "Honeymoon Cruise" at the age of fifty-one, he was already an experienced fiction and television writer, used to depicting enough sexuality to titillate the reader or television viewer without upsetting the censors.

A native of Iowa, Deming served in the army and worked briefly as a social worker and for the Red Cross before becoming a full-time writer at the age of thirty-five. He used seven pseudonyms during a career in which he progressed from writing for pulps to digest-sized mystery magazines, then paperback original novels, and finally to novelizations of the *Charlie's Angels* and *Starsky and Hutch* television series, written under the pseudonym Max Franklin. Under his own name, he turned out novels and short stories centered on the activities of the wisecracking Manville "Manny" Moon and hard-boiled police procedurals featuring Matt Rudd, as well as novelizations of *The Mod Squad* television series. He also penned ten novels using the pseudonym Ellery Queen (as other authors did at the time) between 1962 and 1970. In addition, he wrote nonfiction volumes on subjects as diverse as American spies, civil and criminal law, sleep, and the metric system.

Deming wrote nearly 150 short stories under his own name and as Max Franklin. As Deming, he wrote "Honeymoon Cruise" for *Alfred Hitchcock's Mystery Magazine* in 1966. Reminiscent of Patricia Highsmith's "The Talented Mr. Ripley," published in 1955, the story shows how easy it can be to toss one's scruples—and an inconvenient husband—overboard. A sense of inevitability propels "Honeymoon Cruise" to its ironic conclusion.

Honeymoon Cruise

1966

When the employment office sent me down to the Miami Yacht Club to be interviewed by the owner of the *Princess II*, I had no idea she was tin heiress Peggy Matthews. I was told to ask for a Mrs. Arden Trader.

The *Princess II* was moored in the third slip. It was only about a thirty-five footer, but it was a sleek, sturdy-looking craft which appeared as though it could weather any kind of seas. No one was on deck or in the wheelhouse.

I climbed on deck, stuck my head down the single hatch behind the wheelhouse, and yelled, "Anyone aboard?"

A feminine voice from below called, "Be right up."

A moment later, a slim brunette of about twenty-five came up the ladder. She wore white Capris and a clinging white blouse that showed off a lithe, extremely feminine figure, thong sandals that exposed shapely feet with carmine toenails, and a white sailor hat. Her features were slightly irregular, her nose being a trifle aquiline and her chin line being a little short, but her face was so full of vitality and there was such an aura of femininity about her that she was beautiful, anyway. Lovely dark eyes, a suggestion of sensuality about her mouth, and a creamy suntan probably helped the general effect.

I recognized her at once from news photos I had seen. Only a few months before, on her birthday, she had come into full control of an estimated fortune of twenty million dollars, which had been left to her in trust until she was twenty-five by her widower father, tin magnate Abel Matthews. Matthews had been dead about ten years, but until Peggy's last birthday the terms of the trust fund had required her to struggle along on the piddling sum of about a hundred thousand a year. Now she was one of the richest women in the world.

"Aren't you Peggy Matthews?" I asked.

"I was," she said with a smile which exposed perfect white teeth. "I've been Mrs. Arden Trader for the last couple of days. Are you from the employment agency?"

"Yes, ma'am. My name's Dan Jackson."

She looked me up and down, and suddenly a peculiar expression formed on her face. Even now I can't quite describe it, but if you can imagine a mixture of surprise and gladness and apprehension, that comes close.

I think there must have been a similar expression on my face, except for the apprehension, because I was having an odd emotional reaction, too. Just like that, on first meeting, static electricity passed between us so strongly, it seemed to crackle like twin bolts of lightning.

I still don't believe there can be such a thing as love at first sight, but I learned at that instant that there can be an almost overpowering physical attraction between a man and a woman the first moment they look at each other. I had experienced it a few times in much milder form but never with this sort of thunderous impact.

We stood staring at each other in mutual dismay, hers probably from guilt, mine because she was already married. It was incredible that this should happen with a bride of only two days, but it was happening. There was no question in my mind that my impact on her was as strong as hers on me.

We gazed at each other for a long time without speaking. Finally, she said in a shaken voice, "Did the employment agency explain the job, Mr. Jackson?"

I took my eyes from her face so that I could untangle my tongue. "I understand you need someone with navigational and marine engine experience to pilot the *Princess II* on a Caribbean cruise and also double as a cook."

She turned and looked out over the water. "Yes," she said in a low voice. "It's to be a honeymoon cruise. My husband can pilot the boat all right, but he's not a navigator and knows nothing about engines. Neither of us is a very good cook, either. Incidentally, our marriage is to remain a secret until after the honeymoon because we don't want to be met by reporters at every port."

"All right," I agreed, still not looking at her.

I did risk a glance at her left hand, however. She was wearing both a diamond and a wedding band. I wondered how she expected to keep it a secret when people were bound to recognize her at every port of call. But that was none of my business.

She suddenly became brisk and businesslike. "May I have your qualifications and vital statistics, Mr. Jackson?"

"In that order?"

"As you please."

"I'll give you the vital statistics first," I said. "Age thirty, height six-one, weight one ninety; single. Two years at Miami U. in liberal arts with a B average, then I ran out of money. My hobbies are all connected with water: swimming, boating, fishing, and as a chaser for rye whiskey. No current romantic entanglements."

"I'm surprised at the last," she said. "You're a very handsome man."

I decided to ignore that. It didn't seem a good idea to involve myself as a third party on a honeymoon cruise if the situation were going to become explosive. I wanted to know right now if we were going to be able to suppress whatever it was that had sparked between us at the instant of meeting and keep our relationship on a strictly employer–employee basis.

"Now for qualifications," I said. "I did two years in the navy, the second one as chief engineer on a destroyer. I took an extension course in navigation and chart reading, intending to buck for a reserve commission, but changed my mind before my hitch was up. I finished the course, though, and am a pretty good navigator. I'm also an excellent marine mechanic. I had my own charter boat out of Miami Beach for two years. I lost it in moorage when Betsy hit, and there was only enough insurance to cover my debts, so I've been unable to finance another. Since then I've been odd-jobbing at any sea job I could get."

I looked directly into her face as I spoke, and she gazed back at me levelly. Whatever had caused the lightning to crackle between us was gone now, I was both disappointed and relieved to find. Her manner remained the brisk, almost brittle one of a business-woman conducting a personnel interview. She still held an immense physical attraction for me, but now that she wasn't sending out rays of static electricity, I wasn't responding by sending them back.

She asked, "How about your cooking ability?"

"I'm no chef, but I've been cooking for myself for some years and have managed to remain healthy."

"That's not too important so long as you're adequate," she said. "We'll probably dine either with friends or in restaurants at our ports of call. You can furnish references, I presume?"

"They're on file at the employment office, which has already checked them. All you have to do is phone."

"Very well," she said. "I think you'll do, Mr. Jackson. The salary is five hundred dollars plus your keep for a one-month voyage. Is that satisfactory?"

"Yes, ma'am."

"We'll leave tomorrow morning about ten. Our first port will be Southwest Point in the Bahamas, which should only take about four hours because the *Princess II* cruises at twenty-one knots. I'll outline the rest of the voyage after we're under way. Now, would you like to look over the boat?"

"Sure. Where's Mr. Trader?"

"Shopping for some last-minute supplies. We'll start below with the engine."

I judged the boat to be a couple of years old, but it was in excellent shape. I started the engine and listened to it for a time, and it seemed to be in top condition. There was a separate generator engine for the lights when we were in port, and the main engine was idle.

The galley was clean and shipshape, with an electric range and electric refrigerator, the latter well stocked with food. The food cabinet was well stocked with canned goods, also. There was a bunk room that slept four, and off it was a small head and a salt-water shower.

Just she and her husband would occupy the bunk room, Peggy Trader explained. There was a leather-covered bench in the pilothouse which folded out into a fifth bunk, and I would sleep there.

Her manner was entirely impersonal as she conducted the tour. Once, as we were moving from the bunk room into the galley, she accidentally crowded against me in the close quarters, but I sensed no reaction from her at the physical contact.

She merely said politely, "Excuse me," and continued through the hatch.

I knew the instantaneous physical attraction between us hadn't been just my imagination, but apparently she had decided, after her one brief lapse, to bring the matter to a screeching halt. I couldn't help feeling a bit rueful, but at the same time I was relieved. I needed the money badly enough so that I probably would have risked taking the job even if she had thrown herself into my arms, but I preferred not to break up a marriage before it was even fairly under way. If she could restrain herself, I knew I could.

I reported aboard at nine the next morning. Peggy's husband was present this time. Arden Trader was a lean, handsome man of thirty-five with dark, curly hair and a thin mustache. He had an Oxford accent and treated his bride with the fawning indulgence of a gigolo.

Later, I learned he had been the penniless younger son of an equally penniless English duke and had been existing as one of those curious parasites of the international set who move from villa to villa of the rich as perennial house guests.

I knew he was a fortune hunter the moment he flashed his white teeth and gave me a man-to-man handshake. I wondered why Peggy had allowed herself to be suckered into marrying him. I learned that afternoon.

The plan for the cruise was to sail east to Southwest Point the first day, a distance of about a hundred miles. After a two-day layover, we would head for Nassau, and after a similar layover there, we would cruise to Governor's Harbor. From there we would island hop to Puerto Rico, then hit the Dominican Republic, Haiti, Point Morant on the east tip of Jamaica, then head back northeast through Windward Passage to Port-de-Paix on the northern coast of Haiti.

The last would be our longest single jump, a distance of about two hundred and fifty miles. With a cruising speed of twenty-one knots, we could make it in about ten hours, however, so no night sailing would be required during the whole voyage.

After Port-de-Paix, we would touch at the island of Great Inagua, island hop from there back to Governor's Harbor, then cruise nonstop back to Miami. With all our scheduled stops, ranging from one-day layovers to two or three days, we would spend more time in port than at sea during the one-month voyage.

At noon the first day out, I called Arden Trader to take over the wheel while I went below to prepare lunch. When it was ready, as we were in no hurry, we cut the engine, threw out the sea anchor, and all lunched together.

After lunch, I pulled in the sea anchor and got under way again. The sea was rolling a little, but it wasn't rough, and the sun was shining brightly. We were clipping along at cruising speed when Peggy came into the wheelhouse wearing a red bikini swimsuit.

"Arden wants to try a little fishing," she said. "Will you cut to trolling speed for a while?"

Obediently, I throttled down until we were barely moving. Glancing aft, I saw Arden Trader seated at the stern rail with a sea rod in his hands. Peggy made no move to go back and join him after delivering the message.

"He probably won't troll more than fifteen minutes if he doesn't get a strike," she said. "He bores rather easily."

I didn't say anything.

She moved over next to me in order to look at the chart book lying open on the little ledge between the wheel and the pilothouse window. The nearness of her scantily clad body made my pulse start to hammer so hard I was afraid she could hear it.

"Where are we?" she asked.

I pointed silently to a spot a little more than halfway between Miami and Southwest Point.

She said, "We should be in by cocktail time, then, even if Arden decides to fish as long as an hour, shouldn't we?"

"Oh, yes."

There was no reason for her to remain where she was, now that she had seen the chart, but she continued to stand so close that our arms nearly touched. I didn't have on a shirt. In fact, I was wearing nothing but a pair of my old navy dungarees and a visored yachting cap, not even shoes. She was so close I could feel the warmth of her body on my bare arm.

Although the sea was fairly calm, our decreased headway caused the boat to roll slightly. One swell a little larger than the rest caused a heavier roll to port. Instinctively, I leaned into it, and at the same moment she lost her balance.

She half turned as she fell against me. My right arm went around her waist to steady her as she grabbed for my shoulders. Her full bosom, covered only by the thin strip of the bikini halter, crushed against my bare chest. The bolts of lightning that crackled between us made that of yesterday morning seem like summer lightning. We remained rigid for several seconds, staring into each other's faces. Her lips parted, and her eyes reflected the same mixture of surprise and gladness and dismay I had caught when we first glimpsed each other. Then she straightened away from me and glanced out the aft pilothouse window. I looked over my shoulder, too. Her husband was fishing with his back to us.

"I shouldn't have hired you," she said quietly.

I faced forward and gripped the wheel with both hands.

"I knew I shouldn't have when I did it," she said. "Don't pretend you don't know what I'm talking about."

"We'll head back for Miami tomorrow," I said. "You can have the employment agency send you another man."

"No, I don't want to. It's too late."

With her gaze still on her husband, she reached out and gently squeezed my bicep. I tingled clear to my toes.

"It's ridiculous," I said tightly. "You're a bride of three days. You must be in love with him."

Her hand continued to caress my bicep. "I'm not going to try to explain it, Dan. I was in love with him until you came aboard yesterday. I took one look at you, and everything turned topsy-turvy. It did for you, too. I could see it in your eyes. I can feel it in your muscles right now."

"Stop it," I said, keeping my gaze rigidly fixed ahead. "It's impossible. Why did you marry him?"

"Because I hadn't met you," she said simply.

"That's no answer. You must have been in love."

Her hand left my arm and dropped to her side. "I went into it with my eyes wide open," she said. "I've had a hundred offers of marriage—women with money always do—but I'd given up ever finding the man I dreamed of. The rich ones were all fearfully dull, the charmers all fortune hunters. I'm twenty-five and tired of being single. I hardly needed a rich husband, so I decided to settle for a charmer. Arden has been pursuing me for a year. Last week at a house party in Mexico City, I gave in. We were married there, then flew to Miami to pick up my boat for a honeymoon cruise. On my second day as a new bride, I had, finally, to meet the man I've been looking for all my life."

I continued to grip the wheel and stare straight ahead. The whole situation was incredible. A series of wild thoughts ran through my mind.

I'd always considered myself a confirmed bachelor, but suddenly the thought of having Peggy for a wife was so appealing, I've never wanted anything more. Her money had nothing to do with it, either. I would never marry for money because it had been my observation that men who do usually earn it. It had never occurred to me that I might fall in love with a rich woman.

I wasn't sure this was love, but no woman had ever held as strong a physical attraction for me, and I was sure I wanted to marry her. And it was hardly a disadvantage that she was one of the richest women in the world. Would it be sensible to turn her down merely because a few villas scattered around the world, a few yachts and foreign cars went with the deal?

Then the bubble popped. She already had a husband.

"Aren't you going to say anything?" she asked.

"Uh-huh. Do you plan an annulment?"

"From Arden? Impossible. He would hold me up for a half million dollars."

"Can't you afford it?"

From the periphery of my vision, I could see her frown. "Nobody can afford to throw half a million dollars down a hole. My father spent too many years building his fortune for any of it to be tossed away capriciously. It's not a matter of being able to afford it; it's a matter of principle."

"Then I guess you'll just have to stay married to him," I said.

There was a yell from the stern. "Strike!"

I cut the engine and looked over my shoulder. Trader was straining back in his seat, and a hundred yards behind the boat a sailfish broke water.

Peggy said, "We'll postpone discussion until later," and hurried aft to stand by with the gaff.

There was no opportunity to resume discussion that day, however. Trader lost his fish, and it discouraged him from further fishing. He devoted his attention to his bride for the rest of the day.

About five p.m. we berthed at Southwest Point. Trader and Peggy dressed and decided to go into the settlement for dinner. Trader invited me to go along but I knew the invitation was only politeness, so I refused.

I had a lonely meal and afterward sat on the stern rail smoking a cigarette. The night was warm enough so that I didn't bother to put on any more than I had worn during the day. I had finished my cigarette but was still seated there bare-chested and barefooted when they returned about nine.

Arden Trader had donned a white linen suit to go to dinner. Peggy had put on a dress but hadn't bothered with stockings. She wore thong sandals on her bare feet.

There were two inflated rubber mats with removable canvas back rests on the stern deck. Without the back rests you could lie full length on them for sunbathing. With the back rests in place, they made deck-level lounging chairs. Peggy sank onto the one right in front of me, leaned against the back rest, and kicked off her sandals.

"Let's enjoy the moonlight for a while," she said to her husband. "How about a cigarette?"

He knelt beside her with his back to me, placed a cigarette in her mouth, and lit it. After taking one draw, she took it from her mouth, put her arms about his neck, and drew him to her.

Ever since she had left the wheelhouse that afternoon, I had been stewing about what transpired there. I had finally decided that if she wasn't going to leave her husband, we were not going to have just an affair. I still wanted her as a wife more than I've ever wanted anything, and maybe if she had been married ten years, I might have settled for having her just as a mistress. But I wasn't quite rat enough to cuckold a groom on his honeymoon.

Apparently, my soul-searching had been for nothing. I could think of no reason for her deliberate show of affection in front of me other than that she had decided to let me know in definite terms that the scene in the wheelhouse had been a mistake. I looked away, not wanting to see her kissed by Trader.

I felt something touch my left foot and glanced down. My pulse started to pound when I saw her right foot rubbing against my instep. Her carmine-tipped toes wiggled in urgent demand for some response.

With her arms wrapped around her husband, the gesture seemed more likely to be an invitation for a clandestine affair than a signal that she wanted a more permanent relationship. Since I had already decided against settling for that, my conscience told me to withdraw my foot.

My desire for her was stronger than my conscience. I raised my foot and pressed its sole against hers. Her toes worked against mine and along the sole of my foot in a lascivious caress, all the time her arms tightening around her husband's neck until finally it was he who broke the kiss.

As he started to rise, her foot drew away from mine, and I dropped mine back flat on the deck. Trader sank onto the other mat and lit a cigarette.

"I'm beginning to like this married life," he said to me with a grin. "You ought to try it, Dan."

"I may if I ever meet the right girl," I said, getting to my feet. "Think I'll turn in. It's been a long day."

"Good night, Dan," Peggy said softly.

"Night," I said without looking at her, and headed for the wheelhouse.

The following morning when I climbed down on deck, Arden Trader was screwing some kind of bracket to the timber immediately right of the hatchway which led below.

"Morning," I said. "What's that?"

"Morning, Dan," he said affably. "I'm installing an outside shaving mirror I picked up in town last night. The head's too small and too poorly lighted to get a decent shave."

He lifted a round shaving mirror from a paper bag and slipped the two small vertical shafts at its back into holes in the top of the bracket. Then he moved the bottom of the mirror in and out to demonstrate that it could be adjusted to suit the height of anyone using it.

"Now all I need is a basin of hot water and my shaving equipment," he said as he started below. "You can use it when I'm finished if you want."

I did use it from then on.

I had no opportunity to be alone with Peggy during the two days we were in port because Trader was playing the attentive groom. By the second day, I couldn't stand his constant little attentions to her and, since I wasn't needed aboard because they were taking their meals in town, took the day off and spent it on the beach by myself.

On the third day, we pulled out for Nassau. As the trip would take six hours, we got under way at eight a.m. About ten, Peggy came into the pilothouse, again wearing a bikini.

"He's taking a nap," she said, and with no more preamble moved into my arms.

I spiked the wheel so as to have both arms free. Hers went about my neck, and her body pressed against mine as our lips met. We were both trembling when she finally struggled from my arms and stepped back. It was none too soon.

She backed clear to the pilothouse door. We were both so out of control, if her husband had walked in at that moment, neither of us could have concealed our naked emotion from him.

"What are we going to do?" she whispered.

My good resolutions lay in shreds. I didn't care what we did so long as it meant being together in some way. If she wanted to shed Trader and marry me, I would be happiest. But now I was willing to settle for just an affair if she wanted that. If she had suggested solving our problem by holding hands and jumping over the rail, I would have at least considered it.

I jerked out the spike and gripped the wheel with both hands in an effort to control my trembling. "What do you want to do?"

"Do you love me?"

"Do you have to ask?" I demanded.

"I want to hear you say it."

I took a deep breath. "I love you. I'm absolutely nuts about you."

She closed her eyes. "I love you, too," she said almost inaudibly. "I've never felt such overwhelming love. Do you want to marry me? Answer me truly, Dan."

"There's nothing I want more," I said in a husky voice.

Her eyes opened, and she seemed to get a little control of herself. In a more normal tone, she said, "I couldn't just have an affair, Dan. Despite my behavior, I'm really a quite moral person. I'm not a prude. If I were single, and we were alone out here and planned to get married when we reached port, I wouldn't insist we wait until the proper words were spoken. But there's some Puritan strain deep within me that makes it impossible for me to violate my marriage vows."

"We aren't going to have an affair," I told her. "I've already told you I want you for my wife."

"But I have a husband."

"You shouldn't have any trouble getting an annulment after this short a marriage. Why do you think it would cost you a half million?"

"Because I know Arden. I know him so well, I made him sign a premarital agreement waiving all claim to my estate except whatever I decided to leave him in my will. I didn't think it wise to put him in a position where he could become rich if I died."

I turned to stare at her. "If you thought him capable of murdering you, why in the devil did you marry him? What possessed you?"

"Oh, I really didn't think he might try to kill me. But he's a fortune hunter, and you don't place temptation in the hands of men such as

Arden. Because he is a fortune hunter, I know he'll hold me up if I ask for an annulment. My guess that his price for cooperating will be a half million is based on sound experience. That's exactly what it cost each of two women friends of mine to shed fortune-hunting husbands."

"Wouldn't your premarital agreement cover that?"

"That only applies in case of my death," she said. "Actually, I could get out of paying him a red cent if I wanted a legal battle. No court would grant him any kind of settlement. But there's a pattern of blackmail men such as Arden use. If I refuse to pay him off, Arden will fight me in court with every dirty tactic he knows. He'll drag my reputation through the mud by filing countersuit for divorce and accusing me of infidelity with a dozen men. The tabloids will have a field day."

I said sourly, "You knew all this in advance of marrying him. How the hell did you bring yourself to do it?"

"I assumed it was going to last, Dan. How was I to know you would come along?"

I took my gaze from her and looked ahead again. "If you don't get rid of him, how are we going to marry?"

"Oh, I intend to get rid of him," she said softly.

"By paying him off?"

"There's a much simpler way, Dan. Who would suspect anything if a brand-new groom fell overboard and was lost at sea on his honeymoon? The wife might be suspected after a ten-year marriage or even after a year—but not after just a week, Dan."

A sudden chill doused the warmth I still felt from having her in my arms. "Murder?" I said shakily.

"There wouldn't be a chance of suspicion. Who could suspect a love triangle when I'm on my honeymoon and you and I have only known each other a few days? It's even incredible to me that we're in love. How could the thought ever enter the heads of the police?"

The logic of what she said was penetrating my mind even as I was rejecting the thought. Under the circumstances, who could possibly suspect? My throat was suddenly so dry I had to clear it.

"There would be some suspicion after we announced our marriage."

"Why? No one knows you're only a temporary employee. I'll simply keep you on in some permanent capacity—say as my social secretary. I'm the only woman in my set who has never had one, and it's about time I acquired one. You'll show sympathy for my bereavement, and I'll show appreciation for your sympathy. Gradually, your sympathy and my appreciation can ripen into love. It won't be the first time a sympathetic male friend has ended up marrying a grieving widow. I think it would be safe at the end of as little as two months."

Again her argument was so logical I had no answer, except that it takes more than mere certainty that you won't be caught to condition your mind to murder.

"It has to be that way or not at all," she said in a suddenly definite tone. "I'll leave you to think it over." She turned and left the pilothouse.

I was still thinking it over when it came time for the noon mess. By then, we were passing through Northwest Providence Channel. I had deliberately kept to the center of the channel, and land was barely visible on the horizon on both sides. The water was calm, with only a slight roll, and the sun was shining brightly. There wasn't another vessel in sight.

Arden Trader had emerged from below in swim trunks about eleven o'clock, and both he and Peggy were lying on the inflated mats at the stern, deepening their already rich tans. I yelled for Trader to come take the wheel while I prepared mess. He rolled off his mat, leaned over Peggy, and gave her a long kiss. Jealousy raged through me so hotly I had to turn my back to get control of myself. When he came into the wheelhouse, it was an effort to keep my voice calm while I gave him his bearing.

The sight of his kissing Peggy had brought me to a decision. Peggy came into the galley only a moment after I got there and stood looking at me expressionlessly. "All right," I said.

Her nostrils flared. "When?"

"Right now if you want."

"How?"

"Why don't you go out and suggest a swim before lunch? The water's calm enough. I'll do the rest."

Without a word, she turned and left the galley. I waited a moment, then followed, pausing astern while she climbed to the pilothouse. A moment after she entered, Trader cut the engine, then they both emerged.

"Okay, Dan," Peggy called. "You can throw out the sea anchor."

I was already standing next to it. I tossed it overboard and let down the wooden-runged ladder strung with rope so that swimmers could more easily get back aboard ship. "Think I'll have a dip with you," I said. "I'll put on my trunks."

When I came back out on deck, Trader and Peggy were already in the water. Trader was floating on his back about four feet from the boat, his arms outstretched and his eyes closed. Peggy was treading water near the rope ladder. I motioned her aboard. Quietly, she climbed up on deck. Trader opened his eyes and looked up at her.

"Be right back, honey," she said, and ran below.

Trader closed his eyes again.

It had been my intention to swim up behind him and give him a judo chop, but his outstretched position made him vulnerable to a safer form of attack. Taking a running jump, I launched myself feet first at his stomach, bringing my knees to my chest and snapping them straight again with terrific force just as I landed. The air whooshed out of him, and he was driven deeply under water in a doubled-up position.

I must have caught him in the solar plexus with one heel, temporarily paralyzing him, because when I reversed myself and dove after him to grab his shoulders and push him even deeper, he barely struggled. I forced him down and down until my own lungs were nearly bursting, then reversed again, got my feet against him, and gave a final shove which drove him deeper and shot me toward the surface.

I made it only a microsecond before I would have had to breathe in water myself. Starting under with no air in him, I was sure Trader couldn't possibly survive. But when I recovered my breath and had climbed aboard, I crouched at the rail and studied the water for a good ten minutes just to make absolutely certain. Then I called Peggy from below.

When she came up, her face pale beneath its tan, I said tonelessly, "There's been an accident. I think he had a cramp. I was on deck with my back turned and didn't see him struggling until I happened to glance around. I tried to reach him, but he went under before I got there. I kept diving for nearly an hour in an attempt to spot him, but he must have sunk straight to the bottom. That's my story for the record. Yours is simply that you were below when it happened."

She stared at the gentle swell of water in fascination. "Will he come up?" she whispered.

"Eventually, if something doesn't eat him first, which is more likely. Not for days, probably."

She gave a little shudder. "Let's get away from here."

"We have to stick around for at least an hour," I said. "I spent an hour futilely diving for him, remember? If we head straight on, somebody just might check to see when we left Southwest Point and when we arrived at Nassau. It would look fishy if there weren't enough of a time gap to allow for our hour of waiting around."

"Why say we waited an hour?" she asked. "We'd know after ten minutes he wasn't coming up."

"You're a brand-new bride," I said. "You wouldn't give up hope after ten minutes. We'll do it my way."

"Do we have to kill the time right here?" she asked nervously. "There's no mark on the water where he went down. Run a few miles and throw out the sea anchor again."

With a shrug, I hauled in the sea anchor, pulled up the rope-strung ladder, and went tops to start the engine. Peggy went along with me and stood right next to me, with our arms touching, as I drove the boat through the water at full throttle for about five miles. Then I reduced speed until we were barely making headway, scanned the horizon in all directions to make sure no other vessel was in sight, and finally cut the engine altogether. I went aft, tossed out the sea anchor, and lowered the ladder again, just in case another vessel came along during the next hour and I actually had to start diving.

Peggy had followed me from the pilothouse. She emitted a deep breath of relief and threw herself into my arms, clinging shakily.

We were only about two hours out of Nassau. We arrived about three-thirty p.m.

No one showed the slightest suspicion of our story. As Peggy had surmised, it didn't even occur to the police that it might be a love-triangle murder when they learned she had been a bride for less than a week and she had never seen me until two days after her marriage. Their only reaction was sympathy.

Since we said we had waited in the area for a full hour after Trader went down, they didn't even bother to send ships to look for the missing man. A couple of helicopters scanned the general area for a couple of days in the hope of spotting the floating body, but it was never spotted, and Arden Trader was finally listed as missing at sea, presumed dead.

Since Peggy's secret marriage wasn't revealed to the press until the drowning of the groom was simultaneously announced, both got wide news coverage. But again there wasn't the slightest intimation that it could have been anything but a tragic accident.

Peggy owned a half-dozen villas in various parts of the world, and one of them was at San Juan. When the police at Nassau released us, we continued on to Puerto Rico, where the grieving widow went into seclusion. News reports said that the only people accompanying her to the villa were a female companion and her personal secretary, neither of whose names were reported.

The "female companion" was a middle-aged housekeeper who spoke nothing but Spanish. I, of course, was the personal secretary.

The villa had its own private beach, and we spent an idyllic two months on a sort of premarital honeymoon. Long before it was over, there was no question in my mind about being in love. The physical attraction was just as strong, but that wasn't Peggy's only attraction anymore. I was as ludicrously in love as the hero of some mid-Victorian love novel.

At the end of two months, Peggy thought it safe to emerge back into the world and for us to be quietly married. She had been in correspondence with one of her several lawyers meantime, and the day before the ceremony was to be performed, she presented me with a legal document to sign, a waiver of all rights to her estate except what she voluntarily left me in her will.

"You think I might murder you for your money?" I growled after examining it.

"It's my lawyer's idea," she said apologetically. "While I'm not legally bound to follow my father's request, it was his expressed wish in his will that if I had no heirs, I leave most of my estate to set up a research foundation. If we have children, naturally the bulk of the estate will go to them, and of course I'll see that you're well taken care of. But just suppose I died the day after we married? I have no other living relatives, so you would inherit everything. Would it be fair for my father's dream of a Matthews Foundation to go down the drain?"

"I'm not marrying you for your money," I told her. "If you died the day after we married, I'd probably kill myself, too. But it's not worth arguing about." I signed the document.

The ceremony was performed before a civil judge in San Juan, with our housekeeper and the court clerk as witnesses. Peggy wanted only a plain gold band, and it cost me only twenty-five dollars. The diamond she wore, I discovered, had not been given her by Arden Trader but had been her mother's engagement ring. She said she preferred to continue to wear it instead of having me pick out another.

As in the case of her previous marriage, Peggy didn't want the news released to the press until we had completed a honeymoon cruise so we wouldn't be besieged by reporters at every port of call. I pointed out that she was too well known to escape all publicity, and unless she wanted to pretend deep gloom at each stop, people were bound to guess we were on a honeymoon. She said she didn't plan to withhold the news from friends and acquaintances but was going to request them not to relay it to any reporters, so there was a good chance we could keep the secret from the general public until we completed the cruise.

"It won't be a tragedy if reporters find out," she said. "I just want a chance for us to be alone as long as possible."

For our cruise we decided to complete the circuit of the Caribbean we had already started. This time there would be only two of us aboard, however.

We got as far as the island of Great Inagua when we ran over a floating log in the harbor, broke a propeller shaft, and lost the prop. The spare parts weren't available anywhere on the island, but I knew I wouldn't have any trouble finding them back at our previous stop, Port-de-Paix.

A packet ship plied every other day from Great Inagua to Haiti, then on to the Dominican Republic and finally to Puerto Rico. I checked the schedule and discovered that if I caught the one on Friday, I could catch the return ship from Port-de-Paix to Great Inagua on Saturday.

Peggy knew some people named Jordan on the small island where we were laid up, and as they were having a house party on Friday night, she decided not to accompany me.

I got back with the new propeller shaft and propeller about four o'clock Saturday afternoon. The private boat slips were only about fifty yards from the main dock, and I could see the *Princess II* as we pulled in. A slim feminine figure in a red bikini was on the bow waving to the ship. I doubted that she could make me out at that distance from among the other passengers lining the rail, but I waved back, anyway.

When I lugged my packages aboard the *Princess II*, Peggy was no longer on the bow. She was leaning back into the canvas back rest on one of the air-inflated mats on the afterdeck. A tanned and muscular young man of about twenty-five, wearing white swim trunks, was seated on the stern rail.

As I set down my packages, Peggy said, "Honey, this is Bob Colvin, one of Max and Susie Jordan's house guests. My husband Dan, Bob."

The young man rose, and we shook hands. He inquired how I was, and I said I was glad to meet him.

"Bob was planning to take the Monday packet ship up to Governor's Harbor, then fly from there to Miami," Peggy said. "I told him if he wasn't in a hurry, he might as well leave with us tomorrow and sail all the way home. He can sleep in the pilothouse."

Counting our two months in seclusion at San Juan, our honeymoon had now lasted long enough so that the urgency to be completely alone had abated somewhat for both of us. I don't mean that my love for Peggy had abated. It was just that both of us were ready to emerge from our pink cloud back into the world of people. My only reaction was that it would be nice to have someone to spell me at the wheel from time to time.

"Sure," I said, and knelt beside my wife to give her a kiss.

She kissed me soundly, then forced me to a seated position next to her and pressed my head onto her shoulder. Smiling down into my face, she began to stroke my hair.

With my face in its upturned position, I could look right over her shoulder into the shaving mirror attached to the timber alongside the hatch leading below. By pure accident it was slanted slightly downward to reflect the deck area immediately in front of the inflated mat.

In the mirror I could see Bob Colvin's raised bare foot. Peggy's bare toes were working lasciviously against his and along the sole of his foot.

GABRIEL GARCÍA MÁRQUEZ

(1928–)

Colombian author Gabriel García Márquez has created a body of work that defies categorization. Some of his work may be termed magic realism; much of it has the resonance of fables; all of it is intensely original. Nobel laureate García Márquez admired the work of another Nobel Prize winner in this volume, William Faulkner. Both authors' works grapple with grand emotions and themes grounded in a rich regional foundation: love, pride, power, entrapment, and death. Like Faulkner, García Márquez never set out to be known as a crime writer but has nonetheless written works in which violent death occurs, including "The Last Voyage of the Ghost Ship."

García Márquez was born in Aracataca, Colombia, and attended two colleges before studying law and journalism at the National University of Colombia and at the University of Cartagena. He married, had two sons, and worked as a journalist in Paris, Havana, and New York. Before returning to Colombia in 1982, the same year that he won the Nobel Prize, he had resided in Venezuela, Cuba, the United States, Spain, and Mexico. He has authored novels, short stories, plays, screenplays, journalism, and polemical nonfiction. The Nobel Prize made the world aware of García Márquez as one of the most influential and talented Latin American writers in this century.

"The Last Voyage of the Ghost Ship" demonstrates García Márquez's flair for literary risk-taking. Written in one fantastic sentence, this is the story of a troubled boy's vision of a huge vessel that annually glides by and sinks into "the radiant fishbowl of the bay." This piece is enriched by the author's crafty use of creative repetition, which builds the reader's anticipation of a climactic scene.

The Last Voyage of the Ghost Ship

1972

Now they're going to see who I am, he said to himself in his strong new man's voice, many years after he had first seen the huge ocean liner without lights and without any sound which passed by the village one night like a great uninhabited palace, longer than the whole village and much taller than the steeple of the church, and it sailed by in the darkness toward the colonial city on the other side of the bay that had been fortified against buccaneers, with its old slave port and the rotating light, whose gloomy beams transfigured the village into a lunar encampment of glowing houses and streets of volcanic deserts every fifteen seconds, and even

though at that time he'd been a boy without a man's strong voice but
with his mother's permission to stay very late on the beach to listen to
the wind's night harps, he could still remember, as if still seeing it, how
the liner would disappear when the light of the beacon struck its side and
how it would reappear when the light had passed, so that it was an
intermittent ship sailing along, appearing and disappearing, toward the
mouth of the bay, groping its way like a sleepwalker for the buoys that
marked the harbor channel until something must have gone wrong with
the compass needle, because it headed toward the shoals, ran aground,
broke up, and sank without a single sound, even though a collision
against the reefs like that should have produced a crash of metal and the
explosion of engines that would have frozen with fright the soundest-
sleeping dragons in the prehistoric jungle that began with the last streets
of the village and ended on the other side of the world, so that he himself
thought it was a dream, especially the next day, when he saw the radiant
fishbowl of the bay, the disorder of colors of the Negro shacks on the hills
above the harbor, the schooners of the smugglers from the Guianas load-
ing their cargoes of innocent parrots whose craws were full of diamonds,
he thought, I fell asleep counting the stars and I dreamed about that huge
ship, of course, he was so convinced that he didn't tell anyone nor did
he remember the vision again until the same night on the following March
when he was looking for the flash of dolphins in the sea and what he
found was the illusory liner, gloomy, intermittent, with the same mistaken
direction as the first time, except that then he was so sure he was awake
that he ran to tell his mother and she spent three weeks moaning with
disappointment, because your brain's rotting away from doing so many
things backward, sleeping during the day and going out at night like a
criminal, and since she had to go to the city around that time to get
something comfortable where she could sit and think about her dead
husband, because the rockers on her chair had worn out after eleven years
of widowhood, she took advantage of the occasion and had the boatman
go near the shoals so that her son could see what he really saw in the
glass of the sea, the lovemaking of manta rays in a springtime of sponges,
pink snappers and blue corvinas diving into the other wells of softer waters that were there among the waters, and even the wandering hairs of
victims of drowning in some colonial shipwreck, no trace of sunken liners
or anything like it, and yet he was so pigheaded that his mother promised
to watch with him the next March, absolutely, not knowing that the only
thing absolute in her future now was an easy chair from the days of Sir
Francis Drake which she had bought at an auction in a Turk's store, in
which she sat down to rest that same night, sighing, oh, my poor Olofer-
nos, if you could only see how nice it is to think about you on this velvet
lining and this brocade from the casket of a queen, but the more she
brought back the memory of her dead husband, the more the blood in
her heart bubbled up and turned to chocolate, as if instead of sitting down

she were running, soaked from chills and fevers and her breathing full of earth, until he returned at dawn and found her dead in the easy chair, still warm, but half rotted away as after a snakebite, the same as happened afterward to four other women before the murderous chair was thrown into the sea, far away where it wouldn't bring evil to anyone, because it had been used so much over the centuries that its faculty for giving rest had been used up, and so he had to grow accustomed to his miserable routine of an orphan who was pointed out by everyone as the son of the widow who had brought the throne of misfortune into the village, living not so much from public charity as from the fish he stole out of boats, while his voice was becoming a roar, and not remembering his visions of past times anymore until another night in March when he chanced to look seaward and suddenly, good Lord, there it is, the huge asbestos whale, the behemoth beast, come see it, he shouted madly, come see it, raising such an uproar of dogs' barking and women's panic that even the oldest men remembered the frights of their great-grandfathers and crawled un-der their beds, thinking that William Dampier had come back, but those who ran into the street didn't make the effort to see the unlikely apparatus which at that instant was lost again in the east and raised up in its annual disaster, but they covered him with blows and left him so twisted that it was then he said to himself, drooling with rage, now they're going to see who I am, but he took care not to share his determination with anyone, but spent the whole year with the fixed idea, now they're going to see who I am, waiting for it to be the eve of the apparition once more in order to do what he did, which was steal a boat, cross the bay, and spend the evening waiting for his great moment in the inlets of the slave port, in the human brine of the Caribbean, but so absorbed in his adventure that he didn't stop as he always did in front of the Hindu shops to look at the ivory mandarins carved from the whole tusk of an elephant, nor did he make fun of the Dutch Negroes in their orthopedic velocipedes, nor was he frightened as at other times of the copper-skinned Malayans, who had gone around the world enthralled by the chimera of a secret tavern where they sold roast filets of Brazilian women, because he wasn't aware of anything until night came over him with all the weight of the stars and the jungle exhaled a sweet fragrance of gardenias and rotten salamanders, and there he was, rowing in the stolen boat toward the mouth of the bay, with the lantern out so as not to alert the customs police, idealized every fifteen seconds by the green wing flap of the beacon and turned human once more by the darkness, knowing that he was getting close to the buoys that marked the harbor channel, not only because its oppressive glow was getting more intense, but because the breathing of the water was becoming sad, and he rowed like that, so wrapped up in himself, that he didn't know where the fearful shark's breath that suddenly reached him came from or why the night became dense, as if the stars had suddenly died and it was because the liner was there, with all of its

inconceivable size, Lord, bigger than any other big thing in the world and
darker than any other dark thing on land or sea, three hundred thousand
tons of shark smell passing so close to the boat that he could see the seams
of the steel precipice, without a single light in the infinite portholes, without a sigh from the engines, without a soul, and carrying its own circle
of silence with it, its own dead air, its halted time, its errant sea in which
a whole world of drowned animals floated, and suddenly it all disappeared with the flash of the beacon and for an instant it was the diaph-
anous Caribbean once more, the March night, the everyday air of the
pelicans, so he stayed alone among the buoys, not knowing what to do,
asking himself, startled, if perhaps he wasn't dreaming while he was
awake, not just now but the other times too, but no sooner had he asked
himself than a breath of mystery snuffed out the buoys, from the first to
the last, so that when the light of the beacon passed by the liner appeared
again and now its compasses were out of order, perhaps not even knowing what part of the ocean sea it was in, groping for the invisible channel
but actually heading for the shoals, until he got the overwhelming revelation that that misfortune of the buoys was the last key to the enchant-
ment and he lighted the lantern in the boat, a tiny red light that had no
reason to alarm anyone in the watchtowers but which would be like a
guiding sun for the pilot, because, thanks to it, the liner corrected its
course and passed into the main gate of the channel in a maneuver of
lucky resurrection, and then all the lights went on at the same time so
that the boilers wheezed again, the stars were fixed in their places, and
the animal corpses went to the bottom, and there was a clatter of plates
and a fragrance of laurel sauce in the kitchens, and one could hear the
pulsing of the orchestra on the moon decks and the throbbing of the
arteries of high sea lovers in the shadows of the staterooms, but he still
carried so much leftover rage in him that he would not let himself be
confused by emotion or be frightened by the miracle, but said to himself
with more decision than ever, now they're going to see who I am, the
cowards, now they're going to see, and instead of turning aside so that
the colossal machine would not charge into him, he began to row in front
of it, because now they really are going to see who I am, and he continued
guiding the ship with the lantern until he was so sure of its obedience
that he made it change course from the direction of the docks once more,
took it out of the invisible channel, and led it by the halter as if it were a
sea lamb toward the lights of the sleeping village, a living ship, invul-
nerable to the torches of the beacon, that no longer made it invisible but
made it aluminum every fifteen seconds, and the crosses of the church,
the misery of the houses, the illusion began to stand out, and still the
ocean liner followed behind him, following his will inside of it, the captain
asleep on his heart side, the fighting bulls in the snow of their pantries,
the solitary patient in the infirmary, the orphan water of its cisterns, the
unredeemed pilot who must have mistaken the cliffs for the docks, be-

cause at that instant the great roar of the whistle burst forth, once, and
he was soaked with the downpour of steam that fell on him, again, and
the boat belonging to someone else was on the point of capsizing, and
again, but it was too late, because there were the shells of the shoreline,
the stones of the streets, the doors of the disbelievers, the whole village
illuminated by the lights of the fearsome liner itself, and he barely had
time to get out of the way to make room for the cataclysm, shouting in
the midst of the confusion, there it is, you cowards a second before the
huge steel cask shattered the ground and one could hear the neat destruction of ninety thousand five hundred champagne glasses breaking, one
after the other, from stem to stern, and then the light came out and it was
no longer a March dawn but the noon of a radiant Wednesday, and he
was able to give himself the pleasure of watching the disbelievers as with
open mouths they contemplated the largest ocean liner in this world and
the other aground in front of the church, whiter than anything, twenty
times taller than the steeple and some ninety-seven times longer than the
village, with its name engraved in iron letters, *Haldlcsillag,* and the ancient
and languid waters of the seas of death dripping down its sides.

Translated by Gregory Rabassa

SAHO SASAZAWA
(1930–)

It is impossible to read Saho Sasazawa's "Invitation from the Sea" without remarking on how reminiscent it is, in terms of circumstance and mysterious atmosphere, of Agatha Christie's *And Then There Were None* (1940; originally titled *Ten Little Niggers*, 1939; also *Ten Little Indians*, 1965). Five guests who seem to have no prior connection to one another are invited by an unknown host to a waterside holiday retreat. The invitations are signed only, "The Sea." Sasazawa builds tension among the guests gathered together in a Japanese hotel suite as successfully as Christie and other writers of classic detective novels, who assembled their suspects in country house libraries.

"Invitation from the Sea" represents only one style of writing employed by Sasazawa. According to Frederic Dannay, the Japanese author got his start in mystery writing as a "writer of pure detective stories, though his style was more sensual than intellectual." Sasazawa also wrote "romantic mysteries" before penning works that could be termed hard-boiled, in which the criminal is the protagonist.

Sasazawa was born in Japan's Kanagawa Prefecture in 1930. He worked for a time for the post office. A hospital stay after an accident provided him with the opportunity to undertake extensive reading, after which he took up writing. He published his first story, "The Message in the Dark," at the age of twenty-eight in the December 1958 special issue of *Hoseki (Jewel)*. His first novel, *The Uninvited Guest*, was published two years later. Outside of the detective fiction field, he is known as the author of period novels. His most popular series character is Monjiro Kogarashi, a wandering *ronin*, or sort of freelance samurai of the Edo period. *Ronin* are rarely masterless by choice, but are usually at large because their *daimyo*, or feudal lord, has dismissed them or suffered calamity. *Ronin* are often unkempt, impoverished, itinerant mercenaries. They mask their hunger by ostentatiously sporting toothpicks in their mouths to give the impression that they have just dined well when, in fact, they are starving. Sasazaka's character, Kogarashi, is memorable for using the long toothpick that he carries in his mouth as a weapon when the occasion demands.

"Invitation from the Sea" does not rely on such exotic weapons. Rather, a reporter darts to the truth using a nose for news and a straightforward process of elimination. It is the author's only story to date published in English.

Invitation from the Sea

1978

After reading the short letter, Sadahiko Kogawa figured it must be a new kind of hotel publicity stunt. Then he changed his mind. There was no reason for a newly opened seaside hotel to use such methods on him. He was neither rich nor famous. At thirty-three, he worked for a top-flight entertainment magazine, but only as an assistant editor. Although he was in no financial need, his income scarcely allowed him to satisfy all of his own desires or those of his wife and three children. If the hotel were out for publicity, they would have sent the letter to one of the higher-ups. Judging from the word "Toto" in its name, this must be one of the chain of prestigious Toto hotels, with plenty of capital behind them. If they desired publicity, they would not have to resort to tricks; they could pay whatever cost to advertise.

The letter was written in an elegant hand that set the whole tone:

July 23

Though this may seem abrupt, I have written to extend to you a heartfelt invitation. I should be pleased if you would consent to spend a most enjoyable night in one of the finest suites in the newly opened Toto Kawazu Hotel, at Kawazu Beach, on the eastern shore of the Izu Peninsula. If you accept my invitation, please come to the hotel by five o'clock in the evening, on Saturday, August 1.

Please present this letter at the front desk. You will be guided to the room. I have taken the liberty of including funds for your transportation.

"The Sea"

Along with the invitation, the envelope contained two ten-thousand-yen notes. Perhaps they intended Kogawa to hire a private car. No name or return address was given, only the words "The Sea." The invitation was from the sea.

Kogawa was undecided what to do. If this wasn't a publicity stunt, who had sent it and for what reason? Though it made him uneasy, it was interesting. Maybe it was only a practical joke played by some intimate friend. After all, the person knew his name and address.

Sadahiko Kogawa decided to accept for three reasons. First, he had received the twenty thousand yen. There was no way to return it. If he ignored the invitation, he would have accepted the money without cause.

Second was the natural curiosity of man. The person extending the invitation seemed to be a woman. The letter asked him to spend a summer night in one of the best suites of a brand new hotel. He could not help entertaining the wishful thought of the kind of night only experienced in dreams.

Third was his curiosity as a journalist. A writer who has worked for
years on a weekly magazine specializing in sensational articles comes to
have an abnormal curiosity for everything. He develops a sensitive nose
for secrets.

About a month ago, his nose for news had led him into something
completely unassociated with his work. The editor-in-chief had lectured
him about it. A scandal about a famous singer had come up, and Kogawa
had hurried to check it out at the Shirahama hot-springs resort in Wakayama Prefecture. The singer was supposed to have disappeared because
of a lesbian love affair. While at Shirahama, Kogawa and the cameraman
stayed in the Bokiso Hotel, overlooking the sea. Word had it that the
singer was at Shirahama, but Kogawa was unable to track her down. The
two of them sat in their room drinking until late at night. At about two
in the morning, they heard a commotion outside the window. They were
on the second floor. The lights that burned all night in the garden brightly
illuminated the concrete walkway outside the hotel. Sprawled flat against
the pavement lay a young woman dressed in Western-style clothing. Milling around were several guards and men who likely were hotel employ-
ees.

Kogawa hurried downstairs. He went out through the service entrance
and asked the guard who had found the body, the busboys, and others
about what had happened. He learned that the dead woman was Suzuko
Kume, twenty-five. She had been staying in room 515.

In her handbag, in her room, were found three suicide notes: one to
her parents; one to her younger sister, who was traveling abroad; and one
to her superiors where she worked. They thanked the addressees for all
they'd done and apologized for the trouble her death would cause. She
had decided to kill herself because of an impossible love affair with a man
who was married and had children. The handwriting was identified as
her own.

The window of 515 was open. She must have jumped.

Although her hometown was Kanazawa, in Shirakawa Prefecture, she
had been living with her younger sister in an apartment in Tokyo. The
sister worked for a travel agency that sent some of its personnel out with
tour groups to act as guides. The suicide had taken place while the sister
was in Europe on such a trip.

The hotel log showed that, just before her death, Suzuko Kume had
made an hour-long phone call to her parents in Kanazawa. This seemed
somehow out of keeping with the mood of a person about to commit
suicide.

The suicide notes were in her writing. In her hand she clutched a
handkerchief with the initials SK on it, her own handkerchief. But something warned Kogawa that it was not just plain suicide.

Leaving the alleged lesbian singer up to the cameraman, Kogawa began trying to sniff out the secret behind the young woman's death. After receiving a go-ahead, he went to Kanazawa and talked in detail with Suzuko Kume's parents. Later, he visited the place where she worked and questioned several people there. He learned a few things from them, but nothing that would prove the suicide different from normal. He had, thus, wasted three days on the incident, which brought a scolding from the editor-in-chief.

"Leave stuff like that to the women's magazines. We're in entertainment. If it doesn't concern big stars, it's of no value to us." He repeated this several times.

The unintelligible invitation also had nothing to do with entertainment stars. It might be valueless, but it was impossible to get over habitual insatiable curiosity overnight.

Sadahiko Kogawa had already made up his mind. A week later, at noon on August 1, he faked illness and left the office. He hailed a cab. The driver agreed to drive all the way to Kawazu because Kogawa promised to pay the roundtrip fare.

They traveled along the Tokyo–Nagoya Expressway, then switched to the Atsugi–Odawara bypass. It was a Saturday afternoon and there were long lines of cars at every traffic signal. All along the Hakone Turnpike and the Izu Skyline Drive and finally the shore drive, it was impossible to make any speed because of pleasure drivers. It was sunny and hot outside. Kogawa was happy the taxi was air-conditioned. Looking at the deep blue sea and the clear sky, he found it difficult to believe that so much fuss was being made over the issue of environmental pollution.

After passing several other hot-springs beach resorts, they finally pulled into Kawazu. The undulating green mountainsides seemed to thrust outward into the sea. The town looked cheerful with rows of red and blue roofs. The cream-colored, seven-story Kawazu Hotel was clearly visible halfway up one of the hills. Who could be waiting for him in that building? Why was he invited here? Sadahiko Kogawa was tense as he asked himself these questions.

2

When he presented the letter at the desk, the clerk greeted him politely and called a boy. The clerk seemed almost too polite. This worried Kogawa. It made him think the person who invited him must be very important. Who could it be?

There were many couples and families in the lobby. Children clustered around a large aquarium, admiring tropical fish. The scene seemed to pose no trap. As Kogawa followed the boy into the elevator, he felt sure it was not some kind of trap.

At the fifth floor, they walked down the corridor, thickly carpeted in blue. After several turns, they came to a massive double door with a plaque reading: "VIP Suite." The boy knocked, bowed to Kogawa, then disappeared down the corridor.

Hesitantly, Kogawa touched the doorknob. He was thirty minutes late. He opened the door, stepped inside.

Four people stared at him, seated in the living room. There were two men and two women, unsmiling.

The room was spacious, luxuriously furnished. On the right, a door led to a bedroom; to the left was a Japanese-style room with tatami flooring and a dressing room beyond. At the opposite end, beyond glass windows, was a balcony. The sea lay green-blue beyond. Nearby islands seemed so close one might swim to them. The sky was clear save for light clouds in the direction of Mount Mihara.

Five leather-upholstered chairs were arranged around a large circular table under a chandelier. Four were occupied, one remaining for Kogawa. Making a general greeting, he sat down. He knew none of these people. The chilly mood in the room suggested they were all strangers. Was he in the wrong room?

Presently, three busboys entered with a wagon bearing whisky, sherry, beer. The boys took orders, served drinks, and left without a word. Silence fell again, as everyone sipped drinks.

Across from Kogawa sat a sturdily-built, healthy, refined-appearing gentleman in his mid-fifties. He looked like a company executive. Next to him sat a man of over twenty. His sharp eye and his negative expression concealed his thoughts. Maybe a university student.

To Kogawa's right sat a woman who looked around forty. Dressed tastefully, in expensive clothes with elegant accessories, she was probably the wife of someone with money. Thin, nervous, she gave the impression of being difficult to deal with. Another woman was to Kogawa's left; physically attractive, in her late twenties, with a beautiful face, though heavily made up. Her legs were crossed high and she wiggled the upper one in apparent irritation. Kogawa could barely keep his eyes off the shapely thighs under the short, hiked-up skirt.

By six o'clock, nothing had happened. Kogawa felt anger. It seemed pretty obvious the others had also been invited. The idea of four hosts was absurd. Suddenly brave, Kogawa turned to the younger woman. "Excuse me. But are you here because you received a strange invitation?"

She seemed relieved. "Yes. That's right."

"Any idea who invited us?"

"No. It's weird, really. I didn't even think I'd come. But the letter said something about a very important personal secret. And," she smiled, "there was the forty thousand yen for carfare. I couldn't ignore it."

"Where'd you come from?"

"Nagoya."

She had received twice as much transportation money as he because she had farther to travel.

The older woman spoke up stiffly. "The same thing's true here. I couldn't understand it. Thought I should ignore it. But it said they wanted to discuss a secret about my husband. The envelope contained twenty thousand yen. It scared me, but I came."

She laid an envelope on the table.

"You came from Tokyo?" Kogawa asked.

"Yes." Her tone was cool.

"I came from Yokohama," the executive type said, smiling brightly. "Asked to spend a pleasant day at the beach. I didn't think twice. Crazy about the sea." He placed his invitation on the table.

Turning to the young man who seemed to be a student and who sat with a blank look on his face, he said, "What about you?"

"Same," the young man replied, rather self-derisively.

"Where'd you come from?"

"Matsumoto, Nagano Prefecture."

"What'd your invite say?"

"Stupid seduction stuff about a romantic night awaiting me. It was the stupidity that interested me. Then, too, I'm stupid enough to welcome a chance for a trip when somebody else pays the way." He drained his glass of beer.

It was clear they all had been invited by "The Sea." The invitations varied from person to person to create a situation where the recipient felt compelled to accept. Kogawa had been invited to spend a most enjoyable night. The young man had been told of a romantic night. Both letters were calculated to stimulate male curiosity. To the older man, the invitation offered the more wholesome attraction of a day on the beach.

Such were not the tactics to use with cautious women. They received invitations concerning personal secrets and secrets about a husband. Including the money, it was a strategy designed to inspire insecurity.

Next, everyone introduced himself. The younger woman was Shinobu Komai, secretary of a company president. The older man was, as Kogawa suspected, an executive in a trading firm in Yokohama. His name was Sojuro Koshikawa. The younger man was Shiro Kayama, a student at Shinshu University. The older woman was the wife of the chief surgeon and head of a large Tokyo hospital; her name was Setsuko Kijima.

Why had these five people, who had never seen or heard of each other, been invited here? What could it mean?

Where was the person who invited them?

3

Oshima island began to fade from view. White mists lay along the horizon; the last light of day reflected on treacherously calm waters. The small town seemed prepared for the night. Only the cars on the highway, miniaturized by distance, continued to hurry.

Glancing at his watch with a yawn, Shiro Kayama said, "Seven o'clock." His face was flushed from two beers.

"I figured it might be a practical joke," Shinobu Komai said. She bit her lip. Light from the glittering chandelier fell directly on her.

Setsuko Kijima moved restlessly. "I'm beginning to consider going home." After two glasses of sherry, she appeared red around the eyes.

Sojuro Koshikawa lifted a plump hand. "Let's wait a bit longer. Be patient—see what comes of this." Like Kogawa, he had been steadily sipping whisky-and-water.

Setsuko Kijima was strident. "Why? this is a silly game to make fools of us all. I haven't got time—"

"I don't agree with you, Mrs. Kijima," Koshikawa said, shaking his head, smiling. "I don't believe it's a game."

"Well, what is it, then? We just sit here?"

"You think we've been brought here for no reason?"

"Yes. I do."

"There's got to be a reason. Why bring five complete strangers here, like this? Whoever invited us has already spent over a hundred thousand yen on transportation alone. No. He's serious and has a purpose inviting us here."

"What purpose?"

"I don't know. We'll have to wait and find out."

"He should have appeared at once, then."

"Yeah. But we don't know who he is. There must be some reason behind it all." Koshikawa was no longer smiling as he raised his drink.

Kogawa agreed that it was no mere prank. It was much too elaborate for that. After all, the person who sent the invitations had spent money to summon strangers from Nagoya, Nagano, Yokohama, and Tokyo. But what attracted Kogawa's attention more than anything else was: If the five had been brought together for a purpose, they could not have been chosen at random. He glanced around, said, "I agree with Mr. Koshikawa. This is no simple joke. Not just anyone would do. Only we five received invitations. There has to be a reason."

Koshikawa nodded heavily in approval. "That's right. It had to be us. He knew our names, addresses, ages, and other things. . . ."

Kogawa became a bit tense. He was suddenly realizing the matter was more serious than he'd supposed.

"We know for certain none of us has any connection with the other," Shinobu Komai said, looking insecure and all the more attractive. "What can be the reason for bringing us together?"

Kogawa lit a cigarette. "Maybe what you say is true at first glance. None of us ever met, but there may be some connection—something we're not aware of."

Setsuko Kijima said, "I don't get it."

Kogawa ground his cigarette out in a tray. "Maybe it's something we have in common."

"For instance?" Koshikawa leaned forward intently.

"Oh, place of birth. Or maybe friends. Perhaps we all subscribed to the same magazine years ago."

"Can you think of anything you might have in common with the rest of us?"

"No, frankly."

"We might start by looking for something between you and me. I was born in Kanagawa Prefecture. Finished college in Kanagawa Prefecture. I direct a trading firm, have for thirty-one years. I go abroad every year. I like to swim, play golf, scuba dive—anything between us on that list?"

Kogawa shook his head. "Afraid not."

"Well, we could check the front desk," Koshikawa said. He rose, went to the telephone. After asking a number of questions, he returned, shrugging. "No help. Ten days ago, the rooms were booked in the name of somebody called Nakamura. The following day, a representative of Nakamura showed up. He gave some instructions and paid the bill in cash." Koshikawa sat down again.

"I can't beef about how things are," Kayama said, his eyes sleepy. "I can't go back to Matsumoto now. And I can spend the night free in this hotel."

Turning to the young man, Koshikawa said, "I guess we should look for something in common. You like water sports?"

"In the mountains of Nagano?" Kayama said, closing his eyes.

"A river or lake's just as good. Nothing's as much fun as putting on an aqualung and taking a stroll underwater. *Aqualung*'s really a trade name. In America they call 'em scubas. They were developed as special military equipment during World War II by Colonel Cousteau. Bet he never dreamed scuba diving would become a popular sport. The *aqua* part of *aqualung* is . . ."

"Latin for *water*. And *lung* is English for *lung*."

"Yeah. But it's the lung part that's weak. Its only fault. The amount of time the air in the tank will last is limited. The greater the water pressure, the more air we need to breathe. This means an air tank that ordinarily lasts an hour, lasts only thirty minutes at a depth of ten meters. Twenty minutes at twenty meters. I'm seriously thinking of trying to improve this aspect of the aqualung."

Carried away with enthusiasm, Koshikawa talked on, lighting a pipe, sucking on it after it went out. No one else spoke and he suddenly fell silent, embarrassed.

Shiro Kayama chuckled. The others looked at him. The women seemed hesitant. Kogawa thought for a moment that Kayama was at last ready to reveal himself as the sender of the invitations.

"Everybody's so dense," Kayama said. "It's so simple. Why didn't anyone guess?"

Kogawa said, "You have something?"

Kayama nodded.

"What is it?" Koshikawa asked.

Kayama became serious, looking at them all. "Sojuro Koshikawa, Shinobu Komai, Sadahiko Kogawa, Setsuko Kijima, and Shiro Kayama. Don't you get it?"

No one spoke.

He said, "All five of us have the same initials."

There was a general amazement.

The letters SK.

Then another association with the initials SK struck a note of alarm in the mind of Sadahiko Kogawa.

4

They all sat thinking about the simplicity and undeniable nature of the thing they had in common.

Sojuro Koshikawa asked suddenly, "But why should we all be brought together just because we have the same initials?"

"Must be thousands of people with the same initials," Shinobu Komai said, frowning.

Kogawa was silent. He knew what the initials SK meant. On June 12, at the Bokiso Hotel in Shirahama, Wakayama Prefecture, a young woman had committed suicide. Her name was Suzuko Kume, initials SK. When she died, she had been clutching a handkerchief embroidered with the initials SK. Kogawa had been struck by the letters at the time, since they were his initials, too. When Kayama pointed out the initials as linking the five people in the room, he had recalled Suzuko Kume. It was no coincidence that the person who invited them had selected people with these initials. Something very important related them to each other.

"It's no trick," he said. "It's serious."

They all stared at him.

He went on. "It's true we all have the same initials. But that's only a superficial reason for being here. Something much more important connects us."

"How'd you mean?" Koshikawa wanted to know.

"What we have in common has to do with something we all did in the past. I'm talking about forty days ago. On June 12, we all took a trip to the same place and stayed at the same hotel."

"June 12?"

"Yes. If any of you didn't stay at the Bokiso Hotel, in Shirahama hot springs, that night, please say so."

Kogawa rose and walked to the balcony window. Moths and other insects were thick outside. The room was air-conditioned. Beyond the shore, the sea and sky blended into a vast darkness. He turned to face the room again. They were all staring at nothing. No one denied staying at the Bokiso Hotel that night. Kogawa's guess had been correct.

Shinobu Komai sighed. "How'd you know we all stayed there that night just from the fact that our initials are the same?"

"You probably all recall that, on that night, one of the hotel guests committed suicide by jumping from the window of room 515?"

Kogawa stood behind Koshikawa's chair.

Koshikawa said, "Yes. A young woman."

Kogawa said, "Her name was Suzuko Kume. Initials SK."

"Then why've we been brought here?" Setsuko Kijima said with sudden anger. She was a refined woman, but apparently found it humiliating to be at the mercy of someone else. But she had a point. Why should an unknown person invite them all here just because they happened to stay at a hotel where a young woman committed suicide—just because they had the same initials as that young woman? Kogawa had confidence in his suspected reason. The time he'd thought wasted making inquiries into the history of the young suicide seemed to prove of value. Moving back to his original chair, he remained standing. "I work for a magazine. I'm curious, by nature. At the time of the death of Suzuko Kume, I spent three days making investigations here and there. I probably have more detailed information than any of you. I have an idea about the identity of the person who invited us here." He paused to light a cigarette. They were all watching him.

"Who?" Koshikawa said. "C'mon, who!"

"Probably Suzuko Kume's younger sister. The two of them shared an apartment in Tokyo. But at the time of the suicide, the younger sister was traveling in Europe."

Shinobu Komai looked dissatisfied. "But why should the sister do something like this?"

"They lived together. Probably the sister knew Suzuko Kume better than her parents and certainly better than anyone else. Shortly after Miss Kume's death, the sister returned to Japan and made detailed inquiries. Something about the suicide must've struck her as suspicious."

"Suspicious?" Koshikawa said, loudly crushing ice.

"Yes. Something odd or contradictory to what the sister knew from daily association with Suzuko."

"But—what?"

"We all have the same initials as the dead girl. I'd say something suspicious is connected with those initials."

"You know of any connection?"

"Yes."

"What?"

"At the time of her death Suzuko Kume was clutching a handkerchief bearing the initials SK."

"Well—it was her handkerchief."

"Everybody assumed that. But all handkerchiefs with the same initials don't belong to the same person. What about your handkerchief, Mr. Koshikawa?"

"I don't have initials put on my handkerchiefs."

"There are any number of ways to put on initials. Gothic letters, or even letters made up of flower patterns. Sometimes they're printed on, sometimes embroidered. Some use both initials, some only one. My guess is that Suzuko Kume used only the S, in embroidery. Her younger sister knows this. When she heard her elder sister was holding a handkerchief with the initials SK, she was probably astonished. The handkerchief must have belonged to someone else, not to Suzuko at all."

"Then—it was murder. . . ."

"It'd be odd for a person to hold his own handkerchief at the time of death if suicide were planned. Suzuko Kume didn't jump from that window—she was pushed. To keep from falling, she must've grabbed for the murderer's hand and caught the handkerchief, which she was still holding when she struck the ground."

"Then the murderer and the victim both have the initials SK."

"Not only that, but the murder took place late at night in a hot-springs hotel. As you all know, hotels of that sort close their doors early. There's no going into or exiting from them late at night. This means the murderer not only has a name with the same initials, but was also staying at the same hotel. The younger sister must've gone to the Bokiso Hotel and found out all the names of people with those initials who were there that night. That's how we five were selected."

"She could get our names from registration cards. Addresses, everything."

"Exactly."

"But what's her purpose? She invites us here, but doesn't appear. She can't mean revenge on us all."

"The killer is one of us. She's hoping that, as we talk together, we'll solve the question of the murderer's identity."

Kogawa sat down, feeling tired.

Shinobu Komai still kept up the nervous mannerisms with her leg. She had lowered her eyes, unable to conceal her uneasiness. Shiro Kayama sat with closed eyes, as if he were listening to nothing. Sojuro Koshikawa examined everyone's face eagerly. With stiff shoulders, Setsuko Kijima said spitefully, "What a horrible thing! A murderer right here among us."

5

None of them had a clear alibi. Suzuko Kume's sister must have selected them for that reason. All of them but Kogawa had been alone in single rooms. They could have moved freely about the hotel in the middle of the night. Kogawa had been in a twin room with the cameraman, but this was no proof of innocence. There was nothing to show he had not found a way to keep the cameraman quiet, or that the cameraman might even be his accomplice.

Talking about alibis and lack of motive would not solve the issue. They were all equal in terms of advantages and suspicion. Until the killer was identified, they were all suspects.

"This is really stupid," Kayama said clearly, opening his eyes. He slapped the edge of the table, stood up, and pointed at Kogawa. "It's nothing but your fool imagination. Your guesses. There's nothing as meaningless, boring, and worthless as guesses."

Kogawa kept his voice under control. "Okay. It's my imagination. But it's not without grounds. There's something in what I say."

"You're forgetting the most important thing," Kayama said, scowling.

"What, then?"

"The day after the woman's death, I heard the maids say three suicide notes, in her handwriting, had been found." Kayama stared hard at Kogawa.

Kijima nodded. "I heard that, too." She was assuming the role of Kayama's ally.

"Me, too," Shinobu Komai said.

Kayama was much surer of himself now. "Three suicide notes prove without a doubt that she killed herself. It's irrational to claim the woman was murdered in the face of this kind of evidence."

"Let me ask you this, then," Kogawa said calmly. "Is it possible to say with absolute certainty that a person killed himself because suicide notes were found?"

Kayama shrugged. "I don't understand—"

"Well, even after writing suicide notes, is it impossible that, at the last minute, a person might change his mind about killing himself?"

"Well, I suppose . . ."

"Suzuko Kume was one who did."

"You're talking through your hat again."

"No. It's a fact. Just before she died, Suzuko Kume made a phone call that lasted for an hour, to Kanazawa, her hometown. She spoke with her mother. I met both parents and discussed this with them. Suzuko confessed that she'd come to Shirahama with the intention of killing herself. This shocked her mother, who spent an hour talking and finally succeeded in changing her daughter's mind."

"Maybe she promised her mother to give it up. Then, after thinking it over, she decided to go ahead after all."

"Think about it. She had laughed as she talked with her mother and said suicide was foolish. It takes a little time for a person in that frame of mind to become desperate enough again to die. All the more time for somebody who already initiated suicide plans and then broke 'em off. Only six or seven minutes passed from when she promised her mother and hung up, to when she fell from the window."

This was fact. The hotel telephone log recorded Suzuko Kume's call as ending five minutes after two. The guard had seen her fall from the fifth-story window and had hurried to the spot at eleven or twelve minutes after two. At that time, she had no intention of killing herself. She had not had a chance to dispose of the three suicide notes.

"The killer knew nothing about her original plan to kill herself, the telephone call that changed her mind, or the three suicide notes in her handbag. The murderer must have been happy to learn next day about these coincidences, and about the identical initials. These were the factors that caused the death to be declared suicide."

Kogawa blew a cloud of cigarette smoke at Kayama. Kayama sank into his chair, apparently with nothing more to say. But his next step was to reject the possibility of his having a motive. "I just happened to spend the night at Shirahama hot springs on my way to Wakayama to visit relatives. I'd never seen Suzuko Kume. I have no motive for killing her." His tone was softer now.

"What could be the reason for killing her?" Shinobu Kamai asked, turning timid eyes on Kogawa.

"When it comes to that—" He shook his head, then said, "You ask me, the murderer's a woman." He was blunt.

"What?" Shinobu Komai looked startled.

"How d'you mean?" Setsuko Kijima was shocked, too. She went pale. If the killer was one of the five in the room, and a woman, it had to be either Shinobu Komai or Setsuko Kijima.

Sojuro Koshigawa folded his hands on the table. "Mr. Kogawa, what grounds d'you have for thinking the killer's a woman?"

"Because Suzuko Kume let the person into room 515 without hesitation."

"Maybe the door wasn't locked."

"Think of the time. That late at night, anyone would lock the door as a matter of course."

"Then the murderer knocked?"

"It was no time for casual callers. The murderer must have spoken to Miss Kume and said she had something important to discuss. If the voice'd been that of a man, even without thinking of murder, just natural caution, she would've told the man to wait. She would have arranged a date for the following day, in the lobby, perhaps. She wouldn't have opened the door."

"She opened the door because it was a woman, because there was no reason for caution?"

"Sure."

"That all you think?"

"Nope. There's the handkerchief. In other words, throughout the time in room 515, the killer held a handkerchief. Mr. Koshikawa, we take handkerchiefs out to wipe sweat from our faces, but do men generally go around with handkerchiefs in their hands for no reason?"

"I guess not. They take 'em out when they want to use them."

"You see? But women often use them as accessories. You frequently see women simply hold them in their hands."

"That's right."

"Finally, and most important—the relation between the motive and my belief that the murderer's a woman. Suzuko Kume's reason for wanting to commit suicide was the end of a love affair with a married man with children."

"Not exactly unusual—"

"From what I learned, Miss Kume and the man got along quite nicely until the wife found out and caused a row. This is why they started talking about breaking up, but only three or four days before her death."

"You think the motive's connected with this?"

"Finding out about her husband's young lover made the wife mad enough to kill. Since the breakup had taken place only three or four days earlier, the wife didn't know about it. She thought her husband and the young woman were going on as before. She made up her mind to kill the woman, Suzuko Kume."

Koshikawa asked no more questions. The room was heavy with silence.

Shinobu Komai said loudly, "I'm not married. I don't have a husband. I couldn't have any motive!"

They all looked at her, then slowly turned their eyes toward Setsuko Kijima, who slumped in her chair, shoulders twisting as she sobbed.

"If I'd only known he'd broken off with her. No, if I'd known she had come to Shirahama to kill herself over him. None of this would've happened. He said he was going to Osaka. Then the private detective I hired to follow them told me the woman had gone to Shirahama. I figured they were planning to meet there. I hurried there myself and took a room at the Bokiso." She leaned on the table now, sobbing.

For some time no one spoke.

6

Setsuko Kijima called the police herself and admitted to murder. Two detectives and a policewoman came and took her away.

The remainder of the group ordered late supper. No one had much appetite. Afterward, over whisky, Sojuro Koshikawa said, "Now, I suppose the younger sister of Suzuko Kume has had her wish."

"She must be happy," Kogawa said, imagining the sister as his type of woman.

"A pity the person who invited us still hasn't shown up."

"Maybe we'll see her yet."

"I hope so."

"I'd certainly like to meet a woman who'd do something as crazy as this."

"I agree."

"I have a hunch we'll never get to see her."

"It'd be like her—smart, I mean—not to turn up."

"Let's forget about her. Why not just take what it said on the invitation at face value? It was this beautiful sea that invited us."

"Mr. Koshikawa? You going to spend the night?"

"You bet. I'm going to have a good day on the water tomorrow. Hire a boat and go fishing. Or, maybe diving. How about you?"

"Well, I could."

"Why not? There's room in this suite for lots of people."

"I'm going to spend the night. And I'm going to order anything I want for breakfast. That's why I came all the way from Nagano." Saying this, Shiro Kayama rose and took an erratic line toward the bedroom.

"If you'll excuse me—" Shinobu Komai bowed to Koshikawa and Kogawa and departed. They watched her leave in silence. It wouldn't do to ask a lone young woman to spend the night with three men.

When Shinobu Komai got out of the elevator at the first floor, she was very deeply grateful to Sadahiko Kogawa. She was lucky a man like that had been a member of the group. If he hadn't been there, it would have been more difficult to set a psychological trap for the murderer.

To the man at the desk, she said, "Three people are going to spend the night in the suite. If there's any extra charge, I'll pay now."

"Miss Nakamura, isn't it?" The clerk smiled. "No. We've already been adequately reimbursed."

Shinobu Komai, alias Miss Nakamura, alias Miyoko Kume, left the Kawazu Hotel and walked to the shore. She was not as happy as she thought she would be to have turned the murderer of her sister Suzuko over to the police. Somehow, she felt empty.

Her heart was dark and so was the night sea that spread out before her.

PETER LOVESEY

(1936–)

British author Peter Lovesey dreamed of becoming a great runner but instead won crime and mystery writing competitions with his novels set in the world of odd Victorian sports. Born in Middlesex, England, Lovesey was educated at the University of Reading. He later served as an education officer in the Royal Air Force and was employed by colleges in Essex and London before he entered the writing contest that launched his mystery writing career. Lovesey initially established himself as a writer of period mysteries, building his series around his research into English sports and Victorian police procedure. His best-known sleuths are Sergeant Cribb, Constable Edward Thackeray, and his police superior, Inspector Jowett. These Victorian characters appeared not only in Lovesey's books but in the Sergeant Cribb television series based on the novels and in additional programming that Lovesey and his wife Jacqueline plotted for television.

Lovesey has also written novels in which the fictional storyline is woven into actual historical events, often populating the work with historical characters such as Hollywood's Keystone Cops in *Keystone* (1983), the murderer H. H. Crippen in *The False Inspector Dew* (1982), or Albert, Prince of Wales, in a series of novels launched with *Bertie and the Tinman* (1987). More recently, Lovesey has introduced a new character, Peter Diamond, who heads the Murder Squad in Bath, England. Lovesey continues to produce novels and stories set in the past but has increasingly built an accompanying body of work that proves him equally adroit at plotting contemporary fictional crimes.

Lovesey sees his crime short stories, many of which are collected in *Butchers and Other Stories of Crime* (1985) and *The Crime of Miss Oyster Brown* (1994), as his most accomplished work. Most of these, including "Where Is Thy Sting?," are set in contemporary circumstances that address timeless human foibles and those who take advantage of them. This chilling shoreline story set on the coast of Australia reveals a darker side of Lovesey—and a contemporary author in top form.

Where Is Thy Sting?

1988

The storm had passed, leaving a keen wind that whipped foam off the waves. Heaps of gleaming seaweed were strewn about the beach. Shells, bits of driftwood and a few stranded jellyfish lay where the tide had deposited them. Paul Molloy, bucket in hand, was down there as he was every morning, alone and preoccupied.

His wife Gwynneth stood by the wooden steps that led off the beach through a garden of flowering trees to their property.

"Paul! Breakfast time."

She had to shout it twice more before Paul's damaged brain registered anything. Then he turned and trudged awkwardly towards her.

The stroke last July, a few days before his sixty-first birthday, had turned him into a shambling parody of the fine man he had been. He was left with the physical co-ordination of a small child, except that he was slower. And dumb. The loss of speech was the hardest for Gwynneth to bear. She hated being cut off from his thoughts. He was unable even to write, or draw pictures.

She had to be content with scraps of communication. Each time he came up from the beach he handed her something he had found, a shell or a pebble. She received such gifts as graciously as she had once accepted roses.

They had said at the hospital that she ought to keep talking to him in an adult way, even if he didn't appear to understand. It was a mistake to give up. So she persevered, but inevitably it sounded as if she were addressing a child.

"Darling, what a beautiful shell! Is it for me? Oh, how sweet! I'll take it up to the house and put it on the shelf with all the other treasures you found for me—except that this one must stand in the centre."

She leaned forward to kiss him and made no contact with his face. He had moved his head to look at a gull.

She helped him up the steps and they started the short, laborious trek to the house. They had bought the land, a few miles north of Bundaberg on the Queensland coast, ten years before Paul retired from his Brisbane-based insurance company. As chairman he could have carried on for years more, but he had always promised he would stop at sixty, before he got fat and feeble, as he used to say. They had built themselves this handsome retirement home and installed facilities they felt they would use: swimming pool, jacuzzi, boat-house and tennis court. Only their guests used them now.

"Come on, love, step out quick," she urged Paul. "There's beautiful bacon waiting for you." And tirelessly trying for a spark of interest she added, "Cousin Haydn's still asleep by the look of it. I don't think he'll be joining your walks on the beach. Not before breakfast, anyway. Probably not at all. Doesn't care for the sea, does he?"

Gwynneth encouraged people to stay. She missed real conversation. Cousin Haydn was on a visit from Wales. He was a distant cousin she hadn't met before, but she didn't mind. She'd got to know him when she'd started delving into her family history for something to distract her. Years ago, her father had given her an old Bible with a family tree in the front. She'd brought it up to date. Then she had joined a family history society and learned that a good way of tracking down ancestors was to write to local newspapers in the areas where they had lived. She had managed to get a letter published in a Swansea paper. Haydn had seen it and got in touch. He was an Evans also, and he'd done an immense amount of research. He'd discovered a branch of his family tree that linked up with hers, through Great-Grandfather Hugh Evans of Port Talbot.

Paul shuffled towards the house without even looking up at the drawn curtains.

"Mind you," Gwynneth continued, "I'm not surprised Haydn is used to staying indoors, what with the Welsh weather I remember. I expect he reads the Bible a lot, being a man of the cloth." She checked herself, for she was speaking the obvious again. She pushed open the kitchen door. "Come on, Paul. Just you and me for breakfast, by the look of it."

Cousin Haydn eventually appeared in time for the mid-morning coffee. On the first day after he'd arrived he'd discarded the black suit and dog-collar in favour of a pink tee-shirt. Casual clothes made him look several years younger, say forty-five, but they also revealed what Gwynneth would have called a beer-gut had Haydn not been a minister.

"Feel better for your sleep?" she enquired.

"Infinitely better, thank you, Gwynneth." You couldn't mistake him for an Australian when he opened his mouth. "And most agreeably refreshed by a dip in your pool."

"Oh, you had a swim?"

"Hardly a swim. I was speaking of the small circular pool."

She smiled. "The jacuzzi. Did you find the switch?"

"I was unaware that I needed to find it."

"It works the pumps that make the whirlpool effect. If you didn't switch on, you missed something."

"Then I shall certainly repeat the adventure."

"Paul used to like it. I'm afraid of him slipping now, so he doesn't get in there."

"Pity, if he enjoyed it."

"Perhaps I ought to take the risk. The specialist said he may begin to bring other muscles into use that aren't affected by the stroke, isn't that so, my darling?"

Paul gave no sign of comprehension.

"Does he understand much?" Haydn asked.

"I convince myself that he does, even if he's unable to show it. If you don't mind, I don't really care to talk about him in this way, as if he's not one of us."

Cousin Haydn gave an understanding nod. "Let's talk about something less depressing, then. A definite prospect of improvement. I have good news for you, Gwynneth."

She responded with a murmur that didn't convey much enthusiasm. Sermons in church were one thing. Her kitchen was another place altogether.

It emerged that Haydn's good news wasn't of an evangelical character. "One of my reasons for coming here—apart from following up our fascinating correspondence—is to tell you about a mutual ancestor, Sir Tudor Evans."

"*Sir* Tudor? We had a title in the family?"

"Back in the seventeenth century, yes."

"I don't recall seeing him on my family tree."

Haydn gave the slight smile of one who has a superior grasp of genealogy. "Yours started in the 1780s, if I recall."

"Oh, yes."

"To say that it started then is, of course, misleading. Your eighteenth-century forebears had parents, as did mine, and they, in turn, had parents, and so it goes back, first to Sir Tudor, and ultimately to Adam."

"Never mind Adam. Tell me about Sir Tudor." Gwynneth swung round to Paul, who was sucking his thumb. "Bet you didn't know I came from titled stock, darling."

Haydn said, "A direct line. Planter Evans, they called him. He owned half of Barbados once, according to my research. Made himself a fortune in sugar cane."

"Really? A fortune. What happened to it?"

"Most of it went down with the *Gloriana* in 1683. One of the great tragedies of the sea. He'd sold the plantations to come back to the Land of his Fathers. He was almost home when a great storm blew up in the Bristol Channel and the ship was lost with all hands. Sir Tudor and his wife Eleanor were among those on board."

"How very sad!"

"God rest their souls, yes."

Gwynneth put her hand to her face. "I'm trying to remember. Last year was such a nightmare for us. A lot of things passed right over my head. The *Gloriana*. Isn't that the ship they found—those treasure-hunters? I read about this somewhere."

"It was in all the papers," Haydn confirmed. "I have some of the cuttings with me, in my briefcase."

"I do remember. The divers were bringing up masses of stuff—coins by the bucketful, silverware and the most exquisite jewellery. Oh, how exciting! Can we make a claim?"

Cousin Haydn shook his head. "Out of the question, my dear. One would need to hire lawyers. Besides, it may be too late."

"Why?"

"As I understand it, when treasure is recovered from a wreck around the British coasts, it has to be handed over to the local receiver of wrecks or the customs. The lawful owner then has a year and a day to make a claim. After that, the pieces are sold and the proceeds go to the salvager."

"A year and a day," said Gwynneth. "Oh, Haydn, this is too tantalising. When did those treasure-hunters start bringing up the stuff?"

"Last March."

"Eleven months! There's still time to make a claim. We must do it."

Haydn sighed heavily. "These things can be extremely costly."

"But we'd get it all back if we could prove our right to the treasure."

He put out his hand in a dissenting gesture. "*Your* right, my dear, not mine. My connection is very tenuous, but yours in undeniable. No, I have no personal interest here. Besides, a man of my calling cannot serve God and Mammon."

"Do you really believe I have a claim?"

"The treasure-hunters would dispute that, I'm sure."

"We're talking about millions of pounds, aren't we? Why should I sit back and let them take it all? I need to get hold of some lawyers—and fast."

Haydn coughed. "They charge astronomical fees."

"I know," said Gwynneth. "We can afford it, can't we, Paul?"

Paul made a blowing sound with his lips that probably had no bearing on the matter.

Gwynneth assumed so. "What is it they want—a down payment?"

"A retainer, I think is the expression."

"I can write a cheque tomorrow, if you want. I look after all our personal finances now. There's more than enough in the deposit account. The thing is, how do I find a reliable lawyer?"

Haydn cupped his chin in his hands and looked thoughtful. "I wouldn't go to an Australian firm. Better find someone on the spot. Jones, Heap and Jones of Cardiff are the best in Wales. I'm sure they could take on something like this."

"But is there time? We're almost into March now."

"It is rather urgent," Haydn agreed. "Look, I don't mind cutting my holiday short by a few days. If I got back to Wales at the weekend I could see them on Monday."

"I couldn't ask you to do that," said Gwynneth in a tone that betrayed the opposite.

"No trouble," said Haydn breezily.

"You're an angel. Would they accept a cheque in Australian pounds?"

"That might be difficult, but it's easily got around. Travellers' cheques are the thing. I use them all the time. In fact, if you're serious about this . . ."

"Oh, yes."

". . . you could buy sterling travellers' cheques in my name and I could pay the retainer for you."

"Would you really do that for me?"

"Anything to be of service."

She shivered with pleasure. "And now, if you've got them nearby, I'd love to have ten minutes with those press cuttings."

He left them with her, and she read them through several times during the afternoon, when she was alone in her room and Paul had gone for one of his walks along the beach. Three pages cut from a colour supplement had stunning pictures of the finds. She so adored the ruby necklace and the gold bracelets that she thought she would refuse to sell them. Cousin Haydn had also given her a much more detailed family tree than she had seen before. It proved beyond doubt that she was the only direct descendant of Sir Tudor Evans.

Was it all too good to be true?

One or two doubts crept into her mind later that afternoon. Presumably the treasure-hunters had invested heavily in ships, divers and equipment. They must have been confident that anything they brought up would belong to them. Maybe her claim wasn't valid under the law. She wondered also whether Cousin Haydn's research was entirely accurate. She didn't question his good faith—how could one in the circumstances?—but she knew from her own humble diggings in family history that it was all too easy to confuse one Evans with another.

On the other hand, she told herself, that's what I'm hiring the lawyers to find out. It's their business to establish whether my claim is lawful.

There was an unsettling incident towards evening. She walked down to the beach to collect Paul. The stretch where he liked to wander was never particularly crowded, even at weekends, and she soon spotted him kneeling on the sand. This time he didn't need calling. He got up, collected his bucket and tottered towards her.

Automatically she held out her hand for the gift he had chosen for her. He peered into the bucket and picked something out and placed it on her open palm.

A dead wasp.

She almost snatched her hand away and let the thing drop. She was glad she didn't, because it was obvious that he'd saved it for her and she would have hated to hurt his feelings.

She said, "Oh, a little wasp. Thank you, darling. So thoughtful. We'll take it home and put it with all my pretty pebbles and shells, shall we?"

She took a paper tissue from her pocket and folded the tiny corpse carefully between the layers. In the house she unwrapped it and made a space on the shelf among the shells and stones.

"There." She turned and smiled at Paul.

He put his thumb on the wasp and squashed it.

"Darling!"

The small act of violence shocked Gwynneth. She found herself quite stupidly reacting as if something precious had been destroyed. "You shouldn't have done that, Paul. You gave it to me. I treasure whatever you give me. You know that."

He shuffled out of the room.

That evening over the meal she told Cousin Haydn about the incident, once again breaking her own rule and discussing Paul while he was sitting with them. "I keep wondering if he meant anything by it," she said. "It's so unlike him."

"If you want my opinion," said Haydn, "he showed some intelligence. You don't want a wasp in the house, dead or alive. As a matter of fact I've got quite a phobia about them. It's one of the reasons why I avoid the beach. You can't sit for long on any beach without being troubled by them."

"Perhaps you were stung once?"

"No, I've managed to avoid them, but one of my uncles was killed by one."

"Killed by a wasp?"

"He was only forty-four at the time. It happened on the front at Aberystwyth. He was stung here, on the right temple. His face went bright red and he fell down on the shingle. My aunt ran for a doctor, but all he could do was confirm that uncle was dead."

Clearly the tragedy had made a profound impression on Haydn. His account of the incident, spoken in simple language instead of his usual florid style, carried conviction.

"Dreadful. It must have been a rare case."

"Not so uncommon as you'd think. I tell you, Gwynneth, the wasp is one of God's creatures I studiously avoid at all times." He turned to Paul and for the first time addressed him directly, trying to end on a less grave note. "So I say more power to your thumb, boyo."

Paul looked at him blankly.

Towards the end of the meal Haydn announced that he would be leaving in the morning. "I telephoned the airport. I am advised I can get something called a standby. They say it's better before the weekend, so I'm leaving tomorrow."

"*Tomorrow?*" said Gwynneth, her voice pitched high in alarm. "But you can't. We haven't bought those travellers' cheques."

"That's all right, my dear. There's a place to purchase them at the airport. All you need to do is write me a cheque. In fact you could write it now in case we forget in the morning."

"How much?"

"I don't know. I'm not too conversant with the scale of fees lawyers charge these days. Are you sure you want to get involved in expense?"

"Absolutely. If I have no right to make a claim, they'll let me know, won't they?"

"I'll let you know myself, my dear. How much can you spare without running up an overdraft? It's probably better for me to take more, rather than less."

She wrote him a cheque for ten thousand Australian pounds.

"Then if you will excuse me, I shall go and pack my things and have a quiet hour before bedtime."

"Would you like an early breakfast tomorrow?"

He smiled. "Early by my standards, yes. Say about eight? That gives me ample time to do something I promised—try the jacuzzi with the switch on. Goodnight and God bless you, my dear. And you, Paul, old fellow."

Gwynneth slept fitfully. At one stage in the night she noticed that Paul had his eyes open. She found his hand and gripped it tightly and talked to him as if he understood. "I keep wondering if I've done the right thing, giving Haydn that cheque. It's not as if I don't trust him—I mean, you've got to trust a man of God, haven't you? I just wonder if you would have done what I did, my darling, giving him the cheque, I mean, and somehow I don't think so. In fact I ask myself if you were trying to tell me something when you gave me the wasp. It was such an unusual thing for you to do. Then squashing it like that."

She must have drifted off soon after because when she next opened her eyes the grey light of dawn was picking out the edges of the curtains. She sighed and turned towards Paul, but his side of the bed was empty. He must have gone down to the beach already.

She showered and dressed soon after, wanting to make an early start on cooking the breakfast. She would get everything ready first, she decided, and then fetch Paul from the beach before she started the cooking. However, this was a morning of surprises.

For some unfathomable reason Paul had already come up from the beach without being called. He was seated in his usual place in the kitchen.

"Paul! You gave me quite a shock," Gwynneth told him. "What is it? Are you extra hungry this morning, or something? I'll get this started presently. Would you like some bread while you're waiting? Better give Cousin Haydn a call first and make sure he's awake."

It crossed her mind as she went to tap on Haydn's door that Paul hadn't brought her anything from the beach. She wondered if she'd hurt his feelings by talking about the wasp as she had.

She didn't like knocking on Haydn's door in case she was interrupting his morning prayers, but it had to be done this morning in case he overslept.

He answered her call. "Thank you. Is there time for me to sample the jacuzzi?"

"Of course. Shall we say twenty minutes?"

"That should be ample."

She returned to the kitchen and made a sandwich for Paul. The bucket he always took to the beach was beside him. Without being too obvious about it, Gwynneth glanced inside to see if the customary gift of a shell or a pebble was there. It was silly, but she was feeling quite neglected.

Empty.

She said nothing about it. Simply busied herself setting the table for breakfast. Presently she started heating the frying pan.

Fifteen minutes later when everything was cooked and waiting in the oven, Haydn had not appeared.

"He's really enjoying that jacuzzi," she told Paul. "We'd better start, I think."

They finished.

"I'd better go and see," she said.

When she went to the door, the leg of Paul's chair was jammed against it, preventing her from opening it. "Do you mind, darling? I can't get out."

He made no move.

"Maybe you're right," Gwynneth said, always willing to assume that Paul's behaviour was deliberate and intelligent. "I shouldn't fuss. It won't spoil for being left a few minutes more."

She allowed another quarter of an hour to pass. "Do you think something's happened to him? I'd better go and see, really I had. Come on, dear. Let me through."

As she took Paul by the arm and helped him to his feet he reached out and drew her towards him, pressing his face against hers. She was surprised and delighted. He hadn't embraced her once since the stroke. She turned her face and kissed him before going to find Cousin Haydn.

Haydn was lying face down on the tile surround of the jacuzzi, which was churning noisily. He was wearing black swimming-trunks. He didn't move when she spoke his name.

"I think he may be dead," she told the girl who took the emergency call.

The girl told her to try the kiss of life. An ambulance was on its way.

Gwynneth was still on her knees trying to breathe life into Cousin Haydn when the police arrived. They had come straight round the back of the house.

"Let's have a look, lady." After a moment the sergeant said, "He's gone—no question. Who is he—your husband?"

She explained about Cousin Haydn.

"This is where you found him?"

"Well, yes. Was it an electric shock, do you think?"

"You tell me, lady. Was the jacuzzi on when you found him?"

"Yes." Gwynneth suddenly realised that it was no longer running.

Paul must have switched it off while she was phoning for help. She didn't want Paul brought into this. "I don't know. I may be mistaken about that."

"You see, there could be a fault," the sergeant speculated. "We'll get it checked. Is your husband about?"

"He was." She called Paul's name. "He must have gone down to the beach. That's where he goes." She told them about the stroke.

More policemen arrived, some in plain clothes. One introduced himself as Detective Inspector Perry. He talked to Gwynneth several times in the next two hours. He went into Cousin Haydn's room and opened the suitcase he had packed for the flight home.

"You say you knew this man as Haydn Evans, your cousin from Wales?"

"That's who he was."

"A distant cousin?"

Gwynneth didn't care for his grin. "I can show you the family tree if you like."

"No need for that, Mrs. Molloy. His luggage is stuffed with family trees, all as bogus as his Welsh accent. He wasn't a minister of any church or chapel. His name was Brown. Michael Herbert Brown. An English con-man we've been after for months. He was getting too well-known to Scotland Yard, so he came out to Queensland this summer. Been stinging people for thousands with the treasure-hunting story. Here's your cheque. Lucky escape, I'd say."

They finally took the body away in an ambulance.

Detective Inspector Perry phoned late in the afternoon. "Just thought I'd let you know that your jacuzzi is safe to use, Mrs. Molloy. There's no electrical fault. I have the pathologist's report and I can tell you that Brown was not electrocuted."

"What killed him, then?"

He laughed. "Sort of appropriate. It was a sting."

Gwynneth frowned and put her hand to her throat as she recalled what Cousin Haydn had told her. "A sting from a wasp?"

"In a manner of speaking." There was amusement in his voice. "Not the wasp you had in mind."

"I don't understand."

"No mystery in it, Mrs. Molloy. A sea-wasp got him. You know what a sea-wasp is?"

She knew. Everyone on the coast knew. "A jelly-fish. An extremely poisonous jelly-fish."

"Right, a killer."

"But Haydn didn't swim in the sea. He kept off the beach."

"That explains it, then."

"How?"

"He wouldn't have known about the sea-wasps. That storm washed quite a number on to the beaches. Looks as if Brown decided to take one look at the sea before he left this morning. He'd put on his swimming gear—we know that—and he must have waded in. Didn't need to go far. There were sea-wasps stranded in the shallows. You and I know how deadly they are, but I reckon an Englishman wouldn't. He got bitten, staggered back to the house and collapsed beside the jacuzzi."

"I see." She knew it was nonsense.

"Try and remember, Mrs. Molloy. Did you see him walk down to the beach?"

"I was cooking breakfast."

"Pity. Where was your husband?"

"Paul?" She glanced over at Paul, now sitting in his usual armchair with his arms around his bucket. "He was with me in the kitchen." She was about to add that Paul had come up from the beach, but the inspector was already on to other possibilities.

"Maybe someone else saw Brown on the beach. I believe it's pretty deserted at that time."

"Yes."

"Be useful to have a witness for the inquest. All right, I heard what you said about him normally keeping off the beach, but it's a fact that he died from a sea-wasp sting. That's been established."

"I'm not questioning it."

"I ask you, Mrs. Molloy, how else could it have happened? There's only one other possibility I can think of. How could a jelly-fish get into a jacuzzi, for Christ's sake?"

EDWARD D. HOCH
(1930–)

Edward Dentinger Hoch has said, "I always have my ears and eyes open for story possibilities, especially looking for odd and unusual facts." Hoch's ability to see life in terms of story ideas has made him a rare bird indeed: a writer who makes his living largely from writing short fiction. His publication of nearly 800 short stories is especially remarkable considering that this was accomplished during four decades when magazine markets were folding. At a time when most other writers of crime, mystery, adventure, westerns, fantasy, and science fiction—all genres that Hoch has explored—turned to the more healthy paperback or hardcover novel markets, Hoch continued to produce short stories of reliable quality that gained him recognition as "the most important post-World War II writer of mystery and detective short stories" (*Critical Survey of Mystery and Detective Fiction*, edited by Frank N. Magill). In fact, so steady is Hoch's output that *Ellery Queen Mystery Magazine* has run a story by Hoch in every issue of the magazine from 1973 to the present. With the exception of two stories published in 1992, they were all newly written.

Born in Rochester, New York, Hoch began writing detective stories as a teenager. He continued to write while attending the University of Rochester, while working at the Rochester Public Library, and through two years in the U.S. Army. He then went to New York City in search of a position in publishing but ended up working in shipments and accounts for Pocket Books, hardly the editorial work that he sought. After one year, he returned to Rochester, where he secured a position in advertising and public relations, all the while still turning out short stories. Finally, in December of 1955, when he was twenty-five years old, he broke into print with "Village of the Dead," published in the pulp magazine *Famous Detective*. During the next two years he published twenty-two stories. Over the next forty years, he created twenty-five series characters, writing under eight pseudonyms in addition to his own name. He also became a highly respected anthologist and wrote five novels. He became a full-time writer in 1968, after winning an Edgar Allan Poe Award for his story "The Oblong Room."

"The Theft of the Bingo Card" exemplifies Hoch's flair for finding a story possibility in his own experience. Hoch says that as an invited guest on a mystery cruise on the Holland America Line, he learned that bingo cards were provided in the lifeboats. "The idea of sitting in a lifeboat playing bingo while your ship sinks or you wait to be rescued was so bizarre to me that I had to use it in a story," Hoch recalled, but, as this story proves, he found other mysterious possibilities in the use of a bingo card.

The Theft of the Bingo Card

1990

Some of the most pleasant hours of Nick Velvet's life had been spent sailing with Gloria on Long Island Sound, and that was why he finally agreed to her suggestion that they escape the bitter February cold with a week-long cruise in the Caribbean. The giant cruise ships that traveled the southern routes were nothing like the small yacht he guided through the waters of the Sound, but he thought it was the sort of vacation he could be comfortable with.

"We'll have fun," Gloria said. "And you'll be away from the telephone for once. I won't have to worry about our plans being disrupted by some client wanting you to steal the wig off a mannequin or—"

"That didn't disrupt any of our plans," Nick reminded her. "You're beginning to sound like a wife."

"Don't I have a right, after all these years?"

"We'll go to the Caribbean," he agreed. "I'll leave the travel arrangements to you."

They flew to Fort Lauderdale early on a Saturday morning, leaving behind the snow-dusted expressways of New York and Connecticut. The temperature was seventy-nine when they landed and Nick could feel the warmth begin to thaw out his bones. Their first view of the cruise ship *Antilles* was impressive, and Nick began to understand how someone aboard such a ship could relax and forget the everyday world.

When they were allowed aboard, they found that their luggage had already been delivered to their stateroom. They were on the upper promenade deck, the only one with an outside deck running all the way around the ship. Already, through their stateroom windows, they could see passengers exploring the ship, strolling back and forth as a small band played appropriate music for the sailing.

"How many passengers are on board, Nicky?" Gloria asked as she started to unpack, frowning when she saw his kit of special tools.

"More than twelve hundred, and another five hundred crew members. It's a big ship."

"And we don't know a single one of them. Nothing for you to steal."

"I hope not," Nick said with a laugh. "I didn't come here to meet old friends, Gloria, or to work. Those tools are just force of habit."

The cruise ship had barely left the dock when the loudspeaker blared an announcement that a mandatory lifeboat drill would be held at 5:30 that afternoon. The lifeboat stations were on their deck, and Nick and Gloria helped each other into the bright-orange life jackets that made them bulge incongruously before joining the others at their boat station, number seven.

The boat deck was just above the upper promenade deck, and the oversized lifeboats and ship's tenders hung there on sturdy ropes, waiting to be lowered. Some of the deck stewards called the roll to make certain all passengers were present, then went among them checking and tightening their life jackets. An Englishwoman standing next to Nick made a face as the steward reached around her to retie the jacket.

"What a waste of time!" she told Nick. "I doubt if we'll hit an iceberg in the Caribbean."

She was a slender, good-looking woman in her thirties who managed to wear the unflattering life jacket with a certain style. "Is this your first cruise?" Nick asked her.

"My first for pleasure. We came over on the *QE II* once because Herbert hates to fly. This is my husband, Herbert Black. I'm Marnie Black."

"Nick Velvet. Pleased to meet you." The two men shook hands awkwardly. Black was a grim-faced man, obviously resigned to letting his wife do most of the talking. He was a bit older, probably into his mid-forties, with a stocky build. "I do fly now," he clarified with the sort of deep British accent Nick had always admired. "I decided if I were to be ill, five hours was preferable to five days."

"Do you get seasick?"

"Not any more. The medication they have now is truly—"

He was interrupted by a booming voice over the loudspeakers announcing that several of the lifeboats would be lowered to give the passengers an understanding of them. "All lifeboats and tenders are motor-driven, and equipped with signal flares, radios, bottled water, bingo cards—"

At Nick's side, Marnie Black laughed. "Can you imagine bobbing about in the middle of the Atlantic playing bingo?"

"It's probably meant to keep people calm," Gloria suggested.

"Well, I wouldn't stay calm for long in an open boat. At least the tenders are closed in."

The lifeboat drill came to an end and the passengers scattered. A ship's photographer was busily taking pictures of groups in their awkward attire, and Nick was certain the pictures would be on sale soon, along with those taken when they'd boarded the ship. "I hope we don't need to wear those again," he grumbled as he stowed the jackets away in the closet. "What's next on the agenda?"

"We're in the second seating for dinner," Gloria told him. "That's at eight-fifteen. That leaves us plenty of time to look around the ship."

Nick was getting used to the slight vibration of the engines. They'd be at sea for forty-eight hours until the ship docked late Monday afternoon in Puerto Rico. It wasn't the same as cruising on his yacht, but he was beginning to like it. He and Gloria went down the hall from their state-room to a cocktail lounge that overlooked a dance floor and stage on the deck below. A pre-dinner party was in progress for a group of fifty or so men and women, apparently sales representatives for a computer firm. Nick and Gloria stood at the railing for a few moments looking down at the group. Suddenly she tugged on his sleeve. *"What's that?"*

Her attention had been attracted by a slim man with dark hat and a moustache who had appeared suddenly on the stage in front of the audience. He took two or three steps forward and then collapsed. There was a knife buried deep in the center of his back. A few people in the crowd screamed when they saw him. "Get the ship's doctor!" someone shouted, and a man immediately came forward to examine the body.

"He's dead," he announced in a voice that was a little too loud.

Nick began to doubt what he was seeing. "I think it's a game," he told Gloria. "One of these mystery-party things where the guests try to solve a murder."

"But that knife—"

"There's blood all over the back of his shirt, but the stain isn't spreading. It looks more as if it was painted on. Let's go down and see."

They hurried down the stairs to the promenade deck, just in time to intercept the doctor as he was leaving. "Are you really the ship's doctor?" Nick asked.

"Oh, yes—Dr. William Kites from Omaha," the man said with a slight smile.

"And was that a real murder?"

The smile became a chuckle. "No, no. These people are top sales reps from all over the country. They're being rewarded with this cruise, and the company threw in a mystery game for them to solve. It adds to the fun."

"Who's the man with the knife in his back?"

"Well, that depends. To the group he's an industrial spy from a rival company. In actuality, he's a fellow named Simon Franz, one of the dancers in our nightly cabaret."

"You're not going to help solve the mystery?" Nick asked Kites as some husky crewmen carried off the victim.

"No, they just wanted me to examine the corpse and declare him dead. I was glad to do that."

"We've got an hour before dinner," Nick said. "Would you care to join us for a drink?"

Kites smiled. "I wouldn't mind that."

They found a lounge decorated with a large white statue of King Neptune and ordered cocktails. "Is this a permanent job for you?" Gloria asked the doctor.

"No, I'm on board only for three weeks. That's three round-trip cruises to the islands. Then someone else takes over. It's good duty, though. Most of the time it's simply a vacation, with little call for my services unless the seas get rough."

He was a jovial, friendly man and they spent an enjoyable time with him before dinner. Finally, when the steward's ringing of the chimes signaled them, they went down to the dining room. Their tables weren't far apart and Nick and Gloria were facing the one where the doctor sat with some other ship's officers.

"And there's the couple we met on deck," Gloria said. "The Blacks."

Nick half turned in his chair to see them seated at a large table toward the center of the vast dining room. Their own table was only for four, and the other couple were an older man and woman from Seattle who informed Nick and Gloria they'd been given the trip as a forty-fifth anniversary present from their three children. While Nick was glancing about the room, he saw one of the dinner captains stride quickly to Dr. Kites's side and whisper something to him. Kites was on his feet at once, following the man. "Excuse me," Nick told Gloria, "I'll be right back."

There was no reason to suppose that Dr. Kites's sudden errand concerned him in any way, but Nick had always had an innate curiosity that sometimes got him into trouble. This time it led him to the cramped backstage area away from where he'd seen the men lug the body of the murder-game victim. There he found three or four crew members standing around, looking glum. Nick hesitated, and almost at once Dr. Kites reappeared through a doorway with the ship's officer. The group spoke in low voices and then Kites headed back toward the dining room.

"What happened?" Nick asked, falling in step beside him.

"It's that man, Simon Franz—the one who was the murder victim in the game earlier. He's dead."

"*Dead?* What killed him?"

"I'm not exactly certain. There are needle marks on his arm. It could have been a drug overdose. We'll want to keep this quiet, of course. Please don't tell any of the other passengers . . ."

Nick wasn't a detective, and the death of Simon Franz meant little to him. When he told Gloria about it later, she speculated about whether one of the mystery-game players had taken the role of murderer seriously.

"Did anyone see Franz alive after they carried him out this afternoon?" she asked.

"Apparently not. If an injection killed him, I suppose it might have been administered while he was being carried out, or later. Or maybe it was an accidental drug overdose. Things like that happen."

"I'd hate to think the crew is high on drugs."

"The crew is mainly Indonesian and Filipino. Franz was a dancer with the troupe hired to do the shows. He had no connection with the crew."

"I don't know," Gloria said as she climbed into bed. "It still makes me uneasy. I don't think I'll sleep a wink."

Nick was surprised at how well they slept, lulled by the gentle move-

ment of the ship. In the morning they took a few turns around the deck
before breakfast and spent the rest of the morning relaxing around the
pool.

At the buffet lunch, Nick found himself in line behind Marnie Black,
who turned to him with a conspiratorial whisper and asked, "Did you
hear that someone was killed on the ship last night? One of the performers
in the lounge show."

"Really?"

"They say the police will be meeting the ship in San Juan tomorrow."

Word of the death was obviously spreading. As Nick told Gloria about
his exchange with Marnie Black, she said, "There's a woman watching
you from that table to your left. One of your many admirers, I suppose."

He waited a moment and then casually glanced in that direction. The
woman was dark-haired and a bit overweight, with an attractive face.
Nick's eye was caught by the glitter of diamonds on her fingers and an
expensive-looking bracelet watch on her left wrist. "I have no idea who
she is," he told Gloria.

But he was soon to find out. She approached him as they were leaving
the dining room and asked, "Aren't you Nick Velvet?"

"Yes, I am."

"You helped a friend of mine once. I wonder if I could speak with
you privately."

"I'm—"

"I want to hire you." She spoke intently, lowering her voice.

"I'm on vacation," he told her, watching Gloria's back as she kept on
walking. Down the hall a bit, she stopped to study the photographs of
the passengers that had been taken the previous day.

"What's your usual fee?" the woman asked.

"Thirty thousand," Nick told her, raising it by five thousand because
he didn't want the job.

"I'll pay you forty." Other people were coming out of the dining room
behind them and she was forced to cut their conversation short. "Meet
me at the bingo game this afternoon."

She hurried away and Nick walked on to join Gloria. "Have you
found our picture?"

"Right here. It's terrible of me."

"No, it isn't. Let's order one."

"Who was your girl friend?"

Nick grinned. "Jealous?"

"I told you she was watching you while we ate. What did she want?"

"To hire me."

"Nicky, we're on vacation!"

"I told her that."

"Good! What are we going to do this afternoon?"

"How about some bingo?" Nick suggested.

On the way to the lounge where the bingo game was held each afternoon, Nick and Gloria encountered Dr. Kites again. Nick took him aside and asked, "Have you determined anything about that death last evening? Rumors are spreading that he was murdered."

Kites looked uncomfortable. "As near as I can tell, death was caused by an overdose of cocaine. Whether self-administered or not, I have no way of knowing."

"I thought cocaine was inhaled."

"Usually it is, but some addicts prefer to inject it." He broke off the conversation and moved away. "Good to see you again, Mr. Velvet."

Nick rejoined Gloria and they continued into the lounge where the bingo game was about to begin. He bought just one card for each of them because he didn't intend to stay long. The cards had slides across each number, which could be moved with the finger as that number was called. "That's neat," Gloria decided, working the slides. "You don't need those old plastic markers."

"When's the last time you played bingo?" Nick asked her.

"About twenty-five years ago, when I was in high school."

Herbert and Marnie Black were at one of the tables and motioned for Gloria and Nick to join them. The British couple had three cards each and obviously took their bingo seriously. "They have a game called the snow-ball," Marnie explained enthusiastically. "You win a big prize if you cover all your numbers. If nobody gets it, the prize is added to the following day's jackpot."

Nick covered his free-play square in the center of the card and waited for the first number to be called.

"G-49," a voice called out over the loudspeaker. The game had begun.

Almost at once Nick spotted the dark-haired woman who had accosted him earlier. She was standing near the windows, seemingly more intent on the sea outside than on the bingo game. He excused himself, passing his card to Gloria to play.

"I'm glad you decided to come, Mr. Velvet," the woman said, turning from the window.

"I didn't catch your name earlier."

"Dolores Franz."

Nick frowned. "Wasn't Franz the name—?"

"Simon Franz was my husband, but that needn't concern you. I will pay you forty thousand dollars in cash to steal a bingo card."

Nick let his gaze take in the room. "One of those?"

"Just like those, but it's in one of the lifeboats at the moment."

"Oh? Which one?"

"Sorry, I don't know. As you may have noticed, the bingo cards are numbered in the upper left-hand corner. I want card number 253."

"How do I get in the lifeboats?"

"That's what I'm paying you for. I need the card by Wednesday evening, when we leave St. Thomas."

"I'll need ten thousand as a down payment."

"It will be delivered to your room this evening."

"You're serious about this, aren't you?"

"I certainly am."

From across the lounge came the triumphant cry of *"Bingo!"* There were groans from the other players as a white-haired woman hurried forward with her card to claim the prize. "The word is your husband died from a cocaine overdose," Nick said.

"Simon didn't do drugs. He was murdered."

"Who by?"

"Someone who wanted to keep him from getting that bingo card."

"What makes it so valuable?"

"Just find it," she said, "and deliver it to me."

That night when he and Gloria returned to their stateroom after dinner, there was a small parcel wrapped in coarse brown paper resting on the bed. Nick carefully opened one end and counted out the ten thousand dollars in fifty-dollar bills.

While Gloria relaxed by the ship's pool, Nick spent part of Monday afternoon strolling the upper promenade deck, trying to come up with a plan for locating the bingo card. There were fourteen lifeboats in all, counting the ship's tenders—larger enclosed craft used to ferry passengers to the dock when shallow waters kept the ship anchored out in the harbor. The lifeboats were secured to mooring posts on the boat deck and were lowered when needed. The only way to gain access would be to lower each of them in turn until they were level with the upper promenade deck and could be boarded. Surely that was an impossibility. Nick was certain an alarm would sound somewhere as soon as the first boat was lowered, and the odds were only one in fourteen that the first boat would be the one he wanted.

"Getting your daily workout?" someone asked.

Nick saw it was the ship's doctor, who'd come up beside him. "I was just looking at the lifeboats, Dr. Kites. Is it true they keep a set of bingo cards on each boat?"

"The ships on this line do. If you have a hundred panicky people in a lifeboat in the middle of the Atlantic Ocean, you need to keep them occupied with something until help arrives. These days, it would likely only be a matter of hours, but lives can be lost in a matter of minutes."

"Still, the idea *is* a bit bizarre."

William Kites lowered his voice. "Here comes Mr. Perkins, the organizer of the murder game."

Perkins was a bright-looking man around fifty, with eyeglasses and a receding hairline. Nick remembered seeing him the previous night during the beginning of the murder game, when Simon Franz had been playing the victim he was soon to become in reality. "Dr. Kites," Perkins said.

"Hello, Mr. Perkins. How's the mystery game going?"

"Fine, just fine. But I've been hearing stories that the chap who played our victim is really dead. Can that be true?"

"Mr. Franz did pass away, but I can assure you it wasn't related to your game."

"Was he—murdered?"

"No, it seems to have been a natural death. But the authorities in San Juan will perform an autopsy."

"In my brief dealing with him, he was most friendly and cooperative. I'm sorry to hear of his death."

Perkins nodded slightly to Nick and continued on his way around the deck. "What about Franz?" Nick asked the doctor. "Did he have any family on board? A wife, perhaps?"

Kites shot him a questioning glance. "Not that I've heard. He was with a troupe of dancers hired out of Miami."

"Has there been any trouble with drugs aboard ship?"

"No, we have to be very careful of that. When we return to Florida, the Customs agents go over everything. What are you, a detective or something?"

"Hardly," Nick answered with a laugh.

When the ship docked in San Juan later that afternoon, he went ashore with Gloria, taking one of the tour buses with Herbert and Marnie Black. It wound its way through the city and then followed a road up to El Morro Castle, the harbor's brooding guardian they'd seen from the ship. They spent an hour touring the old fortress, posing for pictures by stacks of cannonballs that had once been the city's defense against pirates and invaders.

At one point, as Nick trudged up one of the castle's ramps with Herbert Black, the Englishman asked, "Did you see them removing the coffin as we docked?"

"No—I missed that."

"I didn't point it out to Marnie. She's upset enough already about the rumors we've been hearing."

"What rumors are those?"

"That there's a killer loose on the ship."

The women rejoined them and the conversation shifted abruptly. "Isn't this a fantastic view?" Marnie asked, pointing out toward a string of small islands that were catching the last rays of the setting sun.

"Beautiful," Gloria agreed.

Nick returned to the ship still wondering how he would manage to steal the bingo card from a lifeboat. . . .

On Tuesday they were anchored off Tortola in the British Virgin

Islands, using the ship's tenders for the shore excursions. Seating and storage on the tenders was quite different from the slightly smaller open lifeboats. Nick assumed they had a full stock of bingo cards on board, but he had no opportunity to check, with other passengers and crew members always present.

As they waited on the dock for their tour bus—a small vehicle with open sides that held about fifteen people—he noticed Dolores Franz standing by herself, away from the other passengers. "Hello again," he said, tipping the peaked cap he'd worn against the tropic sun.

"Good afternoon, Mr. Velvet." She smiled slightly, then asked, "What luck have you had?"

"None, so far."

"You only have until tomorrow night."

"How was your husband going to do it?"

"Climb into the lifeboat and get it."

"He knew where it was?"

"He said he did."

"Where did that card number come from?"

"It was sent to him in a telegram just before we sailed."

"What else did the message say?"

"Nothing else," she insisted. "I saw it. There was only the number."

"Had he done this before, with the bingo card?"

"I don't know. I guess so."

"Was the card always hidden in the same lifeboat?"

"I don't—No, it was in different boats. I remember him saying this one wouldn't be too difficult."

"Nicky," Gloria called, "our tour bus is here!"

"I'll have it tomorrow night," Nick assured Dolores Franz.

They took a winding mountainous road that crossed the island to a lovely sandy beach on the opposite side. Gloria went wading in the gentle surf while Nick watched from a distance, then they sat and relaxed with a couple of beers on the shady terrace of a little cafe.

"It's a good life," Gloria decided. "I could stay here forever."

"You could, but I couldn't. I have a job to do aboard the *Antilles* tonight."

"Be careful. Don't do anything foolish at your age."

"My mother told me the same thing when I was fifteen . . ."

Nick left their stateroom just after midnight and made his way to the boat deck above them. He was dressed in black slacks and sweater to protect against being seen and also to add a layer of warmth against the strong nighttime breeze. The door to the railed balcony by lifeboat ten was kept locked, but opening it presented no difficulty. Getting to the boat itself was another matter. It could be lowered from where he stood, but it was still a good six feet over to the boat itself. Simon Franz had been a younger man than Nick by a couple of decades, and perhaps that distance had presented no obstacle. Nick opened his kit of special tools.

He took two heavy-duty suction cups from the kit and attached them to the palms of his hands. Then he began climbing up one of the metal mooring posts that held the lifeboat in place. Each was shaped like an inverted "J" and with the help of the suction cups he was able to clamber up the left one with ease. Then he swung himself down into the boat, which was uncovered, relying on a drainage hose to remove any rainwater.

Once in the boat, it took Nick only a minute to locate the supply chest with its hundred or so bingo cards. He hoped his hunch about the boat number had been correct.

He missed it the first time through, and cursed his luck. Then he looked more carefully and spotted it, right near the top.

Card number 253.

He slipped it under his sweater and returned the other cards to the supply chest. He climbed back to the deck the same way he'd come, deciding he was still in pretty good shape.

When he reached his own deck, he stopped to examine his prize for a moment before returning to the stateroom. It looked pretty much like all the others he'd seen:

card 253

B	I	N	G	O
3	17	22	47	63
6	20	31	50	66
9	23	W	52	67
11	25	75	55	70
14	27	45	58	71

"Is that you, Velvet?" a voice called to him. He turned to see Herbert Black coming toward him. "Fierce breeze tonight."

"It is," Nick agreed.

"What's that you've got?"

"One of the bingo cards from inside. I forgot to turn it in after the game."

"I didn't know they played at night. Marnie and I have been at the casino ourselves. She won twenty dollars at blackjack."

"Good for her." Nick showed him the bingo card. "You two are familiar with the game. Do you notice anything odd about this card?"

"No, not really."

"It has a W in the center space instead of the words Free Play."

"You're right—it's a British bingo card. We use a W for Win. But why would one of the bingo cards be British?"

Nick shrugged. "Beats me. A mistake, I suppose. I won't worry about it."

Black fell into stride with him. "I enjoy walking the deck just before bedtime. Marnie's always dead tired, but this makes me sleep better."

"I expect to sleep well tonight," Nick told him. "I've had an invigorating day."

Wednesday, on St. Thomas, Nick and Gloria strolled through the crowded streets of Charlotte Amalie, the little portside town filled with jewelry and linen shops. There were passengers off a half dozen cruise ships, many already carrying bags of expensive purchases. "I might see something I like," Gloria decided after looking in a few shop windows.

"Why don't you look around for an hour or so?" Nick suggested. "I'll meet you back at the dock at one-thirty." He'd telephoned Dolores Franz's stateroom before they left the ship, arranging to meet her in front of the Charlotte Amalie post office at one o'clock. The bingo card was inside his shirt, and he planned to deliver it in return for the balance of the money.

"Let's have a quick lunch first," Gloria suggested. "I'm spoiled by that big buffet on the ship every day."

They found a place in one of the narrow shop-lined alleyways. Over a sandwich, Nick asked, "Have you noticed any British people on board besides the Blacks?"

She thought about it. "There's a woman in that group of sales reps—I think her name is Elizabeth something. Elizabeth Armstrong. She seems quite nice. I met her when I was lounging in a deck chair yesterday. Why do you ask?"

"I may want to speak with her."

They parted after lunch and Nick headed along the main shopping street toward the post office indicated on his map across from an unimposing two-story building called the Grand Hotel just around the corner from a small park with a statue of some local hero. He saw Dolores at once, leaning unsteadily against the post-office building as crowds of tourists hurried by.

He hurried up to her. "What's wrong?"

"I—" Her eyes glazed as she tried to focus on him. "My arm—"

He slid up the sleeve of her white blouse and saw the mark of the needle. "Dolores, who did this?"

She was sinking to the pavement and he could no longer hold her up. "She's ill," he told a man who stopped to help. "Call an ambulance!"

He waited with her while a crowd collected around them until the ambulance came. As she was being lifted onto the stretcher, he told one of the white-coated attendants, "She's a passenger on my ship, the *Antilles*. How does it look?"

The grim-faced attendant shook his head. "Drug overdose. I've seen 'em before."

"Stay here," the ambulance driver said. "We'll want your name."

But Nick preferred to fade into the crowd. He knew his money was probably in Dolores Franz's purse, but there was no way he could take it now. Instead, he walked back to the dock and met Gloria.

On their way back to the ship, he told her what had happened. Once they were back in their stateroom, she asked him, "What are you going to do with the bingo card?"

"I don't know. It was valuable to Simon Franz and to his wife. I suspect it's valuable to the person that killed them both, but I don't know who that is."

He took out the card and studied it. "I think I'll go looking for Mr. Perkins," he said.

Nick found the short man with the receding hairline in one of the cocktail lounges, enjoying a pre-dinner drink. "I'm looking for a British lady named Elizabeth Armstrong, Mr. Perkins. I understand she's with your group."

"Certainly. We all dine together and we usually drink together, too. She's right over at that table there."

Elizabeth Armstrong proved to be a stout woman with an infectious laugh. Nick had noticed her earlier without being aware of her name. "Someone looking for me?" she asked. "As long as it's a man!"

The people at her table joined in the laughter as Nick drew her aside. "I want to ask you a question, Mrs. Armstrong."

"It's Miss Armstrong, and the answer is yes!"

Nick laughed, showing he could go along with the joke. "It'll only take a minute," he told her.

She rose and followed him away from the table.

He asked his question and she answered it. Somehow it was the answer he'd been expecting. "Thank you, Miss Armstrong," he said fervently.

He left the lounge amidst more laughter and went out to one of the ship's bulletin boards, near the front office. It was one of several places where a map of the Caribbean was posted, with a red line showing the ship's daily progress. It was on its way back now, heading west northwest toward the Bahamas and Nassau. Next to the map, the exact locations at various times of the day were duly noted.

He read them and nodded, knowing at last what he had to do.

Thursday was spent at sea, a bit roughly, sailing toward the ship's next landfall. Nick spent the day making certain preparations, which involved a ship-to-shore telephone call and a meeting with the ship's captain and chief security officer. Nick wasn't in the habit of working with authorities of any kind, but this time seemed different. When Dolores Franz had died virtually in his arms, something had changed.

Much later, past midnight, as the *Antilles* was cruising through the

Ragged Island Range and beginning to turn north northwest toward Nassau, there was some unusual activity on B deck, where passengers usually disembarked for the ship's tenders. The door in the side of the ship had been opened by one of the cabin stewards and one of the ship's bulky inflatable life rafts was being pushed out into the night sea.

At that moment, Nick stepped into view. "There will be some delay in your delivery," he told the taller of the two men. "The United States Coast Guard has a cruiser out there."

Herbert Black turned from his task. "I should have killed you along with the woman." He started for Nick, and something glistened in his hand, but now the corridor was filled with ship's officers and armed Coast Guardsmen.

"Be careful!" Nick shouted as they moved in. "He has a needle!"

Black dropped the hypodermic to the floor and ground it underfoot as they moved in to take him.

Nick sat in the deserted main deck lounge with the ship's captain, a Coast Guard officer, and a man from the Drug Enforcement Agency, trying to explain at two in the morning how he'd known exactly where fifty pounds of uncut cocaine was to be dropped from the *Antilles* into the Atlantic Ocean.

"It was the bingo card," he told them, passing it around for their examination. "The drug dealers who were receiving the shipment had a virtually foolproof method of arranging delivery. The cocaine was delivered to the ship with ordinary supplies at one of our ports of call. The crew member assisting Simon Franz hid it somewhere below deck. Meanwhile, the drug dealers had hidden a bingo card on board with delivery instructions. Franz was sent the number of that bingo card and nothing more. If he had been arrested or the message intercepted, nothing would have happened. Again, if the bingo card was discovered without knowing the plan, its message would have been unreadable."

"Why was Franz killed?" the DEA man asked.

"Because Herbert Black heard about the scheme and decided he'd take it over. He killed Franz and waited for his wife Dolores to lead him to the hidden bingo card. Unfortunately for her, she hired me to steal it. I ran into Black with the card in my hand and asked him to look at it. Once he'd seen it, he didn't need Dolores Franz alive any more. He injected her with an overdose of cocaine, just as he'd done her husband."

"This card does look a bit strange," the captain commented.

"Of course it does, in two ways. First, there's the W in the center free space, and, second, the four numbers in that N line are 22–31–75–45. Any bingo player will tell you that the numbers are listed consecutively on the cards, so they're easy to locate quickly, and the N row always contains numbers from 31 through 45. On that card, the numbers 22 and 75 are misplaced."

"I'll be damned!"

"The entire middle row is a careful paste-up job. My misfortune in showing the card to Black solved the mystery, even though it also led to Dolores Franz's death. Anyone who'd played bingo like Black did would have spotted those wrong numbers at once when I asked him if there was anything wrong with the card. And when I asked him specifically about the letter W in the middle, he said it stood for Win on British bingo cards. I've been to England a couple of times and I didn't think this was true, but I sought out a British lady and asked her, just to be certain. She told me British bingo cards have no free-play space at all. There are twenty-five numbers on every card. So Black had lied about that."

"But what do the numbers mean?" the DEA man asked. The others didn't have to ask. "And how did you know where to find this particular card?"

"I'll answer the last question first. If the message to Franz contained only the number 253 and that told him not only the number of the bingo card but in which of fourteen lifeboats it was hidden, there could only be one explanation. I added the three digits of 253 together and came up with lifeboat number ten. You may want to check the other lifeboats for similar cards that could be used on future voyages."

"And the numbers?"

"Obviously it was the center, or N, row that was gimmicked. What do we have there? N–22–31–W–75–45. What else could it be but latitude and longitude? Latitude 22 degrees, 31 minutes north, longitude 75 degrees, 45 minutes west. Our exact location, as the crew member could verify to Black, when the cocaine was to be dumped."

The Coast Guard officer said, "We have the yacht that was waiting for the pickup. They had other cocaine on board."

"You'll want to question the crew member," Nick suggested. "He was probably the one who first tipped off Herbert Black." He yawned and got to his feet.

"Where are you going?"

"It's been a long night and my wife will be looking for me," Nick said. "I'm going to try and get some sleep."

Friday morning, as the ship docked in Nassau, Gloria finished hearing about the night's activities. "I'm glad you were working with the law for once," she told him. "Are you giving up that other life?"

"This was special," Nick said. "I owed it to Dolores Franz."

"And you didn't take any money for it."

"Well, I still have my down payment. Come on—" he took her hand "—I'll buy you something at the straw market."

JOHN MORTIMER
(1923–)

Hilda Rumpole is determined to enjoy a second honeymoon on a cruise ship with her long-suffering husband, the "Old Bailey hack" Horace Rumpole. "She Who Must Be Obeyed" prevails, and the two set out for a Mediterranean cruise, which becomes a busman's honeymoon for the barrister when his shipmates—including a despised judge—are convinced that a passenger has mysteriously and suspiciously disappeared. This story proves again John Mortimer's inimitable abilities to entertain while making a serious case for the fundamental tenets of British justice. It is also one of a corpus of stories so substantial that it can be considered a canon in the crime and mystery genre, as are the Sherlock Holmes stories.

John Mortimer was born into a life of literature and the law, the only child of a highly eccentric and literate barrister and his wife. Mortimer's first home was in his parents' flat in London's Inner Temple. The family then moved to England's Chiltern Hills, where Mortimer spent an essentially solitary childhood centered around a house and extensive garden designed by his father. After his father became blind, Mortimer entertained him with readings from volumes including *The Oxford Book of English Verse*, which his character Rumpole would quote from liberally years later. In return, Mortimer's father treated him to memorized recitations of the Sherlock Holmes stories, delivered during long walks in the countryside.

Mortimer was educated at the Dragon School in Oxford, then at Harrow and at Brasenose College, Oxford. During World War II, he worked on documentary films with the Crown Film Unit. Following this, he studied law and was called to the bar in 1948. He began his career as a divorce barrister but eventually exercised his talent as an advocate by serving as Queen's Counsel in criminal cases and defending in some highly publicized cases concerning censorship and freedom of expression. In the meantime, he had launched a career as a novelist, playwright, screenwriter, and literary critic. He also adapted his own works and Evelyn Waugh's *Brideshead Revisited* for television. He was married for twenty-three years to the writer Penelope Mortimer, with whom he raised a family. He is now married to Penny Gollop Mortimer. The couple has two daughters, one of whom is the actress Emily Mortimer. They reside in the Chiltern home immortalized in Mortimer's novel, *Clinging to the Wreckage*, which was made into the play and film *Voyage Round My Father*.

The following story can be considered a voyage toward the truth. It is left to the reader to decide just who is who in "Rumpole at Sea."

Rumpole at Sea

1990

Mr. Justice Graves. What a contradiction in terms! Mr. "Injustice" Graves, Mr. "Penal" Graves, Mr. "Prejudice" Graves, Mr. "Get into Bed with the Prosecution" Graves—all these titles might be appropriate. But Mr. "Justice" Graves, so far as I'm concerned, can produce nothing but a hollow laugh. From all this you may deduct that the old darling is not my favourite member of the Judiciary. Now he has been promoted, on some sort of puckish whim of the Lord Chancellor's, from Old Bailey judge to a scarlet and ermine justice of the Queen's Bench, his power to do harm has been considerably increased. Those who have followed my legal career will remember the awesome spectacle of the mad Judge Bullingham, with lowered head and bloodshot eyes, charging into the ring in the hope of impaling Rumpole upon a horn. But now we have lost him, I actually miss the old Bull. There was a sort of excitement in the corridas we lived through together and I often emerged with a couple of ears and a tail. A session before Judge Graves has all the excitement and colour of a Wesleyan funeral on a wet day in Wigan. His pale Lordship presides sitting bolt upright as though he had a poker up his backside, his voice is dirge-like and his eyes closed in pain as he is treated with anything less than an obsequious grovel.

This story, which ends with mysterious happenings on the high seas, began in the old Gravestones' Chambers in the Law Courts, where I was making an application one Monday morning.

"Mr. Rumpole"—his Lordship looked pained when I had outlined my request—"do I understand that you are applying to me for bail?" "Yes, my Lord." I don't know if he thought I'd just dropped in for a cosy chat.

"Bail having been refused," he went on in sepulchral tones, "in the Magistrates Court and by my brother judge, Mr. Justice Entwhistle. Is this a frivolous application?"

"Only if it's frivolous to keep the innocent at liberty, my Lord." I liked the phrase myself, but the Judge reminded me that he was not a jury (worse luck, I thought) and that emotional appeals would carry very little weight with him. He then looked down at his papers and said, "When you use the word 'innocent,' I assume you are referring to your client?"

"I am referring to all of us, my Lord." I couldn't resist a speech. "We are all innocent until found guilty by a jury of our peers. Or has that golden thread of British justice become a little tarnished of late?"

"Mr. Rumpole"—the Judge was clearly unmoved—"I see your client's name is Timson."

"So it is, my Lord. But I should use precisely the same argument were it Horace Rumpole. Or even Mr. Justice Graves." At which his Lordship protested, "Mr. Rumpole, this is intolerable!"

"Absolutely intolerable, my Lord," I agreed. "Conditions for prisoners on remand are far worse now than they were a hundred years ago."

"I mean, Mr. Rumpole," the Graveyard explained, with a superhuman effort at patience, as though to a half-wit, "it's intolerable that you should address me in such a manner. I cannot imagine any circumstances in which I should need your so-called eloquence to be exercised on my behalf." You never know, I thought, you never know, old darling. But the mournful voice of judicial authority carried on. "No doubt the Prosecution opposes bail. Do you oppose bail, Mr. Harvey Wimple?"

Thus addressed, the eager, sandy-haired youth from the Crown Prosecution Service, who spoke very fast, as though he wanted to get the whole painful ordeal over as quickly as possible, jabbered, "Oppose it? Oh, yes, my Lord. Absolutely. Utterly and entirely opposed. Utterly." He looked startled when the Judge asked, "On what precise grounds do you oppose bail, Mr. Wimple?" But he managed the quick-fire answer, "Grounds that, if left at liberty, another offence might be committed. Or other offences. By the defendant Timson, my Lord. By him, you see?"

"Do you hear that, Mr. Rumpole?" The Judge re-orchestrated the piece for more solemn music. "If he is set at liberty, your client might commit another offence or, quite possibly, offences."

And then, losing my patience, I said what I had been longing to say on some similar bail application for years. "Of course, he might," I began. "Every man, woman and child in England might commit an offence. Is your Lordship suggesting we keep them all permanently banged up on the off-chance? It's just not on, that's all."

"Mr. Rumpole. What is not 'on,' as you so curiously put it?" The Judge spoke with controlled fury. It was a good speech, but I had picked the wrong audience. "Banging up the innocent, my Lord." I let him have the full might of the Rumpole eloquent outrage. "With a couple of psychopaths and their own chamber-pots. For an indefinite period while the wheels of justice grind to a halt in a traffic jam of cases."

"Do try to control yourself, Mr. Rumpole. Conditions in prisons are a matter for the Home Office."

"Oh, my Lord, I'm so sorry. I forgot they're of no interest to judges who refuse bail and have never spent a single night locked up without the benefit of a water closet."

At which point, Graves decided to terminate the proceedings and, to no one's surprise, he announced that bail was refused and that the unfortunate Tony Timson, who had never committed a violent crime, should languish in Brixton until his trial. I was making for the fresh air and a small and soothing cigar when the Judge called me back with "Just one moment, Mr. Rumpole. I think I should add that I find the way that this matter has been argued before me quite lamentable, and very far from being in the best traditions of the Bar. I may have to report the personal and improper nature of your argument to proper authorities." At which point he smiled in a nauseating manner at the young man from the Crown Prosecution Service and said, "Thank you for *your* able assistance, Mr. Harvey Wimple."

"Had a good day, Rumpole?" She Who Must Be Obeyed asked me on my return to the mansion flat.

"Thank God, Hilda," I told her as I poured a glass of Pommeroy's Very Ordinary, "for your wonderful sense of humour!"

"Rumpole, look at your face!" She appeared to be smiling brightly at my distress.

"I prefer not to. I have no doubt it is marked with tragedy." I raised a glass and tried to drown at least a few of my sorrows.

"Whatever's happened?" She Who Must Be Obeyed was unusually sympathetic, from which I should have guessed that she had formulated some master plan. I refilled my glass and told her:

> "I could a tale unfold" Hilda "whose lightest word
> Would harrow up thy soul, freeze thy young blood,
> Make thy two eyes, like stars, start from their spheres,
> Thy knotted and combined locks to part,
> And each particular hair to stand on end,
> Like quills upon the fretful porpentine: . . ."

"Oh come on, I bet it wouldn't." My wife was sceptical. "What you need, Rumpole, is a change!"

"I need a change from Mr. Justice Graves." And then I played into her hands, for she looked exceptionally pleased when I added, "For two pins I'd get on a banana boat and sail away into the sunset."

"Oh, Rumpole! I'm so glad that's what you'd do. For two pins. You know what I've been thinking? We need a second honeymoon."

"The first one was bad enough." You see I was still gloomy.

"It wouldn't've been, Rumpole, if you hadn't thought we could manage two weeks in the South of France on your fees from one short robbery."

"It was all I had about me at the time," I reminded her. "Anyway, you shouldn't've ordered lobster."

"What's the point of a honeymoon," Hilda asked, "if you can't order lobster?"

"Of course, you can *order* it. Nothing to stop you ordering," I conceded. "You just shouldn't complain when we have to leave three days early and sit up all night in the train from Marseilles. With a couple of soldiers asleep on top of us."

"On our second honeymoon I shall order lobster." And then she added the fatal words, "When we're on the cruise."

"On the *what*?" I hoped that I couldn't believe my ears.

"The cruise! There's still a bit of Aunt Tedda's money left." As I have pointed out, Hilda's relations are constantly interfering in our married lives. "I've booked up for it."

"No, Hilda. Absolutely not!" I was firm as only I know how to be. "I know exactly what it'd be like. Bingo on the boat deck!"

"We need to get away, Rumpole. To look at ourselves."

"Do you honestly think that's wise?" It seemed a rash project.

"Moonlight on the Med."

She Who Must became lyrical. "The sound of music across the water. Stars. You and I by the rail. *Finding* each other, after a long time."

"But you can find me quite easily," I pointed out. "You just shout 'Rumpole!' and there I am."

"You said you'd sail away into the sunset. For two pins," she reminded me.

"A figure of speech, Hilda. A pure figure of speech! Let me make this perfectly clear. There is no power on this earth that's going to get me on a cruise."

During the course of a long and memorable career at the Bar, I have fought many doughty opponents and won many famous victories; but I have never, when all the evidence has been heard and the arguments are over, secured a verdict against She Who Must Be Obeyed. It's true that I have, from time to time, been able to mitigate her stricter sentences. I have argued successfully for alternatives to custody or time to pay. But I have never had an outright win against her and, from the moment she suggested we sail away, until the time when I found myself in our cabin on the fairly good ship S.S. *Boadicea*, steaming out from Southampton, I knew, with a sickening certainty, that I was on to a loser. Hilda reviewed her application for a cruise every hour of the days that we were together, and at most hours of the night, until I finally threw in the towel on the grounds that the sooner we put out to sea the sooner we should be back on dry land again.

The *Boadicea* was part of a small cruise line and, instead of flying its passengers to some southern port, it sailed from England to Gibraltar and thence to several Mediterranean destinations before returning home. The result was that some of the first days were to be spent sailing through grey and troubled waters. Picture us then in our cabin as we left harbour. I was looking out of a porthole at a small area of open deck which terminated in a rail and the sea. Hilda, tricked out in white ducks, took a yachting cap out of her hat box and tried it on in front of the mirror. "What on earth did you bring that for?" I asked her. "Are you expecting to steer the thing?"

"I expect to enter into the spirit of life on shipboard, Rumpole," she told me briskly. "And you'd be well-advised to do the same. I'm sure we'll make heaps of friends. Such nice people go on cruises. Haven't you been watching them?"

"Yes." And I turned, not very cheerfully, back to the porthole. As I did so, a terrible vision met my eyes. The stretch of deck was no longer empty. A grey-haired man in a blue blazer was standing by the rail and, as I watched, Mr. Justice Graves turned in my direction and all doubts about our fellow passengers, and all hopes for a carefree cruise, were laid to rest.

" 'Angels and ministers of grace defend us!' It can't be. But it *is*!"

"What is, Rumpole? Do pull yourself together."

"If you knew what I'd seen, you wouldn't babble of pulling myself together, Hilda. It's *him*! The ghastly old Gravestone in person." At which I dragged out my suitcase and started to throw my possessions back into it. "He's come on the cruise with us!"

"Courage, Rumpole"—Hilda watched me with a certain contempt— "I remember you telling me, is the first essential in an advocate."

"Courage, yes, but not total lunacy. Not self-destruction. Life at the Bar may have its risks, but no legal duty compels me to spend two weeks shut up in a floating hotel with Mr. Justice Deathshead."

"I don't know what you think you're going to do about it." She was calmly hanging up her clothes whilst I repacked mine. "It's perfectly simple, Hilda," I told her, "I shall abandon ship!"

When I got up on the deck, there was, fortunately, no further sign of Graves, but a ship's officer, whom I later discovered to be the Purser, was standing by the rail and I approached him, doing my best to control my panic.

"I've just discovered," I told him, "I'm allergic to graves. I mean, I'm allergic to boats. It would be quite unsafe for me to travel. A dose of sea-sickness could prove fatal!"

"But, sir," the purser protested. "We're only just out of port."

"I know. So you could let me off, couldn't you? I've just had terrible news."

"You're welcome to telephone, sir."

"No, I'm afraid that wouldn't help."

"And if it's really serious we could fly you back from our next stop." And he added the terrible words, "We'll be at Gibraltar in three days."

Gibraltar in three days! Three days banged up on shipboard with the most unappetizing High Court judge since Jefferies hung up his wig! I lay on my bed in our cabin as the land slid away from us and Hilda read out the treats on offer: " 'Daily sweepstake on the ship's position. Constant video entertainment and films twice nightly. Steam-bath, massage and beauty treatment. Exercise rooms and fully equipped gymnasium— I think I'll have a steam-bath, Rumpole—First fancy-dress ball immediately before landfall at Gib. Live it up in an evening of ocean fantasy.

Lecture by Howard Swainton, world-famous, best-selling mystery novelist, on "How I Think Up My Plots." ' "

"Could he think up one on how to drown a judge?"

"Oh, do cheer up, Rumpole. Don't be so morbid. At five thirty this evening it's Captain Orde's Welcome Aboard Folks cocktail party, followed by a dinner dance at eight forty-five. I can wear my little black dress."

"The Captain's cocktail party?" I was by no means cheered up. 'To exchange small talk and Twiglets with Mr. Justice Deathshead. No, thank you very much. I shall lie doggo in the cabin until Gibraltar."

"You can't possibly do that,' She told me. 'What am I going to tell everyone?"

"Tell them I've gone down with a nasty infection. No, the Judge might take it into his head to visit the sick. He might want to come and gloat over me with grapes. Tell them I'm dead. Or say a last-minute case kept me in England."

"Rumpole, aren't you being just the tiniest bit silly about this?"

But I stuck desperately to my guns. "Remember, Hilda," I begged her, "if anyone asks, say you're here entirely on your own." I had not forgotten that Graves and She had met at the Sam Ballard–Marguerite Plumstead wedding, and if the Judge caught sight of her, he might suspect that where Hilda was could Rumpole be far behind? I was prepared to take every precaution against discovery.

During many of the ensuing events I was, as I have said, lying doggo. I therefore have to rely on Mrs. Rumpole's account of many of the matters that transpired on board the good ship *Boadicea*, and I have reconstructed the following pages from her evidence which was, as always, completely reliable. (I wish, sometimes, that She Who Must Be Obeyed would indulge in something as friendly as a lie. As, for instance, "I do think you're marvellous, Rumpole," or "Please don't lose any weight, I like you so much as you are!") Proceedings opened at the Captain's cocktail party when Hilda found herself part of a group consisting of the world-famed mystery writer, Howard Swainton, whom she described vividly as "a rather bouncy and yappy little Yorkshire terrier of a man"; a willowy American named Linda Milsom, whom he modestly referred to as his secretary; a tall, balding, fresh-complexioned, owlish-looking cleric wearing gold-rimmed glasses, a dog-collar and an old tweed suit, who introduced himself as Bill Britwell; and his wife, Mavis, a rotund grey-haired lady with a face which might once have been pretty and was now friendly and cheerful. These people were in the act of getting to know each other when the Reverend Bill made the serious mistake of asking Howard Swainton what he did for a living.

"You mean you don't know what Howard does?" Linda, the secretary, said, as her boss was recovering from shock. "You ought to walk into the gift shop. The shelves are just groaning with his best-sellers. Rows and rows of them, aren't there, Howard?"

"They seem to know what goes with the public," Swainton agreed. "My motto is keep 'em guessing and give 'em a bit of sex and a spot of mayhem every half-dozen pages. I'm here to research a new story about a mysterious disappearance on a cruise. I call it *Absence of Body*. Rather a neat title that, don't you think?"

"Howard's won two Golden Daggers," Linda explained. "And *Time* magazine called him 'The Genius of Evil.' "

"Let's say, I'm a writer with a taste for a mystery." Swainton was ostentatiously modest.

"I suppose"—Bill Britwell beamed round at the company—"that since I've been concerned with the greatest mystery of all, I've lost interest in detective stories. I do apologize."

"Oh, really?" Swainton asked. "And what's the greatest mystery?"

"I think Bill means," his wife explained, "since he's gone in to the Church.'

"What I've always wanted," the Reverend Bill told them, "after a lifetime in insurance."

"So you've joined the awkward squad, have you?" Swainton was a fervent supporter of the Conservative Party on television chat shows, and as such regarded the Church of England as a kind of Communist cell.

"I'm sorry?" Bill blinked, looking genuinely puzzled.

"The Archbishop's army of Reverend Pinkos"—Swainton warmed to his subject—"always preaching morality to the Government. I can't think why you chaps can't mind your own business."

"Morality *is* my business now, isn't it?" Bill was still looking irrepressibly cheerful. "Of course, it used to be insurance. I came to all the best things late in life. The Church and Mavis." At which he put an arm round his wife's comfortable shoulder.

"We're on our honeymoon." Hilda said that the elderly Mrs. Britwell sounded quite girlish as she said this.

"Pleasure combined with business," her husband explained. "We're only going as far as Malta, where I've landed a job as padre to the Anglican community."

And then Hilda, intoxicated by a glass of champagne and the prospect of foreign travel, confessed that she was also on a honeymoon, although it was a second one in her case.

"Oh, really?" Swainton asked with a smile which Hilda found patronizing. "And which is your husband, Mrs.—?"

"Rumpole. Hilda Rumpole. My husband is an extremely well-known barrister. You may have read his name in the papers?"

"I don't spend much time reading," Swainton told her. "I'm really too busy writing. And where is your Mr. Rumbold?"

"Oh, well," Hilda had to confess, "he's not here."

"You mean?"—Swainton was smiling and inviting the group to enjoy the joke—"you're having a second honeymoon with a husband who isn't here?"

"No. Well. You see something rather unexpected came up."

"So, now"—and Swainton could barely conceal his mirth—"you're having a second honeymoon on your own?"

But Hilda had to excuse herself and hurry away, as she had seen, through the window of the saloon in which the Captain's cocktail party was taking place, stationed on a small patch of windy and rain-beaten deck, Rumpole signalling urgently for supplies.

What had happened was that, being greatly in need of sustenance and a nerve-cooling drink in my Ducal Class dugout (second only to the real luxury of Sovereign Class), I had rung repeatedly for a steward with absolutely no result. When I telephoned, I was told there would be a considerable delay as the staff were very busy with the Captain's cocktail party. "The Captain's cock up, you mean," I said harshly, and made my way to the outskirts of the port (or perhaps the starboard) deck, where it took me considerable time to attract Hilda's attention through the window. "Make your mind up, Rumpole," She said when she came out. "Are you in hiding or aren't you?" and "Why don't you come in and meet a famous author?"

"Are you mad? *He's* in there." I could see the skeletal figure of Graves in the privileged party around Captain Orde. He was no doubt entertaining them with an account of the Rumpole clientele he had kept under lock and key.

"Really," Hilda protested, "this is no way to spend a honeymoon. Mr. Swainton looked as though he thought I'd done you in or something. Apparently he's doing research on a new book called *Absence of Body*. He says it's all about someone who disappears during a cruise."

"Hilda," I said, "couldn't you do a bit of research on a glass or two of champagne? And on what they've got on those little bits of toast?"

So She Who Must Be Obeyed, who has her tender moments, went off in search of provisions. I watched her go back into the saloon and make for the table where the guzzle and sluice were laid out. As she did so, she passed Mr. Justice Graves. I saw him turn his head to look at her in a stricken fashion, then he muttered some apology to the Captain and was off out of the room with the sudden energy of a young gazelle.

It was then I realized that not only was Rumpole fleeing the Judge, the Judge was fleeing Rumpole.

Back in the cabin, Hilda put on her dress for the dinner dance and added the finishing touches to her *maquillage*, whilst I, wearing bedroom slippers and smoking a small cigar, paced my confinement like a caged tiger. "And

you'll really like the Britwells," She was saying, "He's going to be a parson in Malta. They're quite elderly, but so much in love. Do come up to
dinner, Rumpole. Then we could dance together."

"We did that on our first honeymoon!" I reminded her. "And it wasn't
an astonishing success, so far as I can remember. Anyway, do you think
I want Gravestone to catch me dancing?"

"I don't know why you're so frightened of him, quite honestly. You
don't exactly cower in front of him in Court from all you tell me."

"Of course I don't cower!" I explained. "I can treat the old Deathshead
with lofty disdain in front of a jury! I can thunder my disapproval at him
on a bail application. I have no fear of the man in the exercise of my
profession. It's his friendship I dread."

"His friendship?"

"Oh, yes. That is why, Hilda, I have fled Judge Graves down the
nights and down the days." And here I gave my wife a heady draught
of Francis Thompson:

> "I fled Him, down the arches of the years;
> I fled Him, down the labyrinthine ways
> Of my own mind; and in the mist of tears
> I hid from Him, and under running laughter."

"Well, there's not much running laughter for me"—Hilda was dis-
pleased—"going on a second honeymoon without a husband."

When Hilda was made-up, powdered and surrounded with an appropriate fragrance, she left me just as the Britwells were emerging from
the cabin opposite. They were also in evening-dress and were apparently
so delighted to see my wife that they cordially invited her to inspect the
amenities which they enjoyed. As the Britwell berth seemed in every way
a carbon copy of that provided for the Rumpoles, Hilda found it a little
difficult to keep up an interesting commentary, or show any genuine surprise, at the beauty and convenience of their quarters. At a loss for conversation, she looked at their dressing-table, where, she told me, two large
photographs in heavy silver frames had been set up. The first was a recent
wedding portrait of the Reverend and Mrs. Britwell standing proudly
together, arm-in-arm, outside a village church. The bride was not in white,
which would have been surprising at her age, but she wore what Hilda
called a "rather ordinary little suit and a hat with a veil." The other was
a studio portrait of a pretty, smiling young girl in a sequined evening-
gown. She asked if that were Bill's daughter, to which he laughed and
said, "Not exactly." Before she could inquire further I whistled to Hilda
from our door across the corridor as I had an urgent piece of advice for
her.

"For God's sake, if you see the Judge," I warned her through a chink in our doorway, "don't encourage the blighter. Please, don't dream of dancing with him!"

I was not in the least reassured when She answered, "You never know what I might dream of, Rumpole."

Hilda didn't dance with the Judge that night. Indeed Mr. Injustice Graves didn't even put in an appearance at the function and was busily engaged in lying as low as Rumpole himself.

Most of the dancing was done by the Britwells, who whirled and twirled and chasséed around the place with the expertise of a couple of ballroom champions. "Aren't they good?" Hilda was playing an enthusiastic gooseberry to Swainton and his secretary, Linda. "Don't you think he dances rather *too* well?" Swainton sat with his head on one side and looked suspiciously at the glittering scene.

"I don't know exactly what you mean?" Hilda was puzzled, but Linda told her, "Howard looks below the surface of life. That's his great talent!"

When the husband and wife team came off the floor, perspiring gently after the tango, Howard Swainton repeated, "We were saying you dance unusually well, Britwell, for a vicar."

"Don't forget I wasn't always a vicar. I spent most of my life in insurance."

"Oh, yes. I remember now. You told us that." Howard Swainton seemed to be making a mental note. Hilda said, "Do men in insurance dance well?"

"Better than vicars!" Mrs. Britwell was laughing. The elderly newlyweds did seem an ideally happy couple.

"I was in insurance and Mavis ran a secretarial agency." Bill was telling the story of his life. "Of course, I married her for her money." He raised his glass of wine to his wife and drank her health.

"And I married him for his dancing!" Mavis was still laughing. "Why don't you let Bill give you a slow foxtrot, Mrs. Rumpole?"

"Oh, that would be very nice"—Hilda had not had a great deal of practice at the foxtrot—"but not this evening, perhaps." She was looking anxiously about the room, a fact which the sleuth Swainton immediately noticed. "Are you looking for someone?" he asked.

"Oh. Oh, well. A judge, actually. I happen to have met him before. I'm sure he was at the Captain's cocktail party but I don't seem to see him here."

"A judge?" Swainton was interested.

"Oh, yes. He used to be just down the Bailey, you know," Hilda told them. "But now he's been put up to the High Court. Scarlet and ermine. A red judge. Sir Gerald Graves."

"Graves?" Howard Swainton was smiling. "That's a rather mournful name." But the Reverend Bill didn't join in the laughter. He made a sudden movement and knocked over his glass of red wine. It spread across the tablecloth, Hilda told me, in words I was to remember, like blood.

> Swiftly, swiftly flew the ship,
> Yet she sailed softly too:
> Sweetly, sweetly blew the breeze—
> On me alone it blew.

It blew on me alone because I was taking a solitary stroll in the early morning before the waking hour of the most energetic judge. The good ship *Boadicea* clove the grey waters, seagulls chattered and soared in the sky behind us, hoping for scraps, and I trod carefully in the shadows of boats and deck buildings.

> Like one, who on a lonesome road
> Doth walk in fear and dread,
> And having once turned round walks on,
> And turns no more his head;
> Because he knows, a frightful judge
> Doth close behind him tread.

Coleridge's memorable lines were beating in my ears as I looked fearfully around me and then, almost too late, spotted an energetic old party in a blue blazer out for a constitutional. I ducked into the doorway of the Ladies Health and Beauty Salon, while Graves stopped and peered furtively into the window of the room where breakfast was being served to the Ducal passengers.

I know that he did this from the account that Hilda gave me later. She was at a table with Swainton and Linda Milsom, getting stuck into the coffee and eggs and bacon, when she saw the judicial features peering in at her. She only had time to say, "Ah. There he is!" before the old darling vanished, and she said, "He's gone!" Bill Britwell joined them with a plate of cornflakes he'd been fetching from a central table. "Who's gone?" he asked.

"Mr. Justice Graves. He must be an early bird." The Reverend Bill sat and ate his breakfast and Swainton asked how Mavis, who was noticeably absent, was that morning.

"Well, not too good, I'm afraid. Mavis isn't quite the ticket."

"The what?" Linda Milsom seemed to be listening to a foreign language.

"Not quite up to snuff." Bill did his best to explain his meaning.

"He means she's sick," Howard Swainton translated for Linda's benefit and his secretary looked deeply sympathetic. "What, on her honeymoon?"

"Do tell her we're all so sorry for her." Swainton was also solicitous, and then he turned his attention to Hilda and asked her, with obvious scepticism, "And how's *your* husband, Mrs. Rumpole? Have you heard from him lately?"

"Oh, yes, I have," Hilda told him.

"Still busy, is he?"

"Well, he's on the move all the time."

"Gee, I hope your wife gets better," Linda was saying to Bill Britwell in a caring sort of way. "I've got these great homeopathic capsules. I could drop them into your cabin."

"That's very kind of you but," Bill told them firmly, "I think she'd like to be left alone for the moment."

"Such a terrible shame!" Hilda was also sympathetic. "And she seemed so full of life last night."

"Yes, that's exactly what I thought." Howard Swainton was looking at the Reverend Bill as though he were an interesting piece of research and he repeated Hilda's words, "So full of life!"

After funking a meeting with Hilda in the breakfast room, it seemed that Mr. Injustice settled himself down in a deck-chair, with a rug over his knees, in a kind of passage on the upper deck between the side of the gymnasium and a suspended boat into which his Lordship, in time of trouble, ought, I suspected, be ready to jump ahead of the women and children. There he sat, immersed in *Murder Most Foul*, the latest Howard Swainton, when, glancing up after the discovery of the fourth corpse, he saw Hilda standing at the end of the passage. His immediate reaction was to raise the alleged work of literature over his face, but he was too late. My wife gave a glad cry of "Mr. Justice Graves!" And, advancing towards him with indescribable foolhardiness added, "It is Sir Gerald Graves, isn't it? Hilda Rumpole. We met at Sam Ballard's wedding. You remember he got spliced to the ex-matron of the Old Bailey and astonished us all." Whereupon she sat down in one of the empty chairs beside him and seemed prepared for a long chat.

"Mrs. Rumpole"—Hilda, who is always a reliable witness, alleges that the old Deathshead here "smiled quite charmingly"—"of course, I remember. I had no idea you were on the boat." And he added nervously, "Are you here on your own?"

"Well, yes. On my own. In a sort of way."

"Oh, I see. Oh, good!" His Lordship was enormously relieved, but then, Hilda told me, a sort of hunted look came into his eyes as he inquired anxiously, "Your husband isn't about?"

"Not about? No. Well. Definitely not about. Of course, Horace's got a very busy practice," Hilda explained. "I believe you had him before you quite recently. I don't know if you remember?"

"Your husband's appearances before me, Mrs. Rumpole," Graves assured her, "are quite unforgettable."

"How sweet of you to say so." She was gratified.

"In fact, we judges are all agreed," Mr. Justice added, "there's simply no advocate at the Criminal Bar in the least like Horace Rumpole."

"A 'one off.' Is that what you'd say about him?"

"Without doubt, a 'one off.' We're all agreed about that."

"I'm sure you're right. That may be why I married him. He's a bit of a 'one off' as a husband." Hilda began, strangely enough, to treat the old Gravestone as a confidante.

"Forgive me, Mrs. Rumpole"—Graves clearly didn't want to be let into the secrets of the Rumpole marriage—"I have absolutely no idea what Rumpole is like as a husband."

"No. Silly of me!" And here I believe that She laid a friendly hand on the old party's arm. "Of course, you don't know what it's like to go on one honeymoon with him, let alone two."

"No idea at all, I'm delighted to say."

"But I'll tell you all the nice things you've said about him. About him being 'unforgettable' and a 'one off' and so on."

"You'll tell him?" His Lordship's hunted expression returned.

"When I next see him."

"Oh, yes, of course." And he suggested hopefully, "Back in England?"

"Or wherever. It may encourage him to break cover."

"To do what, Mrs. Rumpole?" There was a distinct note of panic in the judicial question.

"Well, to come out into the open a little more. Would it surprise you to know, Rumpole's really a very shy and retiring sort of person?"

By this time the shy and retiring Rumpole had outstayed his welcome in the entrance hall of the Ladies Health and Beauty Salon and I began to make my way back to the safety of our cabin, taking cover, from time to time, in such places as the children's play area (where I might have been spotted peering anxiously out from behind a giant cut-out clown) and the deck quoits' storage cupboard. Then, getting near to home, I glanced down a passage between a building and a boat and saw Hilda seated on a deck-chair, her knees covered with a rug. The back of the hanging boat prevented me seeing her companion, until it was far too late. "Hilda!" I called. "Yes, Rumpole. Here I am," came the answer. And then, as I moved towards her, the sight I dreaded most hoved into view. We were forced together and there was no way in which a meeting between old enemies could be avoided. What was remarkable was that the Deathshead greeted me with apparent *bonhomie*.

"Rumpole!" He didn't rise from his seat but otherwise he was cordial. "My dear fellow! This *is* a surprise. Your good lady told me that you weren't about."

"Well," I admitted, "I haven't been about. Up to now."

"What's up, old chap? Not got your sea legs yet? I always thought of you as a bit of a landlubber, I must say. Come along, then. Sit yourself down."

I did so with a good deal of trepidation on the seaward side of She Who Must be Obeyed.

"The Judge has been sweet enough to tell me that your appearances before him were 'unforgettable,' " Hilda said.

"Oh, yes? How terribly sweet of him," I agreed.

"And like no one else."

"And I honestly meant it, my dear old fellow," Graves assured me. "You are absolutely *sui generis*."

"To name but a few?"

"Even if you have so very little Latin. What was the last case you did before me?"

"It was an application for bail." And I added, with heavy irony, "With the greatest respect, my Lord."

"Of course it was!" Graves seemed to recall the incident with delight. "You should have been there, Mrs. Rumpole. We had great fun over that, didn't we, old fellow?"

"Oh, yes," I assured him. "It was a riot. Tony Timson's been laughing so much he could hardly slop out in Brixton."

"He will have his joke, won't he, Mrs. Rumpole?" The Judge's cheerfulness was undiminished. "Your Horace is a great one for his little joke. Well, now I've met you both, there's no reason why we shouldn't have a drink together. After dinner in the Old Salts' bar at, shall we say, five minutes past nine exactly?"

At which point, the Gravestone took up his copy of *Murder Most Foul* and left us to the sound of my, I hope derisory, "If your Lordship pleases." When he had withdrawn, I turned a tragic face to Hilda. "The Old Salts' Bar," I repeated. "At five past nine. *Now* look what you've done!"

"I had to flush you out somehow, Rumpole," She said, unreasonably I felt. "I had to get you to take part in your own honeymoon."

But my mind was on grimmer business. "I told you, it's the awful threat of his friendship. That's what I dread!"

That evening, in the privacy of our cabin, Hilda read out an account of the delights of the Old Salts' bar from the ship's brochure: " 'Tonight and every night after dinner,' " she told me, " 'Gloria de la Haye sings her golden oldies. Trip down Memory Lane and sing along with Gloria, or hear her inimitable way of rendering your special requests.' "

"And that's not the only drawback of the Old Salts' bar," I added. "What about 'Stiff sentences I have Passed,' the long-playing record by Mr. Justice Gravestone?"

"Oh, do cheer up, Rumpole. We've got each other."

"Next time you decide to go on a honeymoon, old thing," I warned her, "would you mind leaving him behind?"

"Poor Mavis Britwell getting sick like that!" Hilda's mind flitted to another subject. "She'll be missing all the fun."

"Tonight," I told her, having regard to the rendezvous ahead, "the sick are the lucky ones."

When we left the cabin on our way to dinner, Hilda's mind was still on the misfortunes of Mavis, and she knocked on the door of the cabin opposite with the idea of visiting the invalid. After some delay, the Reverend Bill called from behind the door that he wouldn't be a minute. Then the little man I was to discover to be Howard Swainton, the famous author, came bouncing down the corridor, carrying a bunch of red roses and a glossy paperback of his own writing. "Visiting the sick, are we?" he said. "We all seem to have the same idea."

"Well, yes. This is my husband." Hilda introduced me and Swainton raised his eyebrows higher than I would have believed possible.

"Is it, really?" he said. "I *am* surprised."

"And this is Mr. Howard Swainton," Hilda went on, undeterred, "*the* Howard Swainton."

"How do you do. I'm *the* Horace Rumpole," I told him.

"Your wife says you're a barrister." Swainton seemed to find the notion somewhat absurd, as though I were a conjuror or an undertaker's mute. "I am an Old Bailey hack," I admitted.

"And we've all been wondering when you'd turn up." Swainton was still smiling, and I asked him, "Why? Are you in some sort of trouble?"

Before matters could further deteriorate, the vicar opened his cabin door and Hilda once again performed the introductions. "I'm afraid Mavis is still feeling a little groggy," Bill Britwell told us. "She just wants to rest quietly." Hilda said she understood perfectly, but Howard Swainton, saying, "I come bearing gifts!" and calling out, "Mavis!" invaded the room remorselessly, although Bill protested again, "I'm not sure she feels like visitors."

We followed, somewhat helplessly, in Howard's wake as he forged ahead. The woman whom I took to be Mavis Britwell was lying in the bed further from the door. The clothes were pulled up around her and only the top of her head was visible from where we stood. Howard Swainton continued his advance, saying, "Flowers for the poor invalid and my latest in paperback!" I saw him put his gifts down on the narrow table between the two beds, and, in doing so, he knocked over a glass of water which spilled on to Mavis's bed. She put out an arm automatically to protect herself and I couldn't help seeing what Swainton must also have noticed: the sick Mrs. Britwell had apparently retired to bed fully dressed.

"Oh, dear. How terribly clumsy of me!" Swainton was dabbing at the wet bed with his handkerchief. But Mavis had drawn the covers around her again and still lay with her face turned away from us. "Perhaps you could go now?" her husband said with admirable patience. "Mavis does want to be perfectly quiet." "Yes, of course." Swainton was apologetic. "I *do* understand. Come along, the Rumpoles."

We left the cabin then and Swainton soon parted from us to collect his secretary for dinner.

"She was dressed," Hilda said when we were left alone. "She was wearing her blouse and cardie."

"Perhaps the Reverend Bill fancies her in bed in a cardie."

"Don't be disgusting, Rumpole!" And then Hilda told me something else she had noticed. The two heavy silver framed photographs, which had stood on the dressing-table when she first visited the Britwells' cabin, had disappeared. She Who Must Be Obeyed has a dead eye for detail and would have risen to great heights in the Criminal Investigation Department.

The Old Salts' bar was liberally decorated with lifebelts, lobster nets, ships in bottles, charts, compasses and waitresses with sailor hats. There was a grand piano at which a small, pink-faced, bespectacled accompanist played as Miss Gloria de la Haye sang her way down Memory Lane. Gloria, a tall woman in a sequined dress, who made great play with a green chiffon handkerchief, must have been in her sixties, and her red curls no doubt owed little to nature. However, she had kept her figure and her long-nosed, wise-mouthed face, although probably never beautiful, was intelligent and humorous. She was singing "Smoke Gets in Your Eyes" and, with dinner over, we were awaiting our assignation with Gravestone in the company of Bill Britwell, Linda Milsom and Howard Swainton—Mrs. Mavis Britwell still being, her husband insisted, unwell and confined to her room. Hilda was giving an account of what she would have it thought of as a happy meeting with Sir Gerald Graves.

"Is he someone you've crossed swords with?" Swainton asked me, "in the Courts?"

"Swords? Nothing so gentlemanly. Let's say, chemical weapons. The old darling's summing up is pure poison gas."

"Oh, go on, Rumpole!" Hilda was having none of this. "He was absolutely charming to you on the boat deck."

"What's the matter with the claret, Hilda? Glued to the table?—That was just part of his diabolical cunning."

"Rumpole, are you sure you haven't had enough?" She was reluctant to pass the bottle.

"Of course, I'm sure. Coping with his lethal Lordship without a drink inside you is like having an operation without an anaesthetic."

At which, dead on time, Mr. Injustice berthed himself at our table, saying, "You're remarkably punctual, Rumpole."

"Oh, Judge! Everyone"—Hilda introduced the old faceache as though she owned him—"this is Sir Gerald Graves. Howard Swainton, *the* Howard Swainton, Linda, his personal assistant, and Bill Britwell, the Reverend Bill. Sir Gerald Graves."

"Five past nine exactly." The Judge had been studying his watch during these preliminaries and I weighed in with "Silence! The Court's in session."

"Well, now. Our second night at sea. I'm sure we're all enjoying it?" Graves's face contorted itself into an unusual and wintry smile.

"Best time we've had since the Luton Axe Killing, my Lord," I told him.

"What was that you said, Rumpole?"

"It's absolutely thrilling, my Lord," I translated, a little more loudly.

"I'm afraid"—the Reverend Bill got up—"you'll have to excuse me."

"Oh. So soon?"

"Can't you relax, Bill? Forget your troubles." Swainton tried to detain him. "Enjoy a drink with a real live judge."

"I must get back to Mavis."

"It's his wife, Judge. She hasn't been well," Howard Swainton said with apparent concern. And as Gloria switched from "Smoke Gets in Your Eyes" to "Thanks for the Memory," Bill agreed, "Well, not quite the ticket."

"I'm sorry to hear it." Graves was sympathetic. "Well, I do hope she's able to join us tomorrow."

"I'm sure she hopes so too." Swainton was smiling as he said it. "Give her all our best wishes. Tell her the Judge is thinking of her."

"Yes. Yes, I will. That's very kind." And Bill Britwell retreated from the Old Salts' bar saying, "Please! Don't let me break up the party." Whereupon Swainton came, like the terrier Hilda had described, bounding and yapping into the conversation with "I say, Judge. Horace Rumpole was just talking about your little scraps in Court."

"Oh, yes? We do have a bit of fun from time to time. Don't we, Rumpole?" Graves smiled contentedly but Swainton started to stir the legal brew with obvious relish. "That wasn't exactly how Rumpole put it," he said. "Of course, I do understand. Barristers are the natural enemies of judges. Judges and, well, my lot, detective-story writers. We want answers. We want to ferret out the truth. In the end we want to tell the world who's guilty!"

"Well put, if I may say so, Mr. Swainton!" Graves had clearly found a kindred spirit. "In your tales the mysteries are always solved and the criminal pays—"

"Enormous royalties!" I slipped in, "I have no doubt."

"His heavy debt to society!" Graves corrected me and then continued his love affair with the bouncy little novelist. "You always find the answer, Swainton. That's what makes your books such a thumping good read."

Gloria had stopped singing now and was refreshing herself at the bar.

stranger than fiction. Rumpole was a witness to the fact that when we called on Mrs. Mavis Britwell in her cabin, she was lying in bed with her clothes on! I don't know why it is, but I seem to have a talent for attracting mysteries."

"You mean she wanted you to believe she was ill?" Graves asked.

"Or *someone* wanted us to believe she was ill," Swainton told him. "Of course, one doesn't want to make any rash accusations."

"Doesn't one?" I asked. "It sounds as though one was absolutely longing to." But Mr. Justice Graves was clearly having the time of his old life. "Swainton," he said, "I'd very much like to know how your story ends."

"Would you, Judge? I'm afraid we'll all just have to wait and see. No harm, of course, in keeping our eyes open in the meanwhile."

At which moment, the accompanist pounded some rhythmic chords on the piano and Gloria burst into the ditty whose words I could still remember, along with long stretches of *The Oxford Book of English Verse*, better than most of the news I heard yesterday:

> Who's that kicking up a noise?
> My little sister!
> Who's that giggling with the boys?
> My little sister!
> Whose lemonade is laced with gin?
> Who taught the vicar how to sin?
> Knock on her door and she'll let you in!
> My little sister!
> Who's always been the teacher's pet?
> Who took our puppy to the vet?
> That was last night and she's not home yet!
> My little sister!

"What an extraordinary song!" Hilda said when my request performance was over.

"Yes," I told her. "Takes you back, doesn't it? Takes *me* back, anyway."

When the party in the Old Salts' bar was over, Hilda slipped her arm through mine and led me across the deck to the ship's rail. I feared some romantic demonstration and looked around for help, but the only person about seemed to be Bill Britwell, wrapped in a heavy raincoat, who was standing some way from us. It was somewhat draughty and a fine rain was falling, but there was a moon and the sound of a distant dance band. Hilda, apparently, drew the greatest encouragement from these facts.

"The sound of music across the water. Stars. You and I by the rail. Finding each other . . . Listen, Rumpole! What do you think the Med. is trying to say to us?"

"It probably wants to tell you it's the Bay of Biscay," I suggested.

Her plump accompanist was going round the tables with a pad an
cil, asking for requests for the singer's next number.

"Thank you, Judge. Most kind of you." Howard Swainton was
not above saluting the judicial backside. "But the Horace Rumpo
this world always want to raise a verbal smokescreen of 'reas
doubt.' Tactics, you see. They do it so the guilty can slide away to sa

"*Touché*, Rumpole! Hasn't Mr. Swainton rather got you there?"
was clearly delighted by the author's somewhat tormented prose.

"Not *touché* in the least!" I told him. "Anyway, I've heard it so
times before from those who want to convict someone, anyone, anc
care very much who it is. There speaks the voice of the Old Bill."

"But I don't understand. His name's Howard." Miss Linda M
however rapid her shorthand, was not exactly quick on the uptake

"Detective Inspector Swainton"—I was now in full flood—"di
defending counsel and wants all trials to take place in the friendly
bourhood nick. He's so keen on getting at the truth that, if he can
it, he'll invent it—like the end of a detective story."

"Is this how he goes on in Court?" Swainton asked with a sn
the Judge, who assured him, "Oh, all the time."

"Then you have my heartfelt sympathy, Judge," Swainton said,
could scarcely withhold my tears for his poor old Lordship. "Thank
Graves said. "Tell me, Swainton, are you working on some won
new mystery to delight us?"

Then my attention was distracted by the little accompanist, who
me if I'd care to write down a request for Gloria. I looked across
tall, sequined woman, apparently downing a large port and lemo
I was whisked back down the decades to my carefree bachelor c
was leaving Equity Court, when the Chambers were then run by H
Daddy, C. H. Wystan, for a chop and a pint of stout at the Cock t
and decided to give myself a treat by dropping in to the Old Metrop
music hall, long since defunct, in the Edgware Road. There I mig
jugglers and adagio dancers and Max Miller, the "Cheeky Chappie
. . . At this point I scribbled a song title on the accompanist's pa
looked at it, I thought with some surprise, and carried it back to C
And then, bringing me painfully back to the present, I heard Sw;
tell us the plot of his latest masterpiece.

"In *Absence of Body*," he said, "I am now thinking along these
A woman, a middle-aged woman, perfectly ordinary, is on a cruis(
her new husband. He's a fellow who has taken the precaution of ins
her life for a tidy sum. He tells everyone she's ill, but in fact she's
in bed in their cabin"—here Swainton leant forward and put a ha
Graves's knee for emphasis—"fully *dressed*."

"I see!" Graves was delighted with the mystery. "So the
thickens."

"It's the truth, you understand," Swainton assured him. "It's so

"Is there nothing you feel romantic about?"

"Of course there is." I couldn't let that charge go unanswered.

"There you are, you see!" Hilda was clearly pleased. "I always thought so. What exactly?"

"Steak and kidney pudding." I gave her the list. "The jury system, the presumption of innocence."

"Anything else?"

"Oh. Of course. I almost forgot," I reassured her.

"Yes?"

"Wordsworth."

There was a thoughtful silence then and Hilda, like Gloria, went off down Memory Lane. "It doesn't seem so very long ago," she said, "that I was a young girl, and you asked Daddy for my hand in marriage."

"And he gave it to me!" I remembered it well.

"Daddy was always so generous. Tell me, Rumpole. Now we're alone"—Hilda started off. I'm not sure what sort of intimate subject she was about to broach because I had to warn her, "But we're not alone. Look!"

She turned her head and we both saw Bill Britwell standing by the rail, staring down at the sea and apparently involved in his own thoughts. Then, oblivious to our existence, he opened his coat, under which he had concealed two silver-framed photographs, much like those Hilda had seen on the dressing-table on her first visit to his cabin. He looked at them for a moment and dropped them towards the blackness of the passing sea. He turned from the rail then and walked away, not noticing Hilda and me, nor Howard Swainton, who had also come out of the Old Salts' bar a few minutes before and had been watching this mysterious episode with considerable fascination.

Time, on a cruise ship, tends to drag; watching water pass by you slowly is not the most exciting occupation in the world. Hilda spent her time by having her hair done, or her face creamed, or taking steam-baths, or being pounded to some sort of pulp in the massage parlour. I slept a good deal or walked round the deck. I was engaged in this mild exercise when I came within earshot of that indefatigable pair, Graves and Swainton, the Judge and the detective writer, who were sitting on deck-chairs, drinking soup. I loitered behind a boat for a little, catching the drift of their conversation.

"Photographs?" The Judge was puzzled. "In silver frames? and he threw them into the sea?"

"That's what it looked like."

"But why would a man do such a thing?"

"Ask yourself that, Members of the Jury." I emerged and posed the question, "Is the Court in secret session or can anyone join?"

"Ah, Rumpole. There you are." Graves, given a case to try, seemed to be in excellent humour. "Now then, I believe you were also a witness. Why would a man throw photographs into the sea? That is indeed the question we have to ask. And perhaps, with your long experience of the criminal classes, you can suggest a solution?"

"I'm on holiday. What Britwell did with his photographs seems entirely his own affair." But Swainton clearly didn't think so. "I can offer a solution." He gave us one of his plots for nothing. "Suppose the Reverend Bill isn't a Reverend at all. I believe a lot of con men go on these cruises."

"That is an entirely unfounded suggestion by the Prosecution, my Lord." I had the automatic reaction of the life-long defender, at which moment the steward trundled the soup trolley up to me and Graves, by now well in to presiding over the upper-deck Court, said, 'Please, Mr. Rumpole! Let Mr. Swainton complete his submission. Your turn will come later."

"Oh, is that soup?" I turned my attention to the steward. "Thank you very much."

"Suppose Bill Britwell wanted to remove all trace of the person in the photographs?" Swainton suggested.

"Two persons," I corrected him. "Hilda told me there were two photographs. One was Bill Britwell and his wife. The other was of a young girl. Are you suggesting he wanted to remove all trace of two people? Is that the prosecution case?"

"Please, Mr. Rumpole, it hasn't come to a prosecution yet," Graves said unconvincingly.

"His wife? This is *very* interesting!" Swainton yelped terrier-like after the information. "One picture was of his wife. Now, why should he throw that into the sea?"

"God knows. Perhaps it didn't do her justice," I suggested, and Swainton looked thoughtful and said, in a deeply meaningful sort of way, "Or was it a symbolic act?"

"A what?" I wasn't following his drift, if indeed he had one. "He got rid of her photograph," Swainton did his best to explain, *"because he means to get rid of her."*

"That is a most serious suggestion." Graves greeted it with obvious relish, whilst I, slurping my soup, said, "Balderdash, my Lord!"

"What?" The little novelist looked hurt.

"The product of a mind addled with detective stories," I suggested.

"All right!" Swainton yapped at me impatiently. "If you know so much, tell us this. Where do you think Mrs. Mavis Britwell is? Still in bed with her clothes on?"

"Why don't you go and have a peep through the keyhole?" I suggested.

"I wasn't thinking of that, exactly. But I was thinking . . ."

"Oh, do try not to," I warned him. "It overexcites his Lordship."

"The steward does up the cabins along our corridor at about this time," Swainton remembered. "If we happened to be passing, we might just see something extremely interesting."

"You mean we might take a view?" The Judge was clearly enthusiastic and I tried to calm him down by saying, "—Of the scene of a crime that hasn't been committed?"

"It's clearly our duty to investigate any sort of irregularity." Graves was at his most self-important.

"And no doubt your delight," I suggested.

"What did you say, Rumpole?" The Judge frowned.

"I said you're perfectly right, my Lord. And no doubt you would wish the Defence to be represented at the scene of any possible crime."

"Have you briefed yourself, Rumpole?" Swainton gave me an un-friendly smile. I took a final gulp of soup and told him, "I certainly have, as there's no one else to do it for me."

When we got down to the corridor outside the cabins, the trolley with clean towels and sheets was outside the Graves residence, where work was being carried out. We loitered around, trying to look casual, and then Bill Britwell greatly helped the Prosecution by emerging from his door, which he shut carefully behind him. He looked at Graves in a startled and troubled sort of way and said, "Oh. It's you! Good morning, Judge."

"My dear Britwell. And how's your wife this morning?" The Judge smiled with patent insincerity, as though meaning, We certainly don't hope she's well, as that would be far too boring.

"I'm afraid she's no better," Britwell reassured them. "No better at all. In fact she's got to stay in bed very quietly. No visitors, I'm afraid. Now, if you'll excuse me." He made his way quickly down the corridor and away from us on some errand or other, and Hilda opened the door of our cabin which, you will remember, was dead opposite the berth of the Britwells. "Ah, Mrs. Rumpole." His Lordship was delighted to see her. "Perhaps you'd allow us to be your guests, just for a moment?" and, although I gave Hilda a warning about helping the Prosecution, She ea-gerly invited the judicial team in, although she asked them to forgive "the terrible mess." "Oh, we can put up with any little inconvenience," the Judge boomed in his most lugubrious courtroom accent, "in our quest for the truth!"

So the search party took refuge in our cabin until the steward pushed his trolley up to the Britwells' door, unlocked it with his pass key and went inside, leaving the door open. Graves waited for a decent interval to elapse and then he led Swainton and me across the corridor and through the door, while the steward was putting towels in the bathroom. There was no one in either of the twin beds, and only one of them seemed to have been slept in. There was no powder, make-up or perfume on the dressing-table and, so far as one quick look could discover, no sign of Mrs. Mavis Britwell at all.

"Can I help you, gentlemen?" The steward came in from the bathroom, surprised by the invasion. "Oh, I'm sorry!" Swainton apologized with total lack of conviction. "We must have got the wrong cabin. They all look so alike. Particularly," he added with deep meaning, "those with only a *single* occupant."

That night, in the Old Salts' bar, Graves and Swainton were seated at the counter, and Gloria was drawing towards the end of her act, when I intruded again on their discussion of the state of the evidence.

"Britwell told us a deliberate lie," the Judge was saying.

"He distinctly said she was in the room," Swainton agreed.

"In my view his evidence has to be accepted with extreme caution," Graves ruled. "On any subject."

"I don't see why." I put my oar in and Swainton gave a little yapping laugh and said, "Here comes the perpetual defender."

"We all tell the odd lie, don't we?" I suggested, and then I ordered a large glass of claret, which I had christened Château Bilgewater, from Alfred, the barman.

"Speak for yourself, Rumpole." Graves looked at me as though I was probably as big a liar as the Reverend Bill. I wasn't going to let him get away with that without a spot of cross-examination, so I put this to his Lordship. "When you met my wife on the deck the other morning, didn't you tell her that you had no idea she was on the boat?"

"I *may* have said that," the Judge conceded.

"And I distinctly saw you at the Captain's cocktail party the night before. You caught sight of Mrs. Hilda Rumpole and went beetling out of the room because you recognized her!"

"Rumpole! That is . . ." The Judge seemed unable to find words to describe my conduct so I supplied them for him. "I know. A grossly improper argument. You may have to report it to the proper authorities."

"Gentlemen!" Swainton was, unusually, acting as a peacemaker. "We may all tell the odd white lie occasionally, but this is a far more serious matter. We have to face the fact that Mrs. Britwell has apparently disappeared."

"In the midst of the words she was trying to say," I suggested:

> "In the midst of her laughter and glee,
> She softly and suddenly vanished away
> For the Snark *was* a Boojum, you see."

"The question is"—Swainton was in no mood for Lewis Carroll—"what action should we take?"

"But who exactly *is* the Boojum—or the Snark, come to that?" This, I felt, was the important question.

"The circumstances are no doubt very suspicious." Graves had his head on one side, his lips pursed, his brandy glass in his hand, and was doing his best to sound extremely judicial. "Suspicions of what?" I had to put the question. "Is the theory that Bill Britwell pushed his wife over-board for the sake of a little life insurance and then kept quiet about it? What's the point of that?"

"It's possible he may have got rid of her," Swainton persisted, "for whatever reason . . ."

"If you think that, stop the boat," I told them. "Send for helicopters. Organize a rescue operation."

"I'm afraid it's a little late for that." Swainton looked extremely seri-ous. "If he did anything, my feeling is, he did it last night. In some way, I think, the event may have been connected with the photographs that were thrown into the water."

So they sat on their bar stools and thought it over, the Judge and the fiction writer, like an old eagle and a young sparrow on their perches, and then Graves rather lost his bottle. "The circumstances are highly sus-picious, of course," he spoke carefully, "but can we say they amount to a certainty?"

"Of course we can't," I told them, and then launched my attack on the learned Judge. "The trouble with the Judiciary is that you see crime in everything. It's the way an entomologist goes out for walks in the countryside and only notices the beetles."

Graves thought this over in silence and then made a cautious pro-nouncement. "If we were sure, of course, we could inform the police at Gibraltar. It might be a case for Interpol." But Swainton had dreamed up another drama. "I have a suggestion to make, Judge. If you agree. To-morrow I'm giving my lecture, 'How I Think Up My Plots.' I presume you're all coming?" "Don't bet on it!" I told him. But he went on, un-deterred. "I may add something to my text for Britwell's benefit. Keep your eyes on him when I say it." "You mean, observe his demeanour?" The Judge got the point.

Looking down the bar, I saw Gloria talking to Alfred, the barman, while beside me Swainton was babbling with delight at his ingenious plan. "See if he looks guilty," he said. "Do you think that's an idea?"

"Not exactly original," I told him, "Shakespeare used it in *Hamlet*."

"Did he, really?" The little author seemed surprised. "It might be even better in my lecture."

By now I had had about as much as I could take of the Judge and his side-kick, so I excused myself and moved to join Gloria, who was giving some final instructions to the barman. "A bottle of my usual to take away, Alfred," I heard her say. "The old and tawny. Oh, and a couple of glasses, could you let us have? They keep getting broken."

"Miss Gloria de la Haye?" I greeted her, and she gave me a smile of recognition. "Aren't you the gentleman that requested my old song?"

"I haven't heard you sing it for years," I told her. "Music halls don't exist any more, do they?"

"Worse luck!" She pulled a sour face. "It's a drag, this is, having to do an act afloat. Turns your stomach when the sea gets choppy, and there's not much life around here, is there?" She looked along the bar. "More like a floating old people's home. I'm prepared to scream if anyone else requests 'Smoke Gets in Your Eyes.' I want to say it soon will, in yours, dear, in the crematorium!"

"I remember going to the Metropolitan in the Edgware Road."

"You went to the old Met.?" Gloria was smiling.

" 'Who's that kicking up a noise?' " I intoned the first line of the song and she joined me in a way that made the Judge stare at us with surprise and disapproval:

"Who's that giggling with the boys?
My little sister!"

"That was my act, the long and short of it," Gloria confirmed my recollection. "Betty Dee and Buttercup. I was Buttercup's straight man."

"Wasn't an alleged comic on the same bill?" I asked her. "Happy Harry someone. A man who did a rather embarrassing drunk act, if I remember."

"Was there?" Gloria stopped smiling. "I can't recall, exactly."

"And about Buttercup?" I asked. "Rather a pretty girl, wasn't she? What's happened to her?"

"Can't tell you that, I'm afraid. We haven't kept in touch." And Gloria turned back to the barman. "My old and tawny, Alfred?" She picked up the bottle of port and glasses the barman had put in front of her and went out of the bar. I let her get a start and then I decided to follow her. She went down corridors between cabin doors and down a flight of stairs to a lower deck where a notice on the wall read SECOND-CLASS PASSENGERS. From the bottom of the stairs I watched as she walked down a long corridor, a tall, sequined woman with a muscular back. Then she opened a cabin door and went inside.

In the normal course of events, a lecture "How I Think Up My Plots" by Howard Swainton would have commanded my attention somewhat less than an address by Soapy Sam Bollard to the Lawyers As Christians Society on the home-life of the Prophet Amos. However, Swainton's threatened re-enactment of the play scene from *Hamlet* seemed likely to add a certain bizarre interest to an otherwise tedious occasion, so I found myself duly seated in the ship's library alongside Hilda and Judge Graves.

Bill Britwell, whom Swainton had pressed to attend, was a few rows behind us. Dead on the appointed hour, the best-selling author bobbed up behind a podium and, after a polite smattering of applause, told us how difficult plots were to come by and how hard he had to work on their invention in order to feed his vast and eager public's appetite for a constant diet of Swainton. An author's work, he told us, was never done, and although he might seem to be enjoying himself, drinking soup on the deck and assisting at the evening's entertainment in the Old Salts' bar, he was, in fact, hard at work on his latest masterpiece, *Absence of Body*, the story of a mysterious disappearance at sea. This led him to dilate on the question of whether a conviction for murder is possible if the corpse fails to put in an appearance.

"The old idea of the *corpus delicti* as a defence has now been laid, like the presumably missing corpse, to rest." Swainton was in full flow. "The defence is dead and buried, if not the body. Some years ago a steward on an ocean-going liner was tried for the murder of a woman passenger. It was alleged that he'd made love to her, either with or without her consent, and then pushed her through a porthole out into the darkness of the sea. Her body was never recovered. The Defence relied heavily on the theory of the *corpus delicti*. Without a body, the ingenious barrister paid to defend the steward said, there could be no conviction."

At this, Graves couldn't resist turning round in his seat to stare at Bill Britwell, who was in fact, stirring restlessly. "The Judge and the Jury would have none of this," Swainton went on. "The steward was condemned to death, although, luckily for him, the death sentence was then abolished. This case gave me the germ of an idea for the new tale which I am going to introduce to you tonight. Ladies and Gentlemen. You are privileged to be the first audience to whom I shall read chapter one of the brand-new Stainton mystery entitled *Absence of Body*." He produced a wadge of typescript and Linda Milsom gazed up at him adoringly as he started to read: " 'When Joe Andrews suggested to this wife that they go on a cruise for their honeymoon, she was delighted. She might not have been so pleased if she had an inkling of the plan that was already forming itself at the back of his mind . . . ' " At which point there was the sound of a gasp and a chair being scraped back behind us. Obediently playing the part of guilty King Claudius, Bill Britwell rose from his seat and fled from the room.

"You saw that, Rumpole," the Judge whispered to me with great satisfaction. "Isn't that evidence of guilt?"

"Either of guilt," I told him, "or terminal boredom."

The ship's gift shop, as well as stocking a large selection of Howard Swainton, and others of those authors whose books are most frequently on show at airports, railway stations and supermarket checkouts, sold all sorts of sweets, tobacco, sun oil (not yet needed), ashtrays, table mats and T-shirts embellished with portraits of the late Queen Boadicea, giant pandas and teddy bears, cassettes and other articles of doubtful utility. On the day of the first fancy-dress ball, which was to take place on the evening before our arrival at Gibraltar, the gift shop put on display a selection of hats, false beards, noses, head-dresses and other accoutrements for those who lacked the skill or ingenuity to make their own costumes. In the afternoon the shop was full of passengers in search of disguise in which they could raise a laugh, cut a dash, or realize a childhood longing to be someone quite different from whoever they eventually turned out to be.

"Rumpole," Hilda was kind enough to say, "you look quite romantic." I had put a black patch over one eye and sported a three-cornered hat with a skull and cross-bones on the front. Looking in the shop mirror, I saw Jolly Roger Rumpole or Black Cap'n Rumpole of the Bailey. And then She looked across the shop to where the Reverend Bill was picking over a selection of funny hats. "You wouldn't think he'd have the nerve to dress up this evening, would you?" She said with a disapproving click of her tongue. I left her and joined Britwell. I spoke to him in confidential but, I hope, cheering tones. "You must be getting tired of it," I said sympathetically.

"Tired of what?"

"People asking 'How's your wife?' "

"They're very kind." If he were putting on an act, he was doing it well. "Extremely considerate."

"It must be spoiling your trip."

"Mavis being ill?" He beamed at me vaguely through his spectacles. "Yes, it is rather."

"Mr. Justice Graves," I began and he looked suddenly nervous and said, "The Judge?" "Yes, the Judge. He seems very worried about your wife."

"Why's he worried?" Britwell asked anxiously.

"About her illness, I suppose. He wants to see her."

"Why should he want that?"

"You know what judges are," I told him. "Always poking their noses into things that don't really concern them. Shall we see your wife tonight at the fancy-dress party?"

"Well. No. I'm afraid not. Mavis won't be up to it. Such a pity. It's the sort of thing she'd love so much, if she were only feeling herself." And then Hilda joined us, looking, although I say it myself, superb. She was wearing a helmet and breastplate and carrying a golden trident and a shield emblazoned with the Union Jack. Staring at my wife with undisguised admiration, I could only express myself in song:

> "Rule Britannia!
> Britannia rules the waves, (I warbled)
> Britain never, never shall be ... "

"Is it going too far?" She asked nervously. But I shook my head and looked at Bill Britwell as I completed the verse:

> "Marri-ed to a mermai-ed,
> At the bottom of the deep blue sea!"

There was a sound of considerable revelry by night and as that old terror of the Spanish Main, Pirate Cap'n Rumpole, made his way in the company of assorted Pierrots, slave girls, pashas, clowns, Neptunes and mermaids towards the big saloon from which the strains of dance music were sounding, I passed an office doorway from which a Chinese mandarin emerged in the company of Captain Orde, who was attending the festivities disguised as a ship's captain. As I passed them I heard Orde say, "The police at Gib have the message, sir. So if he can't produce the lady . . ." "Yes, yes, Captain." The mandarin, who looked only a little less snooty and superior than Mr. Justice Graves in his normal guise, did his best to shut the officer up as he saw this old sea-dog approaching from windward. "Why there you are, Rumpole! Have you had some sort of an accident to your eye? Nothing serious, I hope."

Hilda and I have not danced together since our first honeymoon. As I have already indicated, the exercise was not a startling success and that night, with all the other excitement going on, she seemed content not to repeat the experiment. We sat in front of a bottle of the Bilgewater red, to which I had grown quite attached in an appalling sort of way, and we watched the dancers. Howard Swainton, as an undersized Viking, was steering the lanky Linda Milsom, a slave girl, who towered over him. It might be an exaggeration to say his eye-level was that of the jewel in her navel, but not too much of one. Across the room we could see the Reverend Bill holding a glass and admiring the scene. He was wearing a turban, a scimitar and a lurid beard. "Bluebeard!" Hilda said. "How very appropriate."

"Oh, for heaven's sake!" I told her, "don't *you* start imagining things." And then a familiarly icy voice cut into our conversation. "Mrs. Rumpole," said the ridiculously boring mandarin, "might I ask you to give me the honour of this dance?" She Who Must Be Obeyed, apparently delighted, said, "Of course, Judge, what tremendous fun!" My worst fears were confirmed and they waltzed away together with incomprehensible zest.

In due course, Swainton and his houri came to sit at our table and, looking idly at the throng, we witnessed the entry of two schoolgirls in gym-slips and straw hats. One was tall and thin and clearly Gloria. The other, small and plump, wore a schoolgirl mask to which a pigtailed wig was attached. Swainton immediately guessed that this was Miss de la Haye's little accompanist in disguise. "Betty Dee and Buttercup," I said, only half aloud, as this strange couple crossed the room, and Linda Milsom, who was having trouble retaining the liverish-looking glass eye in her navel, said, "Some people sure like to make themselves look ridiculous." A little time passed and then Swainton said, "Well, that beats everything!" "What?" I asked, removing my nose from my glass and shifting the patch so that I had two eyes available.

"An alleged vicar dancing with a bar pianist in drag." It was true.

The Reverend Bill and the small schoolgirl were waltzing expertly. "I think," I said, "I could be about to solve the mystery of the Absent Body."

"I very much doubt it." Swainton was not impressed with my deductive powers.

"Would you like me to try?" And, before he could answer, I asked Linda to cut in and invite Bill Britwell for a dance.

"Oh," she appealed to her boss, "do I have to?" "Why not?" Swainton shrugged his shoulders. "It might be entertaining to watch Counsel for the Defence barking up the wrong tree."

When instructed by the best-selling author, Miss Milsom acted with decision and aplomb. I saw her cross the floor and speak to Bill Britwell. He looked at his partner, who surrendered more or less gracefully and was left alone on the floor. Before the small schoolgirl could regain the table where Gloria was waiting, Cap'n Rumpole had drawn up alongside.

"I'm afraid I'm no dancer," I said. "So shall we go out for a breath of air?" Without waiting for a reply, I took the schoolgirl's arm and steered her towards the doors which led out to the deck.

So there I was by the rail of the ship again, in the moonlight with music playing in the background, faced, not by Hilda, but by a small, round figure wearing a schoolgirl mask.

"Betty Dee and Buttercup," I said. "You were Buttercup, weren't you? The little sister, the young girl in the photograph Bill Britwell threw into the sea? Not that there was any need for that. No one really remembered you."

"What do you want?" A small voice spoke from behind the mask.

"To set your mind at rest," I promised. "No one knows you've been part of a music-hall act. No one's going to hold that against you. Bill can preach sermons to the Anglicans of Malta and no one's going to care a toss about Betty Dee and Buttercup. It's the other part you were worried about, wasn't it? The part you played down the Old Bailey. A long time ago. Such a long time. When we were all very young indeed. Oh, so very young. Before I did the Penge Bungalow Murders, which is no longer even recent history. All the same I was at the Bar when it happened. You know, you should've had me to defend you. You really should. It was a touching story. A young girl married to a drunk, a husband who beat her. Who was he? 'Happy' Harry Harman? He even did a drunk act on the stage, didn't he? Drunk acts are never very funny. I read all about it in the *News of the World* because I wanted the brief. He beat you and you stabbed him in the throat with a pair of scissors. You should never have got five years for manslaughter. I'd've got you off with not a dry eye in the jury-box, even though the efficient young Counsel for the Prosecution was a cold fish called Gerald Graves. It's all right. He is not going to remember you."

"Isn't he?" The small voice spoke again.

"Of course not. Lawyers and judges hardly ever remember the faces they've sent to prison."

"Are you sure?"

I was conscious that we were no longer alone on the deck. Bill Britwell had come out of the doors behind us, followed by Graves and Howard Swainton, who must have suspected that the drama they had concocted was reaching a conclusion. "Oh, yes," I said, "you can come out of hiding now."

She must have believed me because she lifted her hands and carefully removed the mask. She was only a little nervous as she stood in the moonlight, smiling at her husband. And the Judge and the mystery writer, for once, had nothing to say.

"Such a pleasure, isn't it?" I asked them, "to have Mrs. Mavis Britwell back with us again."

The Rock of Gibraltar looked much as expected, towering over the strange little community which can be looked at as the last outpost of a vanishing Empire or as a tiny section of the Wimbledon of fifty years ago, tacked improbably on to the bottom of Spain. The good ship *Boadicea* was safely docked the next morning and, as the passengers disembarked for a guided tour with a full English tea thrown in, I stood, once more at the rail, this time in the company of Mr. "Miscarriage of Justice" Graves. I had just taken him for a guided tour round the facts of the Britwell case.

"So she decided to vanish?" he asked me.

"Not at all. She went to stay with her old friend, Miss Gloria de la Haye, for a few days." And then I asked him, "She didn't look familiar to you?"

"No. No, I can't say she did. Why?"

" 'Old men forget' "—I wasn't about to explain—" 'yet all shall be forgot.' "

"What did you say?" His Lordship wasn't following my drift.

"I said, 'What a load of trouble you've got.' "

"Trouble? You're not making yourself clear, Rumpole."

"You as good as accused the Reverend Bill of shoving his dear wife through the porthole." I recited the charges. "You reported the story to the ship's captain, who no doubt wired it to the Gibraltar police. That was clear publication and a pretty good basis for an action for defamation. Wouldn't you say?"

"Defamation?" The Judge repeated the dread word. "Oh, yes," I reminded him, "and jurys have been quite absurdly generous with damages lately. Remember my offer to defend you?" My mind went back to a distant bail application. "Please call on my services at any time."

"Rumpole"—the Judicial face peered at me anxiously—"you don't honestly think they'd sue?"

"My dear Judge, I think you're innocent, of course, until you're proved guilty. That's such an important principle to keep in mind on all occasions."

And then I heard a distant cry of "Rumpole!" Hilda was kitted out and ready to call on the Barbary apes.

"Ah, that's my wife. I'd better go. We're on a honeymoon too, you see. Our second. And it may disappoint you to know, we're innocent of any crime whatsoever."

SUSAN MOODY
(1940–)

It is not surprising that Susan Moody has penned this story of treachery on the water entitled "Oh, Who Hath Done This Deed?" Moody grew up in Oxford but spent numerous holidays along the hazardous waterfront at Deal, near Dover, England. She has described the view from her childhood holiday home as containing "the spars of wrecked ships," which "stuck up on the horizon like the arms of sailors, not waving, but drowning." Even the sandbar where she played cricket between tides became quicksand as the tide turned.

The daughter of an Oxford don, Moody was born Susan Elizabeth Horwood. She was educated at the Oxford High School for Girls and at the Open University, an educational alternative that Moody describes as "started by the socialists and implemented by the Tories." Moody then spent two years in France, assisting an expert orchid grower. She later married an American biologist and moved to Tennessee, where she lived for ten years. After her first husband died, she remarried and continued to raise three sons in Bedford, England. She has worked as a creative writing teacher at H.M. Prison, Bedford, and has served as vice chairman and as chairman of the British Crime Writers Association. In recent years she has taken up residence again in Oxford.

Moody introduced her sassy black sleuth, Penny Wanawake, in 1984 and continued her adventures in seven novels. Then, in 1991, she wrote *Playing with Fire* (published in the United States as *Mosaic*), the first of four suspense novels. In 1993 she created another series character, the bridge-playing expert Cassandra "Cassie" Swann, who has appeared in several novels to date. Moody also made the English bestseller lists in 1993 with *Love over Gold*, her story of the Nescafé Gold Blend (Taster's Choice) couple, who flirt over the coffee product. In 1995, the versatile Moody wrote *Misselthwaite*, a sequel to Frances Hodgson Burnett's children's classic, *The Secret Garden*.

"Oh, Who Hath Done This Deed?" demonstrates Moody's talents in the short story form. From title to finish, the author steers this poignant story of infanticide and its enigmatic aftermath along the lines of Shakespearean tragedy. Steadied with references to the Bard's *Othello*, this tale juxtaposes dangerous and unreasonable jealousy with a child's innocence, the resulting contrast moving both the development of the plot and the emotions of the reader.

Moody confided, "This story emerged from a conversation I had with a Frenchman on the coast of Brittany. He told me he had seen a rowing boat under the harbor wall with a man and a boy in it, that the boat had capsized and the man had gone under, as had the boy. Neither of them could swim, it appeared, and neither was wearing a life jacket. The Frenchman dived in to rescue them, first the boy and then what he assumed was his father. The chilling thing, he told me, was that, when he had brought the two of them safely to the harbour steps, and emptied the child of sea-water, all the father said was, 'Where's the boy's hat?' ''

Oh, Who Hath Done This Deed?

1992

I couldn't quite place her.

She came out of the shadows beside the old fort and walked across the palm-shaded square to stand on the jetty, looking down at the water. She had strikingly long legs, rounded hips, a face which, although hidden now by sunglasses, possessed the planes of lasting beauty. Yet, as she crossed the square, stepping in and out of the striped shadows, she was neither striking nor beautiful. Her hair was careless, her shoulders, somehow, defeated.

She had leaned towards me once. She had smiled at me, her face alive with love. But when? It was a small puzzle and one which I did not dwell on longer than it took to wonder ruefully whether I had at last reached the age when any young woman reminded me of lost love.

In front of me, wind riffled the oily surface of the little harbour and the fishing boats rocked together, sending ripples towards the jetty. These were working boats; the place was too small for holiday sailors since there were no watering or petrol facilities, nowhere to stock up on whisky and tins. There was only the hotel up on the cliff, built in the thirties by an over-ambitious Frenchman who shortly afterwards went bankrupt, only the miles of empty country behind and the Roman ruins mouldering in the desert among sombre dunes of reddish sand which at sunset seemed to be made of rust-coloured cloud. And there was, of course, a beach, uncluttered, unpolluted, curling away around the coast for half a mile. For the moment, the place remained undiscovered by all but a very few, though I knew it was inevitable that sooner or later some travel writer or tourist agency would happen upon it and another paradise would be lost.

I should have realised she would be staying at the hotel—there was, after all, nowhere else. The following morning, I was sitting on the terrace which had been built out over the sea when she came hesitantly out and looked around for somewhere to sit. It wasn't difficult; at that time of year there were only half a dozen other guests, but the effort of deciding which table to occupy seemed to be too much for her. She bit her lip, frowning, moved towards one table and then thought better of it; moved irresolutely to another. Again she seemed tantalisingly familiar; curiosity made me half rise in my seat, indicating that she was welcome to join me if she wished but as soon as she caught my eye she ducked her head and scurried towards the table furthest from mine.

I shrugged. Obviously she found me a threat even though she wore a wedding ring; I could see it glinting on her finger as she picked up the glass of pineapple juice in front of her only to put it quickly down to lean her arms on the stone balustrade and gaze at the beach below. When the boy came to take her breakfast order, she shook her head and he went away.

There was something about her I recognised . . . was it the shape of the head, the line of her jaw, a sense of nostalgia I couldn't quite grasp? In the end, curiosity won. I got up and went over to her.

"*Excusez-moi, madame . . .*" French seemed the most obvious language to use since the port had once been part of the French colonial possessions and as far as I knew, I was the only Englishman in the place. "*Excusez-moi, mais j'ai l'impression que . . .*"

She turned swiftly, her eyes wide and alarmed, as though she had not heard me approaching and was startled by my voice. "I'm afraid I don't speak French," she said. She had a clear carrying voice, each word meticulously pronounced.

I smiled. "I'm English myself," I said. "I saw you yesterday, down in the square."

"Yes?" She waited, as though my remark must surely be leading onto something more significant.

"Are you here alone?" It was the crassest of questions and I realised as soon as I had made it that she would take me for some remittance man, some seasonal gigolo making a living from lonely women, giving them sex in return for a watch, a silk shirt, a cheque.

"My husband's down there," she said pointing at the beach.

"Ah." I peered over. The brown beach was nearly empty so early in the day though half a dozen people were cresting the long slow waves or swimming lazily in the shallows.

"That's him," she said, pointing at a black head far out on the waves, making purposefully for the land. "He's an actor. He likes to swim for half a mile morning and evening." She turned to look up at me, gave a soft little laugh. I noticed that her own hair was damp. "I don't know exactly how he judges the distance, but he seems to be able to tell."

It was the laugh which did it. "Desdemona," I said.

She looked blank. For a moment I wondered if I'd got it wrong. But no . . . "You were Desdemona. In the Richter film. The most marvellous Desdemona. With Bernard Peters as your Othello and Charles Everett playing Iago."

She looked down at her clasped hands. "It was a long time ago."

"But unforgettable. You were so . . ." I sought for words. ". . . passionate, so innocent, so *doomed*."

I was not the only one to admire her performance. The critics had raved, the film had been a stupendous box-office success, and the little English actress plucked from some obscure repertory company had been guaranteed an illustrious future. There'd been a second, less prestigious film, a third. In all of them her air of fragile resilience had shone through.

And then there'd been nothing. She had vanished; it was one of those Whatever-Happened-To . . . ? show-biz mysteries which occur from time to time and are eventually solved only when someone does a tragedy article or an unexpected obituary appears.

Her name was Helena Garden. I recalled that she had been married at the time *Othello* was made and the mother of a child. There was no reason why I should have remembered—except that she had been unforgettable.

For a while we talked. The boy came over and went away again. She began to watch the door out onto the terrace.

I knew when he arrived. I could tell by the way her eyes widened and then dropped. I turned. He was standing there at the door onto the terrace, in jeans and a white shirt with the collar turned up to frame his handsome actor's face, unable to resist making an entrance.

He caught sight of us and frowned. He came over, taking a pair of sunglasses out of his pocket and slipping them on as he walked between the tables.

I stood. "I hope you don't think I'm intruding," I said, my voice falsely hearty. "I know it's some years ago now, but I recognised your wife and felt I simply had to say how wonderful I thought her Desdemona was." I held out a hand which he ignored. "I'm Martin Howard."

"Jeremy Talbot," he said shortly. He grasped his wife's shoulder.

I smiled. I backed away, left my unfinished breakfast, went up to my room. He did not seem to remember that we had met before. But I did.

I spent the day sailing round the coastline to Moukabi, a spectacular cluster of ruins long since abandoned to sand and wind. Time had rounded and scoured the ancient walls into a series of extraordinary shapes; they reared out of the red soil like natural growths caused by the earth's shiftings. I had been there before and never failed to find the desolation of the place somehow salutary, a reminder of the transitory nature of man. Then, too, the sound of the wind along the crumbled streets was extraordinarily soothing, mournful, resigned, striking straight at the heart.

Yet for once, I failed to respond to the place. Sitting on deck with a drink in my hand before sailing back, I watched the sun begin to lower itself behind the smooth shallow hills along the coast, and let my mind drift back . . .

It had been years before. I'd sailed into a little harbour on the north coast of Brittany—Locquirec or Perros Guirec, I can't remember which—and tied up for the night. It was late. Most people had already gone ashore for their evening meal; those who hadn't were below—I could smell steaks grilling, and onions, hear the clink of glasses. The sun was almost down; the long lines of boats cast shadows across the dirty green water which lapped at the jetty. I was standing on the foredeck, enjoying the feel of tired muscles relaxing and the crawl of whisky down my throat, when I saw a wooden dinghy come nosing out from between two boats moored further up and make ragged progress towards me. There was a man clumsily wielding the oars; opposite him sat a boy of eight or nine, dressed in an anorak and a yachting cap which must have belonged to his father. The boy had one of those tender open faces which vanish with adolescence; his straight fair hair hung in a fringe over his eyes and every now and then he pushed back the peak of the cap, which was far too big. There was something touching about him; I leaned over the rail for a further look, smiling to myself. I'd been like that once: eager, happy, already in love with the sea and boats and everything they embraced.

The man reached the point opposite which slippery steps led up from the water to the jetty and began to manœuvre the dinghy towards them, between two of the moored hulls. He said something to the boy, who stood up and put both of his hands on the side of the nearest boat, obviously with the intention of guiding the dinghy in to the jetty. As anyone who's ever sailed will know, it's a foolish thing to do, and indeed, as I watched, the dinghy swung away from the bigger boat and the boy fell, with hardly a splash, into the widening gap. For a moment, he lay there on the water, held up by his anorak; the yachting cap drifted slowly away and his hair spread out around his head like a halo.

No one moved. The boy uttered no cry, the father, frozen as I was, simply watched, and I, above them, out of sight, said nothing, assuming the man would dive in after his son. Which, as I began to function again, calling down to ask if he needed help, he immediately did. Once in the water, he floundered and splashed—I watched him for a few seconds, not worried because they were no more than fifteen yards from the harbour wall, until it dawned on me that he was in some kind of trouble.

All this took no more than a few seconds, yet already the boy was sinking, his face under the water, his eyes closed. I jumped in, landing almost on top of the man, who turned a white face towards me and said, hopelessly: "I can't swim."

I grabbed the front of his jacket and pulled him through the water to the dinghy, which bobbed a few yards away. "Hang on," I said. "I'll get the boy." I didn't say what I was thinking: that only a criminally irresponsible parent would take a child out in a boat without a lifejacket and then ask that child to perform a potentially dangerous action when the parent himself was unable to swim.

I got hold of the boy, held his face out of the water, swam fast to the side. He weighed nothing; I got him up the steps, laid him out on the flat stones of the jetty, set to work on him. He'd swallowed about a litre of the filthy water; I got it out, banged his chest, watched his delicate eyelids flicker and open to reveal huge grey eyes. When I was sure he was conscious and breathing, I left him and went after the father, now shivering in the water, knuckles clenched over the edge of the dinghy, and pulled him too safely to land.

Having found out where they were staying, I walked them both back to their hotel and, since the father seemed unwilling or unable to do so, asked the receptionist to call a doctor to check out the boy.

For no good reason, we exchanged names. All he said as I turned to go was: "Where's the boy's cap?"

I told myself he was in shock, or terrified of what the boy's mother would say; embarrassed, even, at having put himself in a position of needing to be rescued. Nevertheless, his response both chilled and disturbed me.

As did his behaviour the following day. I met them both walking along the edge of the harbour: the boy rushed up and clung to my hand, the father followed at a slower pace and, not meeting my eyes, mumbled something about being sorry to have inconvenienced me the night before.

I neither expected—nor wanted—effusive expressions of gratitude. Anyone would have acted as I did. But . . . inconvenienced? It seemed a damned cold-blooded way to refer to what had happened.

That evening, I strolled up to their hotel. Since I was leaving early the next day, I bought a drink in the bar and made one last enquiry about the boy. The girl at the desk was not the one who'd been there the night before; when I explained who I was asking about, and why, she told me they had already left. She murmured something about the boy being accident-prone, that it was lucky I had been on hand, that he'd already had a couple of narrow escapes. When I asked about them, she shrugged. He'd apparently tripped in the street and nearly been run over by a lorry. He'd drunk from a bottle of bleach instead of lemonade. Been treated for concussion after falling down a flight of stone steps. She didn't actually say that boys will be boys but it hung in the air between us. When I asked about the boy's mother, she told me she'd left for home two days earlier; father and son were on their way back to her now.

As I walked away, I thought: there's something wrong here. But what could I do? They'd already left; I myself was sailing on the early tide. Besides, the boy hadn't seemed afraid. He was open and affectionate. And who would I have contacted if I really thought there was a serious threat to his welfare?

Around me the hills darkened into scarlet and orange. The crimsoned sea spread flatly towards the horizon. I shivered suddenly. Over the years, I had occasionally remembered the boy and his father, wondered how they were. Now, the thought dropped into my mind with the heaviness of a stone: if I had not spoken from above, like a controlling god, would he simply have watched his son drown? Was there a link between the boy's "accidents" and the sudden break in Helena Garden's career?

She hesitated at the door opening onto the terrace, just as she had the previous morning. She moved towards one table, then to another, as she had yesterday. I watched her, this time making no move to rise. By then, I was pretty sure in my own mind about what had happened to her and the sick anger the whole affair roused in me made it impossible to concentrate on my coffee—or indeed, on anything else. There were two questions to which I needed the answer. If they confirmed what I suspected, then I would have to come to another decision: to tell or not to tell. I would have no real proof, only a string of circumstantial detail. Yet, if I was right, the detail itself might prove strong enough to convict a man of murder.

Eventually, I pushed back my chair and walked over to her.

She turned, startled once more. "My husband's down there." She pointed to the beach. "He's an actor. He swims half a mile morning and evening. I don't know how he—"

"Yes. You told me yesterday," I said gently. Rage filled me for what had been done to this lovely fragile creature.

"—I don't know how he knows when it's time to turn back." She pushed her fingers through her damp hair and laughed softly.

"How long has he done this?" It was one of the questions to which I needed the answer.

She frowned. "Years," she said. "Years and years."

"Eight years? Ten years?" I had to know.

"All his life."

I hadn't realised I'd been holding my breath. The two of us watched the dark head swimming arrow-straight for the shore below. The black-hearted bastard, I thought. There was only one more piece of information I needed.

"Your son," I said. "How is the boy?"

A shadow drifted across her huge grey eyes, so like those of the child I had once rescued. "Charlie?" She moved the wedding ring up and down her knuckle. "He died."

I went cold. "How? What happened?"

"He went swimming. He swam out too far. He couldn't make it back to the shore."

I tried not to think of Charlie engulfed by some cold grey sea. "Was he alone when the ... when this accident—"

"It wasn't an accident," she said.

So she also knew. I wanted to say: why do you stay with him? I wanted to say: I understand the guilt and fear which keeps you tied to him, I realise you blame yourself for Charlie's death because deep down you must have known what he was trying to do and yet you did nothing to prevent it. But for your own sake, you must get away.

There were tears in her eyes now; one of them rolled down her cheek and the gesture was poignantly familiar. Just so had she faced on screen the jealous Othello; just so had she looked as the black hands closed round the white skin of her throat. She must have encountered a similar jealousy within her marriage, and the victim had been someone even more innocent than Desdemona.

Because I could see it all. Jeremy Talbot, small-time actor, unable to cope with his wife's success, had called a halt to her career in the most subtle and terrible way. He must have guessed just how she—how any mother—would react to the shock of losing her child.

Something should be done. But what? I looked down at the swimmer below us, brown arms flashing in and out of the water as he neared the shore.

He appeared on the terrace a little later. His handsome face was frowning as he hurried towards us. His hand grasped his wife's shoulders; his expression was hostile.

"Enjoy the swim?" I asked. I couldn't keep the sardonic note from my voice.

His eyes met mine coldly. He said: "I told you last time we met that I couldn't swim."

So he remembered too.

Something must be done. All day the feeling nagged at me that I ought somehow to be able to release that shining talent of hers from the straitjacket in which her cold-blooded, self-centred husband had locked it. I could think of nothing.

It was about twelve months later that I saw the announcement in the paper. Nothing big, a small paragraph on page 3: FORMER ACTRESS DIES.

According to the report, she'd killed herself. She'd gone out with her husband in a boat at some seaside resort on the south coast of England and thrown herself overboard. He had told the coroner he couldn't swim: weeping, he'd said that there was nothing he could do to save her. A verdict of accidental death was brought in; the coroner commiserated with him for this second tragedy coming so soon after the loss of his son. That was that. The life and death of Helena Garden, wife, rival, neatly tied up and disposed of.

Or so he thought.

The house was old and charming, somewhere near Brighton. He answered the door himself.

"Come in," he said quietly. "I've been half-expecting you."

There were lines of fatigue on his face and I noticed that one of his hands trembled slightly.

"Nemesis?" I said harshly.

"I suspect you think you know what happened."

"I worked it out," I said. "And if I can ever prove it . . ."

"You think I killed them both." It was a statement, not a question.

"Yes."

"She told you I could swim," he said. "She told you I swam half a mile morning and evening."

"Yes."

"I loathe the water," he said. "I nearly drowned when I was a child— I'm terrified of it. She was the one who went swimming every day."

"But that evening in Brittany . . ." I could hear the note of uncertainty in my voice.

"Charlie was desperate to go out in a boat. And I hadn't dared let him go with his mother. It was only after she'd left for home that I . . ." His voice trailed. After a moment, he spoke again: "What you saw was a simple accident. And afterwards, when you'd got us both out of the water—don't you think I was embarrassed at not being able to swim, at being forced to rely on a stranger to rescue my own son?"

"But—"

"Helena—my wife—was sick." It was exactly what I had expected him to say. "When Charlie was born, she adored him. We both did. We were a perfectly ordinary young couple at the start of our careers, struggling to find the way up in what you must know is a precarious profession. And then they made *Othello*. Helena became a star overnight. There was the second film, and the third. And then nothing. It's always like that for actors. There'd have been something else, of course there would. But she thought it had come to an end almost before it had begun. She looked around for someone to blame and chose Charlie. Suddenly he was in her way. Things began to happen to him. It took me a while to realise they weren't accidents."

I remembered Desdemona's voice, saying the same thing about Charlie's death. "How did he drown?"

"It was the day after I heard I'd got the lead in *Mine Is the Glory*. My biggest break."

I remembered it. A smash hit in the West End, with a transfer to Broadway a year or two later.

"I don't recall you being in it," I said.

"I had to let the part go. Because the very next day, Helena took Charlie out in a boat. She said they went swimming and he got cramp when they were half a mile out. She said he panicked and was struggling so hard she couldn't get hold of him." He looked away and swallowed. There were tears in his eyes. "The coroner called it a terrible accident."

"But it wasn't?"

"You know as well as I do that Charlie couldn't swim. After that business in Brittany, he was as terrified of the water as I was. I'll never know how she persuaded him to get into a boat with her."

There was a silence. After a while, I said: "Why did you go on living with her?"

His strong actor's voice was full of sadness. "Because I married her for better or worse. Because I loved her. Not wisely, but too well."

"But poor little Charlie was the one who got hurt."

"She thought that without Charlie she'd be free, she'd become a star again. But of course she didn't. When she lost Charlie, she lost everything."

He walked me to the door and added, not meeting my eye: "So did I."

Did I believe him? I don't know. Certainly he was convincing, but that was what, as an actor, he was trained to be. It must have been a couple of months later that I read about the new RSC production at Stratford. "A triumph!" the papers called it. "English theatre at its superb best!" "Dazzling!" "Impressively moving."

It was *Othello*, of course. With Jeremy Talbot in the name part. "A powerful, poignant performance," the papers said. "Perhaps one of the greatest actors of our generation."

It was a part he'd been forced to turn down only a few weeks earlier because his wife, the former Helena Garden, had been diagnosed as having terminal cancer and needed full-time nursing care. There was a suggestion that she had killed herself in order not to stand in his way.

I thought how easy it would be to knock someone overboard from a small boat. How simple it would be to ward off a dying woman. How useful an oar would be in holding her under until she drowned.

I don't suppose I shall ever know the truth. I can only say that when I was finally able to get tickets, his performance moved me to tears.

CATHERINE AIRD
(1930–)

From the first sentence in Catherine Aird's "The Man Who Rowed for the Shore," the reader knows whodunit. The interest in this little tale of a murder's aftermath can be summarized in the question, "Will he get away with it?"—and in the author's impeccable craftsmanship and wit. Close examination of Aird's story reveals the author's marvelous sense of timing, which shows a wicked sense of humor and also anchors a perfectly executed plot. The comic yet poignant action centers upon a murderous husband, a handful of his late wife's relatives, and their efforts to dispose of the deceased's ashes in as dignified a manner as is possible.

Born Kinn Hamilton McIntosh in an industrial city in Yorkshire, England, Aird was a doctor's daughter raised on conversations about Joseph Bell, the medical professor who is thought to have been a model for Sir Arthur Doyle's Sherlock Holmes. Aird's father instilled in her a scientific approach to observation and a fascination with details of forensic medicine. Aird's aspirations to attend medical school were set aside when, as a young woman, she suffered from a life-threatening illness that confined her to bed for several years. When she recovered, she took up dispensing drugs and managing her father's medical practice from the doctor's house located two miles from Canterbury, where she continues to reside. Over the years, she also engaged in voluntary work for the Girl Guides, now the Guide Association, for which she was made a Member of the Order of the British Empire. Aird has penned local history, scripted video and "son et lumière" productions for her local church, and chaired both her Parish Council and Burial Committee, experiences she has described as "most useful to the crime writer." Aird also chaired the British Crime Writers Association during the Agatha Christie Centennial year, 1991.

Using a pseudonym drawn from her family tree, Aird published her first detective novel in 1964, after discarding three mainstream novels that she had written previously. The work introduced Inspector C. D. Sloan with the intention of making him "an ordinary man, oppressed by his superiors and disappointed in those underneath." Aird good-humoredly dubbed him "Seedy Sloan" and has written him into fifteen novels and a volume of short stories. Aird has also completed writing a biography of Josephine Tey. She has contributed articles and essays to numerous publications and is an editor of *The Oxford Companion to Crime and Mystery Writing*.

The Man Who Rowed for the Shore

1992

Norman Pace only made one mistake when he murdered his wife. That was to engage Horace Boller of the estuary village of Edsway and his boat *The Nancy* for the final disposal at sea of Millicent Pace's ashes. Norman didn't know, of course, at the time he did it, that hiring Horace Boller's motorboat would be his only mistake.

By the time he came to do so he thought—and with good reason—that all danger of detection was well and truly past and that he would very soon be able to give the nubile young lady in Personnel—she who saw no distinction, semantic or otherwise, between Personnel and Personal—more of his attention than would have been prudent as a married man.

Besides which he was then considering something which had turned out to be an unexpected problem. If anyone had told him beforehand that the main discussion point with his wife's family attendant upon her murder would be a sartorial one he would have laughed aloud; had he been the sort of man who laughed aloud—which he wasn't.

The right clothes—rather, the correct ones—to wear to the ceremony of casting Millicent's ashes into the sea had considerably exercised the mind of her brother, Graham Burnett, too. In fact the two men even discussed the matter at length—oddly enough it was manifest that the two brothers-in-law were on friendlier terms now than they had been before Millicent's death.

This was no accident. Norman had realised very early on that his main danger of detection in the murder would come from Millicent's brother Graham—a chartered accountant with a mind trained to expect cupidity in those with whom he dealt—money bringing out the best in nobody at all. In the little matter of averting his brother-in-law's possible suspicions Norman Pace felt he had been really rather clever. . . .

First of all, as all the good books suggested in the matter of winning support from those whom you have reason to suppose do not like you, he had asked Graham a favour. Taking him quietly aside after luncheon on Christmas Day he had said, "I wonder, old man, if I might put you down as one of my executors? I've got to go over to the States in the spring for the firm and I thought I'd tidy up my affairs first. I've never really enjoyed flying and you never know these days, do you?"

"Of course." If Graham Burnett was surprised at the request his professionalism was far too ingrained for him to let surprise show in his face. "Only too happy to help."

"I know you'd look after Millicent anyway if anything happened to me," he had said, "and so it seemed easier to make it all legal."

"Much better," said the accountant firmly.

"By the way," he had murmured as they had rejoined their respective wives, "will you remember if anything does happen that I want to be cremated—we both do, actually."

"I shan't forget," promised Graham Burnett.

And he hadn't.

When Millicent Pace had died while Norman was safely in America, Graham had arranged for his sister to be cremated—as Norman had been sure he would. The fact that Norman was not able to be contacted in the United States of America at the critical moment was also the result of some careful forward planning. After his business was done, Norman had set off for Milwaukee to visit a second cousin there.

Actually the second cousin wasn't there because he had died the year before but Norman had carefully neither mentioned the fact nor acknowledged the letter apprising him of it. Just before the time that he had calculated that Millicent would have died he checked out of his New York hotel without leaving a forwarding address and set off for Milwaukee. That he chose to do the journey by long-distance bus would, he knew, come as no surprise to his wife's family, among whom he had a fairly well-deserved reputation for being "ower careful with the bawbees."

His colleagues would not have been unduly surprised by his economy either. Always very attentive to his expenses claims, he was more than inclined to parsimony when it came to subscription lists and whip-rounds at work. In fact the only person either at work or among his family and friends who might have been surprised at his frugality was the nubile young lady in Personnel upon whom he had already lavished several gifts—but then she had been brought up by her mother on the well-attested aphorism that it was better to be an old man's darling than a young man's slave. . . .

In the United States Norman had been written off very early as a tight-wad, and it was this knowledge of his basic meanness which had led his brother-in-law Graham to turn down the undertaker's offer to keep Millicent Pace's body in a refrigerator until her husband's return. Finding out what it had cost to leave the coffin in the Chapel of Rest (Graham Burnett suspected that most of the time this was the shed at the back of the undertaker's yard) had already seriously alarmed him. As an accountant he was accustomed to breaking bad financial news and he did not relish it. The prospect of adding fiduciary complaint to Norman's personal grief did not appeal to him at all and he accordingly took the responsibility for arranging his sister's prompt cremation—as Norman had been sure he would.

On his visibly distressed return from Milwaukee, via New York where sad messages had awaited him, Norman Pace had listened to a long account of illness and death with suitable mien.

"I can assure you, Norman, everything that could be done was done," said Graham in careful, neutral—but unctuous—tones that he could only have picked up from the undertaker.

"The doctor . . ." said an apparently broken-hearted Norman.

"He was marvellous," said Graham swiftly. "He couldn't do enough for poor Millicent."

Norman had bowed his head. "I'm glad to hear it." In fact his brother-in-law had never said a truer word. The only thing the old fool had been able to do for Millicent had been to write her death certificate. The really important thing was that he had not associated any of her symptoms—abdominal pain and vomiting leading to heart failure—with poisoning by thallium.

Even more importantly, neither he nor the other doctor who subsequently also signed the cremation certificate, had associated those everyday symptoms with Norman, by then in faraway Milwaukee. One of the undoubted attractions of thallium as a poison was the valuable delay in the onset of symptoms—it could be as long as forty-eight hours—as well as the peerless advantages of its being odourless, tasteless and colourless.

The only drawback of thallium known to Norman was that it was not only detectable in bone after death but that it survived in cremated ashes too. The disposal of Millicent's ashes at sea thus became more than mere ceremony. Graham Burnett and his wife, not being privy to the real reason for the scattering of the ashes at sea, saw it only as an occasion. Hence the discussion about what to wear.

"I'm hoping for good weather, of course," said Norman, "but don't forget that it's always colder at sea than ashore."

"That's what Neil says too," said Graham. Neil was his son, a bright lad with all the cleverness of a born clown. "I don't know about you, Norman, but even so I don't think a yellow sou'wester is quite right."

"No," agreed Norman, adding judiciously, "but then neither is my black. Not at sea."

"I hope you won't mind," said Graham, "but Neil says he's going to wear his cagoule."

"I think," said Norman with unaccustomed magnanimity, "that everyone should put on whatever they feel most comfortable in."

"So shall we say that dignified yet practical wear is the order of the day?" said Graham Burnett, who liked summing up.

Horace Boller, boatman, wore his usual working clothes for the expedition. Whether he knew it or not the fisherman's jersey which he had on complied with a long tradition of Aran knitting where each seaman's jersey was of a slightly different pattern, the better to identify the drowned.

Horace's deplorable garment could have been confused with no one else's—dead or alive. Norman Pace regarded him and his cluttered boat with distaste.

"You do understand, don't you, that we must be outside the three-mile territorial limit before it is legal for me to scatter my wife's ashes in the sea?" said Norman, who had his own reasons for being well out to sea before unscrewing the flask containing the mortal remains of Millicent. The said flask was nestling safely in the inner pocket of the new raincoat which Norman had seen fit to purchase for the occasion.

"Leave it to me, guv'nor," said Boller, whose regard for the letter of the law was minimal and for its spirit non-existent. "And watch that bit of coaming as you come aboard, if you don't mind. I've been having a peck of trouble with it. Now, be very careful. . . ."

Conversation on board, stilted to begin with, thawed a little as Boller's boat turned out into the estuary from Edsway and headed for the open sea and Neil Burnett revealed himself as knowledgeable about birds.

"Common sandpiper," he said in response to a question from his mother. She had settled on a tasteful grey outfit with plastic raincoat handy. "And that's a ringed plover."

"I suppose that one's a little twit," said Angela, Neil's fiancée, who had insisted on joining the party to underline her new status as a potential member of the Burnett family. She, too, was wearing a cagoule.

Family solidarity on Norman's side was represented by two late-middle-aged sisters who were his cousins. Old enough to be veteran funeral-goers and therefore experienced mourners, they were kitted out in dark slacks and blazers left over from a Mediterranean cruise of long-ago.

"I think it's a silly little goose," responded Neil, giving Angela a quick hug.

This by-play on the part of the young ostensibly passed Norman Pace by, although he was obscurely gratified by the presence of Enid and Dora, who had not heard about the cremation in time to attend. He had taken up a rather aloof stance at the prow of the boat, looking out to sea, and letting his back give every appearance of a man thinking his own thoughts—if not actually communing with the deep. Horace Boller very nearly spoilt this tableau vivante by opening the throttle of the motor boat without warning just at the moment when they left the saltmarsh estuary behind and hit the open sea.

"Tide on the turn, I expect," said Graham Burnett knowledgeably. He audited the books of several fishing enterprises in Kinnisport and thus felt qualified to give an opinion.

"Why are we going East and not straight out to sea?" demanded Norman, who was more observant.

"Got to get the church at Marby juxta Mare in line while I can still see Cranberry Point, haven't I," said Horace Boller glibly. He paused, craftily waiting for the contradiction which would indicate that anyone on board *The Nancy* knew anything about nautical miles. It was not forthcoming so he went on, "Otherwise I shan't know exactly how far out I am, shall I?"

Norman turned back to the bow. He'd struck a hard bargain with

Boller but he didn't want the fisherman telling the whole party so. Horace Boller was still smarting from it, though, and had no intention of going half a mile further out to sea than he could get away with.

When he had gone nearly as far from land as he deemed necessary Horace put *The Nancy* about just enough to make the motorboat pitch fractionally. Mrs. Burnett was the first to notice.

"It isn't going to get rough, is it?" she asked timorously. "I'm not a very good sailor."

Horace Boller throttled the engine back before grunting non-committally.

One of the effects of slowing the motorboat's speed was that it also began to roll ever so slightly.

Cousin Enid unfortunately chose to be bracing. "Remember the Bay of Biscay, Dora, that time we were on our way back from Lisbon?"

"Don't remind me," pleaded Dora. "It was dreadful, simply dreadful."

Horace Boller went through a charade of examining the sea and sky and looking anxious. He reduced the speed of the motorboat until it was scarcely making any headway at all, saving fuel the while.

"Haven't we gone far enough?" said Graham Burnett.

"Distances at sea are very deceptive," observed Cousin Enid. "It's always further than you think."

"And later," hissed Neil irrepressibly to Angela.

Norman Pace, standing in the prow, was aware that the boat was now beginning to wallow in the water. He patted the flask containing the ashes. How right he had been not to scatter them on land where they might one day have been sought by a diligent constabulary. Strewing them on the waves met every possible requirement. . . .

"Should be all right now," said Boller. "Can't see St. Peter's spire at Collerton any more."

That this was because it was behind the headland he did not see fit to explain. Instead he put *The Nancy* about, switched off the engine and suggested to Norman that he came and stood at the lee side. "Can't strew ashes into wind, can you?" said Boller grumpily. "They'll only blow back at you."

Nothing loath, Norman clambered back into the well of the boat and then, helped by Graham, stepped up onto the seating which ran round the inside of the tiny deck. He took out the flask from the crematorium, still slightly disconcerted that that fine white dust could contain all that had come between him and the young lady from Personnel.

"Steady as she goes," quipped Neil unnecessarily. The nautical double entendre went unappreciated, all eyes being on Norman as he held the flask between his hands for a decent moment before unscrewing it. Enid and Dora, he was happy to see, were standing at attention—at least as far as they were able to in the rocking boat.

In fact, Cousin Enid, always game, appeared to be saying some private prayer—for which Norman was grateful since he found no words coming spontaneously to his own lips and the silence was a bit unnerving.

It was unfortunate that just as Enid had got to "Eternal Father, Strong to save, whose arm doth bound the restless wave . . ." a very restless wave indeed caught *The Nancy* amidships. It was even more unfortunate that this happened just as Norman was about to unscrew the flask containing Millicent.

He lost his footing and the flask at the same moment.

"Butterfingers," murmured young Neil, not quite sotto voce enough.

"Oh, my God!" said Norman, losing his cool as well as his footing and the flask, which was now bobbing briskly away from the stationary boat.

"It's not God's fault," said Dora quietly in the eminently reasonable tones that must have accounted for the deaths—should they have used them, too—of quite a number of Early Christian Martyrs. On religious matters her docility was always trouble-making.

Any naval disciplinary court would have had no difficulty in holding Horace Boller—rather than God—to blame since he should never have allowed the boat to drift in the sort of sea he did, being, amongst other things, a hazard to shipping. As Their Lordships of the Admiralty were not called upon to pay for Horace's fuel—and he was—he remained untroubled.

Until, that is, Norman turned on him. "Quick, start the engine. . . . Look, it's floating about . . . just there. Hurry, man, hurry, or we'll lose her."

With maddening calm Horace Boller applied himself to the engine. Everyone else on board rushed to the port side of *The Nancy*.

"Mind that coaming!" shouted Boller.

"Never mind your blasted coaming," shouted back Norman, who had turned a nasty shade of puce. "Get that engine going. Quickly, quickly . . . keep your eyes on her everyone."

The engine of the motorboat gave a little cough and then reluctantly sprang to life.

"Follow that flask . . ." Norman implored Boller urgently.

"Yoicks! Tally ho!" said Neil.

"Neil, you are awful," said Angela.

"She went that way . . ." said Norman since the flask could now be seen only intermittently bobbing on the waves.

"That way," said Cousin Dora, pointing in a different direction.

"She's over there," said Graham's wife distantly. She'd always rather liked her sister-in-law and thought the whole expedition unseemly.

"Where?" Norman clutched her arm. "Which way?"

Graham Burnett said nothing at all: but his brother-in-law's patent dismay gave him furiously to think.

So did his next exchange with Boller.

"What sort of a tide is it?" Norman demanded, advancing on the boatman.

"Flow," said Boller testily. "Now, which way is it you want me to go?"

It was too late. Of the little flask containing the mortal remains of Millicent there was now nothing whatsoever to be seen.

"If we don't catch her," Norman asked the fisherman, "where will she fetch up?"

"De profundis," murmured Enid.

"Dead man's reach," whispered Neil to Angela, who gave him a little shove in response.

"Billy's Finger," said Boller without hesitation. "Spit of shingle in the estuary where the tide turns. . . ."

"A dead spit . . ." murmured Neil in Angela's ear.

"You'll find her there by morning, guv'nor," promised Boller. "No problem."

There was a problem, though.

For Norman, anyway.

Millicent's ashes had indeed fetched up on Billy's Finger in the estuary of the river Calle by morning but then so had Detective Inspector Sloan and Detective Constable Crosby, advised (Graham Burnett would never have used the expression "tipped off") by Millicent's brother that there might be a message for them in the bottle.

There was.

As Millicent, his late wife, would have said, it was just like Norman to spoil the ship for a ha'porth of tar.

JANWILLEM VAN DE WETERING

(1931–)

Despite the title's playful tone, "Messing About in Boats" by Janwillem van de Wetering bears little resemblance to Kenneth Grahame's *The Wind in the Willows*, from which the title is derived. Cultures and personalities clash with murderous result during a boating outing taken by a Dutch professor of philosophy and his all-too-devoted Japanese secretary. This piece is an excellent example of the author's preoccupation with character and the missed connections that can spark explosive situations. Van de Wetering draws upon his acquaintanceship with Japan, where he lived for a year while studying Zen Buddhism in a Kyoto monastery.

His has been an international existence. Van de Wetering was born the son of a successful businessman in Rotterdam, the Netherlands, where his comfortable life was shaken when he saw his Jewish school friends and neighbors carted off by the Nazis. His awareness of the atrocities that they faced convinced him of the fragility of well-being.

Van de Wetering was educated at the Delft Institute of Technology, the College for Service Abroad, the University of Cambridge, and the University of London. His work in the import business took him to South Africa, Colombia, and Peru. He sold real estate in Brisbane, Australia, and then returned to the Netherlands to manage his family's textile business. He served in the Amsterdam Reserve Police in lieu of military service. There he gained experience invaluable to his series of detective novels set in Amsterdam and featuring the police adjutant Henk Grijpstra, detective sergeant Rinus de Gier, and (in most of the books) the Commissaris. He wrote the books in English first and then translated them into his native Dutch. The series was introduced in 1975 with *Outsider in Amsterdam*. That same year, the author left Amsterdam for Maine where he spent five years with a Buddhist group. He now lives on the coast of Maine with his wife, who is an accomplished sculptor.

Most of the "Amsterdam cop" books are set in that Dutch city, but van de Wetering has taken his sleuths to Japan, the coast of Maine, and New York City's Central Park to solve murders. An unrelated book, *The Butterfly Hunter* (1982), is an international pursuit novel. Van de Wetering has also collaborated on a cartoon book and has written two collections of short stories, chil-

dron's books, a study of the writer Robert van Gulik, and two nonfiction ___ s Zen experience.

___ ing first published a version of this story in 1985, with other ___ ng the Japanese Inspector Saito (in *Inspector Saito's Small* ___ te "Messing About in Boats" in 1995 especially for this volume, creating a more definitive ending without undercutting the story's enigmatic quality and nightmarish sense of inevitability.

Messing About in Boats

1995

Adrian de Roos, Adirano Dorosu as pronounced in Japanese, Dutch professor of philosophy temporarily teaching in Japan, was not in a good mood. He walked ahead of Yoshiko, as dictated by local custom, and had her carry the lunchbasket. He also walked too fast and the girl, off balance on her high heels and hindered by her tight skirt, had trouble keeping up with the tall blond-haired blue-eyed foreigner. "Dorosu-san, please, not so quickly," she called from time to time, in the wailing high little voice used by Japanese women when they surrender to a man. He would slow down a little, look over his shoulder, excuse himself, and forget again that he wasn't the only one on earth. He had wanted to spend the day reading, stretched out on two chairs, with a lot of cigarettes and an endless supply of coffee, but Yoshiko had been whining at him for months now so he might as well have the outing, and be done once and for all. He was about to spend time boating, together with the secretary the university had been good enough to supply him with as part of his income, because in money he didn't earn all that much. That's the way it goes in Japan; a young professor can flatter himself on working for a renowned institute, he is given a free apartment, eats for a dime and a nickel in the canteen, everyone, the older professors excluded, bows deeply when he comes by, and he gets a bit of cash as well.

Good day to you, Adrian thought, he would rather take a lot of money. He wished he was still in Hong Kong; Chinese are practical folk, prepared to pay straight interest in Western philosophy. Over there he had at least felt that he might be employed usefully and that his audience understood what he was talking about. Besides, he spoke good Chinese and now had trouble with Japanese. "Make sure you link up with an intelligent whore," the Chinese colleagues told him when he departed. "A foreign tongue is learned quickest on the pillow." He was also told there would be many prostitutes in Japan, as many at least as in Hong Kong.

Leaving wasn't too bad, arriving was. He had met enough bar girls by now; they all wanted a steady friend but he couldn't face the commitment. In Hong Kong it had been all right to flutter from flower to flower but here the pattern turned out to be more intricate. Even with Yoshiko, whom he hadn't touched with a finger yet, he felt caught by thousand minute hooks, dug firmly into his flesh, working themselv a little more every day. What was his relationship with the girl a

She typed his letters, in correct English, and helped with the Japanese explanations, since he tried, every now and then, to teach in the local lingo. She had lunch with him and liked to "discuss philosophy." He would respond by always taking the negative view so that he could succeed in stripping whatever she came up with of any possible value—a game he had learned at Leyden University while barhopping with his fellow students. That he didn't always believe in his own arguments was his business. He disliked the girl and enjoyed drilling holes in her limited concepts.

Still, Yoshiko wasn't really bad looking, her body was well shaped and her legs fairly straight, not bent as with most Japanese females. That she wore spectacles shouldn't bother him either; they could come off at the right moments, couldn't they? And didn't she always make an effort to be charming? She helped with his shopping, took him to good restaurants, removed stains from his clothes. If he didn't take care she would do anything. *Here I am, Lord, abuse me. Shall I fetch the whip?* It so happened, however, that he wasn't sadistically inclined. Or was he, perhaps? It's risky to state about the self that it is *not* something in particular. He had studied Jung after all, even with much zeal. Every man has a shadow that accompanies him at all times and the shadow is the opposite of what a man thinks he is, hopes to be, insists on believing himself to be. Adrian had always taken himself to be a kindly disposed gentleman, so he could very well be an utter scoundrel; just wait, the shadow slithers along and is forever ready to prove its worth. Never mind, Adrian thought, we're going boating now. He waited until Yoshiko, panting, could catch up. "Dorosu-san, your legs are so long and I'm only little huh, huh, huh."

"*Sumimasen*, Yoshiko-san," Adrian said dutifully. Wasn't he sorry that the poor little thing had run out of breath? "But there are the nice boats waiting for us, dear, see? Your ordeal is almost over."

The boat man shook his head when he saw Yoshiko's thin spiked heels. "My boats are made out of thin plastic, Miss, and they'll fill up in no time if you pierce the hull. There's quite a bit of wind today. There's another rental outfit further along—they have stronger boats."

"No," the girl said, clipping her words nastily, "I'll take off my shoes."

She had gotten in already and Adrian was rowing; the sharp nose of the sleek little craft cut through the waves.

"Ooooh," Yoshiko said. "You're so good at it. You can do everything well, can't you?"

"Can't you row?"

"No, I've hardly ever been on the water. We only used to go once in a while when I was a kid. On a pond that was, and my parents would come too. The water was shallow out there, but this is a real big lake. Shall we go to that island? We could have lunch on the beach."

Adrian looked over his shoulder; the island was some miles away. He saw a hill, suitably surrounded by what would be pine trees.

He rowed on with a vengeance. Three years in the country now and he still didn't like it. The paper-thin politeness that covered all behavior had a tendency to interfere with his breathing and he drank more than he had done even during his student years. Only in drunkenness will the Japanese open up, or so he was beginning to believe. How many more evenings would he still have to spend in artfully furnished bars, between the red grinning faces of his colleagues, assuring him of their everlasting friendship while they fondled the serving girls.

That miserable Yoshiko, would he ever be rid of her fawning approach? She was waiting for him at every corner; she had already stated her love, hiccuping with emotion, after much sake in a romantic inn. Pressed to the edge of a mental precipice, Adrian admitted to Yoshiko that he preferred gentlemen to ladies. It wasn't quite true—his preference for the male sex was incidental—but he had to come up with something and it had better be final. Caught between the paper lanterns, with a view of a full moon detaching itself gently from the embrace of pine branches, could he have been expected to answer, "Yoshiko, you're abhorrent to me, the very sight of you turns me off completely"? He couldn't have said that, could he now?

"Does happiness exist, Dorosu-san?" Yoshiko asked him afterward. The idea! Since when has life been designed to point at happiness? Had he chosen the discipline of philosophy to become happy? He needed happiness as much as he needed love play with this poorly programmed plastic doll.

"I think so, Yoshiko."

"Have you been able to find it?"

"No." He said it sadly, swallowing the contents of another cup of rice wine, feeling the alcohol dull his perceptions—there wasn't much difference anymore between the lanterns painted with characters and the moon cut through by branches.

"So what is the purpose of human existence?"

"No purpose. Life is no more than senseless suffering."

She raised her hands in weak protest but he wasn't done yet. "Suicide, Yoshiko," Professor de Roos said solemnly, "is the only valid way out. And besides," he dropped his voice to a confidential whisper, "that way we can at least create an illusion of free will, and succeed in symbolizing our dignity."

"But you're alive."

"Out of weakness, Yoshiko, but I assure you that I want nothing more than death." He paused significantly. "One day I may gather enough courage. A little more sake, Yoshiko? Drink up, alcohol is death, too, and intoxication a splendid beginning."

Her foot touched his ankle under the table but he withdrew his leg.

The scene was crystal clear in his memory, while he pulled on the oars and the waves breaking across the bow drenched his back, but that evening had slid away long ago, and was no more than a part of an overall pool of misery.

Now, on the lake, she talked to him, like a mother talks to her infant, about the birds flying and swimming around them, the shoreline, partly shrouded in fog, the brilliant red color of a buoy floating by. He knew that she wasn't merely babbling nonsense, and that she might genuinely be impressed by the beauty of the environment, but why go into all those idiotic details?

Adrian's father had been "lost" in a World War II prison camp on the then Dutch island of Java. Starved to death, beaten senseless, who would ever know what the sadistic Japanese guards had done to Papa de Roos? And who would ever know how he, the holy father figure, would have behaved if the roles had been reversed? De Roos Senior as a camp guard, it could well have been possible. Adrian didn't remember his father as having been a pleasant man. One has to be careful with generalizations, transference, and idealism. Didn't Jung say, and probably rightly, that man has great potential for the highest good, and the worst evil? To be motivated now by open or hidden hatred would be a dangerous slip into non-conscious behavior. If only Yoshiko would shut up. The girl jabbered on, however. She looked inviting, he would say that much for her. The tight skirt had crept up to well above her knees, and her breasts, almost completely exposed in the low-cut blouse, were also hard to ignore; he promised himself to keep his hands off her. Two more years waited at Kyoto University and a wrong move now would jeopardize future adventures in the Willow Quarter. All he had to do today was row, eat, listen to the girl's verbal flow of trivialities, and then home, Home.

"Careful Dorosu-san, we're almost there."

He pulled the dory onto the rocky beach and Yoshiko unpacked the hamper, twisting her small, lithe body continuously, providing a selection of cleavage and seductive thighs for his perusal. She offered the food gracefully, illustrating each dish with elaborate verbal labels. Mushrooms from the famous island such and such, known for its autumn colors; seaweed cookies from the far northwest where the snow monkeys live; a salad as made in Okinawa and the fish stew Tokyo Bay is famous for; only the rice had to be plain, for rice is rice.

The rice wine was of exceptional origin again, and came with its own story and in a large stone jug, decorated with bright blue paper cord. It was a little early for indulging but she insisted and poured cups for two, forcing more on him while she drank steadily herself. He was debating whether he would go back on his decision and grab her after all—why not anyway, surely he would find a way to be rid of her afterward— when he noticed that he wasn't only drunk but nauseous. His intestines cramped until he was in pain and he crawled away, aiming for a rock that seemed to offer protection. Yoshiko was also in trouble, staggering about in the direction of another large boulder. Too much sake, Adrian thought, while he vomited and squatted down afterward. He should be used to the stuff now. He rolled away from his own stench and spent a few minutes on his back, breathing deeply, before forcing himself to walk back. The lunchbasket stood on an empty beach, its half-eaten contents waiting in pretty dishes on a reed mat. He found Yoshiko. She was crying.

"Feeling better? That sake must have been off."

"It didn't work," sobbed Yoshiko.

"What didn't work?"

"The poison."

Well, well, Adrian thought and lit a cigarette. He blew smoke carefully. The girl hid her face in her arms.

"Suicide?"

"Yes."

"And you wanted me to go along with you?"

"Yes. You wanted to, didn't you?"

He noted that she was using the intimate word for "you"; the shared experience of coming death had equalized them. A good thinker I am, Adrian thought. So we have studied philosophy and psychology have we? And Chinese literature thrown in? We have lived in the Far East for a number of years now. Hasn't it occurred to us yet that frustrated Japanese females like nothing better than double suicide? To walk the final plank, hand in hand with loverboy? A splendid obituary in the newspaper afterward, suitable mumblings at the university? Glory glory hallelujah. And he, subtle intellectual that he was, had handed her the idea of a joint death himself, during that exotic evening spent in the inn's garden, between the paper lanterns that aped the moon. It would have been better if he and his diligent student could have made love first but because he, how stupid can one get, had insisted on telling her he was gay . . . asshole, Adrian thought.

"So what poison did you use?"

"Snake poison," sobbed Yoshiko. "I bought it at the street market, from a witch. It would work slowly and painlessly, she said, but it's just another throwing-up brew, and she charged me so much money for it."

The sour smell emitted by her body made him back off a few feet more.

"Let's go for a swim."

"Without bathing suits?"

He stared at her unbelievingly. "Yes. Naked. You don't mind, do you, dear?" His voice was sharp with venom.

"I can't swim," Yoshiko said sweetly.

"Who cares? I only want you to wash up—you stink, you know. Why the hell did you have to drag me into this? Couldn't you have at least asked?" He shook her by the shoulders. "Moron. Even if I would be interested in suicide, couldn't you have granted me the grace of at least selecting my own place and time?"

"Don't you want to die, then?"

"What is that to you?" He pulled the blouse roughly off her shoulders and yanked on the thin belt of her skirt. The treatment seemed to please her. She dropped her arms and purred when he took off her bra and slip. He stepped out of his own clothes and pushed her toward the surf. He pushed too hard and she fell but he grabbed her arm and dragged her into the water where he let her go before striking off on his own. When he swam back a few minutes later she was washing herself, dipping water daintily into her hands and pouring it down her back.

While swimming he had been able to reflect and find more reasons to be angry. He picked her up and threw her down on the beach. Professor de Roos raped his secretary Yoshiko, pushing roughly without giving her a chance to ease his way. He saw her eyes turn helplessly away and listened to her groaning with pleasure. The tremendous energy contained in his maleness took only a few thrusts before spurting into her; once his seed was released he pulled back and got up.

"That was that."

She smiled. "You're not gay at all."

He cursed her, using expressions in Japanese that he had picked up in low-class bars. What he said hurt; he saw the tremors in her body while he told her, as impolitely as possible, how much he despised her. "Ten of your type in exchange for one common whore, my slut, and you've no brains either. Your cleverest statements are based on common ignorance. You can only do parrot talk and even then you make mistakes. You should get married to whatever fool accepts your dowry and spend your time with a simple rice cooker, an on and off switch is about the only gadget you can handle. Stay out of my way and spare me your act. All you want to do is make an impression and all you come up with is a lousy imitation of some dumb movie star. Keep your saccharine to yourself and stay away from me."

She rolled away while he shouted at her. He followed her, kicking pebbles. He saw her reach into the hamper and come back holding a revolver. She aimed at his head. The barrel was short but heavy.

Extraordinary, Adrian thought, there are two slits on the sides of the barrel. I wonder why they were put in. But he knew that his mind was trying to ignore the problem and that the problem was pointed at him and that it was death.

"Idiot!" whispered Yoshiko. "And what do you imagine that I think of *you*? Eh? Now that I know that you aren't gay and that I'm not good enough for you." Her voice hissed. "Now I *hate* you. Your arrogance. Your egotism. I only wanted to be your friend. I never expected you to marry me. Foreigners always marry their own kind; they mate legally with pink hippos or giraffes. I knew that all along. You won't accept my gift. Take *this* gift." The revolver came a little closer.

"Easy now, Yoshiko," he tried to say calmly, but his words stuck together. The slightly trembling barrel and its large metal eye were annoying him by her persistence. If she fired, his entire head would come off. Jesus, what a wicked weapon.

"I'm quite calm." Yoshiko said pleasantly. "And I'll kill you first and myself later."

He saw her index finger move steadily. He also saw the plump heads of the bullets mathematically grouped around the barrel, fixing him quietly. There was no shot, only a dry click. The ammo was old, probably. The thought flashed through his brain while he grabbed the revolver and twisted it out of her hand. He reached out to hit her but she was gone, climbing the hill behind her. A moment later he saw her again, pushing against an enormous rock.

Right, Adrian thought. If the poison doesn't work and the gun refuses I have to be smashed.

She came back, what else could she do? The rock weighed tons. She dressed, hiding behind the rock where she had vomited before. Her shoes were on the beach. He picked one up, walked to the boat, and pushed its thin strong heel through the bottom. The hole was quite small. He pulled the shoe back and dropped it next to the other.

He let her get in, pushed the oars into the boat, and shoved it into the water. She sat in the bow, looking away from him. He handed her her shoes, gave one last push, and walked back to the beach. The wind was blowing away from the island. He repacked the hamper, climbed the hill, and sat on the rock she had been pushing a few minutes ago.

The boat sank slowly. As he expected, she panicked and let go of the wreck, preferring to support herself on the floating oars. The boat drifted on, still showing its gunwales, carried by the buoyancy of its plastic material. He saw her head dip, come up a last time, and go under again.

She tried to kill me thrice, Adrian thought, and I only made one attempt, but I was successful, that's the difference. Three against one, that should equal things out. Or am I revenging my father after all? If that murder is added to what Yoshiko tried to do to me the scales should tip my way.

He lit a cigarette and noted that his hands were steady.

The boat man came an hour later, making his speedboat plane gracefully across the little waves of the lake. When he saw the remains of the rowboat he changed course and throttled his engine back before shifting into neutral. He attached the wreck to his boat and looked at the island. Adrian waved his white shirt.

"I had warned her," the boat man said, "those spiked heels penetrate a thin plastic hull easily. How come she was alone in the boat?"

"She wanted to row by herself for a while," Adrian said. "She claimed she had often rowed a small boat before. I went for a walk on the island and when I came back I saw that the boat was nearly sunk. *She* had disappeared altogether. It was too far to swim out. If I had tried I would have drowned myself."

"We'll have to telephone the police. I'm sorry about this misfortune. Did you know the girl well?"

"We were friends, not too close."

Now he'll ask me to pay for the boat, Adrian thought, but the man said nothing. He bowed and pointed at the shore. "Shall we go?"

Guilt, Adrian thought as he got in. The flat powerboat flew over the lake, the fast movement cheered him up. Am I guilty? Of course I am. So will I even my guilt out by spending years and years in a small cell, on a diet of rice and wheat, boiled in water? Isn't that the kind of fare served in jail here?

The powerboat approached the harbor. The engine behind him stuttered and coughed out.

No, Adrian thought. His hand slid into Yoshiko's hamper, grabbed the gun, appeared again and dropped the revolver gently into the water. The boat man was checking his engine, paying no attention to his passenger's doings.

Adrian stepped on the shore. Boating with a fatal end, that's how he would define this succession of events. The definition would be within acceptable truth. He would pass it to the police soon, and repeat his version for as long as he was questioned. No poison, no gun, no rock. No more than a simple, albeit tragic, accident, caused by the stubbornness of a stupid girl.

He would go home afterward, have a shower, smoke a cigar on the balcony of his apartment, and gloat.

He had to restrain himself not to laugh. He knew now what he was capable of doing if circumstances turned against him; the knowledge would be useful, undoubtedly. And Yoshiko? He shrugged his shoulders; he would forget her soon enough.

About two weeks later, in a private room of the fashionable Black Swallow Restaurant in Kyoto's "Willow Quarter," two men faced each other across a low red lacquered table.

Chief Commissioner of the Kyoto Municipal Police Gato was an aristocratic older man in an expensive tailor-made three-piece linen suit. His guest, Inspector Third Class Saito, of Kyoto's Homicide Division, was not yet thirty years old. Both men squatted on the tatami, straw-matted, floor. They were drinking heated rice wine.

"Tell me," Gato said pleasantly, tapping his hearing aid to make sure that it functioned, "tell me, Inspector-san, how you managed Adirano Dorosu's untimely death the other day." The chief smiled approvingly at his neat-looking subordinate, appreciating Saito's simple blue blazer, grey slacks, and silver-colored necktie on a white button-down shirt. "Yes,"

Gato said. "I'm most curious to hear why the Dutch philosophy professor, mildly suspected of having murdered his secretary, chose to finish his life by drinking an exotic mixture of hemlock and . . ." Gato burped, "datura, was it?"

Saito smiled politely. "The laboratory isn't sure, sir. There were various plants involved, it seemed." He narrowed his eyes. "The doctor in charge said that the professor may have swallowed the very substance that ended the life of the Greek philosopher Socrates, sir."

"Of course," Gato said softly, handling his cigar fondly. "How befitting." He looked up. "You don't deny that it was you who set off the course of events that culminated in the imitation of Socrates' final act."

Saito smiled blandly. He cleared his throat. He said "saaaah" in the way Japanese will acknowledge an opponent's remark without committing themselves to any judgment.

"Saaaah," Gato mockingly imitated his subordinate's reaction before looking serious. "Each report ultimately reaches my desk and although I don't read them all I've never missed studying one of yours. I will tell you why I find your method fascinating. You always research your situations impeccably and I know that your investigations usually result in an arrest. In the case of the drowned secretary I did not entertain that hope, for it was clear from the start that there were no indications of proof. You will understand that I have some experience in reading between the lines. You suspected Dorosu of murder although you did not say so clearly. You never arrested the professor either. I surmised you would not pursue the case, incorrectly as it turned out, for Professor Dorosu died yesterday, by his own hand." Gato burped again. "So let's hear how you brought him to that final decision."

Saito did not quite manage to hide a self-satisfied smile. Then he burped too.

"Well?"

Saito lit the cigar that his commanding officer had given him while nodding his appreciation of the tasteful gift. "You must excuse me, Gato-san. I indulged too much and my brain is not clear. I am afraid I cannot follow your line of reasoning."

Gato sipped cognac and smacked contentedly. "Listen, Saito, I assure you that there are no hidden microphones in this room. I admire the way in which you handled the case, but I'm curious too and I insist that you answer my question. A little more cognac, friend?"

Saito's face was set. "No, thank you. I'd rather wait a moment."

Gato's smile broadened. "Very well, last things first then. Saito-san, I have the pleasure to inform you that you are promoted to inspector first class. You know that it's most unusual to jump from third to first class, especially for an officer as young as you are. However, your insight and diligence are clear to everyone. Your immediate chief asked me for the favor of informing you himself but I suggested he should leave the matter to me. I work in a quiet room, Saito, and feel the need to communicate at times."

"Thank you," Saito said. He wished he didn't remember his Zen teacher's admonition. *"Whatever happens to you, worthless student, is not important. All that matters is that you use your circumstances to detach yourself from illusion."*

Gato surmised that his gesture had unnerved the young man. He rubbed out his cigar. "Well, Inspector First Class-san, isn't one favor worth another? Don't forget that there should be no secrecy between colleagues and that both you and I are descendants of samurai. An extra code of honor binds us. The Dorosu solution is too mysterious for me and I need to know how you managed to fit your facts together in such a way that you could set off circumstances causing Suspect to kill himself. Let me break up my query into certain clear-cut questions. How did you know that Dorosu did do away with his secretary Yoshiko?"

Saito spoke monotonously, keeping his voice down, "I was faced by an intelligent opponent, who also happened to be a foreigner whose motivations, way of deciding, and potential activity were formed in an environment I'm not familiar with. As you said just now, the case provided insufficient proof and there was a complete absence of witnesses. If I wanted to pursue it, I would have to work as unobtrusively as possible."

"You suspected the professor immediately?"

"Only in theory, Gato-san. When the boat man phoned that a dead girl had been found floating on Lake Biwa and that he had detained her companion, a foreigner, I happened to be on duty at Homicide and drove out immediately. Dorosu was eating at the sushi restaurant next to the boat place and the boat man was keeping him company. The Dutch professor speaks amazingly good Japanese. He knew how to evaluate my questions, and how to parry my thrusts with repetitive short, precise and innocent-sounding statements. He showed no emotion—an attitude that I could appreciate, for I knew Suspect and could therefore assume that a man of his intellectual elevation would know how to control his behavior in awkward circumstances."

The chief commissioner raised an eyebrow. "You *knew* the killer? Your report did not say so."

Saito shrugged the accusation off. "Only casually, sir. The professor and I had met at university. I take an evening course in the relation between Western anarchy/nihilism and Buddhist thinking. Dorosu was showing us some existentialist aspects that might relate to the subject. We were introduced by the director of the program but Dorosu didn't remember me." Saito laughed boyishly. "To us all foreigners resemble each other. We sometimes forget that we may look alike to them too."

Gato grinned grimly. "Yes." He suddenly looked disgusted. "Bah. I recall that you found some traces on the island, after you allowed Dorosu to leave. The boat man took you out to the island, didn't he?"

"Yes, Gato-san. But I did not dwell on those traces in my report. I found vomit and excrement, smeared on two rocks, and deduced from the position of the rocks that the professor and the girl must have been hiding from each other while they threw up and emptied their bowels. I thought of a possible poisoning. Food poisoning perhaps. A picnic containing rotten fish maybe. But then I also found signs of what could have been hectic lovemaking, or rape."

"And the imprint, on wet sand, of a handgun."

"A short-barreled revolver. Yes, Gato-san. Later I also found the gun. By that time I had worked out a hypothesis that would fit the facts."

"The gun was found?"

"Yes, sir. By a police diver, in the vicinity of the jetty. We were lucky. The lake is deep in most places but shallow around the island and near the boat rental place. The divers only looked in the easy places."

"Good luck comes to those who keep trying," Gato said.

"Good luck," Saito, emboldened by alcohol, said, "comes to those who are lucky." He bowed excusingly. "So says my Zen teacher, sir. I wouldn't know anything like that myself."

"Aha," Gato said, reluctantly choosing not to pursue the challenge between his own positive and a Zen master's free thinking. "But the gun hadn't been fired, so it wasn't much good to you, except to point out that there was something wrong with the couple's relationship, yes?"

"Exactly," Saito said obediently, "why bring a deadly weapon to a romantic outing?" He paused, then looked up. "By the time the laboratory had checked out the gun and come up with nothing interesting I decided to stop wasting time and change the direction of my inquiry. It's a well-known fact that women discuss intimacies with girl friends. Discreet enquiries, via my university contacts, led me to the wife of one of the assistant professors, a lady called Suga. Suga-san was Yoshiko's intimate and trusted friend."

The cognac had enthused Gato. His laughter interrupted Saito's report. "Clever, very clever. I bet Suga is beautiful. I understand Yoshiko wasn't too attractive. My wife isn't either, you know. I didn't select her myself, of course. I was disappointed with my parents' meddling at the time, but then I realized how lucky I was, for she always had beautiful girl friends. Getting to know my wife's friends was a most pleasurable occupation." He frowned. "You aren't married, are you, Saito?"

"No, sir."

Gato nodded. "Interesting. I will talk to my wife. We might help you there. Facilitate your spectacular rise to high office." He shook his head. "To business, though. So you met Suga, Yoshiko's confidant."

"I understood," Saito said, "that Yoshiko worried that Dorosu might not find her physically attractive but she firmly believed that she was Dorosu's spiritual soul mate. Suga was interested in the relationship because, I surmised . . ."

Saito smiled, ". . . she herself was interested in the professor."

Gato nodded happily. "Exactly. Suga used her friend Yoshiko's confessions as substance for her own dreams. By the way, how attractive *was* the professor?"

Saito shrugged. "Hard to say, sir. I'm not a woman. Dorosu was tall, had blond hair and blue eyes. An exotic man here, but I dare say he would be attractive to European women too."

Gato poured himself more cognac. "Blue-eyed demons we used to call them. But go on, so Suga was helpful, was she?"

"Suga-san told me," Saito said, "that the relationship between Dorosu and Yoshiko only continued because Dorosu had to work with the girl. As she was a kind of gift from the university Dorosu-san couldn't fire her without making everybody lose face. In order to make the best of a bad set of circumstances Dorosu amused himself by teasing the unfortunate secretary. He was a bit of an alcoholic and Yoshiko found him romantic bars. While drinking they played a game: discussing the possible lack of meaning of human existence. Dorosu defended the position that there is no purpose . . ."

"A Buddhist dogma . . ." Gato interrupted.

"Buddhism goes even further, sir. It believes in nothing, not even in the denial of meaning, Buddhism points out that . . ."

"Yes," Gato interrupted, "or no, as you like, just tell me how we get to a corpse floating on Lake Biwa, if you please."

Saito kept smiling. "Easy enough. Dorosu knew that Yoshiko was a Buddhist and that Buddha said that life is suffering. By refusing to live a meaningless life more suffering is prevented."

Gato scowled. "I see. So Yoshiko was stupid was she? She didn't see that Buddha's so-called enlightenment goes beyond the dualism we keep getting ourselves stuck in." His eyes opened widely. "And Dorosu was equally stupid?" He slapped his cheek. "Ah, I see how Suspect tricked himself, and how you helped him along." He laughed. "Go on, colleague, this is beginning to be really interesting."

"You've got it, sir." Saito sucked his cigar. "Dorosu was having his way with the girl. He forced his witless disciple to accept that, because of the philosophic concept that 'nothing matters,' suicide is the only dignified way out. Suga tells me that Dorosu was quoting Western philosophers too. David Hume, for instance. David Hume posited that because ultimately only Nothing exists all human values have to be fabricated."

Gato nodded. "But that's a very pleasurable thought."

Saito poured a little more cognac. "Not too many people seem to see that. But this is abstract and enlightened philosophy, sir. Dorosu had his adventure on the lowest physical level. My theory is that he was, unconsciously, trying to get rid of the girl. He wanted to kill her all along but wasn't aware of what he was really doing by consenting to go to that island with her."

Gato had trouble lighting a fresh cigar. He blew on his finger where the match had burned his skin. "She had decided on a double suicide, had she? She would die because he didn't love her and he would die because he couldn't face that life has no purpose. As he couldn't do that by himself, she, his soul mate, would help him choose the dignified way out." Gato laughed. "Double suicide, the stereotyped ending of impossible romance, as shown nightly on the cheaper channels."

"Yes, sir. Yoshiko didn't actually tell Suga she was planning something like that but Suga guessed, and didn't worry. She didn't think Dorosu would allow Yoshiko to go that far."

"The poison Yoshiko mixed in the lunch didn't work?"

"The gun didn't either, sir. I understood that the gun had to belong to Yoshiko because why would the professor arm himself for a picnic? The gun was irrelevant, however, and Dorosu decided to get rid of the thing. Its presence would alert us."

Gato nodded. "We forget the firearm, Saito. *Then* what did you do?"

"Up till that moment I hadn't faced Suspect directly, sir. We did have the interview in the sushi restaurant next to the boat place but I wasn't making any moves yet. I was merely listening, not reacting. I thought it was time to get to know Dorosu personally. Suga was kind enough to invite us both to an intimate dinner party at her villa near the Daitoku-ji temple."

"Villa," Gato said thoughtfully. "A beautiful lady who lives in Kyoto's best quarter. That Suga shows up too often, Saito. How far did you go to secure her cooperation?"

Saito shook his head firmly. "Suga is married, sir."

"So what else is new?"

Saito didn't smile. "There is nothing between the lady and me, Chief Commissioner-san. During dinner Dorosu and I talked. He knew that I was the police inspector in charge of the investigation around Yoshiko's natural death and Suga told him I am a graduate philosophy student. The combination didn't worry Suspect. He was friendly enough. I even got the impression that the professor took a liking to me. My original theory was confirmed. Dorosu was rather a jolly fellow, eager to enjoy himself while on Earth. He certainly wasn't the depressive melancholy mental patient Yoshiko had made him out to be when she was confiding to her friend Suga. I was tempted to define Suspect as an intelligent active man, eager to penetrate the great mysteries of our seeming existence, a true philosopher who was using his opportunity to explore Eastern thought. Unfortunately he still insisted on being centered in what he assumed to be his own ego."

Gato nodded. "That's where you caught him."

Saito spread his hands. "I had to, sir. We can't have unexplained bodies on the most beautiful lake of this country."

"Quite quite," Gato said. "So, in a manner of speaking, you must have gotten Suspect's so-called ego to get rid of his so-called ego. And the professor kindly left a note, admitting to having killed the unfortunate girl. But how did you bring that about, my dear fellow?"

Saito couldn't help grinning. "I staged an experiment. I know a stage director who likes to be helpful. He put on a play, written by me, and performed by university students. Dorosu had to go because I made sure he was personally invited by the university's dean. The hero in my play is a foreign manufacturer who is doing a Japanese project. The actor is a fat fellow wearing a brown wig. His local girlfriend is a bar hostess played by one of the university's stunning beauties. I changed the facts there as I didn't want Professor Dorosu to catch on too quickly."

Gato nodded his approval. "Hmm, hmm, well done, Saito-san. Never be too obvious. Get them with your backhand."

"Yessir," Saito said brightly. "I did aim for some recognition, however, so I put in the picnic, and the boat. *Messing About in Boats* the play was called, after *The Wind in the Willows*, a British children's book."

The chief commissioner wasn't familiar with literature to be enjoyed by British toddlers. He waved Saito on.

"Very well, sir. I also rather harped on the suicide/murder combination. Lovely, but silly, girl of pleasure dies, superior man goes home to Holland."

"Superior foreigner?" Gato asked, frowning.

"No, sir, the foreign part wasn't important, really. I believe the professor saw himself as a superior man in any environment, also at home. Quite an arrogant fellow."

"Rather like the *Madame Butterfly* syndrome yes?"

"Indeed," Saito said. "I even had parts of that opera played as background." Saito grinned. "Jazzed up somewhat. My friend Sasaki was playing the trumpet. He sometimes gets quite good. He is an emotional player."

Gato, an opera fan, hummed a few lines, sung by the hero as he leaves Japan. He looked at Saito. "Not a very realistic scene, I thought. I hope you did better."

"My play was realistic, sir."

Gato frowned. "Are you telling me you made your two actors shit and puke?"

"No, sir. The actress vomited a little, but discreetly, behind a rock. The realism was contained in the rape scene, caused because the foreigner does not understand the subtle feelings of the girl. I made the dialogue rather coarse but I confess I also overdid that scene to unmask the so-called daintiness of our women. Under extreme circumstances even Japanese ladies can be coarse, I believe."

"Can't they ever," Gato said. "Good, so you're also a literary genius, I understand. If I follow you correctly you first made Dorosu feel safe, because he isn't some fat trader, and the real Yoshiko was unattractive, but then, with the rape scene, you made Suspect aware that the Kyoto police were on to him all right. Carry on, Inspector."

"Suga," Saito said, "provided me with photographs of Yoshiko and she also told me what clothes the secretary was wearing on the day she was murdered. I selected three girls who had about the same posture as Yoshiko. In the play the fat foreigner gets away, that's to say he isn't arrested, but he does go mad when his victim appears to him in a dream. After the play was over I intended to lure Suspect into a nightmare."

Gato sat up straight. "You used Yoshiko look-alikes?"

"Yes, sir. Suga and I dressed the three girls in identical clothes, the same clothes Yoshiko had been wearing when Dorosu killed her by not saving her when the boat sank. Suga made sure our models were wearing a Yoshiko-like make-up. We even copied the perfume. I knew what Dorosu would do after leaving the university theater, of course. He is addicted to alcohol so he would drive to the nearest bar. First he'd leave the theater and Yoshiko appeared to him, quickly, just a glimpse, in the building's lobby. Then there she was again, in the parking lot, another glimpse as she disappeared into the botanical garden behind it, and then there she would be again, in the bar."

"And that would be physically impossible?" Gato asked. "She couldn't have moved so quickly, I mean? Dorosu has long legs and he walks quickly, and the third part of his route would have been in his Mazda sportscar, tearing along at a hundred kilometers an hour?"

"Exactly, sir," Saito said. "Moreover, Yoshiko is dead. And there she appears to her killer, three times, very much alive, especially in the bar where she is a presence, talking and laughing."

"With who?"

"With my own assistant, sir, Sergeant Kobori." Saito looked concerned. "I wanted the model to be safe. Kobori is an athlete."

"You were there too?"

"I was, sir."

"You're good at karate, I hear."

Saito smiled shyly. "I study the old-fashioned form of unarmed combat. Jiu-jitsu, sir. My teacher specializes in defensive movements, he never allows me to be aggressive."

"Sure," Gato said. "And you're probably a black belt too." He sighed. "How can a man as young as yourself excel in so many different things at once? I'm glad you have those jug-head ears, Inspector-san. If you'd look like a movie star I would have to fire you. Ideal people irritate me. They make me jealous."

Saito felt his ears that did indeed stand out from his head somewhat. "Jug-head, sir?"

"Yes," Gato said. "So you were creating visions for your victim. Where did you get that idea, Inspector?"

Saito was still feeling his ears. "I first came across the method in a manual on detection, *Parallel Cases Under the Pear Tree*, a thirteenth-century Chinese treatise."

"I've heard of it. The old magistrates used living corpses to frighten their suspects?"

"Sometimes, sir. They would also dress themselves up as judges of the netherworld and suddenly appear in a suspect's cell. There would be eerie music in the jail's corridors. They usually prepared their prisoners by withholding food and afflicting pain."

Gato's long hair was hanging in his eyes. He brushed it back impatiently. "Torturing is out these days but you're getting fairly close, my man. However, no matter. So did you crack the professor's defenses?"

"Yes sir. I activated his guilt."

"Really?" Gato asked. "You believe in guilt? You surprise me. I thought you would, as a philosopher who is interested in Western nihilism and Eastern negativity, deny all values."

Gato pointed at Saito's nose. "How can we feel guilty when there weren't any rules to break in the first place?"

"I feel guilty," Saito said quietly. "I have felt guilty ever since Dorosu drank the poison."

There was a long and awkward silence.

Gato nodded. "Yes. I see. But we did come up with some rules of behavior in our society, here, Inspector, and you and I were hired to enforce them. A silly girl's body floats in Lake Biwa because a psychopath felt he could use his intelligence to kill her. The psychopath is a genius, we can't catch him officially, so he will kill again, but in this case we found an unofficial way to prevent that."

"So you approve, sir?" Saito leaned forward eagerly.

Gato was paying the bill, complimenting the restaurant's owner, handing out tips to the serving girls.

"Sir?" Saito asked.

"Yes, Inspector First Class-san?" Gato asked, tapping his hearing aid that seemed to malfunction. "Yes, I do think we need a taxi."

MARTIN EDWARDS
(1955–)

A conference in Nottingham, England, the restoration of the underground headquarters of the Allied Command in Liverpool, and Martin Edwards's legal expertise all led to the creation of this tale that turns on a point of law. According to Edwards, soon after he was invited to create an original story for this volume at the 1995 World Mystery Convention, or Bouchercon, in Nottingham, he took a tour of the World War II military nerve center. "I had an idea for my shipboard story then but going underground gave it more body," Edwards recalled.

Edwards was born in Knutsford, England, a town important in English literary history, since it formed the model for Elizabeth Gaskell's famous nineteenth-century novel *Cranford* (originally published in *Household Words*, 1851–1853). The son of a steel worker and a teacher, Edwards grew up in Northwich, one town over from Knutsford. As a boy, he attended local schools and discovered a fascination with books and writing early on. At age six, he knew he wanted to become a writer, and at age nine, when he discovered the works of Agatha Christie, he knew that crime writing was for him.

When he was admitted to Oxford, however, he decided to pursue a course of study that "would make it possible for me to eat while I wrote," Edwards said. "I was simply fortunate that I enjoyed the law more than I think I might have expected." After receiving a First Class Honours Degree in Law at Balliol College, Oxford, in 1977, Edwards qualified as a solicitor in 1980. He joined the law firm Mace & Jones Grundy Kershaw, where he specializes in labor law. His firm is based in Liverpool, as is his character Harry Devlin's much smaller firm, but Edwards insists, "The resemblance ends there!"

Edwards has published five books and many articles on legal subjects, and five novels featuring the earnest solicitor-sleuth Devlin, who was introduced in *All the Lonely People* (1991). Edwards has also edited and coedited regional and national anthologies of short stories by members of the British Crime Writers Association, including *Perfectly Criminal* (1996) and the forthcoming volume *Whydunit?*

With a Little Help from My Friends

1997

Harry Devlin was reading the obituaries. For the past couple of hours he had been killing time at Liverpool's County Court, waiting for his case to be called. Apart from his client, a taciturn market trader who was being sued by two ex-employees for back wages, Harry had only a copy of *The Times* for company. He had long since exhausted the sports news and main stories. Now he was left with a choice of death or taxes. Unable to face any more speculation about the Chancellor of the Exchequer's forthcoming budget, he found himself studying the columns detailing the lives of the recently deceased.

Suddenly one of the obituaries caught his eye. A wealthy woman called Ianthe Ogus had died. Why did the faintly ridiculous name ring a distant bell? He glanced through the paragraphs which recorded her passing. She had been born in Liverpool but spent most of her adult life in London. Her first husband had become chairman of the Byzantium Shipping Line and after his death, five years ago, she had married an old friend of the family. When he too died, she had returned to her native Merseyside, spending the last eighteen months of her life in affluent Blundellsands. She had been well known for her work for charity and generous patronage of the arts. The Byzantium Gallery of Maritime Art had been established at Greenwich in honour of her first husband and she had funded an annual prize for the best picture devoted to ships and the sea.

The newspaper had reproduced a photograph of her, taken by Cecil Beaton in the early fifties. She was a woman of breathtaking beauty, with high cheekbones and hypnotic eyes. Although her hair and clothes were in the style of another age, Harry was fascinated by the portrait—not merely captivated by her beauty but also intrigued by her Mona Lisa smile.

Why did the obituary puzzle him—why did he think there was something disturbing about it? He shut his eyes, trying to force himself to remember. Something had stirred within the recesses of his memory, but he could not be sure what it was. Several of the names in the report seemed vaguely familiar from the past, but he could not place them. He had no connection with Byzantium, its chairman or his widow. Nevertheless, the piece conjured up associations of mystery and murder.

A court clerk tapped him on the shoulder. "You're on now, Harry. But make it snappy, will you? The judge is keen to get away for the big match in Manchester tonight."

Within half an hour, his client was taking the bus home, a sadder, wiser and poorer man, and Harry was on his way back to the office, reflecting that his firm would soon be joining the market trader's long list of creditors. Walking through India Buildings, he saw the signboard of Maher and Malcolm, the city's most prestigious firm of solicitors and was unexpectedly reminded of Ianthe, the woman he associated with a puzzle yet to be solved.

Harry had trained as a lawyer with Maher and Malcolm. The relationship had been improbable from the outset, rather as if Robert Mitchum had been apprenticed to Sir John Gielgud. Yet within an instant

Harry became convinced that he had come across the name of Ianthe Ogus during his time at the firm where he had been articled.

For the rest of the day he racked his brains, but he could not remember any more about Ianthe. Was she a client he had seen at the behest of his principal? He thought not. When he bumped into Jim Crusoe—another alumnus of Maher and Malcolm—he asked if the name of Ianthe Ogus struck a chord, but his partner's face remained blank.

"No one I remember, old son. Why do you ask?"

"She died a couple of days ago."

"So what's bothering you?"

"I'm not sure. I read her obituary in *The Times* and I knew straight away that something wasn't quite right."

Jim sighed. He was accustomed to Harry's flights of fancy. "With you, everything has to be a conundrum, doesn't it?"

"I won't be able to sleep until I've fathomed it."

"Well, if you're really troubled, why not give Toby Jones a ring? When we were with Maher and Malcolm, he knew everyone who mattered."

As his partner returned to his own room, Harry reflected that, not for the first time, Jim had set him on the right path. During their time with Maher and Malcolm, Toby Jones had been the head of the wills, tax and probate department. He had been a solicitor of the old school, courteous and genteel. Every afternoon at precisely four o'clock, he had left the office, saying that he had to see an old lady about her will. Opinions in the firm were divided as to whether this was true or simply an excuse for an early trip home, but no one denied that Toby was an expert in his field, a knowledgeable lawyer whose greatest gift was his bedside manner. Generations of the firm's private clients had placed their trust in him and he had deserved it. He knew more secrets about the great and the good of Liverpool than any other man alive, but he had always been the soul of discretion. He had retired from day-to-day practice years ago, but he still lived locally, in a mansion on the road to Southport.

Harry arrived at the house at nine that evening. Ever the gentleman, Toby had professed on the telephone that he was delighted to hear from his former trainee.

"I have heard that you cannot resist the temptation to keep playing the detective."

"It beats working. And I must be honest. It will be grand to see you again, but the reason for this call was that I read in the papers that a woman called Ianthe Ogus had died."

There was a pause. "Ah," Toby said.

"Maher and Malcolm acted for her, didn't they?"

Toby was famous for choosing his words carefully. At the age of seventy-nine, he had not yet lost the knack. "Not exactly," he said.

"Then why do I remember her name?"

"I am not sure," Toby said deliberately, "that it is the name of Ianthe *Ogus* that you remember."

He refused to say any more on the telephone. Harry realised, as he rang Toby's front door bell, that he was tense with suppressed excitement. He was still unsure why the obituary of a woman whom he had never met had made such an impression on him. There were no direct clues in the text. She was an old lady, who had been born in the dockland area of the city and worked as a secretary after leaving school. Throughout the war she had worked at the Western Approaches headquarters, plotting the course of convoy ships, their escorts and the German submarines sent to destroy them. On the first anniversary of V-E Day, she had married a businessman and, although they had had no children, she had during the years that followed developed a passion for art. She had a reputation for philanthropy: the obituary writer made it clear that she would be sadly missed.

Toby greeted him like an old friend and Harry could not help feeling flattered. At Maher and Malcolm he had been something of a gatecrasher, a local lad employed by a firm which customarily employed the brightest and best from Oxford and Cambridge. True, his own examination results had been good, but he had never found it possible altogether to shake off a feeling of inferiority when surrounded by clever contemporaries who possessed social graces he could never hope to acquire. Toby Jones was as blue-blooded as anyone in the firm, yet he had also been prepared, when Harry spent six months in the department discovering how to make wills for the rich and famous, to spend time with his trainee. He would talk about the law and emphasise the importance of developing people skills which were never taught at college. Toby had forgotten more about human nature than most lawyers ever knew and Harry sometimes reflected that if he had failed to make the most in financial terms of his early years with a leading commercial firm, it was no fault of Toby's. By the same token, much of the sympathy for others which made him a good listener and solver of puzzles derived from the lessons he had learned from his mentor.

"Come in, come in. It is so good to see you. Winnie has left us a pot of coffee in my study. May I take your coat?"

Toby limped briskly along the hallway, his guest trailing in his wake. Although he had lost his leg during the war, he remained remarkably spry. Harry allowed himself to be shepherded into a room he found more reminiscent of the city library than a typical study. Its ceiling was high and the shelves of books on each wall stretched from floor to ceiling. Each volume evidenced the breadth of Toby's interests, from the complete works of Victor Hugo to treatises by Stephen Hawking and Socrates. For every legal text there were dozens of books on every other subject under the sun. Toby Jones, Harry thought, had never fallen into the trap of believing that his own field of expertise was the only one that mattered, and he was a better man for it.

For a few minutes they exchanged reminiscences and sipped the excellent coffee that Winifred Jones had made for them before Harry turned the conversation to the subject of the obituary.

"Ever since I read that Ianthe had died, I've been wondering why the news captured my attention. It's so long ago that I'm very vague, but I seem to think she was involved with a murder case. What puzzles me is that Maher and Malcolm never handled criminal work. Can you put me right? I'm hardly an expert in old ladies with a taste for maritime pictures. Who was Ianthe—and why do I think there's a mystery about her?"

Toby Jones stroked his chin with a slender, age-spotted hand. "Her Christian name is unusual. I suppose that is what must have stuck in your mind. Rather pretentious, I always thought. In the days when I knew her, she was unmarried and her surname was Shuttleworth. As for Ogus . . ."

"Yes?"

To Harry's intense surprise, Toby looked embarrassed. His leathery cheeks had flushed and he was averting his gaze. If it had not been unthinkable, Harry would have described the old man's expression as shifty.

"I take it you have forgotten the file?"

"All I know is that at some point during my time with Maher and Malcolm, I came across this woman and there was some connection with a murder. More than that, I simply can't recall."

Toby sighed. "The law of probate was never your favourite subject. As I remember it, I had to try to hold your interest by telling you anecdotes about the curious cases I had encountered over the years."

Harry grinned. "I bet you never had so much trouble with Jim Crusoe, did you? I'm sorry if I wasn't a good pupil. Was Ianthe the subject of one of your stories?"

"Yes. I expect I mentioned her case as an example of those rare cases when the law of succession dispenses with the formality that so many unthinking people regard as needless bureaucracy."

Harry narrowed his eyes as he tried to think back. "Something about a will?"

"Correct. I used to call it the tale of the murder on the HMS *Frodsham*."

"Of course!" Harry said. Mention of the ship's name was enough to bring the story rushing back to him. How could he have forgotten? "The man who killed a fellow sailor and then fell overboard whilst being pursued by his victim's friend. They were officers on the *Frodsham*, weren't they?" He paused. "So refresh my memory. Was Ianthe the lady the two men quarrelled about?"

Toby shook his head. "No, her name was Betty Higgins. She was a pretty Liverpool girl with whom a man called John Prentice had fallen in love. Prentice came from a wealthy family; he was the only son of the chairman of Prentice Munitions. The firm made a fortune during the early years of the war. Maher and Malcolm had always been the company's solicitors and I joined them after I was invalided out of the army. John never worked in the business and he took a commission in the Royal Navy as soon as war broke out. His parents were killed in the Blitz and I met him then, when he came home to sort out the arrangements. Betty was working at the Western Approaches HQ in Derby House when she met John. They became engaged, but John was at sea for long stretches of time. The *Frodsham* returned to port irregularly. Its main task was to protect the convoys—difficult and dangerous work. The U-boats were a terrible threat and there was a real risk that each voyage might be his last."

As Harry sipped his coffee, the old man said quietly, "I am talking about a time long before you were born. It must be difficult for you to imagine what it was like here in war-time. Liverpool was a prime target for the Luftwaffe and Hitler's bombers destroyed most of the city centre." He paused. "And the post-war planners and architects did for the rest. But I digress. We all lived day by day. There was no choice: no one could be sure that tomorrow would ever come. When life seems so fragile, people are careless of the consequences of their actions. As, for example, Betty Higgins was."

"She had an affair with a pal of Prentice's, didn't she?"

"His name was Samuel Kitson. He had been at school with John Prentice and he served on the *Frodsham* as well. Although he couldn't match John for money, Sam was a handsome, strapping fellow by all accounts and it seems that during one shore leave when John was briefly struck down by a stomach bug, Sam seized his opportunity and took Betty to bed. I don't believe it was a great romance. They were simply two young good-looking people who were thrown together in war-time and did what so many other couples did."

"How did Prentice find out?"

"Not through Betty. She was no fool. But Sam was a different kettle of fish. He loved to boast of his conquests and within twenty-four hours his affair with Betty was common knowledge. John was not a popular officer—he was quick-tempered and wealthy enough since the death of his parents to attract the envy of a good many of his colleagues on board the ship. I imagine that someone took a good deal of malicious pleasure in making him aware that his fiancée had slept with a man who was not only a fellow officer but also, supposedly, a friend."

"And how did he take it?"

"By all accounts he went out and got drunk and talked about finding a girl who would offer him the chance to pay Betty back in kind. In that, he evidently succeeded. He does not seem to have challenged Sam Kitson in the short time left before they were due to re-embark. Betty claimed later that he gave her no indication that he had learned the truth about her brief affair. She hoped she had got away with it. In a sense she did, but Kitson was not so lucky."

"What exactly happened?"

Toby shifted his artificial leg into a more comfortable position and closed his eyes for a few moments. Harry sensed that the old man was re-living the longago days of his youth. The war had cost him his fitness, but it must have been a thousand times more exciting than the peaceful working life of a probate practitioner, tidying up the estates of clients who were in no position to quibble or complain.

"As the *Frodsham* sailed back to Liverpool, the two men encountered each other on deck one night. The precise sequence of events was never altogether clear, but it seems that John Prentice could contain his anger no longer. At around midnight, he accosted the man who had slept with his girlfriend. There was a vigorous altercation and blows were exchanged. Prentice hit his head on a guard-rail and slumped onto the deck. A third man, another Liverpudlian who knew them both, saw the whole sorry business. His name was Eric Delabole. He'd been feeling ill and had come out on deck to get a little air. To begin with, he kept out of the way. The other two hadn't seen him and he thought it wiser not to interfere. He had heard Sam bragging about his performance with Betty and he reckoned that Prentice was entitled to give the fellow his comeuppance. However, he said that as soon as he saw Prentice collapse, his instinct told him that the worst had happened. Prentice was lying motionless, like a broken doll. Delabole called out to Kitson: 'You bloody fool! You've killed him!' And Kitson glanced at him in blind panic and then ran to the side of the ship. Within seconds he was over the rail. By the time Delabole had reached the place where Kitson took the plunge, there was no sign of him. It was a February night and the Atlantic was freezing. Delabole wasted little time in raising the alarm, but nothing could be done. Prentice was dead and there was no hope of recovering Kitson's body."

For a little while neither of them spoke. Harry was picturing in his mind's eye the scene on the *Frodsham* and he guessed that Toby Jones was doing the same. Death had come in the darkness to the ship, but not in the way that those on board would constantly have feared. Rather than being annihilated by a torpedo or by gunfire, two of their number had died as a result of a *casus belli* as old as the hills. It was easy to imagine Delabole's despair as he saw the shadowy figures' struggle end with one man's head smashed beyond repair and the other surrendering to the cold and the waves.

And yet—surely something was wrong with the picture. What else could he think after studying the obituary of Ianthe Ogus?

"The aftermath," he prompted gently. "You were involved directly, as I recall."

"Since the death of his parents, John Prentice had become one of our wealthiest private clients. He had no brothers or sisters. As soon as we learned about the tragedy of his death, we had to consider who would have a claim to inherit his estate. An answer was soon forthcoming. Even in those days, when sudden death was commonplace, the loss of the Prentice Munitions heir caused quite a stir. The authorities tried to massage the facts, but word soon leaked out about the quarrel. As I have mentioned, it was widely known that Sam Kitson had slept with Betty Higgins. Prentice was seen as the injured party and Betty as a common tart. But very few people were aware that Prentice himself had bedded a pretty young girl during his last period of leave. He had, however, confided in a couple of old chums of his. They happened to be cousins and they came forward with a remarkable story."

"What exactly did they have to say?"

Toby struggled to his feet. He moved over to a mahogany sideboard, opened a drawer and extracted a thick and yellowing file of papers. "For that, you should properly consult the official source. When you told me what you were interested in, I called up the office. I've been spending part of my retirement tinkering with a history of the firm of Maher and Malcolm. It is one of the oldest legal practices in the United Kingdom, as you know. There are many good stories to be told and the present partners have always been willing to grant me access, within reason, to any archived files that I believe may assist me with my researches. I asked for a copy of the Prentice Estate papers and, thanks to the wonders of technology and modern archiving systems, this little fellow was couriered here within a couple of hours. I must say it is a far cry from my earliest days in articles, when our post book contained a manuscript record of every letter and parcel that we ever despatched."

Harry took the file. "This really is very good of you, Toby."

"Think nothing of it. I am intrigued by your interest in the case. And I must admit that although I do not share your talent for sleuthing, I have myself been wondering about the implications of the report in *The Times* about the death of Mrs. Ogus."

Inside the file were a couple of bulky affidavits. Harry slid them out and began to study the first. "Yes, I remember reading this now. This man, Geoffrey Shaw, said that he and his cousin met John Prentice for a drink a few hours before Prentice was due to re-embark on the *Frodsham*. Prentice was still evidently dismayed by the behaviour of Betty and Sam Kitson. He said he had not tackled Betty directly, because he feared the consequences of his own temper, but his mind was made up. He intended to break off the engagement. She had betrayed him and any feelings of his for her had been destroyed."

Toby said, "Yet Geoffrey and his cousin, Ronald, made it clear that Prentice's mood was, on the whole, surprisingly jovial. He even said at one point that perhaps he owed Betty and Sam a favour. For if he had

not learned about their affair, he would not have become besotted with
the beautiful young woman who had so quickly captured his heart. Iron-
ically, Betty had introduced him to her. She too worked in the Western
Approaches, but she was lovelier than Betty."

"And her name," Harry said softly, "was Ianthe Shuttleworth."

Toby nodded. "Her beauty was important. It was easy to believe what
the two men told us. They knew Prentice, Kitson and Delabole, but neither
of them appeared to have any particular connection with Ianthe. I remember that they explained how Prentice had become sombre as the time to
leave approached. He told them that he was afraid that the *Frodsham*'s
next voyage would be its last. It was not a morbid fancy, you know, but
a matter of grim realism. Prentice was no coward, but he was desolate to
think that, so soon after meeting Ianthe and falling in love with her, he
might lose her."

"So he did his best to look after her?"

"Correct. He told the cousins that, if the worst did happen to him, he
wanted Ianthe to have everything."

"But he wrote nothing down?"

"Not a word. Even so, the two men were adamant. He had left them
in no doubt. They were quite sure he was not drunk. Melancholic, yes,
but thinking clearly. He had come to his decision and he asked them to
assure him that, in the event of his death, they would make sure that his
wishes were fulfilled."

"They didn't betray his trust," Harry said thoughtfully as he studied
the affidavits. "Their evidence is consistent and unambiguous. Prentice
wanted Ianthe to inherit all his worldly goods."

"You must understand," Toby said, "it was commonplace in war-time.
Death was everywhere. Servicemen about to engage with the enemy were
bound to turn their minds to the question of what would become of their
worldly goods if they failed to return home. Which is why the law makes
a special concession for people in such circumstances."

Harry nodded. "This is the legal nicety you explained to me all those
years ago, isn't it? The Prentice file illustrated it perfectly."

"Yes." Toby took a breath. "The textbooks state the principle suc-
cinctly: *A soldier, sailor or airman in actual military service is entitled to a
special privilege as regards the making of a will: no formality whatsoever is
required.*"

"So there need be nothing in writing at all," Harry said softly.

"That is right. The courts show great indulgence. During the First
World War, a soldier fresh out of Sandhurst told his fiancée: 'If I stop a
bullet, everything will be yours.' He was killed in action and the will was
upheld. The precedents are endless and there is even a special terms for
wills of this kind: *nuncupative.*" He rolled the word off his tongue, sa-
vouring it for a few moments before continuing. "In Ianthe's case, the
evidence of the cousins about Prentice's intentions was convincing and

the fact that he was on dry land at the time did not matter: the law regarded him as being on service. He had no close family. The only other person who might have expected anything was Betty and in view of her ill-fated fling with Sam Kitson, she scarcely had grounds for complaint."

"So Ianthe got the money?"

"Eventually, yes. The estate was quite complicated, as is always the way when there are extensive assets. But she was patient. A pleasure to do business with, I thought." He hesitated before adding, "She was a remarkably attractive woman, as you will have gathered from the photograph in the newspaper today. Quite flawless. I was young and impressionable. I suppose I was a little bit in love with her. There was never any question, though, of the two of us . . ."

He left the sentence hanging in the air. Harry said, "Did you keep in touch with her after the estate had been distributed?"

"Oh no, there was no reason to. Towards the end of the war I met Winifred and thoughts of Ianthe faded from my mind. I heard somewhere after the war that she had married. A local man who worked for a shipping line, I gathered, but I never had any details."

"And as far as you knew, they lived happily ever after?"

Toby inclined his head. "To me, the case became nothing more than a legal curiosity, which is why I told you—and a good many other clerks before you—about it."

"So you never learned the identity of the man Ianthe married?"

"Not until I read the obituary in *The Times*. I see that they moved from Liverpool to London not long after the wedding." Toby paused for a moment. For the first time in their acquaintance, his lined face was deeply troubled. "I simply had no idea that her first husband was Eric Delabole, the man who had witnessed the killing of her lover. Or that after his death she married Ronald Ogus, one of the cousins in whose presence John Prentice made his nuncupative will."

Harry arrived home at the Empire Dock flats after eleven. It was a cold night, but crisp and dry, and he decided on a walk along the waterfront before bedtime. His mind was whirling and he knew that sleep would elude him until he found answers to some of the questions that arose from his conversation with Toby Jones.

What must it be like to live through a war? To fear that death might at any time drop out of the sky? When life was cheap, when hundreds might die in a single air-raid or because of the sinking of just one ship, murder might seem a less shocking crime. And there would always be the dream that one day the war would be over and the survivors would inherit the earth.

He stared at the inky expanse of the River Mersey. Everywhere was so quiet. Hard to imagine that the Battle of the Atlantic had been fought from Liverpool. An underground bunker a few hundred yards from his own office had housed the Citadel, the combined headquarters of the Western Approaches and the place where Betty Higgins and Ianthe Shuttleworth had worked. They were both plotters in the map room, Toby had explained, members of a team of women who had tracked the movements of allied and enemy shipping on huge charts. Far from the theatre of war, they had played their part in the sinking of the *Bismarck* and provided the link between the code-breakers of Bletchley Park who had cracked the Enigma cipher and the forces who had exploited the intelligence to turn the course of the battle for mastery of the high seas. They were the unsung heroines who had worked long hard hours in cramped and airless conditions, dedicated to the cause of freedom.

And yet, he thought as he listened to the black water lapping against the river bank, even heroines had lives of their own. Private lives in which they might, like anyone else, succumb to the temptations of lust and greed. He wondered what secrets Ianthe's enigmatic smile had concealed. Had she, he asked himself, been a plotter in more senses than one?

A theory was beginning to form in his mind and as he lay in bed that night waiting for sleep to come, he decided that his best chance of gleaning more clues would be to attend Ianthe's funeral. The following morning he telephoned a friend on a local newspaper and learned that she was due to be cremated that afternoon. He could not be sure that there would be anyone present at the service who had known her during the war years, but there was only one way to find out for certain. Delabole and Ogus were dead—but what about Shaw, the other witness to the will? Might he be persuaded, after all these years, to talk?

His court cases lasted longer than he had expected and he arrived at the crematorium mid-way through the vicar's eulogy about all the dead woman's good works. When the service was over, Harry tagged on to a group of people who were inspecting the floral tributes. From their accents, he deduced that many were friends from London, come up here to pay their last respects.

He found himself standing next to a stout man in a cashmere overcoat. Time to start firing a few long shots. "I say, do you know if Ronald's cousin is here, by any chance? Dear me, what was his name—was it Geoffrey? Geoffrey Shaw?"

The man shook his head doubtfully, but an elderly woman tapped on Harry's shoulder. "Geoff Shaw are you asking about?" she demanded in broad Lancastrian tones. "Lord, I haven't seen him since Ianthe married Ronald. Last time I heard, he was suffering from chronic emphysema."

"Oh dear." Harry did not have to fake the dismay in his voice. If Shaw was dead, the chances of discovering what had actually happened on board the *Frodsham* were slim. "Is he . . ."

She anticipated his question. "No, no, he's still alive. That is, he was ten days ago, the last time I paid Ianthe a visit. She mentioned she had been in touch with him and planning to call on him the following week. I remember she said she felt guilty about not having seen him for a long time. She was such a decent woman, God rest her soul. And that weekend, she looked the picture of health. Who would have thought that so soon afterwards she would suffer a massive stroke? The only consolation is that she did not linger on. She was such an active woman that to be a permanent invalid would have been torture for her."

"There are worse ways to go," the stout man confirmed. "I remember . . ."

"Sorry to butt in," Harry said quickly, "but I would be glad of a word with Geoffrey if it's possible. Does he still live on Merseyside, do you know?"

"Oh yes," the woman said, "he recently moved to a nursing home on the main road only a couple of miles from Ianthe's house. I thought it was rather nice that two old friends who had lived at different ends of the country for so long should finish up as near neighbours. She pointed the place out to me when we took a taxi into the city centre."

"You don't happen to remember what it was called?"

She searched her memory. "Yellow Broom House, I believe." Frowning slightly, she added, "Are you another friend from Liverpool? I don't recall Ianthe mentioning you, Mr. . . ."

"Devlin." Harry smiled and said shamelessly, "I suppose you could say I knew Geoffrey Shaw just as well as I knew Ianthe."

But then his smile faded as he read one of the neatly typed cards which accompanied the flowers.

Dedicated to the memory of Ianthe—please forgive your old friend. Geoffrey Shaw.

He drove quickly to Yellow Broom House. It seemed to him that no time should be lost: he had a sense that over the last few days events had been moving to a climax. A meeting between Ianthe and Geoffrey Shaw had been followed by her death. What did the note at the crematorium mean? What did Shaw have to reproach himself about?

He had no idea whether he would be allowed to see the old man, far less whether he would be able to persuade him to talk about the past. Yet his luck was in. The matron said that Geoffrey Shaw had few visitors and would be glad of a little company. He had seemed out of sorts lately, as if something was preying on his mind.

Five minutes later Harry and Geoffrey Shaw were sitting together in a large and airy room which looked out upon a tiny pond. Carefully, Harry explained the chain of events that had brought him out to the nursing home. Even as he spoke, he still did not dare to hope that he would finally solve the mystery of the *Frodsham*—and he was careful not to reveal everything that he had guessed. When he had finished, he sat back in his chair and waited for Geoffrey Shaw to reply.

The old man thought for a few moments before saying, "It's as if my prayers have been answered."

Harry wasn't accustomed to such a response. So often his questions met with evasion and lies. He said cautiously, "You don't mind telling me what really happened?"

"I need to tell someone before I die, Mr. Devlin. You are obviously interested in the case and you have already made several intelligent deductions of your own. I can't imagine a more suitable confidant."

And so the old man began to tell his tale. He was frail and short of breath; it seemed to take an effort of will for him to force the sentences out. But there was no doubting how much he wanted to share the guilty knowledge that he had for more than half a century kept to himself and the people with whom he had conspired.

"It's been on my conscience all this time," he said hoarsely. "And now that Ianthe is dead, I suppose I'm the only survivor. Eric was the first to go, of course. Then my cousin. And finally, poor Ianthe. Hard to believe that she's passed on. She always seemed so alive. She was a very beautiful woman, you know. Even in old age, you could see it. Yes, a very beautiful woman—and a loyal friend."

"She owed you a good deal," Harry said.

"I know it was wrong," the old man said. He might have been talking to himself. "We all did. Yet it did not seem—*criminal*. After all, no one else suffered. John Prentice had no close relatives, no heirs. Betty Scott had forfeited any moral claim to his estate. And Ianthe wanted it badly." He paused to suck some more air into his lungs. "She was ambitious, she didn't want to stay in Liverpool all her life. Eric was the same. And give them credit. Once they had the money, they didn't waste it. They made the most of the opportunities it brought—and they weren't tight-fisted, either."

"If I'm right, it's an extraordinary story."

"Yes. At least it can't hurt anyone now. I'm the only survivor. I never thought I'd outlast Ianthe, it seems incredible. But I know I don't have much time left. You are a bright fellow, must be, to have put two and two together from a piece in a newspaper."

"I haven't been able to fill in all the gaps. That's why I'm here."

The old man closed his eyes for a few seconds. "Ronald and I had known Eric Delabole for many years. We were at school together. The three of us had always been keen on ships and sailing and when war broke out, we had ideas about joining the Navy together. It didn't work out that way. Ronald and I were employed as draughtsmen in a steelworks. It was a reserved occupation."

"Meaning what?"

"We were more use to the war effort working in the steelyard than pretending to be sailors." The old man wheezed; it was as close as he could manage to a laugh. "Eric worked for the bus company, so he was dispensable. His ship was the *Frodsham*. He introduced us to Prentice, though I never cared for the fellow. He was rich, he didn't need to be liked and made no effort to be agreeable."

"And his fiancée?"

"Betty was a nice-looking girl," the old man said slowly, "though hardly in Ianthe's class. She liked to have a good time and I suppose she thought Prentice offered the passport to it. The trouble was, she tired of him. Sam Kitson wasn't the first young man she'd had a fling with—and a couple of days before the *Frodsham* sailed, it was perfectly clear that her relationship with Prentice was finished."

"What happened?"

The old man closed his eyes again as he travelled back in time. "A group of us met in a bar. Ronald, Eric and myself, together with Prentice and Betty. She'd brought along a girl she worked with, a lovely young blonde called Ianthe Shuttleworth. It should have been a happy night out, but Prentice and Betty rowed and she walked out. Soon afterwards, he left. The three of us who stayed on along with Ianthe all flirted with her, but it was obvious where her preference lay. In the end, she disappeared with Eric. Ronald and I were envious, I can tell you."

"So you and your cousin were the only people who knew about the two of them?" Harry thought for a moment. "When did someone have the bright idea of inventing a will for John Prentice?"

"After the ship returned to port. Everyone was agog when word got out about the deaths of Prentice and Sam Kitson. The authorities tried to hush things up, but bad news travels fast. Betty was humiliated. Everyone regarded her as a scarlet woman. She took ill—tuberculosis, I think. Working in that underground bunker can't have done her much good. All that damp air. And then she'd lost both Prentice and Kitson. She had to give the work up and I heard towards the end of the war that she'd died." He coughed. "Anyway, I'm losing my thread. Eric got in touch and asked if Ronald and I could meet him at a little pub out in Cheshire. When we arrived there, he was with Ianthe."

"I see. They had arranged a rendez-vous where you were most unlikely to bump into anyone who knew you. Presumably because Eric needed to hide from the world the fact that he and Ianthe were close?"

"Of course. And it worked, Mr. Devlin. I'm sure that no one ever suspected the truth. I sometimes think Eric richly deserved all that money. He had to steer clear of the girl he loved for long enough, until it was safe to come into the open. In the end, it was only after he was demobbed that the two of them pretended to fall for each other."

"Who thought up the idea?"

"Ianthe. She had a smattering of legal knowledge. Before she started with the Western Approaches, she had worked as a secretary in a firm of solicitors."

I might have known that the legal profession would be implicated somehow,

Harry reflected. Aloud, he said, "And you and your cousin were persuaded to swear that Prentice had said he wanted to leave everything to
her?"

"There was no one to gainsay it," Geoffrey Shaw said simply. "We
were promised a share of the money, naturally, and Eric and Ianthe more
than kept their word. They were good friends—and more than generous
people."

Especially with money that did not belong to them, Harry thought, but
again he kept it to himself. "They needed to make sure that you would
not give the game away."

"No danger of that. I suppose both Ronald and I were a little in love
with her."

She had that effect on men, thought Harry, remembering the impression
she had made upon Toby Jones.

"Perhaps it was because of that that we were so glad to help, Mr.
Devlin. And the four of us remained in regular contact as the years
passed."

"So everyone lived happily ever after?"

"No need to sound so cynical, Mr. Devlin." Infirm as he was, the old
man was struggling for dignity. "Eric was a talented man, prepared to
work long hours. He would probably have succeeded whatever the circumstances, but the money did help. Before long he was on the board of
the Byzantium Line and eventually he reached the very top. They moved
down to London early on and Ianthe became quite the society hostess.
She took an interest in art and encouraged young painters to specialise in
maritime subjects. Ronald and I both found good jobs in management in
peace-time. Each of us got married. Ronald's wife died six or seven years
ago, mine eighteen months back. Ianthe was very kind to him after
Molly's death; I wasn't surprised when they tied the knot. A pity they
had so little time together before he died."

The old man leaned back in his armchair. He was evidently exhausted,
but at the same time there was a glint of satisfaction in his eyes. Harry
said, "You've been very frank with me."

"Why not? Believe me, this conversation has done me good. I've
wanted to get it all off my chest before . . ."

Harry was tempted for a moment to offer false cheer, to say that Geoffrey Shaw would be around for a long time to come. But he could not do
it. The old man belonged to a generation that was emotionally tough. He
had lived through the worst that war could bring and he knew all about
death. There was no point in pretending. Harry sensed that now his companion felt he could face his Maker unafraid. He was prepared for the
end.

"I'm grateful."

"Just glad to put the record straight." Geoffrey Shaw paused and then said defiantly, "Anyway, even though what we did was wrong, we never hurt anyone. Eric and Ianthe promised that with a little help from us, they could make sure that everyone would gain. We were friends; we trusted them. And they did not let us down. As I said, no one suffered."

Harry hesitated. Did the old man really believe that—or was he still trying to convince himself?

He said gently, "*No one suffered*. You've said that more than once, Mr Shaw. But it simply was not true, was it? You and your cousin might not have realised it, but you were pawns in a murder plot."

There was a long silence and then the old man said, "You are even more perceptive than I realised, Mr. Devlin. What have you deduced?"

Harry leaned forward. He had the sense of excitement that comes when a horse backed at long odds romps past the winning post. "The way I see it, Eric Delabole's account of the murder on the *Frodsham* relied too much on coincidence for comfort. I find it impossible to accept that he witnessed Kitson killing Prentice and then, most conveniently, jumping overboard. Once you know that Delabole was by then already besotted with Ianthe, the other pieces fall into place, don't they? By far the likeliest scenario was that something Ianthe had told him about privileged wills had given him an idea for a perfect crime. He had murdered Prentice and then caught Kitson, the scapegoat, unawares and turfed him over the side of the ship. You and Ronald were the couple's dupes, persuaded to lie about the will that never was. So with a little help from her friends Ianthe inherited with a minimum of fuss and bother, and after a decent interval, the lovers had married. Easy. My only question is—when did you realise what they had done?"

"I suppose—in my heart, I've always known. But I didn't want to believe it. I pushed it to the back of my mind. Ronald was more trusting than me. He believed everything Eric and Ianthe told him. Of course, she could have told him the moon was made of green cheese and he would have taken it as gospel."

"But you never confronted her?"

"Not until the end."

"Can you tell me about it?"

"She wrote to me a little while ago, said she would look me up. We could talk about old times. I hadn't seen her for a year or two and my health had taken a turn for the worse. I felt I might not have another chance to put to her what I had suspected for so long. It was good to see her. I waited while we talked about her two husbands and then I asked her about the killing on the *Frodsham*. I said that there was no need for her to hide anything from me. I simply wanted to know. But she flew into a temper. That's one thing you won't have read in the obituary. She was a sweet woman when she got her own way—which was most of the time. But woe betide you if you crossed her."

"What did she say?"

"She said that the very idea that she and Eric could have conspired in murder was abominable. She even suggested I must be going senile."

"And did you accept her denial?"

The old man said simply, "I had no doubt that I'd struck a nerve. Even after all this time, she was terrified that the truth about the *Frodsham* deaths would come out. I realised, though, that I'd made a mistake. With Ianthe, I should have let sleeping dogs lie. If I had done so, I am sure she would be alive today. You realise, don't you, that she suffered her stroke only a few hours after she left here, vowing never to return?"

"Hence your note at the crematorium?"

"I killed her, Mr. Devlin. To my eternal shame. Despite what she and Eric had done, I did not want her to die. Prentice and Kitson were no great loss."

Harry bowed his head and for a little time neither of them spoke. Presently the old man said something, but he spoke so faintly that Harry had to lean over him to hear.

"All's fair in love and war," Geoffrey Shaw repeated.

He closed his eyes and Harry sensed that he would never open them again. He called the nurse and as he waited for her to do her duty, he repeated to himself the old man's slogan. *All's fair in love and war.* What an absurd notion. Yet many people had once believed it excused murder. And even today, some still did.

CHRIS RIPPEN
(1940–)

Finally, the editor has the pleasure of introducing a new discovery to English-speaking readers. Written especially for this volume, "Ferry Noir" is the work of Chris Rippen, a Dutch writer well-established in his native Netherlands and in Germany, where his work appears in translation. This is his first story published in English.

Rippen was born during World War II in Haarlem in the Netherlands, where he spent his boyhood and youth. He recalls his hometown, located in the western part of his country near the North Sea, as a place famous for its historical center, magnificent pipe organs, and nearby blooming bulb fields. He also retains "less sharp memories of German soldiers in the streets, fire, an execution in the neighborhood." His first published novel, *Sporen* (1987), uses themes of resistance and betrayal during that time. Its title, translated into English, means "traces." Rippen said, "The war and occupation are part of the memory, history, and grief of most Dutch people of a certain age and therefore a main theme in many books and stories."

Rippen attended teacher training college and then served for two years as an officer in the military. Following this, he studied Dutch language and literature at the University of Amsterdam, where he also received his doctoral degree in medieval literature. Along the way, he married and with his wife raised three sons. His academic career included lectureships and managerial work at various universities. As head of the Department of Dutch Language and Literature at the Hogeschool Holland in Amsterdam, he created a popular four-year writing program and has taught short story writing there himself since 1990.

Rippen was forty-seven years old when *Sporen* was published. His second novel, *Playback* (1991), won the prestigious Dutch crime writing award De Gouden Strop '92 (The Golden Noose). Although its title is an English word, *Playback* is not yet translated into English. A third novel, *Met de Grond Gelijk* (Leveled), was published in 1993. His short stories are collected in *Zuidelijke Streken* (Mediterranean Ways) (1995). He is chairman of the association of Dutch crime writers, or Genootschap van Nederlanstalige Misaadauteurs.

Rippen said his literary influences include Raymond Chandler and especially Ross Macdonald. He also enjoys the work of John Le Carré, Georges Simenon, Maj Sjowall and Per Wahloo, and Heinrich Böll, along with "more canonized compatriots" like Hemingway, James Baldwin, Washington Irving, Evelyn Waugh, and Graham Greene.

Most of the action in "Ferry Noir" takes place during a nighttime ferry crossing. This dark tale is viewed through the character's paranoia. In it, Rip-

pen demonstrates his masterful manipulation of visual detail by creating a
literary production shadowed with a film noir atmosphere.

Ferry Noir

1996

He'd almost missed it. The last one of the cars that had been standing in
four lines waiting to drive onto the car deck when he had gone to pick
up his ticket had just gone through the bow doors. They said something
about his booking but in the rush he had not understood what it was. He
didn't care either, as long as they got a move on. He started the car in a
hurry and drove right across the white lines marking the lanes towards
the ramp. The rain pounded the greasy asphalt and sent gusts through
the shine of the arched street lamps along the dock. They'd really be in
for it with this wind when they got to open sea. The tires pounded the
corrugated ramp and the car tipped forward as he put on the brakes
before crossing the sill to the gaping hole. A man in dripping yellowish-
white oilskins was gesturing impatiently to him, then he suddenly raised
one hand and held a portophone to his ear with the other. Brake lights
flashed inside the belly of the ship, he saw the massive backside of a truck
which was blocking the way. It had big, grey, meaningless lettering on
its billowing canvas. Full up? It couldn't be, certainly not on a weekday.
They would have known about that at the ticket office. The man was
beckoning authoritatively and he squeezed his car between the truck and
the steel wall, manoeuvering until it was between the yellow lines. The
last one. But as he turned off the engine, the reflection from the headlights
of another car swept across his mirrors and he turned around alarmed.
He turned off the engine, and as he sat motionless behind the steering
wheel, the stench of exhaust fumes and oil slowly permeated the car.
Rainwater was pouring down the windscreen, distorting the shadowy
figures trying to find their way to the doors in the artificial light from the
bull's-eyes between the cars. Behind him, the folding ramp creaked as it
was raised. He was in. For an instant, relief pushed out the feeling of
repulsion that always crept up on him as he drove onto a ferry. Even
though it would be at least another nine hours before he could be certain,
he was safe for now. There were hollow metallic sounds all around him:
chains rattling into place, wheels being turned producing a grinding
noise, hydraulic groans. He saw a yellow shadow and a hand tapped his
windscreen in passing, while a voice uttered something unintelligible. Un-
willingly he opened the car door and shivered in the cold rush of air
whistling through the hold. He would have preferred to stay where he
was, having an unreasoned feeling that he could keep things under control if he did. But he knew the regulations. Aside from which he had to

get some sleep. Ferries were bad news he thought as he went up the stairs to the key desk, especially night ferries, but not as bad as the tunnel. Silently he handed his boarding-pass to the woman behind the desk. She looked up his name and crossed something off on her floor plan. He looked too, leaning over the desk.

"There's been a mistake," he said. "I've booked a single cabin."

The woman looked at the ticket and consulted her list again.

"Sorry sir," she said. "Everything checks out. An inside cabin for two." She spoke in her best English. Her eyes were clear and her expression neutral in her heavily made-up face; her shift had only just started. As she explained he looked at the dark line around her glistening lips and felt his eyelids close. He was one of the last passengers, the booking could not be changed, everything was full up except the over-priced Captain's Class. He thought about sending for the purser but decided against it. Attracting too much attention wasn't a good idea. "There are some sleeper chairs available," she said, "but you'll have to pay extra. After all you did reserve."

His shoulder-bag slipped forward and he shifted the strap. "No thank you."

The man behind him coughed impatiently and he felt a suitcase being pushed into the back of his knees. He picked up the key-card and nodded to the woman. "Leave it, it's all right," he said and walked over to the floor plan down the corridor. It wasn't all right at all, he thought, but he was too tired to find out who or what had caused the mistake.

The cabin was located past the second transverse passage, almost at the front of the ship. The numbers on the card swam before his eyes as he checked them again. He waited a moment, then slid the card into the lock and opened the door. The light was on. On the duvet of the upper bunk lay a folded coat with a small, leather overnight-bag next to it.

He kept looking at it as he hung up his coat. He inspected the shower and the toilet, felt the towel hanging beside it and kept looking over his shoulder at the sleeping-quarters, as though he expected someone to come in. He then stooped over the lower bunk and put his hands on the sheet. His left leg cramped and he sat down to stretch his muscles. Sleep was the only thing he wanted now. He had used the prospect to keep himself awake during the last hour in the car; he'd driven with the window open because he was really already too far gone. A sleep that would last the entire journey, the only way to survive a trip like this. He pushed himself onto his feet again and looked at the things on the upper bunk. An intruder. What you risked by a last-minute booking. He should have known better, should have checked his ticket while he was still on the dock, but tired as he was and in the rush he had assumed that everything was all right. Of all the times, it had to be now. Was it a coincidence? Someone was sharing his cabin, would be so close to him that he could not avoid, let alone ignore him. A perfect stranger. He himself knew he would feel inhibited, watched, caught out. In a space measuring barely a metre and a half by two metres there would not be any way to avoid physical contact. There would be sounds during the night, uncontrolled sounds, you'd breathe in each other's air. A forced, claustrophobic intimacy. He felt his stomach constricting. Did he still talk in his sleep? For years there hadn't been anyone to blame him for it in the morning, the way Doris used to do.

What kind of man was he? He stretched out his hand towards the bag on the upper bunk, then withdrew it again. The floor beneath his feet started to vibrate and he looked at his watch. Five past ten. He put his ear to the door and listened for sounds from the corridor. Then, with a swift movement he pulled the overnight-bag toward him and pressed down the lock. Locked. He stroked the leather, felt the shapes of the objects inside. His hand hovered over the coat, he was tempted to check the pockets, look at the label, find out something about the man who would enter shortly, have a head start, but his courage failed. He carefully wiped down the bag with the ferry company's bath-towel which was on his pillow and put it back the way he thought it had been before.

He could just lie down for a bit. Chances were that the other man would not come in for the next few hours, would hang around the bar or even take in the show advertised in the corridor. He would simply catch up on a few hours of last night's sleep which he'd missed, and then see what happened. He looked at the lower bunk, bent over and smoothed down the sheet. A soft irregular sound juddered through the cabin walls and floor, in sudden haste he grabbed his coat and shoulder bag and left the cabin. The ship had already separated itself from the continent. On the aft deck he saw the angle between the ship's hull and the quayside increase, filling with a track of foam. Over the dock the air was dirty grey, but out behind the refinery with its windblown red plumes the clouds lit up in an eerie artificial sunset. Down in the railroad yard the empty windows of the boat-train glided slowly out from under the roof. Destination Utrecht? He didn't know, it didn't matter any more anyway, what did he have to do with Utrecht now?

The rain had stopped and some of the passengers had come on deck, in spite of the icy wind which was coming from every side and made all attempts to find shelter useless. He walked along the railing, his shoulders hunched, slowly getting chilled to the bone in his thin coat, already half numbed by the roar of the chimney high above the deck. Had he done it after all? Everything depended on whether they had followed him when he left Utrecht.

He had taken the bus to the campus as usual, twenty minutes past eight, a punctual man, they must have thought. Even a wakeful night wasn't enough to put him off schedule. Very British. He had put his toiletries in the shoulder-bag he always carried, among today's lecture notes. Tomorrow, at home he would call the hotel to have his bags sent after him and to arrange payment. They wouldn't object, he'd stayed there so many times. Almost four years. At eleven o'clock he had said he felt ill and arranged for a colleague to take over the exam. His car was where he'd left it the previous night, at the side entrance next to the space set aside for the handicapped, out of sight. He hadn't seen anyone on the way. First he had made the booking by phone from his room and then he'd called Karen by way of goodbye. She had not been irritated, as he expected, but concerned. Why hadn't he turned up yesterday? She had waited for an hour. Later on she had called the hotel but he wasn't there. Was anything the matter? At their last meeting at the restaurant he had behaved differently too. . . . Her questions had cut his off, her voice had confused him and he had even started an explanation not too far from the truth. When someone had entered the room and he wanted to cut the conversation short, she had pressed for another date soon—tonight, same time, same place—their usual joke. "You're leaving tomorrow anyway . . . aren't you?" Did she suspect anything? Just as usual he had said. If all went well, he would be on the ferry by then.

A car with a rotating roof light was zigzagging among the obstacles scattered about the dock, now hundreds of metres behind them. It was passing the terminal and the nearby sheds at high speed. Jon stared at the flashing lights, but the distance was too great to distinguish anything in the dusk. The Dutch police had blue rotating lights; was this a customs car? Or was it nothing—only his nerves getting the better of him? A large dark shape glided between the ferry and the dock, obscuring his view. It was a homeward-bound vessel, its sparingly lit deck blurring its outline. When it had passed he couldn't see the flashing lights on the dock any more but the leaden feeling in his stomach didn't wear off. Suddenly he became aware of the cold and struggled against the wind, towards the doors.

All the seats on the inside deck and in the central hall were already taken. Uneconomically placed luggage marked people's territories for the night; officially no sleeping was allowed there but everybody ignored this rule. The key desk was closed, which put paid to any chance of his making other arrangements, unless he spoke to the purser. His cabin was situated one deck down. It seemed as if the cold had dispelled his sleepiness, but his body was groaning with fatigue and he knew he had to get some sleep or things would not go well in the morning. He looked for the lounge with the sleeper chairs on the floor plan in the corridor. Maybe it would be quiet there for the next few hours, while people were still roaming the ship or awaiting night in the bar. But two decks down the whoops were already reaching him and members of the staff were busy checking tickets and comparing them. He walked past without checking for an empty seat. Spending the night in a room packed with sleeping bodies was totally impossible. A female voice was routinely giving an outline of the evening's entertainment in three languages, over the intercom. As he stared indecisively at a sign on a door saying Crew Only, the metallic sounds mingled with the noises in his head and for a minute he felt dizzy. The strap of his bag was cutting into his shoulder. He thought of the overnight-bag on the upper bunk. He would grab a pint and then just go to his cabin. Why not? The ship was already rolling as he walked back, he had to find support twice.

The bar was already full of activity. The stage at the back was still empty but couples were already moving around the small oval dance floor to the music from the sound system and all the tables around it were occupied. Moth-eaten whining pop music. Later on there would probably be one of those duos trying to suggest the sound of a full band with just a little electronic background support, playing the same kind of music. Seemingly it was necessary to entertain people. Silence was death. He ordered a pint of stout and sauntered past the miniature roulette table where a woman croupier was dividing her attention between a chatting colleague and the solitary customer across the table. He stared at the people at the tables and when he got to the bar he wondered who the man occupying the upper bunk in his cabin could be. It had to be someone like himself, alone, possibly even a loner. Someone who didn't socialise. Not one of the truck drivers, you could spot them a mile off with their roll-your-own cigarettes and the quick beer before going to sleep. The neat overnight-bag went with a business traveller, if such people still existed, but of course they would take a plane nowadays. Unless they needed to take their own car, the way he did. Behind him a bar stool became vacant and as he seated himself he caught his own reflection in the mirror: pallid. Did the other passengers see what he did? An almost middle-aged teacher who had gone off the rails. Probably not. "One can't tell you're a teacher straight off, Jon," Karen had said once. "You could just as well be an architect or an editor of some sort. As long as you keep your mouth shut that is." Her compliments always had sharp edges.

Someone touched his shoulder, a man leaned forward and beckoned to the bartender. Jon moved a little. The man looked up and smiled at him.

"Sorry," he said. "It's pretty busy in here tonight." He was probably Dutch. His English was correct but his pronunciation was sloppy.

Jon forced himself to nod an affirmative. "Indeed." Then he looked straight ahead of him again. "But what else can you do on a barge like this, right? Spending the whole night in bed isn't great fun either." The man picked up his glass and held it up against the light. "Cheers," he said to nobody in particular and took a swig. "Isn't that what you English say? You are English aren't you?" He had a broad, slightly podgy face and friendly eyes. Small drops were glistening on his balding head. "You express yourself very well," Jon said. It took an effort to get the words out. He spread himself out behind his glass and the Dutchman stood back a little, half facing the room.

Jon felt his eyes close again. It was just past eleven, everything slowed down on a crossing like this. Time adjusted itself. When he first started doing this he had sometimes wondered who on earth would travel by ferry these days. Even women on a shopping spree, looking for a bargain, travelled by plane now. The ferry was full up every trip though. Well outside the holiday season. In the beginning he'd taken a plane of course, that was fast and efficient, it was really the only way to go, four times a year for a week and a half on an exchange programme, otherwise you wouldn't have any spare time. The University even paid for the expensive Dutch taxis. After a while he had taken the tunnel on the way over and the ferry back. It made sense. The customs check at the tunnel was much stricter. Besides, you had to pass the paranoid French customs twice. He had told people some story about how much easier it was to have your own car. He didn't mind the price difference, the job paid enough. He spent most of those extra hours on the ferry asleep. But this time, when he needed the sleep more than ever, they had given him a double, when he changed his booking to a day earlier. His glance in the mirror crossed that of another man and he looked down.

Karen. He had only known one of the roles she was playing, until yesterday. It was just as well he hadn't met her today, because he might have, in a moment of weakness, told her what was bothering him. That he had, purely by chance, seen her at Bluff's as he was coming from the library, looking in in passing. That he had known the man sitting across the table from her, not his name though, only by face. A dark sharp face which was etched into his memory in spite of the uncertain light of a street lamp. And he now knew his trust in her had been a mistake. But he would probably never have been able to withstand her. Her eyes which made him feel reckless, her sultry voice which could whisper things to him in school English, he didn't even dare think about. He would have been capable of disclosing his own escape plan, which was the last thing that should happen.

He wasn't in love with her, he never had been, but when he was with her he felt a kind of obsession he had never felt before. He'd noticed her during his second trimester at Utrecht, but as he now knew, she had planned it that way. Before he left they'd arranged their first date, and later, when she was no longer enrolled, and why should she be, they had continued their relationship. They hadn't been in love, otherwise he could not have handled seeing her at such long intervals. He himself had called it a quarterly affair. That's why never seeing her again didn't hurt him. He would experience missing her as an empty space, and he would with-draw within himself even more. Neither did he blame Karen. She had not betrayed him, she had simply never been on his side. She was on the side of the man he had seen the previous night when he got home. The tiles glistened with rain, there was hardly anyone on the street, but the man had paced to and fro as though he were waiting for somebody. Now and then he looked at his watch impatiently and suddenly he had taken off as if he'd had enough. But Jon had not fallen for that trick. In the dark, behind the curtain he had waited: five minutes later the man had returned, this time showing great interest in a shop-window exactly between two lampposts, a figure in a long, dark coat, shiny with moisture, standing very innocently with his back towards him. But he knew enough.

A group of men entered the club, yelling and cheering. Hot, giggly faces above red and white striped scarves and sweaters, close together like a herd of cattle, as they yelled at each other as though they were miles apart. They immediately took over the bar, claimed the counter and drowned out the music with cheers. Jon was nudged in the back, a man leaned half across him and called something to the bartender. He grabbed his shoulder bag and as he edged his way toward the exit he saw the Dutchman who had just been standing next to him, looking at him in amusement. In the corridor he stood still, undecided. The couches and armchairs were all taken. People were sitting or slouching against each other, some were asleep, others staring straight ahead, looking at him glassy-eyed. A group of people were playing cards in a corner. It was not yet eleven-thirty, they were well out to sea, this couldn't go on all night.

He stared at his watch as though he expected a solution from it. The ship moved under his feet and because of the sick feeling in his stomach he realised he hadn't eaten for nearly half the day. Perhaps the cafeteria would still be open.

The crew member who stopped cleaning the tables to settle up for his two plasticized sandwiches and bottle of beer warned him that he was closing in a quarter of an hour. He cleared a window table for him, and, while chewing, Jon stared through his reflection into the darkness outside. A grey deposit was sticking to the window panes, salt, mould and moisture penetrated everywhere. His eyes closed, he made a mental leap and suddenly sat bolt upright. The bread stuck to the roof of his mouth and he washed it down with the beer. Actually, he hated ferries. Compared with passenger ships and even freighters, they looked like some sort of mongrels. The superstructure was top-heavy and inside they had the artificial look of a third rate nightclub. The hollow space behind the unsightly bow doors jam packed with cargo on wheels. There was nothing romantic about a crossing like this, having to sit it out with hundreds of others who used the ship for one night, devastated it and then disappeared again. The seawhores and their transients; there for a night, a day. They wore the traces of it too, beneath the veneer and the gaudiness you could see the dilapidated carcase, the decay.

But it was over. This would be his final crossing. The letter in which he had asked to be relieved of his post lay ready and waiting. Tomorrow night he would request the faculty board to terminate the assignment. They would not understand. Who wouldn't want a trip to Holland four times a year, a light teaching assignment that required little preparation.

Internationalisation was the magic word, everyone was after a job as an exchange teacher, but he must have his reasons.

He did indeed. But they would not get to hear them. He didn't want to travel any more, however much he would miss the variety, in future he would teach only at Mildenhall, take the monotony in his stride, hoping that all that other business would be over too. And why shouldn't it be? He was of no interest to them any more.

He should never have agreed in the first place. He could still see the face of his predecessor, Jameson, after he had followed him across to take over at the end of the first trimester. "There's something else I want to ask you, my dear colleague . . ." After the introductions and the tour of the campus they had gone over the teaching material together. It had been late afternoon, the sherry had materialised out of nowhere. After all, traditions were there to be upheld, weren't they? The searching look, the smile that looked a bit guilty, the air of male solidarity. "This assignment won't make you rich you know. . . . What would you think of a little money on the side?" Had they pressed him to find someone to take over that department too? He would hardly have to do a thing and he wouldn't notice. The only condition was that he take his car with him in future, the tunnel on the way there and back by ferry, that would be best. Four days before leaving he had to leave his car on a certain spot in a multi-storey car park in Utrecht overnight and pick it up again the next morning. Two days after his return he was to do the same thing in England. That was all. Four times a year. He didn't need to know any more, he wouldn't see any of it and he would earn a fortune. The word wasn't used, things were not named, he had not asked any questions because he felt intuitively that he had better not. Jameson had picked up the bottle again and changed the subject. After the return trip, his colleague's last, he had consented. And he had never noticed anything. He left his car, picked it up. That was all. On the first crossing after that he was so tense he hadn't been able to sleep and when he had walked into the garage in Newmarket three days later, he had fully expected to be arrested, but nothing had happened. He was not involved at all. The only proof that there was something going on was the recurrent envelope under the mat. It was a considerable amount so it had to be worth something. It worked out very well for him at the time because his divorce from Doris had wiped out his bank account. He didn't know what he was transporting, although he had his suspicions. He didn't even know where it was stashed. Once he had combed out the car, in his garage, with the door locked, but with no results. It was fine with him, the less he knew the better. After that it became routine, he almost forgot and in doing so, silenced his conscience. It was almost as if it didn't exist. Until he had the car crash.

He jumped. Behind him the grill was rattling down onto the counter. When he turned around, he saw a man sitting at a table in the back. Dark eyes were looking past him and Jon knew he'd seen them before. In the bar mirror. He turned back to face the window and tried to find the man in the mirrored interior but the reflection was too vague. He pushed his chair back and made a business of putting on his coat so he could look at the other man without appearing to. Was he turning away deliberately? A round head with thick dark hair brushed forward. Well-kept, his clothes too, a black turtle-neck under a brown sports coat. His fingers were playing with his glass and he didn't look up. But as Jon walked towards the exit, he felt the man's gaze on his back. The glass was empty, he thought, maybe he had come in right behind him. He also thought of the overnight-bag on the upper bunk and how well it matched someone who looked like this.

On the inner deck a cold wind was blowing past his head and he shivered as he walked down the stairs to the cabin section. While walking he looked at the key-card, banishing all other thoughts. Like the first time, he waited for a moment before sliding the key-card into the lock.

The first thing he noticed was that the upper bunk was empty. He pushed the door closed with his back and put his bag on the lower bunk, looking at the lock of the bathroom door. Vacant. He pressed the latch down and pulled. The space was dark. On the edge of the bed he untied his shoe laces and then let himself fall backwards. The man wasn't coming back, that much was clear. Why else would he have taken the bag? Perhaps he too had preferred a single cabin, and the price of Captain's Class had not been an obstacle to him. His feet came up and he seemed to float as though he were drunk. Not altogether unpleasant. His eyes closed. Now stay down, keep your clothes on, what did it matter? But he still had to turn off the light.

Two minutes later he was in bed, in his underwear. He'd had to force himself to hang up his clothes. The ferry was tossing on the waves, the hangers in the luggage compartment behind his head jingled as they slid together and apart again from one side to the other. He lay facing the door, feeling the bag behind his back, his wallet in the pillowcase beneath his cheek, everything within reach. There was every chance that the man wouldn't come back. Enough anxiety, tomorrow he'd be home, tomorrow he wouldn't even understand what he'd been so worried about any more. If only they let him be.

Cheltenham Crossing was notorious; there was an accident there nearly every day, so he was always very careful. But he had not been able to avoid the green Rover which had shot out onto the road from behind the truck. Oddly enough, he had only realised when they had towed his car away. One more day and it would not have mattered except for the usual inconvenience that went with a car crash. In a sudden panic he had snapped at the woman who had stood helplessly before him with the damage claim form. They had phoned the next evening. In a neutral tone, a voice had asked why he hadn't kept the appointment. He explained about the car crash and the other person had asked where the car was and how long it would take. The connection was broken before he could ask what to do next. It had been the first contact between him and the other side, the first sign that he was involved in something, apart from the envelope under the mat. It had only increased his panic. He couldn't for a moment forget the fear that they would come upon the hidden cargo either during the damage investigation or the repairs. Every day he had left the bus two stops too soon in order to walk past the garage. On the first two days his car had been outside, the right front wheel a little lopsided under the crumpled mudguard. On the third day it had no longer been there, but he hadn't dared look in through the doors and walked on. During the days that followed, which he had mainly spent looking out for the police, he had decided to quit. He wouldn't do it any more. It was pure anxiety. For the first time he had actually realised what the consequences could be if the contraband was detected, and he had not tried to tinge his reasoning with morality, at least he was that honest with himself. He had forfeited that right the moment he had agreed to Jameson's proposal. He had done it for the money, to add comfort to his life, and now he realised that he was jeopardizing that very existence and more, he was quitting.

He had felt so much better after making this decision that, oddly enough, he was sure all would be well this time. And it was. A week and a half later he had picked up the car and gone over the bill with the head mechanic without noticing anything resembling suspicion or doubt. The next day the stranger had telephoned again, and he had taken the car to the car park later that night and picked it up the next day. For the last time, he had promised himself, and smothered the slight feeling of regret that had come over him when he had opened the envelope, such a waste of money. But then he'd discovered they weren't going to let him go that easily. The day before he left, the phone had rung again, the same voice, he'd recognised it immediately. For the first time there was a change in procedure. Would he mind waiting until he was called after returning in future? Apparently they had been just as nervous as he was. He had barely started his statement when the other person interrupted. "Quit? I wouldn't if I were you. . . ." Nothing else; he had been disconnected at once, but the words had stuck in his mind for days. He had wondered how Jameson had managed. Had he been able to get out just because his contract had been terminated? Or maybe they still had a hold on him. Were there others like himself? How big was this organisation?

The bag pressed against his back, he was really quite uncomfortable. He turned onto his other side and pushed it to the foot of the bed. Now he was finally in bed, he couldn't sleep. The duvet was a little too narrow. He grabbed the edge behind his back and kept rolling over until it was wound tightly around him. Surely the man wouldn't come in now? He used to lie like this at St. Patrick's, listening anxiously to hear if they would come again, the others, pulling the blanket off him dragging the mattress onto the floor. Again he felt the suffocating weight of the boy sitting on his chest, hands holding his legs, pulling his pants down. The smothered laughter, the body odour, sweat, urine, semen. When they were finally asleep, he lay awake, the ragged edge of the blanket against his cheek, and around him, their breath like that of a sleeping monster. Karen had noticed something. "You don't like to be touched. . . ." That was in the beginning. His feet rose and fell again, he became light-headed; a pleasant dizzy sensation he slid into.

When he awoke, he thought for a minute he was at the hotel. He stretched out his arm, his hand touched a smooth surface, underneath him the bed moved. A ship at sea. The headboard creaked, metal scraped metal, the hangers jangled together. He held his watch up to his eyes. Ten to three. He felt a burning sensation in his throat and his bladder was about to burst. When he turned over onto his other side he saw a vague gleam close to the floor. He bent over the edge of the bed. A thin strip of light was visible from under the shower room door. Had he forgotten to turn it off? He pulled the duvet up over his shoulder and lay motionless. The ferry was tossing on the waves. There were sounds everywhere, a soft vibrating drone from the depths, the groaning of the walls, air being sucked in and blown out, a constant stream inside the ship. Breathing. Carefully he turned onto his back. There was somebody in the upper bunk. He stared up in the dark. How could he have slept through the sound of the door opening? Had the light been turned on? Had he slept that soundly? He tried to block out the background noises. Had he been mistaken? Then he heard the toilet being flushed.

Without moving his head, he shifted his gaze to the far corner, so far that it hurt. He didn't hear the door, but the light disappeared and the noise of the cistern increased, then died down. He took an inaudible breath and held it. Where was that man? The mattress moved, he saw the vague contours of legs, one foot sought support on the edge of the bed, then he felt it pushing off and the movement of the bunk. Slowly he released the air in his lungs. For minutes he lay motionless. With his eyes wide open he stared upwards, his gaze got lost in the dark, the bed overhead took on enormous proportions. He was in a box, a cellar, enclosed by walls. He was going to suffocate.

Far off down the corridor there were voices and he listened to them greedily, clutching at the sound. "We are the Champions . . .," a wailing song that moved away and died down. The man in the upper bunk sighed and turned over. He smothered a cough and then snorted. Jon felt the contents of his stomach burning at the back of his throat and when he swallowed there was a grinding noise between his ears. In this small room the other must have been able to hear him too, he thought, everything was exposed. He knew from experience that the night would be endless.

After a time he lifted his head and listened. Then he cautiously pushed back the covers and slid out of bed. He knew exactly where he had put his clothes and he put them on in the dark without fastening a button or tying a shoelace, his back towards the bed, bracing himself against the wall when the ship moved. He groped around for the lock and very slowly turned it clockwise, pushing his shoulder against the door panel to release the catch. He expected a voice behind him, a hand grabbing him, but nothing happened and he slipped into the corridor like a thief. While he was straightening his clothes, he remembered he had left his bag on the bed. At the end of the corridor he had to step over some tangled sleeping bags to reach the loo. A man was standing at the zinc urinal, his legs apart and his face upturned while his body bent with the ship's movements. The cold airstream from the ventilators was as strong as a breeze, as though they had opened the doors fore and aft to clear the air. Jon stared at the foam swilling back and forth in the trough and held his breath until he was outside. On the upper deck, the football supporters were lying in their own mess. Beer cans, wrappers, containers for all sorts of junk food, brought from home and already eaten. Some of them were asleep, others staring blankly in front of them as though the match had already been played and lost. Jon sauntered to the tax-free shop amidships and read the ads in the window without remembering any. The feeling of oppression slowly died down. He looked at his reflection. This was part of him, it was just the way he was, and usually he knew how to adjust. At Mildenhall they only thought he was a little reclusive. Distant. That's the way it ought to be. So he would never know who his cabin mate had been. There was no face, which would make it easier, an empty space to add to the collection of empty spaces in his mind. In the end it wouldn't exist any more. He would not get the bag until the ship was moored and the passengers were clamouring to get across the gangplank. Unseen. A clock on a wall said quarter to four. He compared the time with his watch, hesitated whether to put it back already. Leaving the bag had been pretty stupid, now he didn't have his book either. He sank into an easy chair in a corner across from the shop. This was the second night in a row.

He'd underestimated them. He had taken the bus to the campus on the day he was supposed to take the car to the car park at the Vreeburg. The following evening he had sat in his office preparing the end of trimester exams until the building closed. Afterwards he had ducked into a random cinema at the shopping centre, halfway through the film. When he got back to the hotel he saw his car standing in one of the reserved spaces; it had not been moved. Before he went to sleep and later that night, he had looked at it through a gap in the curtains. The next morning he had driven it to work and felt relieved all day, as though he had put paid to something. In the evening, at their bistro, Karen had looked at him searchingly a couple of times, but said nothing, not even when he ordered a second bottle of wine. At the time he had taken her surprise at his coming by car as a sign of excessive concern, and lightheartedly refused to let her drive on the way back. "I don't know what's wrong with you today but I hope you're not doing anything foolish," she said as she got into a cab. It had been their first argument and he had driven to the hotel a bit sobered. The reserved spaces were all taken and he had to leave his car in a side street, something he usually didn't like to do because of the junkies hanging around there. As he walked back, standing across the quiet street, he saw a man in a long, dark raincoat. The next morning, on the way to the bus stop he saw a brown envelope on the front seat of his car, the same kind he usually found under the mat after a shipment. He still hadn't cottoned on, he'd been surprised rather than alarmed. There was some resistance when he opened the car door, as though it stuck on something, then there had been a sharp noise, which had deafened him for a moment. Some of the passers-by looked up but at the same time the bus he should have been on went past and everything was drowned out by the roar and the smell of traffic. There was a smell of gunpowder inside the car. The note in the envelope consisted of two sentences. "It's up to you. Next time it will be a real one." There were pieces of string dangling from the arm rests of both front doors, fishing line or something. When he tried to pull them off they cut into his skin. It must have been a cracker, he remembered them from his childhood. The seriousness of it had taken another minute to sink in. At first he thought, a silly little boy's toy as a warning. Then he had realised that the principle was the same as that of some car bombs. A booby-trap. A bomb waiting to go off. It was up to him, if he did anything wrong, he would destroy himself. They had not lost sight of him for a moment then, they were everywhere, had access to everything, he was completely at their mercy. He hadn't entered the classroom until half an hour after the exam had started, but his Dutch colleague waved away his apologies.

That afternoon he hired a nondescript van. After he'd left his own car in its usual spot in the car park he parked the hired van half a floor up. From the back door window he had watched his own car for hours. He didn't know exactly what he had wanted to do. He wouldn't interfere, he couldn't do anything on his own. In any case, he'd follow them to see where they were going, where they would hide the goods in his car and perhaps do something, anything, with that knowledge. He had wanted to see with his own eyes what went on unknown to him, predominantly driven by curiosity. But when, after a couple of hours, it became clear to him that he was waiting in vain, it also dawned on him that the circumstances were bizarre. What was he doing in a draughty car park smelling of urine, in a foreign country, at three o'clock in the morning? For the first time he realised he had entered a strange, dark world. He had disorganised a smuggling ring and now he was trying to put it right again. They were using his insecurity, playing with him. He had to get out. Leave Holland permanently, as fast as possible, get back to familiar ground before they had him entirely in their clutches.

It was too late to catch the day boat but the night boat should be possible, if there was room for his car. His premature departure would be a nuisance for his students, but he could send them their exam results and the department would just have to handle the rest. At a quarter past seven he was back in his hotel room. His car was parked out of sight on the campus, he'd taken the van back to the hire company, which cost him two long walks and a taxi ride, but he didn't feel tired. After having packed, he followed his usual routine; nobody was to notice what he was up to. He didn't know whether he was being followed or not, he hadn't seen anyone on all the detours he made on his way to Rotterdam, nor during the hours he had spent at Maassluis, in his car, awaiting nightfall. He had boarded the ferry as late as possible, to reduce the chance of attracting attention. The ship tilted, then straightened up. He stretched and stood up, rubbing his lower back. It looked like he had succeeded. Another three hours to Harwich, he'd get through those as well, only preferably not in these chairs. Maybe he could already see the lighthouse.

The wind almost sucked him out when he opened the heavy door to the passenger deck. On the metal stairs to the upper deck he had to hold the railing with both hands and a shower of fine droplets sprayed his face. He caught his breath in the shelter of a glass partition. Under the ship's lights, brownish-yellow heads of foam rose up high beside the ship. They flowed on, sank and dissolved into elongated trails. The whirling wash disappeared into the night after a few metres. Salt water streamed down his face and into his mouth as he peered through the window. There were lights in the distance. Land? He looked along the bow and compared it with the motion of the ferry. It was probably another ship. There was a lighthouse at the point by Harwich wasn't there? Or was that wrong? He saw some movement near the shiny tarpaulins of the lifeboats. It seemed he wasn't the only one who had ventured to go out-side in the middle of the night. His sodden trousers stuck to his legs and he made them billow with his back to the wind. It would really be better for him to go back inside, he hadn't brought any other clothes. If all went well at customs he would be home by nine-thirty, have a hot shower, a stiff drink and go to sleep for a couple of hours, before starting on the second part of his plan. Maybe the heater would already be on. Moody often turned it on a day early in cold weather. It had to work, nobody knew he was back yet, and he'd be on home ground. He didn't have to worry about customs this time, he was clean, as they called it. And he would see to it he stayed that way. He heard something behind him, voices blowing away, and looked round. Two figures were shambling across the upper deck supporting each other, beer cans in their hands. They leaned against the wind with their mouths wide open, a long col-oured scarf fluttering behind them. Idiots. What were they doing on deck sozzled? The minute they disappeared around the corner of the super-structure, he saw someone else at the top of the stairs. A long, dark coat gleamed as the man passed through the circle of light from a deck lamp. Because of the artificial floodlight and the way the man hunched his shoulders, protecting himself against the rain, Jon was reminded of the dark figure in the street across from his hotel. He pressed himself against the window and stood motionless. The man turned his head, the high collar of his coat blew open and Jon recognised him immediately as the man from the cafeteria, in spite of the wet, windswept hair which made him look less well-groomed than earlier that evening. And before that he had seen his dark eyes in the mirror behind the bar, only in a flash but so penetrating, so focused on him that he'd remembered them. This was more than a coincidence. Jon carefully sidled to the corner of the window where he'd be out of sight. Except for a few football maniacs who had slept it off everybody was inside, asleep. How could that man have known he wasn't in bed? Only if he'd been in the same cabin, in the upper bunk. In spite of the cold he was sweating all over. How could he have been so naive? They hadn't lost sight of him for a moment. Ever since the moment he'd given them notice, three months ago, he had been a risk and his behavior in Utrecht had caused them to write him off for good. What had the note said? The next one won't miss. Something to that effect anyway. Karen, who knew everything of course, had been allowed one last try. The last attempt at holding on to him. His flight had been anticipated, the early booking had been checked, and they had simply waited for him at the Hook. An anonymous overnight-bag on the upper bunk. And he had been naive enough to think he could outwit them. A criminal organisation, professionals who made a large profit smuggling hard drugs on a small scale, who used and discarded couriers where it was convenient. Weak links in their chain were replaced and then eliminated. No risks. The only question now was when and where it would happen.

The section of deck he could see from his corner was empty. As far as he could tell the man hadn't noticed him yet, but that was only a matter of time, unless he got out of there, down the stairs. There was an air vent five metres in front of him, next to the railing. He carefully edged forward with his back against the metal wall. There still wasn't anybody around. Stooped over, he crossed in two, three paces, a gust of wind nearly knocking him over, but he clung to the broad metal pipe and hid behind it. A humid suffocating odour brushed his face when he straightened up. The upper deck was deserted.

Why hadn't the man struck while he was asleep? Had he been ordered to wait until they got to England, because two passengers in the same cabin was too risky? The other one would be suspected immediately, the trail was too clear. Or maybe it did have to happen there but at the last moment, just before debarkation, allowing the perpetrator to leave the ship immediately?

Suddenly he realised he had a head start. They'd lost him. They hadn't foreseen that he would flee his cabin in the middle of the night. So he had to keep his lead no matter what, stay lost, find a place where he could wait for the ferry's arrival unseen. The doors to the car deck were locked during the crossing, but perhaps he could reach his car through the crew passageway.

He leaned over the railing of the upper deck. The gangway below was not four metres down; if he held on to the railing he could let himself drop. It was risky though, given the ship's movements. The space between the lifeboats and the wall was narrow and the floor very slippery. He looked to one side and rose slowly and carefully until he was back behind the air vent. The man in the dark coat was diagonally below him; he must have used the other stairs and walked around. It looked as though they were searching systematically. Perhaps it would be best if he stayed behind him, at a distance, until he got to the car deck.

Hugging the wall, staying in the shadow as much as possible, he crossed to the other side of the upper deck. He stayed in the lee of the cabins for a bit. Was he imagining things or was the eastern sky above the waves getting a little lighter? He bumped into the football supporters by the port stairs, there were four of them now, holding on to the railing and each other. As he passed, one of them turned round unsteadily and put a heavy arm around his shoulders. A drunken voice said something in Dutch. He tried to push the arm away but the others crowded around him, their dripping faces close to his. He could smell the booze in spite of the wind. They were slurring their song, the one he'd heard before, but this time it was unarticulated, a shapeless drone blown away by the wind. They wanted him to join in, with drunken obstinacy they pushed the sounds at him, forced him to sway with the beat, a lumbering ritual dance. He saw the stairs just beyond them very near. He pushed their arms away but they kept hanging heavily on to his shoulders almost causing him to lose his balance. He freed one of his arms, flailing wildly in an attempt to tear himself loose and his hand struck one of them on the jaw. The man reeled back and rubbed his chin. The others let go of him in surprise, he was a party pooper, their good humor disappeared instantaneously. He had suddenly turned into the enemy, an Englishman, which was what they were yelling now, bloody English or something like that; they stood in front of him, threatening, their hands shoving, thumping, they challenged him: bloody English. The deck tilted, the ship dove into a trough and one of the men fell against him, dragging him down with him. Jon reeled back and the man fell flat on the deck, his hand clawing past his legs. He jumped aside and dodged the others, but a tackle knocked his legs out from under him. He grabbed one of the rails as he fell, hoisted himself up half blinded by the storm and in a panic he ran towards the stairs. His foot slipped on the first step, he was thrown against the railing and kept sliding, but in spite of the nauseating pain in his knee he struggled back to his feet. Then, a few metres below a shape in a dark coat coming up the stairs, stooped over, each hand firmly gripping a rail. He heard screaming behind him. The man looked up. Jon saw the face that had been haunting him for the past few hours, had driven him from his cabin; under the uncertain light the jaw and thin mouth looked strangely distorted. Was he smiling? For a minute it seemed as though the wind had died down. Jon pushed himself up and grabbed the railing. As the other man put his foot on the next step, he shifted his weight to his arms, pulled his legs up high and then stretched them with all his strength. His feet landed right on the man's shoulders. The shock made the other man lose his balance, his body bent backwards, and he went crashing down, arms flailing, head first. Jon felt a thump on the back, a hand groped in his hair, he ducked and then jumped down the steps, two at a time. The man was lying on the deck, very still, his legs at an odd angle to his body; the blood running down his face looked black.

He locked himself into a stall in the first washroom he found. It was him or me, he thought, him or me. As soon as he sat down, a deathly fatigue paralysed his movements. His clothes were sticking to his body, but he seemed numb, petrified. He'd like to sleep, a merciful sedation which would put an end to this terrible night, to his thoughts going over that one image, a body on a deck, dark as night, dead. He was convinced that the man was dead. Him or me, he thought. After some time he got up and let warm water flow over his hands and face for minutes, at a sink. He was aware of his reflection but avoided looking at it. A man came in, laid out his shaving kit and slowly started to lather his face without looking at him once. Then he realised his cabin was now empty.

In the corridors the first sleepers were waking up. At every corner he watched for the supporters, they'd seen what had happened, no matter how drunk they were. He had to get his bag before the alarm was raised, they'd look in the man's cabin first. The key-card fell as he tried to slide it into the lock, and his powerless fingers scraped the carpet until he could pick it up. The lock clicked, he stepped over the threshold into the dark room and pushed the door shut with his shoulder. He felt around the doorpost for the light switch with his left hand but didn't find it. He stepped aside and hit his foot against something. His bag? The light switch was on the right. For a second he blinked at the bright light, then he saw. A pair of shoes. On the upper bunk a man sat up blinking at the light, supporting himself on his elbow as he held his watch to his eyes. He looked at Jon, his rugged face pale and patchy with sleep. "For God's sake, what time is it? Have we docked yet?"

He spent the last part of the crossing in a concealed corner of the lounge behind the tax-free shop, with his bag on his knees, facing the wall. He thought of nothing. He felt calm return to the slackening movements of the ship, the calm under the Felixtowe coast, he registered when the shutter of the engine stopped, half steam, and in his mind's eye he saw the harbour looming up, the white houses on the hill, the slow turn northwards which brought the ship into the mouth of the river. Like a slow motion film playing in his head. Now and then the sound of voices or a slamming door would register. The announcements over the intercom went in one ear and out the other.

When the ship had docked he could see the birch outside his workroom window quite clearly, he was seated at his desk, the heat of the fire warming his back; down the road Moody went past on his tractor and raised his hand.

With downcast eyes he stood in line at the stairs to the car deck, his bag clenched under his arm. He was startled by an arm pulling him back, he hadn't noticed people were making room to let a stretcher on wheels through. It was flanked by two crew members, but there was nobody under the grey canvas with straps. He heard someone say something about a fight. A bunch of hooligans against a single man. They shouldn't sell tickets to that sort of trash, they were nothing but trouble. A policeman no less, a Dutchman. Looks bad, landed head first on the deck, what do you expect. When the doors opened, he allowed himself to be swept downstairs by the stream of passengers, he was met by the smell of exhaust fumes and oil. On the car deck it took him a while to get his bearings. He had taken different stairs than last night, and when he had finally located his car, the last one in the outside line, he stood and looked at it from a distance. Around him people got into their cars, doors slammed, engines started, while his eyes wandered over the blue-grey Ford Orion. Over the closed doors and the tinted glass. As the first line started to move, he crossed over, ducked down and looked inside. The front seats were empty, the folded rug lay in the back, he didn't see anything out of the ordinary anywhere. He put the key in the lock and turned it. The central locking clicked sharply. He opened the back door and put the bag on the seat, then looked forwards between the seats. Nothing to be seen. Behind him a voice called out, a car in the line next to his wanted to pass and he closed the door. Then he opened the front door and got in. The lane ahead was already empty, he was the last one out and his tires screeched across the metal as he accelerated.

In front of the customs office an official motioned to him to get out of line. He parked next to two cars with Norwegian licence plates, the drivers watching as their luggage was searched. To his own surprise he was not tense at all while his papers were checked. "No," he said, he had nothing to declare, looking past the official at the gangway connecting the ferry to the terminal. Cleaners were going on board and a crew member was hosing down the aft deck. A container ship passed and although the ferry was now higher in the water than last night, it seemed smaller than at the Hook, less intimidating, and he could see all the way through it. One of the Norwegian cars drove into the customs shed, onto the bridge. When he had to open the trunk something quivered within him, he hesitated for an instant, with his fingers on the lock, but nothing happened. The official turned around and motioned him on his way.

While driving he fought off sleep. The previous night's images shimmered before his eyes, an echoing voice-over on an intercom repeated that it had been a policeman. Karen's face appeared, she turned and walked away, and he knew that he was dreaming. Past Ipswich he chose the by-roads for variety's sake, and the familiarity of the landscape pushed the images to the back of his mind. It had been raining heavily here too, the ditches were full of water and at the foot of hills little streams were running down the road. Sometimes he looked in the mirror, there was a chance he was being followed, although he didn't know why anymore or by whom. He was vaguely aware of something he had to do when he got home, but didn't allow himself to think about it. Sleep first.

As he drove along the ridge he saw the village, lying under a veil of rain, a group of houses in a valley. At the farm at the crossroads, he honked the horn and Moody, who was working in the yard, looked up in surprise and waved. A hundred metres on he drove into the shower and as he drove up the garden path raindrops were drumming on the roof of the car. The shutters on the ground floor were still closed, a pity; Moody hadn't expected him home until tomorrow and the house would still be freezing for the next few hours. He aimed the remote control at the garage but the doors remained closed. He pushed it again, then threw the apparatus on the seat beside him. Useless object. This was the umpteenth time. He opened the car door, but remained seated for a minute, slumped down, arms at his side, as the raindrops blew into the car. Then he swung his legs out, one by one. With his coat draped over his shoulders he walked to the side door of the garage and as he stuck the key in the lock he saw Moody arriving by road, bent over the steering wheel of his bicycle. Through the rain no less, that really wasn't necessary. And he would immediately start in about useless modern gadgets, he knew his old neighbour. The lock was jammed. He took out the key and tried again, kneeing the door to reduce the pressure on the lock. Moody's bike clattered against the gate and Jon heard his footsteps on the gravel. He grabbed the latch in a final attempt and found that it yielded. The door was already unlocked.

"Jon!" There he was, panting, his breath rasping in his throat.

Jon looked up smiling. "Hey, neighbour," he said. "Don't hurry like that. It's not good for your health you know, not at your age."

He pushed down the latch and pulled. A scorching flash of light blinded him and for a second he seemed to be floating. Then a sweeping blaze rolled out which lifted and then sucked him down and crushed him.

Translated by Emmy Muller

CREDITS

INDEX